Praise for
Trauma Plan and Candace Calvert

"Candace Calvert has crafted another gut-grabbing medical thriller. *Trauma Plan* kept me engrossed from beginning to end as I immersed myself in the characters' lives, felt their pain, and rejoiced in their victories. The faith message was clear, the medical traumas heart-stopping, and the romance heart melting. I loved everything about the story, especially little Hobo and his two-wheeled cart. A great read and one for your keeper shelf."

—LYNETTE EASON,
award-winning, bestselling author of the Women of Justice series

"Candace Calvert paints an exciting story on a canvas she knows very well—the world of medicine and the people who inhabit it. *Trauma Plan* is a novel that will grip your heart and keep you turning pages."

—RICHARD L. MABRY, MD,
author of the Prescription for Trouble series

"Spine-tingling suspense and a power-packed shot of adrenaline heat up Candace Calvert's *Trauma Plan*. Calvert's tight writing and well-developed characters made for a story I could not stop reading. *Trauma Plan* doesn't disappoint, so grab your parachute and take a dive into an amazing story packed with solid characters, including Calvert's Rx for great fiction—a heartthrob hero!"

—RONIE KENDIG,
author of the Discarded Hero series

D0052587

"[*Critical Care*] flows well and keeps the reader's attention. . . . Characters find not only psychological healing, but also spiritual renewal."

—**CHRISTIAN RETAILING**

"If you need an infusion of hospital drama, *Code Triage* is just the prescription."

—**IRENE HANNON,**
bestselling author of the Heroes of Quantico series

"Good-bye, *ER*. Hello, *Critical Care*! Candace Calvert delivers a wonderful medical romance that peeks inside the doors of an ER to discover a cast of real-life characters who learn to love and live and discover God's truths, all in the high-stress world of medicine. If you like *ER* and *House*, you'll love Logan and Claire and their friends at Sierra Mercy. Give me another dose, and soon!"

—**SUSAN MAY WARREN,**
award-winning author of *Happily Ever After* and *The Shadow of Your Smile*

"[In *Disaster Status*] Candace Calvert succeeded in thrilling me, chilling me, and filling me with awe and respect for ER trauma."

—**DIANN MILLS,**
author of the Call of Duty series

"*Code Triage* is an adrenaline high, ripped from today's headlines, with enough romantic tension to spike your pulse."

—**JULIE LESSMAN,**
award-winning author of the Daughters of Boston series

GRACE MEDICAL

TRAUMA PLAN

GRACE MEDICAL

Candace Calvert

Tyndale House Publishers, Inc.
Carol Stream, Illinois

Visit Tyndale online at www.tyndale.com.

Visit Candace Calvert's website at www.candacecalvert.com.

TYNDALE and Tyndale's quill logo are registered trademarks of Tyndale House Publishers, Inc.

Trauma Plan

Designed by Stephen Vosloo

Edited by Sarah Mason

Published in association with the literary agency of Natasha Kern Literary Agency, Inc., P.O. Box 1069, White Salmon, WA 98672.

This novel is a work of fiction. Names, characters, places, and incidents either are the product of the author's imagination or are used fictitiously. Any resemblance to actual events, locales, organizations, or persons living or dead is entirely coincidental and beyond the intent of either the author or the publisher.

Library of Congress Cataloging-in-Publication Data

Calvert, Candace, date.
 Trauma plan / Candace Calvert.
  p. cm. — (Grace Medical ; 1)
  ISBN 978-1-4143-6111-6 (sc)
 1. Nurses—Fiction. I. Title.
 PS3603.A4463T73 2012
 813'.6—dc23   2011047421

Printed in the United States of America

18   17   16   15   14   13   12

7   6   5   4   3   2   1

For my husband, Andy, a fifth-generation Texan

and my real-life hero

Acknowledgments

Heartfelt appreciation to:

Literary agent Natasha Kern—you are a true blessing.

The entire Tyndale House publishing team, especially editors Jan Stob and Sarah Mason—you are amazing.

Critique partner Nancy Herriman—talented author, dear friend.

My son, Bret MacKinnon—for love and encouragement and for his expert advice on the mountain bike scene.

Fellow nursing, medical, fire, rescue, law enforcement, and chaplaincy personnel—you are true heroes.

The Texas hill country city of Boerne and especially St. Helena's church—you will always have a special place in my heart.

My family and dear friends—love for you infuses every book.

And with special appreciation to my loyal readers—you are a joy, and it is an honor to offer you stories of hope.

When I am afraid, I put my trust in you.

PSALM 56:3

"MAN ON FIRE!"

What?

Jackson Travis hurled his Army duffel to the floor and charged out the clinic door, his mountain boots pounding the splintered wooden porch. He squinted into the April sun; the parking area was swarming with people. A car swerved toward the San Antonio Street curb, brakes screeching. He vaulted over the porch rail as honks joined a rising barrage of screams and shouts.

"Someone's burning up—quick, film it!"

Jack bolted toward the crowd, clenching his teeth against a whiff of smoke and singed hair—far too reminiscent of his weeks in Kandahar. There was a terrified howl and he pressed forward, impeded immediately by a teenager in a knit cap who wedged in front of him to raise a cell phone overhead.

"Stand back," Jack ordered, familiar anger prickling. He gave the kid two seconds to comply before shoving his shoulder into him. "Let me get by!"

"I called 911," an older African American woman told him, tugging at Jack's uniform sleeve as he passed. "Fire department's coming, sir."

"Good . . . thanks," Jack huffed, breaking through the crowd at last. It had been no exaggeration—an elderly man's clothing was on fire. "Hold still! Don't move!"

"Please, God . . . help me!" the man begged, flames licking at his stringy, unkempt hair. He staggered backward, wild-eyed, waved his arms, then lost his balance and sat down hard.

Jack was there in a heartbeat.

"Don't move, sir," he repeated, dropping down beside the man—and feeling an immediate jab of pain as his right knee touched the ground. Jack ignored it and went to work, blinking against the smoke and flames as he stripped off his field jacket. "Hang in there. I've got you," he promised, using the camouflage fabric to smother the still-hungry flames. That accomplished, he swaddled the man inside the jacket and eased him to a lying position on the dusty asphalt. "Easy, buddy. Stay still. Let me help you now."

"Okay, ohhh-kay," the man groaned, the last word stretching into a puff soured by cheap wine and bad teeth. His tear-filled eyes studied Jack's face, and then his body relaxed. "It's you. Oh . . . bless you for being here."

There was a smattering of claps from the bystanders, but a

kid holding a skateboard hooted, "Yeah, well, GI Joe better pray he don't get some ugly disease. You wouldn't catch me touchin' that."

"That"? Jack glared at the boy as sirens wailed in the distance. The call to 911. At least someone had done that for . . . *Gilbert.* Yes. Jack recognized him now. Former hardware salesman. Alcoholic, a smoker with emphysema, and a clinic patient on several occasions. Jack glanced at a nest of smoldering bedding and a grocery basket piled high with empty aluminum cans. On the ground nearby was a broken half-gallon wine bottle, translucent green shards scattered. Probably the reason for the jab in Jack's knee and even more evidence that this homeless man had spent the night on clinic property. Jack cursed under his breath. If word got out, it would be one more item on a long list of complaints that the clinic attracted unsavory elements and depreciated property values.

He turned his attention to the victim, who'd begun to tremble uncontrollably. One of his ears was blistered, the eyebrow and lashes on that side singed: a red flag for risk of airway burns. Had the man inhaled much smoke? *No audible wheezing, lips pink* . . . Jack estimated the man's respiratory rate at thirty, then reached for his wrist: pulse rapid but regular. Panic was probably taking more of a toll than the burns.

"The ambulance is on its way, Gilbert." He made a point of using the man's name, hoping it would make him feel like more than the ugly public spectacle he'd suddenly become. *I know how that feels, buddy.*

Jack glanced toward the clinic porch, debating carrying the man inside. No staff there yet, and the supply cupboards would be locked. Besides, the paramedics were moments away. They'd get this man on oxygen, transport him to the ER where he belonged. Maybe there weren't more burns than those visible. Hopefully the poor man hadn't been lying here in flames for too long.

Jack fought a searing rush of anger and glared at the gathered crowd, including the kid in the knit cap who'd backed off a few yards but was still avidly filming. All of them were no better than scavengers around a rotting carcass. Two dozen or more people had responded to shouts of "Man on fire!" yet no one had attempted a rescue. Not one person had stepped up.

Jack jabbed his finger toward a man talking on a cell phone, then swept it across the crowd like he was drawing a line in desert sand. "*Do* something helpful or get out of here! You hear me? What are you, vultures?"

He rose to his feet, fighting an urge to grab one of the gawkers and shake him, just as the engine company first responders pulled to the curb. The siren yelped. A strong hand clapped onto his shoulder from behind.

"Jack, I almost didn't recognize you in uniform. What's going on here?" San Antonio police sergeant Rob Melton surveyed the scene, radio mic squawking on his shoulder. "Fill me in."

Jack grimaced. "I go to Dallas for my Reserve weekend and come back to find a disaster in the parking lot." He glanced down at Gilbert and lowered his voice. "Homeless alcoholic who probably fell asleep with a cigarette in his hand. Set himself on fire." Jack stared at the receding crowd being dispersed by a second police officer. "And he would have burned to a chicken-fried death if your heartless citizens had their way." He sucked a breath through his teeth. "Heartless and gutless. I've got no use for people like that."

Rob's gaze met Jack's, his compassion as evident as the telltale bulk of his body armor. "I hear you, Jack. But there are plenty of decent folks here. If you give them half a chance."

"Yeah, well . . ." Jack waved at the firefighter crew making their way with equipment bags in hand. "Over here, hustle! And watch out, there's broken glass everywhere."

Jack stepped back as a paramedic attended to Gilbert. Then he gave a brief report to a young firefighter who'd begun to make notes. "Second-degree burns from what looks like a bedding fire. Mild respiratory distress. Alcohol on board. History of emphysema. Where are you taking him?"

"Alamo Grace Hospital."

"Good. I'll grab my things and follow you in."

"Uh . . ." The firefighter's eyes swept over Jack's uniform, settled on his name tape. "We appreciate your offer, Major Travis, but . . ."

Rob Melton smiled. "*Dr.* Travis. He's director of this clinic."

"It's Jack." He extended his hand to the firefighter. "Emergency medicine is my day job. I'm working a shift at Alamo Grace this afternoon."

"Good thing." Rob pointed to Jack's leg. "You're bleeding."

Jack flexed his knee. A warm trickle and mild sting confirmed the observation—a puncture from that broken wine bottle. He'd grab the medical records and close up the clinic. The wound could wait until he got to Alamo Grace. Right now it was far less important than what he'd glimpsed out on San Antonio Street: A trio of news vans. And a white Lexus.

He knew the car. It belonged to the head of the action committee that wanted his clinic torn down. The city council was
meeting in three weeks to discuss the neighbors' issues, which
boiled down to the fact that they preferred people like Gilbert
in another zip code. Meanwhile, they were building a fortress-
size security gate; the block had been torn up for weeks.

Jack stood watch as the paramedics loaded Gilbert and then
made his way toward the clinic. As he started up the wooden
steps, he saw something out of the corner of his eye and sprinted
back down.

He caught the kid in the knit cap before he got to the San
Antonio Street curb, startling him enough that he dropped his
cell phone. It clattered across the sidewalk. The kid grabbed for
it, then attempted to lurch away.

Jack grasped his arm, whirling him around. "I see that film
clip on the Internet—" he jabbed a finger into the short space
between them, barely missing the boy's nose—"and I track you
down. Count on it."

Jack released his grip and watched the kid scuttle away before
turning his gaze on the white Lexus. His jaw tensed.

Close this clinic? Over my dead body.

- + -

Trauma chaplain Riley Hale straightened her elbows and leaned
over her patient's bare chest, using her left hand to sink her right
palm as deeply as she could into his pliable breastbone. Her
long hair swung across her shoulders with each focused effort.
"Twenty-one, twenty-two, twenty-three . . ." She pushed again,
counting cardiac compressions while visualizing the patient's

failing heart squeezed between sternum and spine, her rescue efforts delivering essential blood to his brain and vital organs. "Twenty-four, twenty-five, twenty-six . . ."

Riley compressed again, felt sweat trickle beneath her tailored shirt, then glanced at her patient's pale, waxen face. She told herself that she was saving his life with her bare hands. *My own two very capable hands.* A registered nurse performing exactly what she'd been trained to do, had done a hundred times during her years in the ER. Nothing had changed, except . . .

"*Aagh!*" Riley yanked her hands away as the right hand cramped mercilessly, fingers curling inward beyond her control. She whirled to face ER charge nurse Kate Callison. "I'm working on a dead body, right? He's dead because I'm doing a pathetic job trying to save him. Tell me the truth, Kate."

"Well . . ." The petite brunette took a long swig from her vitaminwater, then leaned back in the conference room chair. "It's not looking good for Mrs. CPR Training Manikin—she should probably buy a nice black dress. But on the bright side, the chaplain's already here."

Riley tried to smile . . . and failed.

"Look—" Kate nudged her lunch plate aside—"you have spinal cord damage that affects your arm. It's weak; you can't help that. The truth is that I'm amazed you're doing as well as you are."

Riley took a slow breath, refusing to let disappointment get the best of her. She'd asked Kate to be honest. In the four months since Riley began work at Alamo Grace, she'd come to admire this California native a lot. She was a skilled critical care nurse and a hands-on leader who could be counted on to roll up her sleeves and work alongside her staff. Plucky, dependable, and honest. She was far less gregarious than the other nurses, yet Kate and Riley had connected immediately. She was the one person Riley had confided in about her injury. And if Kate ever finished packing, she was going to be Riley's new roommate. A good thing. Still . . .

Riley traced her right index finger slowly across the training manikin's plastic shoe and felt nothing. Dull as wood, completely numb. Her life had begun to feel that same way. Numb, except for unrelenting frustration and the stabs of guilt that came every time people applauded her "brave" journey to recovery. Was it selfish and ungrateful to want to be healed completely? Was she supposed to be happy that a horrifying assault left her with "only" a permanently weakened arm?

"Riley?"

"It's been a year now." Riley's eyes connected with Kate's. "Physical therapy, occupational therapy . . . *every* kind of therapy. I want to be back in the ER—" she glanced at her suit jacket draped over a chair—"in scrubs. I want to be a real part of the team."

"You are. You're great at what you do." Kate cocked her head, offering Riley a teasing smile. "You know I'd be the first one to vote a preacher off this island. Or a slacker. I run a tight ship. You're the best trauma-chaplain-slash-assistant-safety-officer we've ever had."

Riley sighed. She was the *only* employee to ever have that position at Alamo Grace. Your basic overpaid gofer, because the Hale Foundation was a large contributor to this medical system. *Thank you for not saying that embarrassing truth: that I'm broken, useless . . . and skating by on my family name.*

Riley scanned the array of training devices scattered across the conference table: adult, child, and infant CPR manikins; an intubation head with simulated lungs protruding; Ambu bags; and a big arm—bicep to fingers—for practicing IV insertion. Each a plastic replica of the real thing. Exactly how she felt about herself right now. But she was determined to change that. Whatever it took.

"How's it going with your IV practice?" Kate checked her watch. "I've got a few more minutes on my break. Want to give it a try?"

"I guess." Riley frowned. "But I could poke that rubber arm a hundred times and it wouldn't be the same as on a live patient. How am I ever going to prove that I'm capable if the hospital won't even give me a chance to—" She stopped short as Kate pulled off her scrub jacket and began wrapping a tourniquet around her own arm. "What are you doing?"

"Giving you a chance. If I'm going to talk you up at the charge nurse meeting today, I'd better have something to base it on."

"I . . . Really?"

"Yeah—wait, hang on." Kate answered her buzzing hospital-issued cell phone with the tourniquet still dangling from her arm.

Riley listened to the one-sided exchange, distracted by the fact that her pulse had quickened like a first-year student nurse's. If Kate could report that Riley's dexterity was improving, it might help her chances. It had been a year since she'd used this skill, given that direct patient care was no longer part of her job description. Prayers, yes; needles, no.

"Something in the ER?" she asked as Kate disconnected.

"Ambulance coming. Seventy-two-year-old man with burns and possible smoke inhalation. Basically stable." Kate shook her head. "Bizarre—it happened in the parking lot of Jack's free clinic."

"Jack?"

"If you have to ask, you've never met him. Jackson Travis, trauma doc, rabid defender of the oppressed. And mountain bike lunatic and . . ." Kate clucked her tongue. "People call him Rambo behind his back. I met him when I helped at the clinic. He works in a couple local ERs, and now he's picking up some shifts at Alamo Grace. This afternoon, in fact. He'll probably parachute in." Kate glanced down at her arm. "I'm turning purple from this tourniquet, and we've got seven minutes before the ambulance arrives."

Riley reached for an iodine swab. "You're sure about this?"

Kate settled her forearm on the table. "Prep me and grab a needle before I change my mind. And no praying out loud, Chaplain Hale."

2

+

JACK SHOVED THE CPR MANIKIN ASIDE, then rolled up his pant leg. The camouflage fabric was stiff with dried blood.

He scraped his chair closer and propped his boot on the conference room table. Awkward and less than sterile, but it would suffice. The overhead light was decent, and the wound on his knee wasn't that big of a deal. L-shaped, maybe 2.0 by 2.75 centimeters, and shallow. He'd have closed it with Dermabond skin glue or Steri-Strips, but it was over a joint and Jack had a skydiving appointment in San Marcos he wasn't about to miss. You never knew how you'd land after falling thirteen thousand feet. A rough one could rip the wound open again. A few nylon sutures would hold better. But he wasn't going to take up an emergency department gurney for something he could do himself right here.

Jack glanced at the cache of supplies he'd snagged from the ER: sterile gloves and drapes, 4-0 suture, disposable instrument kit, syringe, vial of Xylocaine, bottle of saline irrigation, needles, and gauze dressings. Plus some prep supplies, though it turned out he didn't need them. Someone had left several iodine swab packets on the conference table. Along with a whole-grain bagel and fat-free cream cheese.

Fat-free. He smiled, thinking of his unofficial but irreplaceable building manager, Bandy Biggs. The sixty-three-year-old former bull rider would laugh Jack out of the clinic if he brought bagels for the staff; he'd say, "Krispy Kremes or get outta Dodge." Bandy always bragged that he'd cut his teeth on corn dogs and cotton candy. And started down the road to high cholesterol and heart disease, Jack continued to remind him. They made some compromises for the sake of Bandy's happy longevity . . . and became close friends.

Jack glanced at his watch, wondering if the police and fire departments still had the clinic parking lot cordoned off. There had been several incidents of arson in the neighboring community of New Braunfels, and though this fire looked purely accidental, they were required to investigate. He'd warned tonight's clinic volunteers to stay clear of reporters, to give no statements. He'd handle that himself. The first thing on Jack's list had been to get Gilbert to the ER, and he'd done that. The man had been treated, fed lunch, and was fast asleep in the ER's observation room. Now Jack would stitch this wound, grab a shower, and trade his uniform for scrubs before his ER shift began.

He pulled on a pair of exam gloves, ripped open two packages of iodine swabs, then filled a syringe with local anesthetic and changed the needles. After the skin prep, he'd punch a hole in the top of the bottle of irrigating saline and start squirting the wound like crazy, rinsing out any debris that he might have picked up from the clinic parking lot. A time-consuming, messy, and tedious procedure—a nurse's job. He reminded himself to be respectful of the next one he saw. Especially if that nurse had decent skills and could be cajoled into volunteering at the clinic. The downturn in the economy had them in a pinch. He needed staff. And donations. But mostly he needed that pain-in-the-rear action committee to back off before they inspired some eager-beaver news reporter to start digging around in Jack's past. He didn't want to go through that mess again. Anything else, no problem. He'd handle it.

Jack grabbed the iodine swabs and scrubbed the edges of his wound. Then he reached for the syringe of Xylocaine. He pulled the cap off with his teeth, held his breath, and jabbed the needle through his skin.

- + -

Riley froze in the doorway, all thoughts of retrieving her bagel gone. She stared in disbelief as a man dressed in desert camouflage injected something into his leg. She shrank close to the doorframe and studied him: huge shoulders, sandy-blond hair cropped short, shadow of beard growth. Head down, intent on what he was doing.

And what exactly was that? Searching for a vein so he could . . . ? Riley squinted, taking it in.

The man handled the syringe like he'd done it countless

times before. If he was injecting illegal drugs, he'd have to be desperate to risk doing it here, where anyone could walk in.

Desperate means dangerous. She'd just covered that subject in safety instruction to the nursing staff. *Be safe; don't confront.* Policy required that they have the operator page "Mr. Strong," the code for help needed with a potential . . . assailant. Riley fought a shiver and an unbidden memory of her own assault a year ago. She backed up a step, holding her breath. But before she could turn away, the man in uniform raised his head and stared directly at her.

"I'm . . ." Riley yanked her hospital cell phone from her pocket and held it out like a weapon. "I'm going to call—"

"Call who?" he asked, holding the half-empty syringe in midair. His voice was deep, calm, and controlled. But his eyes seemed to dare her to take him on.

"Hospital security," she said, though it sounded far less confident than she'd hoped. Her heart rose to her throat as the man set the syringe down, shifting in the chair as if he might suddenly stand. It occurred to her that he could be armed. She told herself that her injury didn't affect her ability to run. Or scream her head off.

"Oh, right." He glanced down at the syringe, frowning. "You think—"

"I don't think; I *see* it. Very clearly. You're injecting yourself."

"Numbing myself."

She raised the phone, kept her eyes on him. "Whatever you call it and whatever reasons you may think you have for doing it, that can't happen here, sir."

The man lifted his palms. "Whoa there. Wait. You're riding

that horse in the wrong direction. I'm a doctor. I lacerated my knee and I'm repairing it." His fingers flexed. "Think about it: ever see a junkie wearing gloves?"

Riley lowered the phone very slightly, hating that the man's lips were twitching toward a smirk. She cleared her throat. "I've never seen a doctor suture himself either."

"First time for everything, ma'am. The point is that I trust myself more than I trust anyone else. And I didn't want to take up a gurney in the ER—they're busy. If you don't believe me, then go ask the director. I'll be starting a shift down there at three. I'm—"

Rambo. Riley nearly groaned aloud.

"—Jack Travis," he finished, shifting his leg on the table. "I followed the ambulance in with a burn patient. The uniform's because I just got back from a Reserve weekend and didn't have time to change. Or catch the sleep I needed. And you're . . ." He seemed to scan her tailored business attire. "Hospital administration?"

"Trauma chaplain. And assistant safety officer," Riley added, supposing that, if he really was a staff physician, the courteous thing to do would be to step closer and offer her name. She decided against it. "Regardless of who you are, it isn't safe to have surgical equipment, soiled gloves and gauze—any of that—in a nonclinical area. A public area. And . . . I'm going to do exactly what you suggested." She lifted her chin and met his gaze full on.

He sighed, suddenly looking far more fatigued than menacing. "Do what?"

"Ask the ER director to verify who you are."

"Good. And while you do that, I'll stitch my knee." He was definitely smirking. "We're back to square one, Chaplain."

Riley gave a curt nod and escaped down the hallway, trading her initial anxiety for a growing sense of irritation. His being there unexpectedly had frightened her, but that fear was gone. Right now she was simply angry. At herself for being unprofessionally flustered, and at Jack Travis because . . . he'd apparently enjoyed it. She didn't need anyone to confirm his identity. It was obvious now. Their brief encounter had underscored what she'd learned on the nurses' lounge TV not twenty minutes ago.

A spokeswoman for a neighborhood action committee had been interviewed on the grounds of a free clinic. It was operating out of an old private residence, apparently the last such structure to resist a bulldozer in The Bluffs, a community boasting upscale shops and impressive custom homes. The TV interview was preceded by a dramatic camera-phone film clip of an elderly man with his clothing in flames, screaming for God to help him.

As it ended, the spokeswoman had peered into the camera, looking perfectly coiffed and undeniably sincere. "We feel for that poor soul. Of course we do. But he should never have been allowed to sleep on those grounds. There are shelters for that purpose. Downtown. This fire could have spread across the entire Bluffs community and endangered our homes and our children." She pointed into the camera lens. "It happened because Dr. Jack Travis allowed it. He's a reckless, irresponsible maverick who thinks he can make his own rules, regardless of the safety and well-being of others. I can assure you that the generous donor of this property never intended it for these purposes. And I guarantee that we will see this clinic closed."

Riley knew nothing about the history of the dispute, but she'd already seen enough of Jack Travis to suspect that rules were indeed a foreign language to him. And arrogance second nature. She suspected, too, that danger was something he would embrace, not avoid.

So different from Riley. She hated, marrow-deep, that the conference room incident had rattled her. Almost as much as she hated that she'd failed at three attempts to insert an IV needle into Kate Callison's vein. How could Kate talk her up at today's charge nurse meeting after that?

Riley picked up her pace along the corridor toward the chaplain's office, realizing that she'd told Jack Travis she was a chaplain and safety officer, but not that she was a nurse. Surprising, since all her efforts were focused on proving that. But for the first time she was glad she wasn't part of the medical team down in the ER. Working alongside someone like Jack Travis was the last thing she needed.

- + -

Jack jogged toward the ambulance bay as its doors flew open. The medics shoved a stretcher through, shouting a report to him as they went. "Sixty-two-year-old woman found in her yard by a postal worker. BP 174 over 88. Pulse 90. Slurred speech, facial droop, confused and combative." The young medic, wire-rimmed glasses askew, swiped at a bleeding scratch on his cheek. "She's been fighting us the whole time. Can't keep the oxygen on, couldn't get an IV." He pointed to where they'd attempted to cut away clothing to expose her right arm. "It was a short ETA, so we just rolled. Fire's following us in with her meds.

I hope. Her place was locked up behind her like Fort Knox. She finally settled down, stopped fighting so much, about the time we pulled in."

Jack glanced down at the woman as the stretcher rolled toward the exam room. A second medic was doing his best to gently restrain her arms. *Moving both arms. Less suggestive of stroke.* She was glassy-eyed, pale as a fish belly; her skin glistened with sweat, and her well-cut ash-blonde hair was wet. Jack brushed his fingers against her forearm: cold to the touch. "Her name?"

"Vesta," a balding EMT answered as they lined the stretcher up with the hospital gurney. He checked his notes. "Vesta Calder. That's birdseed in her hair and all over the stretcher. She must have been carrying a sack of it when she went down."

Jack patted the woman's shoulder. "Vesta, I'm Dr. Travis. I'm going to help you."

She stared up at him with a blank expression, saliva trickling from the corner of her mouth.

Jack signaled to Kate Callison. "We'll need the works: labs including blood alcohol and tox screen, Foley catheter, EKG, portable chest films, arterial blood gases, brain CT." He nodded as one of the other nurses grabbed the IV start tray and a bag of normal saline. "Get that line in and grab a blood sugar." He turned back to his patient as the team prepared to transfer her to the ER's gurney. "We're going to move you, Vesta. It's okay. The nurse will get a warming blanket, too. Bear with us."

Kate slipped a tourniquet around the patient's arm. A nurse's aide got busy peeling away the remaining layers of clothing, while trying not to skid on birdseed spilling to the floor. Another tech warned Vesta about a finger stick, then poked, trying his best to eke a drop of blood from the woman's ice-cold fingers.

The cardiac electrodes were placed, blood pressure cuff and pulse oximetry probe attached, and a staff nurse began reporting vital signs. "Sinus rhythm at 88, Dr. Travis. BP 140 over 70. Pulse ox . . . can't get it yet; she's too cold. I'll get a temp and the warming system going as soon as we get this last sleeve off her arm."

Kate slid the needle into the vein and pulled a vial of blood; she passed a droplet off to a tech to use for the glucose meter.

Vesta's eyes rolled ominously sideways. Jack moved toward the head of the bed, watching her carefully. *Easy, Vesta . . .*

The aide pulled the last of the clothing from the patient's arm, bent close to stare at her wrist. "Dr. Travis, there's a medical alert band here for diabetes—"

"Blood sugar's reading low," the tech interrupted.

"She's twitching, Doctor, and—"

Vesta Calder's body convulsed violently.

"Seizure!"

3

"GIVE THE FULL AMP OF DEXTROSE," Jack ordered, sliding a suction tip into the corner of Vesta's mouth. "And pull out the intubation tray. Let's have some lorazepam standing by in case we haven't got this right. But I suspect . . ." He watched for a moment, then released a slow breath as the seizure ended. "Okay then, good. She's settling down. There now." He smiled as his patient's face infused with pink color and her eyelids fluttered. "Nothing like the miracle of intravenous sugar—except maybe those pecan pralines at Tia Rosa's."

Jack glanced at the monitor, satisfied that the heart rhythm hadn't changed. "I'm going to need that EKG, folks. And then the brain scan. Did we get a temp yet?" He stroked a gloved fingertip across Vesta's cheek, brushing away a fine sprinkle of millet seed. "Can you hear me, ma'am? Feeling better?"

The patient opened her eyes and nodded, mumbled beneath the fogged oxygen mask, then closed her eyes again. But her fingers curled around his and stayed there. She smiled very slightly, and he was reminded of Gilbert's face in the parking lot this morning, when he realized Jack was there to help him. Nothing—*nothing*—felt better than that. And it was worth any bureaucratic battle he had to wage.

Jack glanced at the clerk entering information into the bed-side computer. "Have you located any past medical records?"

"Yes, sir." The diminutive woman tapped the keys. "It looks like Mrs. Calder changed addresses four times in the past fifteen years but fortunately remained local. And within the Grace Hospital system. She's been hospitalized twice for diabetes problems." The clerk scanned the screen. "Let me make sure I've got the most recent records. Yes, this one has her listed under her current Bluffs address."

Jack raised his brows. "The Bluffs?"

"That snooty community off San Antonio Street." Her eyes widened. "Oops. If you live there, Dr. Travis, I'm sorry."

"If I lived there, *I'd* be sorry."

"Anyway," she continued, "I recognize the street name. My hubby and I took that Street of Dreams tour. Amazing homes. Some folks gotta have the whole enchilada, you know?"

Jack knew all too well. The action committee represented The Bluffs. And its members lived there. Not all of the residents were opposed to what the clinic was doing; a few had even inquired about volunteering. Unfortunately, they tended to be less vocal. He glanced down at the woman still holding on to his hand, wondering—

"Dr. Travis? Excuse me, but may I slide this machine in there?"

Jack stepped aside so the tech could set up the EKG equipment. Then he scanned the department's assignment board on his way back to the physicians' desk: orthopedic patient with a too-tight cast, asthmatic on a breathing treatment, lawn mower versus toe needing sutures, and that psychiatric patient waiting for his injection to kick in. Typical day, no surprises. Except for the birdseed . . . and his being mistaken for a drug addict, that is.

Jack settled into his chair and began to review Vesta Calder's history and current medications. Afterward, he'd do a complete physical exam.

He shook his head. Vesta Calder lived in The Bluffs. Which side was she on?

Jack reached for a pen, and his knee bumped into the side of the desk. He was glad he'd covered the sutured wound with a thick padding of roller gauze. Glad, too, that he escaped his makeshift treatment room before that hospital chaplain called for his arrest. From what he'd seen, the woman was attractive, maybe even beautiful. An intriguing possibility. Eclipsed, of course, by the way she'd pointed her cell phone like it was an M16. And by the stubborn jut of her chin as she dismissed him as unsafe before striding away. A gutsy woman. Who'd left no doubt at all which side she was on: any side but his.

- + -

Riley settled onto a cedar bench, hearing the grackles' raucous squawking from the parking lot trees. She was grateful for the shade provided by the hospital's limestone gazebo; early April and already San Antonio temperatures were approaching eighty, with humidity moving toward sticky as a gecko. She smiled, remembering her favorite nanny's colorful saying. *"Sit awhile, child. And have mercy, I'm already sticky as a gecko from chasin' you around your daddy's big yard."*

Of course, Riley never did sit still. Or have mercy, apparently, because as far back as she could remember, she'd tried her best to pierce the protective insulation that came with being an only child. And a Hale—a family that had known unspeakable tragedy at the hands of a kidnapper. Though her sister's death happened long before she was born, it shaped Riley's life. While other kids worried about the bogeyman under their beds, Riley was cautioned endlessly about abduction. Taught that there were godless, greedy people who would do anything to get what her family was blessed to have.

Everything was centered on keeping Riley safe. And it was the reason she launched a quiet, well-mannered, polite rebellion. Not rowdy enough to truly frighten her parents; she loved them too much for that. But just enough to *breathe*. She needed to feel that if any of the truly horrible things she'd been warned about really did happen, she could stand on her own. Survive them.

So Riley tested the boundaries of her privileged and protective world, even if it only meant climbing to the highest branch of the lightning-struck pecan tree at her grandfather's summer home. Or switching names with her best friend during vacation Bible school; writing private, childish poems about Alejandro, the dark-eyed gardener's son; and becoming a nurse.

Riley touched her hospital badge. Being a nurse was her adult act of rebellion, or at least it began that way. Her parents had expected something far different from their only child.

"Watch out! I'm gonna get you!"

A little girl raced toward the gazebo, letting out a howl that was half shriek, half giggle. She wore a yellow tutu, striped tights, and a rainbow-hued wreath of paper flowers in her hair, its ribbons trailing down her back—and snatched at by a boy running close behind. He caught her inches from where Riley sat, crowed with delight, and then cracked a purple egg over the little girl's head. Confetti spewed from inside it, sprinkling the children like ground pepper on a grilled rib eye. They giggled and took off running again.

A woman, heavily pregnant, hurried behind, murmuring a breathless apology to Riley. "My kids haven't stopped squealing since we got back from the field trip to the River Walk. I shouldn't have scheduled my doctor's appointment during Fiesta." She glanced at Riley's hospital badge. "Can you please tell me where the lab is?"

Riley gave the mother directions, then checked her watch. Time to get back; there was paperwork to finish. She stood and brushed confetti from her jacket, along with a bit of broken purple eggshell. *Cascarones.* Fiesta eggs. Lovely, traditional—and great, silly weapons. She'd made them at her Christian grade school in Houston. Poked holes in the egg, blew out the slippery insides. Then decorated the shell with Easter dyes, glitter, crayon, and filled it with colored bits of confetti, sealing the hole with tissue paper. The toughest part was trying to do all of that without breaking the shell.

No . . . the hardest part was finding out she was the only one in the class who'd never been to San Antonio Fiesta. *"Too far, too crowded, not safe,"* her mother had said, dismissing the idea. It didn't take long for Riley to figure out that most truly fun things fell into those categories.

She shook her head at the ugly irony. Despite all her parents' efforts to protect her, keep her close, she'd been viciously attacked and nearly killed in a parking garage barely five miles from her home. The assault that rocked the Houston hospital, validated her parents' fears, and put Riley in the situation she was in now. She crushed the shard of *cascarón* between her fingertips and let the tiny bits fall. She'd been treated as carefully as a fragile eggshell and had been broken anyway. Now her parents wanted her back in Houston. More than that, they wanted her to give up nursing completely, take a position on the board of the Hale Foundation.

Riley couldn't do that. Being part of the trauma team had been the first time in her life that she felt competent and valued. Worthy in her own right. She had to have that back. She'd make it happen. Even if . . .

She raised her eyes toward the ceiling of the gazebo, pressed her palms together, strong against numb. *You know that I need this. You know how hard I've tried. Why aren't you helping me? Please—*

Her prayer was interrupted by a buzzing from her jacket pocket. A text message requesting a chaplain in the ER.

Riley pocketed the phone, checked her watch. It was an hour past change of shift for the emergency department physicians.

Ugh. Jack Travis would be there. The last thing a department steeped in chaos should welcome was a reckless physician. Any more than Riley should be expected to tolerate another arrogant smirk.

Where was a crate of *cascarones* when you needed one?

- + -

"What was that last glucose reading?" Jack swiveled the chair enough to watch through the exam room door as yet another staffer tried to calm Vesta Calder. Without success, it seemed. The woman had started to pick at the tape on her IV. Yanking the needle out was probably part of her current plan. That and climbing over the gurney rail. Why was she so agitated?

"Her blood sugar is normal at 97. I had the tech check it twice to be sure." Kate glanced down at the CT report on the nursing station desk. "We can't blame this new behavior on her brain, either. Completely normal too."

Jack frowned. "So are the labs, except for that first glucose. And her gases and EKG are excellent for her age. I'd wonder about early onset dementia, except that there's no mention of it in her records, and . . ."

"She's not the least bit confused," Kate said, finishing his thought. "She recited her name, address, the current date, and the name of the president. She even told me the breeds of the last five First Dogs—she loves dogs. No, Vesta's not confused. Unless wanting to get out of *here* counts as that." Kate's nose wrinkled. "I can't really blame her. Seven o'clock can't come soon enough for me." She reached up to push back an unruly lock of her short, dark hair. Then her eyes widened as Jack caught hold of her arm. "What?"

"That's what I was going to ask," he answered, pointing at her forearm. "Why are you so bruised?"

"Oh. It's nothing. I let one of the nurses practice IVs on me."

He shot her a look. "Our nurses need practice? Don't tell me that."

Kate started to speak, then hesitated. Jack got the feeling she was being protective. "She's been out of clinical practice for a while, recovering from a work injury."

"What sort of injury?" he asked.

"Cervical fracture with spinal cord involvement—her dominant arm." Kate looked down, and Jack was even more certain she was cautious about this nurse's privacy. He respected that. Jack hated people poking around in his past.

Kate met his gaze again. "But she's doing pretty well."

He peered at her bruises. "Not that well."

Kate nodded reluctantly. "The tough thing is that she was an ER nurse. You know how we are. Just try and make us work anywhere else; not gonna happen. I can relate to how she feels. She's hoping that administration will let her work here in the department as a triage nurse. Get a toe in there to start. But . . ."

"But what?"

"I can't count the number of times I've manned a desk in triage and ended up doing CPR on that floor. Or had a panicked mother come running into the waiting room carrying a child in a blanket, scream that he's not breathing, and shove him into my arms." She swallowed. "What if that happened to her? What if she had to run to the resuscitation room carrying an unconscious toddler? She can't lift her right arm higher than halfway, and it's weak and numb even after a solid year of therapy. I'm afraid she'd . . ." Kate bit her lower lip.

Drop that kid on his head. "And I'm guessing this injured nurse wants you to be a reference when she applies for a job at Alamo Grace."

"She's already working here. As a trauma chaplain and—"

Jack smothered a groan. "Let me guess: safety officer."

Before Kate could answer, a tech interrupted. "Excuse me, but Mr. Farrell—that patient from the mental health facility—is awake again and asking for more medication. He took his gown off and stuffed it into the toilet. I talked him down, but it's not going to last." The tech raised his voice as the sharp whine of a cast cutter rose from the ortho room. "And Mrs. Calder's asking for her clothes. She says she can't stay here any longer."

Jack shook his head. "Tell Mr. Farrell I'll be there in a few minutes." He turned to Kate. "Vesta needs insulin dosages adjusted and a consult with the dietician, probably overnight observation. See if the clerk can get her doctor on the line. I'll go in and explain things to her one more time."

"Wait." Kate plucked at his sleeve. "Let Riley talk with Vesta. I asked her to come by and help."

"Riley?"

Kate nodded. "The chaplain I was telling you about." She glanced toward the department doors. "Ah, here she is."

Jack turned to look.

The Alamo Grace trauma chaplain strode toward the nurses' desk, dark-blonde hair brushing her shoulders, chin held high—tall, confident, and looking anything but sadly impaired. Her dark-lashed blue eyes scanned the room before settling directly on Jack.

"She'll get through to Mrs. Calder," Kate assured. "Riley has a real knack for connecting with people. I've never seen anybody quite like her."

Even a second time around, neither had Jack.

4

RILEY APPROACHED THE DESK, determined to feel far more in control than she had during the conference room skirmish with Jack Travis. It wasn't going to be easy. He was as imposing in faded scrubs as he'd been in Army camouflage: muscled shoulders, strong jaw, wide-bridged nose, dark brows. There was a surprising hint of olive in his complexion, at odds with his sandy hair. And those eyes . . .

He stood as Kate began the introduction. "Dr. Jack Travis . . . Riley Hale, our trauma chaplain."

A corner of Jack's mouth tugged upward. "And you're also the safety officer, I understand." He offered his hand.

Riley extended hers, grateful that it was a handshake she couldn't feel. His gaze already held her in an inescapable grip.

Jack Travis's wide-set eyes were an unusual color—almost amber-brown, like burnt toffee—and framed by inky lashes. A small scar slashed one dark brow as if boasting rugged conflict. Completely fitting; she hadn't missed the fact that he was still wearing his military boots.

Riley cleared her throat. "Assistant safety officer," she clarified, suspecting Jack wasn't going to reveal that they'd met earlier. She wasn't sure if she was relieved by that. Sharing a secret with this man felt too personal and anything but safe. Riley slid her hand from his and turned to Kate. "You needed some help here?"

"Yes. A diabetic patient who wants to leave against medical advice. Jack's tried to convince her, but that just seemed to make her more anxious. Her name's Vesta Calder. She's in room 7. I thought that you might be able to—" She turned at a keening howl coming from the hallway.

A man staggered from an exam room. "Ahhhh . . . my skin's crawling! Make it stop . . . make it quit! I'm gonna do something bad if it doesn't stop. I'm warning you, I'll tear this place up!"

Jack bolted from the desk.

The young man was naked except for orange boxers and clawed at his skin, raising angry red scratches on his chest. In an instant, he lunged toward the opposite wall, ripped equipment off. He hurled a plastic suction canister, oxygen masks, then grabbed at—

"He's got an oxygen tank!" Riley shouted to the clerk. "Page Mr. Strong. Get security here!"

Two techs whipped past as Kate and the other nurses closed exam doors and cautioned patients to stay back.

Riley's heart hammered, her mouth going dry as Jack approached the screaming and incoherent patient. He spoke calmly, keeping his hands quiet and visible. "Easy, easy . . . I'm here to help, buddy."

"I don't trust you!" the man shrieked, clutching the heavy tank. His bleeding chest heaved. "You're all trying to kill me. You're—"

"I'm a doctor." Jack widened his stance and hunched slightly as the wild-eyed patient hefted the oxygen cylinder shoulder-high, quite obviously threatening him. Jack waved a tech back, then took a step forward. "Mr. Farrell, put that down. Now."

The PA system squawked with static and the patient startled. He jerked the green tank overhead, muscles straining and anxious eyes riveted on the ceiling tiles.

"Mr. Strong, ER. Mr. Strong to the emergency department."

Jack saw the opportunity and lunged forward. The patient howled as he heaved the metal tank, missing Jack's head by inches. The cylinder hit the floor with a thunderous metallic thud and skidded, letting out an explosive hiss as the flow meter struck the wall. Screams echoed from the exam rooms.

Jack tackled the patient, pulled him down. He dodged a flying fist and flipped the man onto his stomach, one big hand holding his face to the floor. In seconds, the techs and two security officers were on the floor beside him.

Jack raised his head, called toward the nurses' station, "Grab the Haldol!"

A surge of adrenaline carried Riley halfway to the medicine cupboard before she realized that, of course, she had no keys. Kate was beside her in an instant, grabbed the vial and syringes, and jogged toward the huddle of staff on the floor.

Riley watched from the desk as the drama subsided. She was trembling; the last time she'd witnessed an attack on hospital staff, two men had died. She'd been a chaplain then, too, her arm still in a sling from her own assault six months prior. She rubbed her left hand over her right, telling herself that she was much better now. Stronger. No sling, and not nearly as clumsy with her fingers. If she'd had access to those keys, she'd have retrieved the Haldol and the syringes. She'd have been a member of the team kneeling on the floor beside Jack Travis. But she was here as a chaplain, not a staff nurse. She sighed and then squared her shoulders.

Riley caught the attention of the clerk. "Excuse me; I'm supposed to look in on a patient named Calder."

"Room 7."

"Thank you."

Riley glanced toward Mr. Farrell's room, saw Jack standing watch as a tech secured temporary soft limb restraints for the safety of both patient and staff. Then she walked toward Mrs. Calder's room, pausing outside briefly as she'd been taught to do in chaplain's training. *Be present, Lord. Let me listen with compassion, not try to fix or judge. Just . . . listen.* It would be especially important now. If this woman had been agitated and frightened to begin with, hearing the violent scuffle in the hallway would only make it worse. Riley took a soft breath, opened the door.

The room was empty.

She scanned it, her stomach sinking. The side rails of the gurney were locked upright, the bedside table and tray of cafeteria food shoved aside. An IV hung overhead, its tubing dangling uselessly into the rumpled bedsheets. A trail of red droplets led from the sheets to the vinyl floor to the doorway where Riley stood. Blood. Like a telltale scene from a *CSI* episode.

Vesta Calder was a runaway.

- + -

Jack dragged his stethoscope back and forth across the nape of his neck, watching as the chaplain continued with her call to hospital security. She held the desk phone receiver in her left hand.

Jack studied the long curve of Riley's neck, visible now that she'd tilted her head to one side. A cervical spine injury . . . and surgery maybe? Likely, if there had been bone fragments that impinged on the fragile spinal cord, and . . . Jack stilled the seesaw of his stethoscope. Kate had said that it was a work-related injury. What had happened? Statistics would point to a serious fall if Riley were a much older woman. But young people tended to break their necks in motor vehicle accidents or as a result of sports mishaps. He frowned, thinking of a young soldier who'd survived two tours in Afghanistan only to become a paraplegic after rolling his ATV into a ditch on his grandparents' ranch.

The chaplain looked athletic. Jack's gaze swept from the shoulders of Riley's tailored suit jacket past her shapely hips to toned calves, and—

"Nothing," she said, turning toward him and effectively halting his clinical assessment. "They've found no trace of Mrs. Calder. No response to the overhead pages, not a sign of her in the cafeteria. And no taxis have arrived front or back."

The chaplain gave a quick nod. "I checked all the first-floor lavatories and left a message on her home phone."

Jack felt an irrational urge to salute. Injured or not, Chaplain Hale was impressively on task. He glanced at the nurses' station clock. "It's been at least thirty minutes. She could have called for a ride." To his annoyance, an image of the white Lexus intruded. Jack scraped his fingers through his hair. "At least she ate some food. But I still can't figure out why she left."

Riley cleared her throat. "Did she seem to have any issues with the staff?"

He raised his brows. "You mean with *me?*"

Her blue eyes met his, unblinking. "It happens."

He started to smile, but it gave way to irritation. "No. She didn't have issues with me or any of the staff as far as I know. She was relatively cooperative, intelligent, and as lucid as a person can be after bouncing back from a serum glucose of 39. And a seizure."

Riley's eyes widened.

"That's right. Which is why it's important that she gets follow-up."

"Of course."

Jack glanced around the ER, doing a quick assessment of patient status, and then turned back to Riley. "Look, I don't know why Mrs. Calder hightailed it out of here without letting us know. And, frankly, I don't know why Kate involved you. I needed a dietician, a callback from her internist. In hindsight, maybe a security guard watching that exam room door."

"But not a chaplain."

"Not a chaplain." Jack sighed. "She wasn't dead or dying. She just needed her insulin adjusted."

Riley's lips parted, then closed as if she'd changed her mind about something she was going to say. She held his gaze for a moment. "I understand what you're saying."

He seriously doubted that. "Well . . . thank you for leaving a message on her phone; that helps. I'll handle the rest. I won't keep you any longer."

"Fine."

The chaplain started to walk away but turned back instead. She strode up to him, close enough that Jack smelled the scent of peaches in her hair.

"Tell Kate I'll be in my office for another half hour or so," she said, her voice lowering to a throaty whisper. "In case anyone *dies*."

- + -

Please don't let me die. Not here. Please, God . . . let me get home.

Vesta Calder stumbled along the darkened wall, her damp palm sticking to its cool enamel surface as her vision blurred and the familiar wave of dizziness threatened to drown her. She sucked a ragged breath, gasped, and tried again, the suddenly too-humid air smothering her like a heavy, sodden towel. Her knees weakened and she leaned against the wall to keep from falling. If she rested a few minutes, caught her breath, she could make it to the hallway again, then across the lobby to the front door. And somehow . . . make it back home. When she got home, she'd be okay. Safe in familiar surroundings. She knew that was all she needed. Unless it was different this time . . .

Vesta squinted in the dim light, her vision still blurry and narrowed as if she were staring through the wrong end of her birding binoculars—and the lens was smeared with Vaseline. She had no idea where she was, only that it was so much better than the emergency department exam room with the bright lights, noise, shouts, and screaming. She'd navigated the hallways, ducked into the first quiet place she could find.

Where am I?

She drew in another breath, willed her heart to stop pummeling her ears, and forced herself to look around. She tried to focus on each detail as if she were identifying a wild bird by its markings: primary feathers, secondaries, ear patch, eye ring, crown, and flanks. She concentrated. Carpeted room, chairs, but no tables. No, there was one table at the end of the room, though it was more of a podium. And a tall vase of Texas bluebonnets. Sconce lighting, an arched window—with no light coming through. Was it a glass mosaic . . . with a white bird?

Concentrate. Yes, a dove. Vesta tried to swallow, ran her tongue over her lips, and realized her legs were numb, toes already cramping viciously. *God, please . . . don't let me die here. Let me go home.*

She slid slowly down the wall to the carpet, felt her hands begin to tingle. One of them was sticky with dried blood. She groaned as her lungs fought, each breath coming like an old locomotive through a dark, airless tunnel. Faster, faster. Gasping, chugging—

"Vesta?"

A young woman, blonde, with beautiful blue eyes, knelt close, startling Vesta for an instant. Then she touched Vesta's shoulder very gently. "Are you Mrs. Calder?"

"Yes," Vesta whispered, lips numb, tears filling her eyes to brimming. *Thank you, God.*

The woman's smile was warm. "Vesta, my name is Riley. I'm a hospital chaplain." She reached in the pocket of her jacket and pulled out a cell phone. "I'm going to call for help, but I won't leave you, even for a minute. I promise. I'll make sure you're safe. Okay?"

Vesta nodded, felt a tear slide down her cheek.

"It looks like you're hyperventilating. That happens when you breathe too fast. It makes you feel anxious and tingly. Has that happened to you before?"

Vesta nodded again.

"Okay." Riley lifted her phone. "I'm going to run some interference and see if I can have help come to you. Right here, in the chapel. I understand that it was hard for you to wait down there in the emergency department. It's not an easy place to be."

A first glimmer of hope eased Vesta's anxiety. Her breathing relaxed. *She understands. This beautiful child knows how I feel.*

"Here we go." The chaplain punched in a number. "Take hold of my hand while we wait."

"My . . ." Vesta's voice emerged in a scratching croak. "Fingers . . . are numb."

Riley's hand, warm and reassuring, found hers. She smiled. "That's all right. So are mine."

The chaplain nestled the cell phone between her shoulder and cheek. Her expression was confident, determined, as she said, "Dr. Jack Travis, please."

5

JACK CROUCHED BESIDE THE HOSPITAL WHEELCHAIR, grimacing as his bandaged knee connected with the worn carpet. He glanced to where Riley Hale stood, telling himself that just because he was currently in a chapel—down on his knees—it didn't mean the chaplain had won this round.

Won? When had he started competing with this woman?

"Looks like you're feeling better now." Jack slid two fingers along Vesta Calder's wrist, noting that her skin was warm and dry and pulse rate was mid-80 range and regular. Her respiratory rate had normalized as well. Good. Though she seemed far from serene, at least the panic had receded from her eyes. *Except for when she looks at me? Am I imagining that?*

"Tingling all gone?" he asked gently.

Vesta nodded, avoiding his eyes—he wasn't imagining it. "I'm sorry to have caused all these problems. I'm fine now. And once I'm home . . ." She turned to Riley. "My neighbor's here?"

"Waiting at the curb with her car. The aide's in the hallway ready to wheel you out. We're all set, and—" Riley's eyes met Jack's—"as soon as Dr. Travis gives us the official go-ahead, you'll be back in The Bluffs in ten minutes flat."

The Bluffs. Jack stood, felt his stitches protest. "Your doctor will be calling you this evening. And you have the dietician's recommendations. No skipping meals. Rest tonight. Check your blood sugar before bedtime." He glanced at Riley. "What was that reading you got just now?"

"It was 128."

"Right. Good."

Vesta glanced at the tidy pile of monitoring equipment sitting on one of the chapel chairs. "I never knew that a hospital chaplain did those things: blood pressure readings and checking sugar levels."

"I'm a nurse, too." Riley's chin lifted a fraction of an inch. "I was a nurse . . . *first.*" Her left hand moved to cradle her right arm, her expression almost wistful. Then she turned to Jack. "Vesta's good to go?"

"Absolutely." He extended his hand to his patient. "It was a pleasure to meet you, Mrs. Calder."

"I . . ." Vesta hesitated, then took his hand. There was no mistaking the discomfort in her age-lined eyes. "Thank you for your kindness, Dr. Travis." Her voice dropped to a halting whisper. "And . . . I'm . . . so sorry. Please forgive me. For . . . everything."

Forgive you?

Jack watched as the nurse's aide wheeled Vesta from the chapel. Riley followed, resting a hand on the woman's shoulder and dipping her head to talk as they moved along. Trying to ease her anxiety, Jack supposed. It was what Riley had been doing since Jack arrived to find her beside Vesta Calder, the patient huddled against the chapel wall in a panicked state. She'd probably have done the same things in the ER if she'd had the opportunity to speak with Vesta earlier. Jack had told Riley in no uncertain terms that he had no need for a chaplain because his patient wasn't dead or dying.

He frowned. Though he'd probably sounded dismissive, he'd been telling the truth. It was only when the life-saving frenzy ebbed into silence and Jack found himself armed with nothing but an industrial-size box of Kleenex that he ever thought of summoning chaplaincy services. Or acquiesced to what they might offer to a patient or family member—"spiritual support." Prayer. He wouldn't argue that it had its place in hospitals . . . and on the battlefield too. But only when there were no viable options left, nothing for a doctor to *do*. No action, no answer, and no life-stealing enemy to grab by the throat and wrestle to the ground. Whether that enemy came in the guise of disease, injury, a roadside desert bomb . . . or as a consequence of inexcusable cowardice.

Action was what Jack understood. Prayer was passive at best. At worst it was surrender, an admission of defeat. If Jack could help it, he would never go down that road. And he certainly wouldn't be *here*, in a chapel.

Except that, in a complete turnabout, he'd been summoned here by a hospital chaplain. To care for a patient who wasn't dead or dying but had fled his care in a panic. *Why?* He thought of Vesta Calder's increasing agitation after regaining consciousness in the ER. And the look in her eyes when she'd accepted his handshake a few minutes ago. A combination of fear and pain.

"Please forgive me. For . . . everything." Strange comment. Had she been apologizing for leaving the department against medical advice?

Jack pulled out his hospital phone and informed the ER clerk he was on his way back to the department. He headed out of the chapel, determined to stop imagining that the neighbor who'd come for Vesta Calder was driving a white Lexus, that his patient had hyperventilated because she'd recognized him as the "maverick" whose negligence nearly set her neighborhood on fire. And that she was a card-carrying member of The Bluffs' action committee.

He shook his head at conjecture that amounted to no more than fatigue-induced paranoia. Vesta Calder was a woman who was uncomfortable in the hospital setting, a diabetic who'd had an insulin-induced seizure. She had no personal connection to Jack or his clinic; she was simply one in a long line of patients he would treat today. Once he got back on track.

His Vibram boot soles squeaked against the vinyl flooring as he marched down the corridor, mentally assigning priorities to the tasks ahead. Coffee, black. Reevaluate the psych patient and the asthmatic. Stitch the lawn mower injury. Call the clinic. Check on Gilbert. Snag himself a tetanus booster. And then figure out a way to smooth things over with the gutsy and beautiful nurse-chaplain that wouldn't look too much like surrender. She'd helped him by finding his patient despite their personal conflict. And Jack had far bigger battles to fight.

- + -

"You managed it okay, then?" Kate Callison handed Riley half of her organic oatmeal cookie. "Mrs. Calder's vital signs and the finger stick for her blood sugar?"

"Well . . ." Riley leaned back against the gazebo bench, noticing the raisin-brown freckles dotting her friend's nose and feeling thankful to have someone she could confide in. "No problem with the Velcro on the blood pressure cuff. The unit's automatic, so—" Riley poked her finger against the cookie half—"just a punch of a button."

"And the finger stick?"

"More than awkward. It took me three pokes because this maddening numbness makes it hard to tell how much pressure I'm using." Riley held the cookie in her left hand and attempted to break off a piece with her right index finger and thumb. "See?" She tensed her lips, tried again. "Too little and nothing happens at all. Too much and—" Pulverized oatmeal speckled her shirt, then settled into her lap.

Kate nodded. "And the cookie crumbles."

"Or the cookie bruises. Horribly." Riley glanced at Kate's battered arm and winced. "I'm—"

"Making progress," Kate insisted, dodging Riley's apology. "You're making steady progress." Her lips curved toward a smile. "And you kept Jack Travis from having to fill out a patient elopement form. The man's already struggling with community PR; now on his second shift at Alamo Grace, he tackles one patient, has another go AWOL . . ." Kate's dark brows nudged together. "Seriously, thank you for finding Vesta. I was worried even before she ran off. That's why I called you. Do you think she has an anxiety disorder of some kind? And maybe the incident with our psych patient made her panic and run?"

"Maybe." Riley swiped at the crumbs on her jacket, then glanced toward a pair of long-tailed black grackles. They strutted along the edge of the ER parking lot, beaks raised straight up and piercing yellow eyes staring at the sky. Common for them, but a quirky behavior that made it look as if they, like Chicken Little, expected the sky to fall at any moment.

For as long as Riley could remember, she'd hated those birds.

"Vesta had a full-blown panic attack," Riley explained, turning her attention back to Kate. "She's had them before. My concern would be how much this is affecting her life overall. Especially her ability to access medical care. I plan to talk with her about it when I make my home visit."

"Visit?"

Riley read the surprise on Kate's face. "Not to poke her fingers; don't worry. I'm going to Vesta's home as a chaplain." Riley sighed and her hand rose instinctively to support her weakened arm. "There's a whole different set of expectations when you're not responding to the wail of sirens. But I'm not complaining. I love having the luxury of time to listen—really listen—to my patients. You know?"

Kate shrugged. "Maybe I'm more like Jack. Get the job done and be prepared to tackle when necessary. Don't get bogged down with the emotional . . . side dishes."

Side dishes? Riley trusted that Kate wasn't really equating her job as chaplain with coleslaw, Texas ranch beans, sweet corn, guacamole—or whatever healthful and organic accompaniments they served in northern California. Besides, if everything worked out the way she hoped, it was only a matter of time before Riley was hired as an Alamo Grace emergency department triage nurse. Time and an all-important medical clearance. It was in the works.

"Oh, I forgot," Kate said, after checking her watch. "Your mother called." She rolled her eyes. "Of course, it took me a minute to figure out that she wasn't identifying the capital of North Carolina."

Riley raised her brows.

"She asked for 'Rah-lee,' as in *Raleigh*." Kate grinned widely, an event worth any teasing. "With an accent that still escapes me after nearly a year of living in this state. Anyway, she said she'd try your cell phone."

"I'm sure she will." Riley sighed. "To tell me one more time that I should move back to Houston."

"And work at a hospital there?"

"Nope." Riley grimaced. "To take a position on the board of my family's charitable organization. Some of that involves grants for hospitals and clinics and scholarships for medical education." She shook her head. "That's the carrot, anyway—that I'd still be involved with medicine. But it would be a more 'civilized environment.' Which in Hale parentspeak translates into 'safe.'"

"Maybe they have a point. Jack did dodge a flying oxygen tank today. And I've only been a nurse for five years, but I've been bitten and swung at, knocked over by gurneys, spit on, pushed—" Kate bit her lip. "I'm sorry. I don't have to tell you that our work can be dangerous. You almost died on hospital grounds." Her dark eyes were gentle. "But would it be so bad?"

"Going back to Houston?" Riley's stomach tensed. "You mean giving up?"

"I mean not having to worry." Kate glanced down at the trio of purple bruises on her arm. "About crumbling cookies. Or passing your next CPR recertification." She met Riley's gaze. "Being a chaplain's one thing, but . . ."

"As triage nurse, I wouldn't have to do those things." Riley noted Kate's sudden change of expression. "What?"

Kate was silent for a few seconds. "It's just that no one can predict what will happen, Riley. You know that better than anyone. And so does nursing administration. A triage nurse is a staff nurse too, so—" Kate's cell buzzed. She slid the phone from her pocket, scanned the text, and sighed.

"The ER?"

Kate stood. "Paula needs help holding a kid for treatment. Confetti under his upper eyelid. Or a piece of broken eggshell." She wrinkled her nose. "Fiesta eggs. What do they call those things?"

"*Cascarones.*"

"Right. Supposed to bring luck if you get hit over the head with one. I think I'll take my chances with a fortune cookie— never caught one in the eye." Kate tossed her apple core into the pebbled trash can. "You're off shift now?"

"Yes." Riley stood and brushed the last lingering crumbs from her jacket. "But I need to pack up those training manikins in the conference room."

"Have a housekeeping tech do that for you."

"No need." Riley hoped she was imagining the look on Kate's face. *Like someone with a gimpy arm can't manage that task.* "I got the equipment out, and I'll put it back."

"Sure." Kate's forehead wrinkled. "Did I say something wrong?"

"Of course not," Riley said quickly, hating that she'd sounded defensive enough for her friend to pick up on it. "Thanks for the cookie."

"Anytime . . . Rah-lee."

Riley watched as Kate jogged the pavement toward the ambulance doors, stethoscope bouncing against her blue scrubs. A nurse going back to her team, fully capable of handling whatever came through those doors, knowing that her strength, intelligence, and skills could very well mean the difference between life and death for someone today. A woman confident in the face of that daunting challenge.

That used to be me.

Riley hugged her arms around herself, numb fingers gripping at the fabric of her jacket. Could Kate have any idea how much Riley wanted what she had? To feel whole, not broken . . . She thought of what Kate had said earlier this morning when Riley had failed to perform adequately on the CPR manikin. That as chaplain Riley *was* part of the emergency team, that she was great at what she did. What if she'd said that because she thought Riley would never be able to return to emergency department nursing? *"Being a chaplain's one thing, but . . . A triage nurse is a staff nurse too . . ."* What had Kate meant by that? Was she still willing to talk with the other charge nurses about Riley's job proposal?

Riley pushed the thought aside and headed toward the side entrance to the hospital, the route closest to the conference room. She'd load the manikins, left-handed, onto a rolling cart and push them back to the storage closet in the ER. Easy, quick.

She frowned. Unless Rambo Travis had left a mess after suturing himself at the conference room table. It seemed like the incident had happened weeks ago, not hours. And they'd been thrown together twice since.

She'd felt Jack watching her in the chapel as she struggled to prick Vesta's finger, slide the blood droplet into the monitoring machine. Long, breath-holding moments, while she silently prayed she could do it—and that he wouldn't notice how hard the simple task was for her. Riley had steeled herself against the real possibility that Jack might be impatient, make some snide criticism. But he didn't. He'd been quiet, professional . . . completely respectful. And there was something about the way he'd knelt on the floor beside the wheelchair, military boots on the chapel's carpet, rugged profile silhouetted against the golden glass mosaic with its white dove, his voice so deep and gentle . . . It had taken her by surprise—an intriguing contrast to what she'd seen of him before.

Riley's lips tightened with irritation. There was no reason to give Jack Travis credit he didn't deserve. The truth was he hadn't even bothered to thank her for finding Vesta Calder. Which meant he still had trouble accepting the fact that a chaplain had been useful to a patient who wasn't "dead or dying." He made his opinion on that very clear. Fortunately, Dr. Travis had nothing to do with Riley's plans to return to the ER as triage nurse. And even when she accomplished that—was back in scrubs—she'd have to tolerate him only rarely. According to Kate, Jack worked primarily in other hospitals. And at his clinic, of course. Riley shook her head. She'd heard more than she'd cared to about his handling of that place.

She stepped onto the hospital sidewalk just yards from the door, skirting a sizable flock of grackles. Most of them, as usual, stared ominously at the sky. Waiting for it to fall . . . expecting the worst. Exactly what Riley had been taught all her life. *My entire life.*

She walked on, stomach churning as she recalled Kate's reaction to the idea of her moving back to Houston—giving up nursing: *"Would it be so bad?"*

Yes. It would, and—

"Ugh!" Riley sucked a breath through her teeth, whirled away from the door, and stomped her feet on the cement, sending the grackles into a shrieking flurry. Black feathers scraped the air, inches from her face. Frantic yellow eyes glared, but she squeezed hers shut and stood her ground. "Stay away from me!"

"So noted."

Who . . . ? Riley blinked, turned back toward the door.

Jack Travis smiled.

6
+

"YOU STARTLED ME." The chaplain eyed Jack warily, a hint of color infusing her cheeks.

"I think those birds might say the same." Jack glanced toward his dusty black Hummer, parked mere yards away. "And looks like my car could prove it—pretty good shelling." He turned back to her. "Don't worry; I won't expect you to wash it."

Riley crossed her arms. "I wasn't going to offer."

"I see that." Jack shook his head, studied her face for a moment. Blue eyes, dark brows and lashes, the pink flush on her cheeks at odds with the very determined set of her mouth. And with the way she'd just tugged her jacket close, squared her shoulders, and turned—"Hey, wait. Don't go. I wanted to . . ." Jack cleared his throat. "I want to thank you."

She turned back, eyes widening.

"For finding my patient," Jack explained. "She needed those instructions, and frankly, I don't need any more controversy. I won't bore you with the details, but it's already been a long day."

"I saw the news. A film clip of the man on fire at the clinic."

"Film?" Jack ground his teeth together as he thought of the young man with the camera phone.

"Yes." Riley stared at him for a moment. "And there was an interview with a woman who claimed to be representing the surrounding neighborhood."

"Let me guess—she wasn't organizing a barbecue in my honor."

The chaplain's lips twitched toward a smile that didn't materialize. She met his gaze, expression growing serious. "She was pretty free with descriptions of you, like 'maverick,' 'irresponsible,' and 'reckless.'"

"I'm sure," Jack said, noticing that Riley had planted her hands on her hips. "But that's only one opinion, so—"

"And then I got an earful from Mrs. Calder's neighbor."

Jack groaned. "Do you think Vesta is part of that group? And that's why she ran off? Because of the campaign against me?"

"I'm not sure. It could have been a trigger. Regardless, she sure didn't need the added drama of her neighbor's rant. I defused it as quickly as I could."

He didn't bother to hide his surprise.

"I explained that you'd done exactly the right things in treating Vesta's emergency, that if she hadn't been fortunate enough to have such skilled care, the outcome could have been . . . well, tragic. And that Alamo Grace Hospital wouldn't have you on staff if you weren't more than competent—" her mouth twitched—"and caring, of course."

"So this neighbor . . ." Jack hesitated, stunned that she'd defended him. "She believed it?"

"Let's say that she believed *me*—after she realized that she knew my parents. Small world." Riley shrugged, then glanced down to check her watch. "I've got to put some equipment away before I go home. I'll get a written report to you after I meet with Vesta again. Maybe I can shed some light on her anxiety. All subject to confidentiality, of course."

"You're meeting with her?"

"A home visit. As part of our Senior House Calls program." She sighed. "Anyway, I'll let you know if I learn anything medically helpful."

"Okay, then. Good." He scraped his hand through his hair. "Look, I know we haven't seen eye to eye on much . . ." He shook his head. "Okay, on anything. But I do appreciate your finding my patient, getting me out of that jam. And I especially appreciate that you went to bat for me with the neigh—" He stopped short as Riley raised her palm.

"Hold it," she said, her expression intense. "You've got that wrong—all wrong. I didn't find Vesta Calder to help *you* out of a jam. I went looking for her because that poor woman was distraught and frightened enough to yank a needle from her arm and run, bleeding, down the hall to find someplace safe. I was concerned about *her*."

"I . . ." Jack paused as twin splotches of color deepened on her cheeks.

"Please. I'm not finished." Riley swiped at an errant strand of her bangs. "The other thing you got wrong is assuming that I 'went to bat' for you. I hardly *know* you. And I'll be honest: what I do know makes me more than a little wary. The reason I smoothed that neighbor's ruffled feathers was to keep Vesta from being frightened all over again about the quality of her medical care. And because portraying a positive, caring image of Alamo Grace Hospital is part of my job as chaplain. Which I do for the living as well as the dead." Riley's lips pursed. "Campaigning for Dr. Jackson Travis *isn't* my job."

She punched in the door's security code and then disappeared into the hospital. Leaving Jack with the feeling that she'd stomped him as handily as she had that flock of stupid birds.

Gilbert DeSoto was propped on the observation room gurney as regally as a king on his throne. Except for the oxygen tubing, slathered burn ointment, and singed-off left eyebrow—which made him look comically off balance.

Gilbert smiled, revealing toothless gums, as Jack approached. "Doc, excuse my flappin' gums. They took away my teeth. Said they had to watch my mouth for more swelling." He pointed to a plastic denture cup on the bedside table. "Didn't stop me from eatin' pie, though." He shook his head with a loud murmur of appreciation. "Coconut cream—crust nearly as fine as my own sweet Helen's, bless her soul. And a double shot of strawberry Ensure." He pulled a Kleenex from a box and folded it carefully, then slid it between the pages of the small book he'd been reading. "They promised me my teeth before supper. Something with meat. Hope I get to stay."

Jack smiled, remembering Vesta's equally eager desire to flee.

He grabbed a chair, pulled it close while he scanned Gilbert's monitoring equipment. Cardiac rhythm—a-fib, which could indeed keep him here for supper—oxygen, blood pressure cuff, IV . . . probably some morphine, considering the pinpoint size of his pupils. And his talkative good humor in the face of considerable pain.

"Glad they're treating you well, Gilbert."

"No complaints. They've been real kind to an old man who got drunk and set himself on fire with a cigarette he dug outta some trash can." He squeezed his eyes shut for a moment, and when he opened them, they were filled with tears. "I'm sorry I caused so much trouble, Doc. You and Bandy and the folks at the clinic have been nothing but good to me. And how do I pay you back? By starting a fire that coulda burned that place of mercy down."

And still might close it, pal. "It's okay, Gilbert. No real harm done. And you're going to be fine. That's what matters."

A tear slid down the man's face, beading on the burn salve. "Thank you for bein' there, Doc. One of the medics said you sliced your leg open trying to help me."

"He exaggerated. Band-Aid, tetanus shot. Don't worry about it. Let's just get you well and out of here." Jack smiled. "After supper. Did they get you set up with a place to stay?"

"Got a list of shelters, some new ones. And treatment centers for the booze. Guess they're obliged to offer that. Been in and out of those places for more than thirty years; I can recite that Serenity Prayer backward. Truthfully, I'm not sure it will ever stick." He shook his head, tapped the book with his finger. "But that lady chaplain said we never get too old for hope. It was a good thing to hear."

"Riley came to visit you?"

Gilbert lifted the book. "Brought me this Bible. Beautiful young woman, face like an angel. And you have to admire that she's here mingling with folks like me. Considering."

"Considering what?"

"You know. Her family and all. I asked as soon as I saw her name tag." Gilbert touched a tentative fingertip to his blistered lower lip. "What? You never heard of the Hales?" He raised his brows, one gray, the other no more than a sooty smudge. Then he let out a cackle that exposed his gums, smooth and pink as a newborn piglet. "Hale Ranch and Hardware. That's her granddaddy. I used to sell his goods from Brownsville to South Padre. Even bowled on the Hale Hardware league for a while. I was pretty good, too—more than a couple of 600 series." Gilbert raised his thumb. "She got a kick out of hearing that. Then there's Senator Bascom Hale, the uncle. Grooming him for a future presidential run, I heard. But I don't always get the latest politics—sometimes my newspapers are wrapped around fish innards." Gilbert showed his gums again. "Plus Hale & Associates, her daddy's business."

"And Hale Medical Foundation . . . those Hales?"

"Yup." Gilbert nodded. "Lots of cement and steel in that young lady's family. She could be sipping tea, with her pretty pinkie up, anywhere she wants. But here she is, talkin' hope to an old man who smells like a burnt corn dog." He clucked his tongue. "Which reminds me, do you know when this place serves supper?"

- + -

Kate set her bottle of water on the nurses' station desk and then pressed her hands to her lower back, stretching against its achy stiffness. She would never go two days without her Pilates work-out again. A floor full of moving boxes at home was no excuse. Neither was the return of that familiar slogging-through-mud sadness she'd tried so hard to leave behind in California. She hated—despised—its tenacious, cruel attempts to mire her in the past. That part of her life was over. And the way it had ended was for the best. *All of it.*

Kate's throat tightened and she reached for her water. In a couple of hours she'd be off duty, so—

She turned as Jack Travis arrived beside her.

"No need for that second dose of 'vitamin H,'" he said, refer-ring to the Haldol he'd prescribed for their tank-tossing psych patient. "He's fairly lucid in there now. And willing to volun-tarily admit himself for evaluation." Jack's brown eyes crinkled at the edges. "Maybe you'll get to finish out your shift without any more incident reports, Callison. I'm guessing you don't welcome them either."

"Like a scorpion in my shower." Kate grimaced. "Don't ask. I'll never get used to Texas. But I *am* glad Riley's following up with Vesta Calder."

Jack's smile was replaced by an expression Kate couldn't quite read. Skepticism? She could understand his concern about the role of spiritual support in the chaos of the ER. She still felt that way. Defibrillator paddles first; prayer way down the line. Offered by someone else, not her. Still—"Riley's good at what she does, Jack."

"And thus wants to give it up?"

"She wants to practice clinical skills, too. Hands-on patient care. As part of the ER team in the way she was before . . ."

Before that monster broke her neck, nearly killed her. Kate took a breath. "Before an injury that was beyond her control. It's not fair. Riley loved being an ER nurse; it's hard to accept never being able to do that again." She met Jack's gaze. "What if something hugely important to *you* was just snatched away?"

Jack glanced around at the bustle of the ER before asking, "Is Riley still capable?"

Kate raised her brows.

"Of performing the physical tasks required of an ER staff nurse," Jack explained. "Giving medications, doing treatments—" he ticked a list off on his fingers—"clearing an airway, pumping stomachs, handling a defibrillator, starting IVs . . ." His gaze dropped toward her bruised arm, and Kate reminded herself to wear her scrub jacket to the charge nurse meeting.

Kate swallowed. "She's proposing a position as a triage nurse."

"You reminded me that you'd done CPR on the triage floor. And wondered how Riley would cope if someone shoved an unconscious kid into her arms." His expression softened. "Right?"

Kate's stomach sank. "Right."

Jack dragged his stethoscope back and forth against his neck. He was quiet for a while, then pinned Kate with his gaze. "As charge nurse, do you really want her out there in triage? Do you feel comfortable with that?"

Thanks a bunch, Rambo. "Please, give me a scorpion in my shower, but don't ask me . . ." Kate tugged a short wisp of her hair. "Look, Riley's a friend. And she's going to be my roommate, too. She's sharp, dedicated, and incredibly perceptive. I have complete confidence in her assessment skills. But she's had almost no opportunity to practice clinical tasks." She stared at

Jack, wanting him to understand how trapped-in-the-middle she felt. "I've never known a triage nurse who wasn't expected to be certified and competent in *all* emergency department skills. But then we've never had a chaplain assigned exclusively to the ER either. Maybe administration will make an exception in this case, too."

"Because . . . ?"

"Because . . ." Kate stopped herself. "Because Riley's an exceptional person."

"I see."

Kate wasn't sure he did, but she wasn't going to bring up the subject of the Hale family's connections to the Grace Hospital system. Or Riley's obvious discomfort with their protective hovering. She finished her water, then glanced up as the triage strobe flashed. "I'd better check on that. I told the nurse to take a break. She's still having trouble with morning sickness."

"Right. Oh, hey . . ." Jack reached into the pocket of his scrub top and pulled out a medication-filled syringe. "I picked up a dip-tet from the pharmacy. When you get back, can I get you to give it to me?"

Kate smiled slowly. "What's the matter, Dr. Travis? Don't you trust anyone else?"

- + -

Riley punched in the security code, pushed her hip into the door leading to the emergency department corridor, then pulled the equipment-laden cart along behind her. She'd piled the CPR manikins—Adult Sani-Man, Buddy Infant, and Toddler Tim— three high and tucked the rubber IV arm and other equipment

on the shelf below. She chuckled, glad the hospital hadn't pur-
chased the heaviest manikin, Fat Old Fred. The training device
was used to simulate the challenge of performing CPR on an
obese, elderly patient.

Riley pulled the cart along the last stretch of hallway toward
the storage closet just beyond the ER doctors' combination
office and sleeping room. She rested her right hand on the cart's
handle, using it alternately with her left. It was weaker but pulling nevertheless. With her particular injury, pulling was easier
than pushing. Riley wheeled on, heard the bustle of the ER in
the distance, felt her pulse quicken slightly. It wasn't quite a
gurney, but she was doing it.

She thought of Kate's advice to call a housekeeping tech
and felt a small surge of pride. She hadn't needed help. The
plastic manikin family was no problem to transport, nor had
the conference room cleanup been difficult. Surprisingly, Jack
Travis had tidied up after—

Oh no. Riley stopped the cart abruptly as Jack stepped from
the ER physicians' office into the hallway. The IV arm slid to
the floor, palm up.

He jogged forward to help.

"Thank you," she said, suddenly wishing it were Fat Old
Fred who'd been catapulted to the floor. In flames. It would
have been a nice diversion while she ran off and called housekeeping to finish up. She'd had one too many run-ins with
Rambo Travis today.

"You're welcome." Jack slid the arm back onto the cart, then
stood looking down at Riley for long enough that she felt the
heat rise in her face. He reached into his scrub shirt pocket. "Do

me a favor now?" He pulled out a small, preloaded syringe and smiled at the look on her face. "A tetanus shot, Safety Officer. I swear."

"I don't understand."

"I need a tetanus shot. You're a nurse. Unless you fibbed to Vesta Calder."

Riley squirmed. "Of course not. But . . ."

"You've given shots?"

"Hundreds."

"So, please. Help me out?" He glanced into the office. "I have an alcohol swab, a Band-Aid—everything I need but you." He stepped back into the office, leaving her in the doorway. "I'm sitting down. Six hours into my tragic risk of lockjaw. Which is almost always fatal."

She smiled despite the fact that she'd begun to tremble—deep inside, where she knew that the only injections she'd given in more than a year were into a dozen H-E-B grocery store oranges. She'd developed a left-handed system and, in fact, hadn't done too badly. No complaints from any injected produce. But . . .

Jack held out the syringe. "Six hours and forty seconds. My jaw's feeling tense."

"Oh . . . fine."

She strode into the small office, refusing to acknowledge the sound of her heart pounding in her ears. Or that it kicked up more than a notch as he lifted the sleeve of his scrub top to reveal a smoothly muscled left shoulder. *Very* muscled. "Be a gentleman and open that alcohol swab?"

"Sure." He handed her the syringe. "And no, I don't have any drug allergies."

"Thanks. I was about to ask." Riley read the label on the medication before taking the offered swab. She rubbed it briskly against his deltoid. "Relax your muscle."

"It is."

It is? She ignored the heat in her face, said a silent prayer, then uncapped the syringe. And—"A little stick here"—sank the short needle left-handed into his muscle. She held her breath and used her numb fingers to depress the plunger. All the way until the syringe emptied. When it was over, it was all she could do not to leap up and down and shout, "Hallelujah"—or cry. But she managed it. And Jack Travis had no idea he'd just been an unwitting lab rat.

"Good job. I didn't feel a thing." He handed her the opened Band-Aid.

"Me either," Riley said, finally meeting his gaze. She was surprised again by the burnt-toffee color of his eyes. And by the genuine kindness in his expression, the same look that she'd noticed earlier when he was kneeling in the chapel. *It looks like he really cares.*

"So," she said, turning her attention back to the Band-Aid, "you're good for another ten years or ten thousand miles, whichever comes first."

He laughed. "You've said that before, Chaplain."

"Hundreds of times."

Riley stepped out into the hallway and Jack followed.

"Need help with that?" Jack pointed to the cart.

"No," she answered, feeling a ridiculously heady wave of confidence. "I've got it. No problem."

"Quite a pile you have there," he said, lifting the toddler

manikin from the cart. He walked a few steps farther across the corridor, hefting it in his hands, turning it over. "Realistic. About the weight of a three-year-old, I'd say."

"Um, sure. Well, I'm going to tote my little plastic family back to the closet and head home." Riley glanced down the hallway, anxious to get away—out of the hospital—before the blush of her small victory began to fade. "So . . ."

"Here . . . catch!"

Riley flinched and then lurched forward with arms raised as Toddler Tim hurtled through the air.

7

+

JACK WATCHED RILEY GRAB INSTINCTIVELY with her right arm, then clutch again with both hands as the manikin slipped from her grasp. She quickly raised a knee to awkwardly pin its plastic legs between her elbow and her midsection, stopping its head from striking the floor. By less than an inch.

"Nice recovery," he said, instantly wishing he'd chosen another word. Especially when she straightened up and he saw the look on her face. "Sorry—instinct. I was raised by two generations of football coaches."

"I would . . . have guessed . . . *wolves*." Breathless and flushed, Riley shifted Toddler Tim into the crook of her left arm. Her eyes narrowed. "What were you thinking? This manikin costs over four hundred dollars. What if I'd dropped it?"

But you didn't. So . . . "You're right. I shouldn't have done that," he said, noticing that she'd begun to jiggle the plastic boy very slightly as if comforting a child. For some reason, it touched him.

"No, you shouldn't have." She sighed. "I'm going."

He watched as Riley added the manikin to the others, telling himself that he'd probably blown his chances with the tossing stunt. Besides, the idea that had been tumbling in his brain since his conversation with Gilbert was crazy at best. He shouldn't go ahead with it, but—"Hey, one more thing?"

She looked up at him.

"Come work for me?"

Her mouth fell open. "What?" If she were still holding Tim, he'd be looking at a skull fracture.

"At the free clinic," he explained, stepping closer. "Volunteer there. As a staff nurse." He saw her initial disbelief morph into wariness. "I think you'd like it. And—" he gentled his voice— "I think the patients would like you, Riley. In fact, I'm sure they would."

"I haven't . . ." She hesitated, her left hand rubbing her right. "I haven't been working as a clinical nurse for a while."

"We're not an ER," he said quickly. "Sore throats, sprained ankles, high blood pressure." He smiled. "And the occasional tetanus shot. We're providing everyday care—the kind of safety net that most people take for granted—to folks who don't have that luxury in their lives. Because they're transient, down on their luck, underemployed, or victims; we're preventing them from falling through the cracks. It's important work."

"Even if the neighbors don't want you there?"

"Even then." Jack's lips tensed, but he made himself smile. "But that's only because they think the same thing you do."

Riley raised her brows.

"That I was raised by wolves." Her faint smile propelled him on. "There are a couple other volunteer docs, so you could come in on their shifts and completely avoid me, and—"

"Wait." Riley lifted her palm to cut him off. "I'm sorry, but I really can't work at your clinic."

"Can't or won't?"

"Can't. I'm out of town a lot on my days off. My responsibilities as chaplain require time beyond my hospital hours. There's a safety review coming up, and . . ." Her gaze dropped to the equipment cart for an instant. "I'm hoping to secure a new position here at Alamo Grace."

"As triage nurse?" Jack asked, his rising irritation making him dump the subtlety he'd striven for.

"How did you know that?"

Jack hesitated, but only for a moment. "Kate Callison."

"Kate told you about me?" Riley's face paled.

He wasn't going to win this one. Jack shoved past a prod of guilt. "I saw the bruises on her arm. I asked where they came from."

Riley closed her eyes.

"Look," Jack offered as gently as he could, "Kate wasn't gossiping. Far from it. She only said that you'd had an accident a year ago. And that it's been difficult finding opportunities to practice your clinical skills."

"So you offer yourself up as a lab rat with that tetanus shot. Then—" something close to a growl rumbled deep in her throat—"you heave a manikin at me? To see if I could keep it from smacking me in the face? So you could tell me 'nice recovery' if it didn't?"

"Hey, don't." Jack glanced down the hallway, took a step closer.

"No," she said, grabbing for the handle of the cart. "*Don't you.* Don't you dare think that you can dismiss me as a chaplain one minute and then swoop in to rescue me the next. I am not on fire in your parking lot, Dr. Travis. And I'm not even close to 'falling through the cracks.' I don't need to tolerate crude aptitude tests or your offer of a pity job. I don't need *you.* Period. What I need is the privacy I'm entitled to. And to go home. Now."

Jack told himself that he didn't see a shimmer of tears in Riley's eyes before she turned and walked away, towing the manikin family behind her. He reminded himself that his clinic offer had been to effect a win-win, not an attempt at rescue— or humiliation. She was wrong.

When she disappeared into the equipment closet, he walked back to the ER. After the next patient, he'd call the clinic to see if the fire investigation was still going on. Then take a peek at the evening news. Hopefully any coverage about him would be concerning current-day conflict and not an unearthing of his monumental past mistakes.

He agreed completely with what Riley had said about privacy. She deserved hers. And he felt the same way about his.

- + -

Safe . . . I'm safe here.

Vesta lowered the binoculars and set them on the windowsill beside a tulip-shaped sherry glass. She scanned the view unaided, willing its familiar peace to wash over her. It was only a modest one-third acre, tucked between her cozy guest cottage and the owners' much-larger home, but it held a treasure trove of foliage. Cedars, live oaks, mesquite, several crepe myrtle, a young redbud, an old hollowed-out black walnut stump—destined for destruction by the eager ladder-back and golden-fronted woodpeckers. As well as an array of wispy Texas grasses and flowering sage and salvia, jewel-bright splashes of color irresistible to the native black-chinned hummingbirds and several other species that migrated through south Texas on their way to Mexico.

The Bluffs cottage was a balm for Vesta's soul in every season. A peaceful, private haven. And her fourth lease in the fifteen years since she'd sold her own home . . . and begun to hide.

I'm safe here. Even though . . .

She picked up the binoculars again, adjusted the focus, and strained to see the slice of San Antonio Street visible beyond the trees. A few cars. None of them police or fire vehicles, though they could have used the Crockett Street route; construction for The Bluffs' security gates had a good section of the road in upheaval. The evening news assured viewers that the routine investigation was winding down. But was it routine? Or was it . . . *arson?*

Vesta's throat tightened. The video of the man on fire in the clinic parking lot had been horrific, his screams for help desperate, chilling. Far too much a reminder of . . . *No, don't think about it.*

Her hands began to tremble and she set the binoculars down, reminding herself to breathe slowly. *I'm home. Safe. It's long past time to let it go.*

She had made some progress toward that in recent months. No panic attacks, only rare nightmares. She'd even ventured farther into the wooded yard to hang hummingbird feeders on the redbud tree. Then laced on her hiking boots to make cautious loops around the small property, leaving a worn path—proof she was better. It had begun to feel like she could finally breathe again, that perhaps there was hope. Until the news started to report suspicious fires in neighboring New Braunfels. Then today . . . The familiar mix of shame and fear brought a wave of nausea. The same as when she'd cowered in that hospital chapel, paralyzed and gasping like a bird that had struck a windowpane—helpless, terrified, and certain she would suffocate and die.

Vesta reached for the glass of pale, straw-colored fino sherry and used both hands to steady it as she raised it to her lips. Crisp, nutty, strong—always better at calming her nerves than any prescribed medication, but something she enjoyed only rarely because of her diabetes. And shouldn't be touching tonight because of the danger of it leading to another deadly plummet in her blood sugar. Dr. Travis would absolutely disapprove, but then . . .

Vesta took another sip, closed her eyes, willed her heart to stay steady, her breathing to cooperate. The irony was that Jack Travis was the reason she needed this forbidden remedy. Because seeing him—meeting him finally—brought the awful memory back as if it had happened yesterday, not nearly fifteen years ago.

Please, God, have mercy. Spare me this.

Vesta downed the last of the sherry, eyes watering, then

picked up the binoculars and glanced toward the street in time to catch a glimpse of Andrea Nichols's white Lexus. Stirring things up, no doubt. Andrea was after Dr. Travis's clinic like a woodpecker on that walnut stump. Even though it was suspected to be accidental, the fire at the clinic had already prompted the media to repeat statistics about suspicious fires in neighboring communities. And with Jack Travis's name in the news, how long could it be before they dug into much older cases?

An unsolved arson-murder would be far more interesting.

Vesta shivered. *I'm safe . . .*

- + -

Riley pulled her sun-faded Honda Civic into her condo's driveway at dusk, watching as the garage door opened to reveal the quartz-blue Mercedes E550 parked inside. She knew she should drive the coupe around the block once in a while to keep the oil from settling. Her trips to Houston had been less frequent lately, and she only drove the car there to please the man who'd gifted it to her. Grandfather Hale—*Poppy*. She smiled, thinking of him.

He'd surprised her with the convertible when she graduated with her bachelor's degree in nursing. And was the one relative who'd always applauded her attempts at independence. From the days she climbed out onto the highest branches of the pecan tree to when he saw her in that hospital after the assault, bruised and battered with a halo brace bolted into her skull. Even then, he'd leaned close and whispered, "You're still my brave little tiger. Remember that."

Brave . . . Her gaze swept over the letters on the car's vanity plate—*TYGRR*—and to the Scripture reference on the silver frame holding it: 1 Corinthians 16:13. *"Be on your guard; stand firm in the faith; be courageous; be strong."* Her grandfather's favorite Scripture . . . locked in the dark. Guilt jabbed. She eased the Honda into the garage, reminding herself that she didn't drive the coupe because flaunting wealth had always made her uncomfortable, because driving a luxury car invited vandalism and theft, and because the Honda was less conspicuous, more gas economical.

Riley frowned with impatience at her fumbling attempt to turn off the car's ignition, then yanked her purse from the passenger seat. The TYGRR-mobile was a moot point; Kate was moving in soon and she'd need the parking spot. Riley would have to find a place to store the Mercedes until she could figure out how to tell her grandfather that she couldn't keep his generous gift. It might be harder than telling her parents that she wasn't moving home. But both things had to be done. The fact was that she was staying in San Antonio and resuming her nursing career at Alamo Grace Hospital. Moving on with her life at long last, and—

"Hi there!"

Riley whirled toward the driveway, body tensing, and then felt immediately foolish. She managed a casual smile. "Hi, Wilma."

Her next-door neighbor clutched a handful of envelopes against her purple blouse, the other hand holding fast to the leash of her rambunctious border collie. "Got some of your mail delivered to my box." Wilma stepped closer, blinking as Riley's string of motion sensor floodlights lit her hair like moonlight on Colorado snow. "My goodness, you've certainly got wattage. Between those and your walkway lights you could land a 747 here."

"I'm sorry," Riley said, embarrassed. "I hope the lights aren't a problem for you."

"No. No problem—I understand." Wilma held out the mail, her kind eyes showing compassion. "I remember how hard it was to come home to an empty house when Gene was traveling for work." She glanced down at the dog. "And now we have Oreo, of course . . . not that she couldn't be distracted with a Milk-Bone. But these days, it's wise to be cautious."

For some reason, Riley thought of Jack Travis. "Right. Better safe than sorry." She took the mail from her neighbor. "Thank you, Wilma. I appreciate this."

"You're more than welcome."

Riley closed the garage door and entered the condo before the last of the daylight dwindled. She tapped in the code on the security alarm system, triple-locked the door behind her, and then leaned back against it. She hated that her knees still felt rubbery from an everyday encounter with a friendly, helpful neighbor. In a community tucked behind security gates. She shook her head, recalling Wilma's remark about her garage lighting, then glanced down the hallway of the condo toward the interior lights timed to switch on at dusk—along with the TV, to sound as if she were home. She supposed most people would call those things overkill, paranoia even. But how could Riley explain the helplessness she'd felt that night in the hospital parking garage?

She closed her eyes and flattened her palms against the locked door, unable to stop the collage of images, textures, sounds, and smells that had repeated over and over in dreams this past year. Her quick glance at the parking garage clock—past midnight, into overtime. The *brrring* sound of the bell on the always-sluggish elevator. Her decision to take the stairs instead. The rustle of her scrubs and the hollow slap of her Crocs against the cement stairs as she descended two levels. The dim, bluish blink of fluorescent lights. Cold, dank air. Faint, distant squawking of grackles. Then a sound behind her and a sudden stomach-dropping sense that something wasn't right. Her hope that it was the security guard. Rising panic, thoughts of what-if tumbling in her brain. Then a confirming deep, feral grunt . . .

Her hair yanked from behind. Confusion as she staggered backward. Her gargled scream as strong fingers found her throat. Ski mask, foul breath . . . her frantic prayer. Followed by a desperate thought: *rape* . . . was that better than death? *Poppy, help* . . . Her head whipping side to side, teeth catching her tongue, a coppery taste of blood. Her rasping, futile struggle for breath. Legs giving way . . . the eerie, quiet sense of floating . . . and the final, brutal shove that sent her down the stairs, each agonizing cement step taking its toll on knees, ribs, shoulder, and hip. Then her skull smashing against the oily, cold garage floor—and blackness.

Riley opened her eyes as the memory faded, feeling the prickle of anger that had finally replaced the tears. A confusing new hostility that seemed to shift trajectories, constantly searching for another target: her parents' expectations and influence, her own limitations, this demoralizing fear, the uncertainty of her nursing career, and ridiculously, even the sight of that license plate on the Mercedes. Because of the way it taunted her to be a "brave tiger" and because of the Scripture, too.

Because I can't seem to "stand firm in the faith"?

Riley's stomach twisted. Was that it? Was it possible that the bull's-eye for her confusing new anger was God himself?

- + -

Kate pushed a damp chunk of hair away from her face and sat up on the exercise mat. She pressed a button on the remote, switched from the *Pilates for Dummies* DVD to the evening news, knowing that she was stalling. She'd packed three boxes of shoes, brushed her cat's teeth, and sweated through forty minutes of exercise, all to keep from calling Riley. It was wrong; telling the truth was a valued part of their friendship. She took a long swallow of her vitaminwater and hit the speed dial on her cell phone, wincing as her friend answered. "Hey, Rah-lee."

"Kate, how's it going in the ER?"

"I'm home, actually. Char wanted a few extra hours on this paycheck, and I needed to pack." Kate smiled. "My new roommate's hounding me to get it done. I left right after the charge nurse meeting." She held her breath, anticipating the next question.

"And how'd that go? Did you test the water about me?"

Kate swallowed. "It didn't go too well."

There was a short silence. "Meaning?"

"Meaning Lil, from nights. You know how she is. She brought up the fact that there's never been a permanent triage nurse, and . . ."

"And never an ER trauma chaplain before me. She made it

about my family?" There was no mistaking the frustration in Riley's voice.

"It's a fact, Riley." Kate took a soft breath, continued. "And it wasn't only Lil. You know how fast war stories start flying. Someone mentioned an incident that happened because a tech was allowed to work in a walking cast; then the oxygen tank fiasco from today came up." Kate sighed. "It dissolved into a whole 'who's got your back?' safety issue. So I didn't push it further. But then it's up to administration to accept or reject your proposal, anyway."

"They'd listen to the charge nurses."

Meaning me. "Probably, but the final decision will depend on your performance of skills." Kate glanced down at her bruised arm.

"Which I'm not allowed to practice. But I've requested a medical clearance from my doctors. That should help things along."

Kate plunged ahead. "Jack told me about the tetanus shot. And about asking you to volunteer at the clinic." There was a silence so long that she was certain Riley had disconnected. "Riley?"

"He said that you told him about my injury."

Kate's throat tightened. "No—I mean, yes. But only that you'd had an accident. Not about the assault; I would never do that. I just told him that you wanted to be back in the ER as a nurse."

"Did he tell you that he threw a manikin at me?"

"What?"

"Completely out of the blue. He shouted for me to catch and hurled that CPR toddler dummy at me."

The toddler. Because I told him I was worried about . . . Kate squeezed her eyes shut against a wave of guilt. "So you . . . ?"

"Caught it. Barely. But the point is that he's a maniac, Kate. And you don't even want to know the things that Vesta Calder's neighbor said about him."

"He's giving you a way back to the ER."

"You don't know that, Kate. You don't know that it would help."

"It can't hurt."

There was a soft moan. "You don't know that either."

Kate reached for her water. "Well . . . I know that he'll be at the ER until eleven tonight."

- + -

Riley held her breath and pushed her hands hard against the bedroom's lush carpet, straining to lift her chest from the floor in a bent-knee push-up. Equally balanced over both arms this time, not collapsing toward the right side like a kid's wagon that lost a wheel. She groaned, pushed harder, and tipped toward the numb arm, her shower-damp hair sticking to her neck. "No!" she breathed through clenched teeth. "I . . . *will* . . . do this." She leaned harder onto her left arm but still felt her right hand cramp and the elbow begin to buckle. *Hold on, hold on—*

"Ugh!" She crumpled onto her right shoulder and kept rolling until she was flat on her back, glaring up at the airy vaulted ceiling. She lifted both arms toward it, watched the right one sag lower, and then smacked her bare feet defiantly against the soft carpet pile. "Why, why, why?" *Why me, Lord?*

A tear slid from the corner of her eye, and Riley swiped at

it with numb fingers, not sure if she'd halted it. Until warm water pooled in her ear. *Numb, weak, clumsy.* She bit her lip against more humiliating tears, thinking of what she'd said to Kate about catching Toddler Tim. That she'd barely kept him from hitting the floor. *Barely.* It seemed to be a key word in her life lately. Barely healed, barely a nurse, barely . . . a believer? Riley glanced toward the open study Bible on the bamboo table beside her bed. Her chest tightened. Since she was a chaplain, barely believing would make her a fraud.

Am I a fraud?

Riley jerked to a sitting position, then stood upright and padded across the carpet to her bed. She sat on the edge of the blue silk duvet and took a deep, slow breath, which did nothing at all to ease the growing ache in her chest. An emptiness that always came when her targeted anger subsided, a vacuum that stubbornly remained despite every kind of therapy that money could buy. Filled only by doubts that whispered, *I'll never be whole again.*

Riley traced her numb fingertips slowly up her cheek to the scar on her forehead, usually hidden discreetly beneath her newly styled bangs. It was one of twin divots left by the cold metal pins that had screwed the halo brace to her skull for three long months. A device designed to help her fractured neck mend, but one that also proved—with exquisite, unrelenting pain—that violence had skewered her life.

Riley could barely feel the scarred hole with her nerve-damaged fingers, but she felt it deep in her gut—in her soul—as if it were still new, bleeding and raw. She was broken and wasn't fooling anyone with clever makeup, well-cut bangs, or her current position as the very first Alamo Grace trauma chaplain. The hospital's ER charge nurses had testified to that painful truth at their meeting today. And Kate had confirmed it. Riley wouldn't feel whole again until she recovered everything the violent attack had taken from her. She had to do it. With or without the support of the nursing staff. Even if that meant . . .

Riley glanced at the clock: ten forty-five. She scooted toward the bedside table and closed her Bible so she could grab the phone lying under its cover. She scrolled through her contacts and tapped the number. Then asked that the call be transferred to—

"Jack Travis," he answered.

"It's Riley Hale," she whispered, heart in her throat. She squeezed the phone even tighter than she'd gripped Toddler Tim, slipping from her grasp. "I want to see your clinic."

8

+

"OKAY." Jack stuck the computer printout to the clinic's aging refrigerator with a Tylenol magnet. "We've got a working plan." He glanced to where his building manager, Bandy Biggs, sat bowlegged astride a cracked vinyl chair. A steaming mug of coffee rested on the table beside the man's small, well-worn Bible. "Rob Melton will have one of his patrol cars swing by a few times each night, show a presence. You'll walk the parking lot before you lock up, make certain those new motion sensor floodlights are working."

"And we'll blind a half-dozen raccoons, a few squinty-eyed armadillos . . . and maybe Miz Andrea Nichols's fine, pedigreed Persian cat." Bandy lifted his worn ball cap, resettling it as a grin creased his sun-weathered face. "Cat's here most nights. That fancy critter has no compunction about hangin' out with us ordinary stock. Right, Hobo?" He reached down to tickle his terrier's chin. Then adjusted a strap on the homemade cart supporting the little dog's hips and withered hind legs. "Yessir. Miss Lah-De-Dah Kitty thinks we're all cut from the same cloth."

When Bandy looked back up, his expression was sober. "I understand what you're doing, Doc. And I see the bind you're in. I do. But we never had a problem here before Gilbert's accident. The clinic board members know that. Our patients have always been respectful. And grateful, bone-deep . . . *soul*-deep." He shook his head. "There's something mighty unfriendly about posting those No Loitering signs. And when folks see that second line, 'Police Enforced'—"

"I know," Jack interrupted, raising his hands. The signs, bright red on reflective white, were equally inhospitable in Spanish. "I agree that a certain number of our patients will be put off by that."

"Scared off, more like." Bandy blew on his coffee, then raised a graying brow. "Not sure Hobo and me would be here now if those signs had been plastered around this place a year ago."

I'm certain of it, buddy. And it would be my genuine loss. Jack spread his palms. "The city owns the property, Bandy. They post the signs. It's not like I could ask for a pink, heart-shaped 'Mosey Along, *Por Favor*' edition."

"Too bad." Bandy glanced around the fifties-era pink- and cocoa-brown-tiled kitchen. "It would fit right in." He tossed Hobo the last crumbs of his toast. "I'm just sayin' that Gilbert slept on that pavement out there because he was drunk, lonely, sick . . . desperate. I've been to all those ugly addresses myself."

His blue eyes studied Jack's face, compassion softening his crusty features. "I don't pry, but I'm guessing you might have traveled some painful roads too, Doc."

Jack glanced toward the window, sure Bandy would like nothing better than to open his Bible and offer a hopeful verse, the same way Jack dispensed free samples of medications. But while the old bull rider knew very little about Jack's past, he knew in no uncertain terms that his boss would welcome Scripture about as easily as—

"Unbelievable!" Jack lunged toward the window. "They're out there. Right on the lawn!"

"Who?" Bandy stood, making his way toward the window with Hobo—wheels of his cart squeaking—close behind. "The action committee?"

"Andrea Nichols. With the neighbor who's a real estate broker and that woman who owns the new dress shop down the street and—" Jack's teeth ground together—"the developer who's been pestering the city about purchasing this property."

Bandy wedged in beside Jack at the window, gave a low whistle. "And his new contractor. See the young man holding the roll of papers? That's Griff Payton, the developer's son. Just moved back to the area from Odessa. Home to help with his daddy's business." Bandy saw the question on Jack's face. "Hobo and I get out some; we hear things."

"And now they're going to hear a few things from me." Jack stepped away from the window.

Bandy grasped his arm. "Hold your horses, Doc. You don't want to do that."

"Watch me." He frowned as Bandy's grip tightened with

surprising strength for a man whose head barely reached Jack's shoulder. "They have no business being there, Bandy. The city council doesn't meet for two weeks; no decisions have been made about the clinic. If I don't squash this now, Andrea Nichols will be rolling a bulldozer in, whether her idiot cat likes Hobo or not."

"I'm only saying that you'll snag more flies with honey than vinegar, son. Every time." Bandy pushed back his cap. "I know that schmoozing doesn't come natural, but every time you lock horns with these folks, you're only shootin' yourself in the foot."

"And every time that heartless bunch circulates a petition or stirs up the media, my patients suffer. And I lose support for the clinic. I need funding, volunteers . . ."

Bandy glanced out the window. "I'd say you need a PR person more."

"And I've got her," Jack said, beginning to grin. He laughed at the expression on Bandy's face. "Or almost have her." He glanced down at his watch. "I said she could come by and have a look around before we open for clinic hours. So that means any time now. Trust me, she's the prompt type."

"Who?"

"A woman from Alamo Grace who's been acting as trauma chaplain." Jack enjoyed Bandy's confusion for a moment, then let the name drop. "Riley Hale. Of the Houston Hales."

Bandy's eyes widened. "Rodeo sponsor Hales?"

Jack nodded. "Secret-weapon Hales. She already smoothed things over with one of The Bluffs neighbors. And if the Hale name is associated with this clinic . . ." He grinned at Bandy. "Better than a pedigreed cat?"

"I don't understand. A chaplain? Why is she coming here?"

"Riley's a nurse, too. But she had a bad accident, a broken neck that left her with weakness in her dominant arm. The hospital hasn't let her return to clinical duties. So I offered—"

"To use her as a sacrificial lamb."

"To help her regain her skills. It's a win for all of us, Bandy. *If* she agrees to volunteer." Jack glanced toward the street. "Good. The Lexus is pulling away. Now I'm going to make myself scarce too. I'll be in my office. You'll show her around."

"Why me?" Bandy peered at Jack out of the corner of his eye.

"Because you know this place like the back of your hand, and—"

"Why?"

Jack sighed. "Okay, because she doesn't like me. We've butted heads a few times. She thinks I'm anti-chaplain, that I have issues with rules, and . . ." Jack frowned. "That basically I act as if I've been raised by wolves."

"Ha!" Bandy doubled over and slapped his cap against his knee. Hobo barked.

"It's not that funny. She's a pain in the behind. You'll see."

"Can't wait." Bandy swiped at his eyes. He chuckled again, then sighed and glanced up at the kitchen ceiling—a habit that Jack knew meant Bandy was acknowledging some heavenly presence. "Quite a plan. Yessir."

- + -

Riley waited for the flagman to wave her past the construction area before driving the remaining half mile to the clinic. She pulled the Honda off San Antonio Street and into the parking lot, surprised by her first real look at the controversial establishment. A decades-old wooden residence with a sagging porch and peeling white paint, its trim, shutters, and window boxes were a vivid pink, making it look more like a child's birthday cake than a medical facility. Her mouth sagged open as she took it in. It was impossible to imagine Rambo Travis here. Combat boots, camouflage, surly attitude . . . and pink frosting? Nothing could be more incongruous. *Except maybe that I'm here . . . after all the run-ins we've had.*

She eased into a parking place, easily recognizing the area she'd seen on the TV coverage of the incident with Gilbert DeSoto. Dumpster, graveled area, oversize lot with trees, grayed cedar fencing. There was an older-model truck-camper much farther back. And official-looking signs she hadn't seen on TV. Lots of them. She scanned the nearest, a terse warning in Spanish: *No se permite vagabundos. Se llamará a la policia.* "No vagrants permitted. The police will be called."

Riley switched off the engine, thinking that the recent fire must have prompted this new signage. As well as pressure from The Bluffs neighbors. The tacky tinderbox was indeed the last vestige of decay in the newly upscale community—a single snaggletooth in a cosmetically engineered set of pearly whites. Even during an economic downturn, The Bluffs remained a sought-after zip code. Only a block from this clinic was the exclusive new dress shop her mother raved about; Riley had an unused gift card tucked into her sock drawer. A few doors down from it was the trendy New Orleans–style eatery featured in *San Antonio Magazine* last month. The scent of spicy, blackened seafood had drifted through the car's open window as she drove past. Riley glanced toward the residential end of the street, idly wondering how far away Vesta Calder lived. And which home belonged to the woman who'd driven her home from the hospital—the neighbor who knew Riley's family.

What would my parents think if they knew I was here?

Riley's stomach sank. What was she doing? It was crazy. A man had nearly died right where she was parked, the neighbors were about to march on this property like torch-carrying villagers outside Frankenstein's castle, and a certifiable madman was in charge of the place. She was a safety officer, and this was a war zone. So why on earth was she—

"You're here. Hello!"

"Oh!" Riley peeled her hand from her chest and blinked at the sun-browned man bent low at her car window. "Um . . . hello." She managed a shaky smile.

He smiled back and quickly pulled off a tattered cap. "I'm Bandy Biggs, building manager. Doc Travis asked me to show you around." His blue eyes were warm. "That is, if you are Miss Riley Hale."

"I am," she said, not at all sure she wanted to be. "Dr. Travis isn't here, then?"

"Ah . . ." Bandy hesitated. "Not sure if we'll see him. But I know this place like the back of my hand. Happy to do the honors." He opened the Honda's door and swept an arm toward the clinic as if he were a royal page welcoming her to the castle. "Follow me."

She did so, deciding that up close the chalky-pink paint resembled Pepto-Bismol far more than frosting. And then had serious concerns she would fall through the creaky porch.

The window boxes, however, were an unexpected delight. "Tomatoes?"

"Early girls are coming right along; tryin' my hand at heirlooms. We'll see—lots of sun out here." Bandy pointed farther down the porch. "And that's cucumbers over there, some peppers, and cilantro. Corn out by my camper truck, but the armadillos have been turning things up a bit. Not sure if it will survive. The geraniums are just for pretty." He smiled. "Figured our patients wouldn't mind taking fresh goods home with them, and I enjoy digging in the dirt. Must be part armadillo myself."

He opened the front door and waved her ahead.

Riley stepped across the threshold into an old parlor, greeted by the tantalizing aroma of freshly brewed coffee and what she would swear was buttery cinnamon toast. Along with the eager, warbling whine of a small dog. Her eyes widened. *Pulling a cart?* Yes. It was supporting his hindquarters. She watched as the animal's front paws clicked across scarred hardwood flooring, the wheels of the cart brushing against a couch topped with tatted doilies. His tail gave friendly thumps on the cart.

"That's Hobo," Bandy explained. "Our version of a Walmart greeter. Or if anyone official asks: therapy dog. The stubborn pup was dragging those legs for months after being stomped by a steer; wouldn't give up. Doesn't hurt his attitude either. I think that's a good thing for folks to see."

"Mm." She bent down and stroked his furry head as she surveyed the cozy room, its mauve walls boasting crayon art and several old photos of a white-haired woman serving food to long lines of people. There were a half-dozen or so mismatched chairs as well as several floor cushions. A vintage magazine rack held pamphlets and printed information sheets in both English and Spanish. A Busy Zoo Activity Center, plastic table and chairs, and a makeshift shelf of children's books were tucked into one corner. "So this is the clinic's waiting room?"

"Right. By the time we open this afternoon, it will be filled and there'll be a string of needy souls leading right past the porch."

Needy souls. Riley stood, remembering Vesta's neighbor's poisonous rant. *"A steady stream of indigents, prostitutes, drug addicts, and illegal aliens. Not in my neighborhood!"*

"That pass-through window leads to the receptionist," Bandy continued, pointing. "Which is mostly me these days." He shook his head. "Tough economy means fewer volunteers. Right now we have—" he counted on his fingers—"three retired nurses, a pediatrician who comes by for two hours on Thursdays, an Army medic who hasn't been able to find a paying job, a dentist once a month, a retired veterinarian who draws blood . . . and one of Doc Travis's mountain bike buddies." He laughed at the look on Riley's face. "Who's an internist over in Fredericksburg."

He led Riley through the small reception office, down a hallway that opened into three exam rooms. Once bedrooms, they were painted in Easter-egg colors of lavender, yellow, and green. Each was outfitted with an old-style, paper-covered examination table and basic medical supplies: gauze, alcohol swabs, otoscope, tongue depressors, and percussion hammers, all neatly organized on paint-layered bedroom dressers. Here, too, childish art decorated the walls. The largest of the rooms boasted a hanging quilt—and a shiny new multidrawer crash cart.

Riley's gaze swept over the defibrillator, adjacent EKG machine, twin IV poles with bags of solution, and Ambu bag. "Do you—" she cleared her throat, surprised to feel her pulse quicken—"get many critical cases?"

"Hardly ever." Bandy raised a calloused finger. "See this? Fastest finger to hit 911 you ever saw." His gaze held hers for a moment. "Let me show you the mudroom we call a lab. It's right off the kitchen, and I make the best coffee this side of the Pecos."

Riley followed him down the short hallway past a closed door, a bathroom perhaps. Bandy gave her a quick tour of the combination supply room and laboratory and an adjacent laundry room also utilized as the medication room. Then he led her back into the sunny kitchen with frilled curtains, fruit-print wallpaper, pink- and brown-tiled counters, and speckled linoleum. Riley accepted a mug of strong black coffee laced with cinnamon and a chair at the kitchen's chrome-and-Formica table. A khaki scrub jacket was draped over the back of the chair; its name tape read *Major Jackson Travis, MD*. Riley settled against it, wondering if she'd been wrong about the closed door in the hallway.

"So that's the tour," Bandy said after feeding Hobo a dog treat. "And here's the part where I say that no matter what you might hear on the TV, we're doing important work here. The woman who donated this property to the city—that's her in the waiting room photos—meant it to be used for a charitable purpose. She headed the Loaves & Fishes Food Pantry downtown for forty years. A church community did some of that work out of this house after she passed. Then the building changed to a charity thrift store and finally it sat vacant because . . ." He sighed.

"Because the new housing development didn't like 'needy souls' quite so close." Riley's heart tugged, remembering Gilbert DeSoto. "But if this woman designated the property for charitable use, how could a developer expect to turn it into high-rent condominiums?"

"Well . . ." Bandy hesitated. "I only heard it secondhand, but apparently Mr. Payton has floated the idea that the city council could be persuaded if the homeowners' association offered to host an annual charity event. You know, one of those shindigs where rich people lock the security gates and drink champagne in honor of the poor folks, and—" Bandy's face flushed and genuine remorse sprang to his age-lined eyes. "I'm sorry. That was plain mean-spirited."

"I understand," Riley said. "Really. That's a big part of why I became a nurse. To offer help, hands on." She glanced back toward the hallway, thinking of the pink window boxes filled with vegetables and the children's artwork on the walls. Then, with a stab of guilt, admitted that she was also remembering what Kate had said about Riley's proposal for the position of Alamo Grace triage nurse. *The final decision will depend on your performance of skills.* And that Jack Travis's offer to let her work here at the clinic could be her only chance to practice those skills.

"I'd like to volunteer here. But . . ." Riley set her coffee cup down. "I don't know if Dr. Travis told you; I had an injury that's left me with some weakness in one arm. And—" She stopped as Hobo gave a short bark and wobbled toward the hallway door, his cart's tiny wheels rolling neatly over her foot.

Bandy grinned. "I think we can work around any physical difficulties, Miss Hale."

"Riley," she insisted, smiling back at him. "I promise I'll do the best I can. And if the medical cases are as straightforward and basic as you indicated—"

A barrage of honking stopped her short, followed by furious barking from the front of the house. Bandy hustled for the door and she followed him to the waiting room.

Riley's stomach lurched. "Oh *no*."

The front door was flung wide and a teenage girl in a glittery pink raincoat lay sprawled on the porch. She was desperately pale, her long hair matted with congealed blood, face battered, and one heavily made-up eye swollen closed. She groaned, gasped for a breath, then made a gargling noise as blood bubbled from her lips.

"Call 911!" Riley shouted, pushing past Bandy.

"On it—and I'm grabbing gloves!"

Riley dropped to her knees beside the girl, heart pounding as rescue protocols buzzed through her brain. *Airway, breathing . . .* She gingerly opened the top buttons of the raincoat—*careful, don't move her; her neck could be broken*—exposing a small green-and-yellow tattoo of Tinker Bell just below the girl's collarbone. Riley confirmed the shallow rise and fall of her chest beneath a thin T-shirt.

Next . . . circulation. Riley pressed her fingers to the girl's neck to check for a pulse, confirmed it, then jerked her gaze toward the hallway at the sound of heavy footfalls.

Jack Travis barreled toward her.

9

"SHE'S OBTUNDED—brain hemorrhage, probably." Jack frowned when the young victim gave no appreciable response to firm pressure against the thin fabric covering her breastbone. He tried again, then palpated her neck to locate the carotid. *Pulse strong but slowing.* "Beaten to a pitiful pulp and dumped on my porch." He shifted his knees on the hard floor, glanced at Riley kneeling on the other side of their patient.

She nodded mutely, her hand on the girl's shoulder.

"Let's see this eye . . ." Jack touched a gloved fingertip to their patient's grossly swollen eye and retracted the lid. "Dilated, sluggish." The victim's ragged breathing gurgled ominously behind the high-flow oxygen mask. "Got that portable suction ready?"

"Yes. If you'll lift the non-rebreather mask, I'll . . ."

He watched as Riley slid the rigid, hissing catheter into the corner of the patient's mouth. Her gloved right hand trembled very slightly with the effort; she bit her lip and continued on. He noticed that the front of Riley's tailored jacket was smeared with blood—and that she didn't seem to care. He nodded. "Good, thanks. But I still don't like the quality of that breathing. I'm going to intubate."

"But if the assault injured her neck . . ." Her face paled, dark pupils suddenly huge against the blue of her eyes.

"I'll put the tube in nasally," he clarified. "You'll find a transport cervical collar in that mobile kit. We'll slide it on before I intubate."

"The police are here," Bandy announced from the porch steps. "And the medics should arrive any minute." He sighed. "Along with a passel of neighbors, I expect."

"No doubt." Jack frowned, then caught Riley's eye. "Make sure the oxygen's on high flow. Pull out the collar, a few adult endotracheal tubes, and the Ambu bag. I want her airway protected in case she vomits. And this way, the paramedics can get on the road faster."

Bandy hurried forward. "I'll help you with the collar, Doc."

"Oxygen's cranked high," Riley reported, her expression a fraction more confident. "I'm getting the airway supplies and switching the suction tip."

Bandy squeezed in beside her. "Here's the collar, Doc. Tell me what to do."

"Great, let's do this then," Jack said as a blur of dark uniforms appeared in his peripheral vision.

Rob Melton crossed the porch and glanced down at the

victim, his expression compassionate. "We're checking for witnesses. Need any help?"

"No, we've got it. Thanks."

Rob shook his head. "Heard that Hobo barked the alert. Quite a team you have there, Jack."

"You bet." Jack turned to Bandy. "Here we go, like this." They slid the collar into place without moving their patient's head; then Jack reached for one of the endotracheal tubes that Riley had placed neatly on the girl's chest.

Jack paused for a moment, shook his head. *Bull rider, chaplain, and a dog pulling a cart.* He'd worked with far less help in military scenarios. But . . .

Jack's jaw tensed as he glanced at his patient's battered face. He wished he was wrong about her chances for a hopeful outcome. And wished just as earnestly that he could get his hands around the throat of the low-life bottom-feeder who was responsible.

- + -

"I've got the suction," Riley said, whispering a silent prayer that her numb fingers would stop cramping and that she could control her shaking well enough to pass the catheter through the tube protruding from the unconscious girl's nostril. "Just say when."

"Now."

Riley fed the suction catheter in, assisting her clumsy fingers with her other hand, then activated the suction and drew back, sucking bloody mucus from the airway. "I hear sirens," she said, relief making her dizzy. *Please hurry. I don't know how long I can do this.*

"I want to hear clearer breath sounds. Bag assist her, will you?" Jack pulled the stethoscope earpieces away and raised his brows, clearly amending his question: *Can you?*

"I . . ." Riley reached for the football-size resuscitation bag, difficult to squeeze under ordinary circumstances. Could she do it left-handed? She struggled and got the bag fitted to the nasal tube. Felt Jack watching her. *Help me, God.* She supported the bag with her numb and shaky fingers, spread her good left hand across its surface.

"Here." Jack handed Riley his stethoscope. "I'll bag. You listen."

Her stomach sank. "Okay."

Jack's huge hand compressed the bag effortlessly, and Riley pressed the stethoscope to their patient's chest, confirming equal exchange of air in all lung fields—initial proof that the tube was properly placed. "Sounds good," she said, meeting his gaze. *And I'm sorry.*

"Medics are here!" Bandy reported from the end of the porch.

"Good. We'll leave the IV to them." Jack gave the bag another squeeze. "Glad we got the tube in, though. She's quitting on us now."

No, please don't die. Riley slid her gloved fingers quickly under the patient's jaw. "Pulse is there, but it's faster now, a little thready." She looked down at the girl's too-pale face. "She's so young. All made up to look older, but I don't think she's more than a teenager. How could she end up—?" She heard Jack's smothered curse. The hostility in his eyes chilled her.

"Runaway," he growled, a muscle on his jaw bunching. "Put to work by any one of a dozen ruthless pimps who make it their business to 'rescue' these poor kids. I see it way too often. Most of the girls are barely fifteen years old, maybe thousands of miles from home. And scared. They'll come here if they're sick or hurt, knowing they don't have to provide documentation the way they do at the hospital. I try to—"

A police officer stepped close. "I'm going to move aside for the medics, but any chance you could check for some ID on this girl?"

Riley nodded. "There wasn't a purse, but I'll check her pockets."

"Careful," Jack warned quickly. "Could be needles."

Needles? Riley swallowed, trying not to imagine what her parents would think of this situation. She warily patted the pockets of the girl's raincoat. "Nothing here. Let me check her pants."

She undid the coat's remaining buttons, swept the thin fabric aside.

Riley gasped. "She's pregnant—and there's a lot of blood down here."

"Medics coming through!"

In mere moments the paramedics surrounded the patient, taking over with the Ambu bag and obtaining a report from Jack. The clinic's once-homey parlor was a sea of uniforms as police mingled with fire rescue, boots thumping across the hardwood floor and radios squawking. Within four minutes "Jane Doe" had two IVs, automatic blood pressure and pulse oximetry equipment, as well as a cardiac monitor. She was scooped up with cervical spine precautions and high-flow oxygen continuous.

Riley winced at the sight of her lying on the stretcher. A

discarded, broken doll, glittery raincoat snipped into tatters. *Little Tinker Bell . . .*

The ambulance pulled away from the clinic parking lot with lights and siren, blasting its horn when a gathering crowd of onlookers was slow to yield the right of way.

Father, go with . . . her.

Riley stood alone in the quiet vacuum of the waiting room, wishing she knew the girl's name so she could add it to her prayer. She wondered if what Jack had said was true, that Jane was a runaway turned prostitute. Or if the girl had instead been a victim of a brutal assault by a stranger. Riley trembled, her teeth beginning to chatter.

"Here, take these," Jack said, arriving beside her with a set of scrubs. "You can change in the hall bathroom. Bandy will find you a plastic sack for those clothes." He pointed at her suit. "Don't think you want to go out of here like that."

Riley noticed for the first time that her linen jacket, shirt, and the knees of her slacks were stained with blood. She shivered again, remembering the clotting puddle under the girl's narrow hips. Had she been kicked in the abdomen? She must have been scared to death. Riley's stomach lurched. She pressed the back of her hand to her mouth and breathed slowly through her nose to dispel the haunting scent of the dank hospital garage, the memory of merciless hands around her throat. *No, don't start remembering . . .*

"Thanks," she said finally, reaching for the scrubs. "Are you going to the hospital?"

"No." Jack studied her face for a few seconds, concern in his expression. "I called and spoke with the ER doc, reported what I know. We'll have patients to see here in a few minutes if they aren't frightened off by the police cars. If we get clearance, Bandy will set it up so that we can guide patients in through the back door and not disturb the detectives." He frowned. "Two investigations in a week."

Riley glanced down at the littered floor. "They're taking her to Alamo Grace?"

"Yes. It's closest and they're equipped to handle high-risk obstetric cases. From the look of her, I'd say she could be seven or eight months along. Certainly viable if the trauma didn't—" Jack's fists clenched, the earlier anger back. "Beating a pregnant girl! The cowardly, low-life son of a—" He bit off the words.

Riley shifted the scrubs in her arms. "So . . . I change in the bathroom?"

"Second door on the right."

"Thanks. I think I'll go on to the ER. See how she's doing."

"Yeah, well . . ." Jack dragged his fingers across his jaw, met her gaze. "Don't take this the wrong way, but that's probably a good idea. I'm afraid our Jane Doe is going to need a chaplain much more than a doctor."

Heart cramping, Riley turned away and walked toward the inner hallway.

"Riley?"

She paused.

"This isn't our normal day. But all things considered, will you be back? To work?"

"I . . ." Riley was quiet for a moment, hearing the distant, clattering sound of Bandy in the kitchen making another pot of coffee for the investigating officers. She glanced at her jacket sleeve, stiff with blood, before meeting Jack's gaze. "I'll be back to return the scrubs. I'll let you know then."

- + -

Thank heaven . . .

Vesta followed the fire truck with her binoculars—a limited glimpse, but long enough to see that it was heading back to the station. The truck's short turnaround time and the fact that she hadn't smelled smoke on the trek around her secluded yard meant fire wasn't an issue this time. The crew had no doubt been dispatched as first responders . . . for that poor girl. *Oh, dear Lord.*

Vesta set the binoculars on the windowsill and fought a chill. Attempted murder half a block away. According to the action committee. She glanced at the screen of her laptop, the urgent mass mailing from Andrea Nichols still open:

Bluffs neighbors:

I feel it my duty to inform you that today a teenage girl was beaten and left near death at the free clinic. It's entirely possible that this victim suffered her critical injuries on that property, as did the vagrant who was burned only a few days ago. I'm sure none of you need to be reminded how close the property is to our homes. Our safety is at risk. As are the tender psyches of our children. Dr. Jack Travis treated this girl on the clinic porch in full view of impressionable Bluffs youngsters! Yet another example of his reckless insensitivity. I urge you to be present at the upcoming special city council meeting, which will convene to hear arguments in favor of closing the clinic. I will be sending out reminders. Remember, too, that tickets are still available for Fashion Fiesta, the spring style show featuring clothing and accessories from Bunny Merrit's darling new dress shop. A portion of the proceeds will benefit local charities. A worthy cause, dear neighbors.

Vesta closed the laptop, groaning at the obvious, sad irony.

She settled into the rose plaid chair near the window, reached for her tea, and then glimpsed a colorful flurry of feathers in the redbud tree. She snatched up her binoculars and adjusted the focus. She hoped it was a painted bunting—vivid scarlet beneath, blue head, brilliant yellow-green on top, black wing bars, red-circled eyes. In her opinion, the most beautiful of Texas birds. Vesta needed that joy right now, because . . .

No. Don't remember.

She shoved the ugly images down, refusing to let them bring suffocating panic again. She shifted the glasses, switched her focus to another graceful tree branch, and scanned its lush, round foliage, still needing the bunting's jewel-bright and elusive joy. And a merciful distraction from the frightening truth: today's incident wasn't Jack Travis's first brush with murderous violence.

- + -

Riley parked the car and headed to one of the hospital's side doors, the same entrance she'd used the day she made a fool of herself shrieking at the grackles . . . and at Jack Travis. That had been only two days ago, but it seemed so much longer. Especially after all that had happened today. She glanced toward the emergency department's ambulance bay and saw the advanced-life-support rig parked close, metal scoop stretcher leaning against its open back doors. A medic she recognized from the clinic sprayed it with a bottle of disinfectant, scrubbing away the blood. Two SAPD patrol cars were parked nearby, officers still hoping to ID the young victim, no doubt. And waiting to see if her assailant could be charged with murder.

If they ever catch him. . . . They don't always catch them.

Riley shivered and entered the door's security code. In moments she'd covered the stretch of corridors leading to the ER to find Kate outside the trauma room. Her expression was grim, and she did a double take when she saw Riley.

"Scrubs?"

"I was at the clinic when . . ." Riley glanced toward the trauma room's closed double doors, heard the telltale *whoosh-sigh* of a ventilator, monitor beeps, and a chorus of staff voices, some reporting numbers, others barking curt orders. "I went there for a tour. Ended up helping with the resuscitation. I changed my clothes afterward because—" Riley stopped short, noticing the deepening distress in the charge nurse's expression. "Are you okay?"

"Fine," Kate said quickly, dragging her fingers through her short hair. "Completely." She forced a smile that did nothing to dispel the troubled look in her eyes. "Skipped lunch. I'll grab some coffee after we finish in there—rough case. But we've got it under control."

"What have you found?"

Kate's lips pinched together. "Still unresponsive, Glasgow scale maybe 5 at best. Neck's not fractured. So we reintubated her, put her on the vent. Doctor says he found an area on her scalp that's 'mushy as a ripe melon.' Depressed skull fracture, he thinks. And probably an extensive brain injury. The neurosurgeon's champing at the bit, but things are doubly complicated because—" Kate winced—"there's a live baby despite the belly trauma. And it's stressed with all that bleeding. The perinatologist wants that baby out, stat. So the plan is—" She stopped as the trauma doors slammed open behind them.

"Let's roll, guys. Coming through!" an ER tech shouted.

Riley stepped aside and Kate moved to help as the gurney, squeaking and clattering, burst from the room. A respiratory therapist squeezed the Ambu bag, and IVs swung above pole-mounted pumps—one infusing dark blood. Riley watched as a flurry of scrubs followed, a faded rainbow of colors representing ER, OR, OB, neurosurgery, and neonatal ICU. All focused on the nameless patient, no more than a child, deathly pale, deeply unconscious . . . and barely clinging to life.

She turned as Kate reappeared beside her. "Emergency cesarean?"

"Yes. And then she goes immediately into the hands of neurosurgery."

And God. "Did the police make an identification?"

"Still Jane Doe so far. They said they'd get fingerprints, DNA. The TV news will broadcast a general description, and the police are going door to door in neighborhoods adjacent to the clinic."

The Bluffs residents will love that. "Jack thinks she's a runaway."

"Mmm." Kate cleared her throat, then tugged at her wispy hairline, face paling enough to make her freckles stand out.

"Whoa there." Riley touched her arm. "You don't look so good. Let's go to the lounge and sit down for a few minutes. Find you something to eat."

"No." Kate's hand fluttered across her stomach. "Couldn't eat anything. Not now. And I should check on the rest of the staff."

"Kate, I want to do something to help you. Let me."

"You can't. Really. I'm fine."

"Well . . ." Riley hesitated, telling herself not to push her stoic friend. "I'll bring you some coffee—with enough cream and sugar to qualify as Southern pudding." She smiled gently. "Now don't you argue with Rah-lee, hear?"

"I hear," Kate said, trying to smile.

Riley squeezed her friend's hand, then turned toward the hallway. She hadn't taken more than a few steps when Kate called her name.

"Maybe you *can* do something."

"Anything—name it."

"Pray they find that girl's family. She's just a kid. And no matter how badly she's screwed up her life, no matter *what* she's done . . ." Kate shivered. "That little baby shouldn't be handed over to strangers . . . tossed away like table scraps. He should have a chance to know his family."

Tossed away? Riley had no idea where that had come from but knew she should tread carefully. She wanted to fold Kate into a hug, but her friend would resist just as stubbornly as she was fighting to hold back the tears shimmering in her eyes. Riley nodded. "I'll go to the chapel—right after I bring that coffee."

"Thank you." Kate took a deep breath, adjusted her stethoscope, and walked back toward the ER nurses' station.

Fifteen minutes later, through the doors of the chapel, Riley heard the PA system play a few bars of Brahms's Lullaby. Alamo Grace Hospital's announcement of a baby's birth.

- + -

Jack opened his condo's front door, made somewhat difficult because he'd neglected to change the burned-out porch light for weeks now and had to fumble in the dark every time he came home late. Which was maybe six out of seven days. Unlike his neighbors, he wasn't much for security systems and motion sensor lights. He smiled, thinking of what Bandy had said about the newly mounted lights at the clinic blinding Andrea Nichols's Persian cat when it came slumming onto the property. Then he realized, as always when he came back to his dark residence, that he was envious of Bandy settling down for the night at the clinic. In his long johns and worn-out cowhide slippers, with a mug of tea—Jack chuckled—and a smuggled donut, probably. He'd do one last round to check the doors, then climb into the office's lumpy sofa bed and put one of his gospel albums in Jack's CD player. The old bull rider had called the ramshackle clinic building home for nearly a year now.

Home. It felt like that to Jack, too, more than he cared to admit to anyone. He'd picked this condo because it was an easy commute to both the clinic and the hospitals and because it had a secure garage for the Hummer and his sports gear, but apart from that . . . He switched on the entry light and frowned at the condo's glass, chrome, and battleship-gray interior. Furnished, cold, anonymous. It didn't help that in a year of living there he'd never completely unpacked; he fell asleep most nights fully clothed atop the bed in front of cable news.

Jack glanced at his duffel and briefcase tossed on an end table, still untouched after his Reserve weekend, thinking he should gather things up so the cleaning service could dust. He scraped his hand across his beard-stubbled chin, heard his stomach growl. It had been a long day. And he had no doubt he'd be seeing the worst parts of it replayed on the late-night news. He dropped his keys on the entry table and headed for the refrigerator, remembering what Rob Melton had said—that tire tracks on the clinic's patchy lawn and damage to the lower step of the porch suggested a car had pulled up as close as possible in order to dump Jane Doe. Barefoot, brain-injured . . . pregnant, hemorrhaging, hardly breathing, and—

Jack slammed his palm against the refrigerator door. "Oxygen-wasting bottom-feeder!"

He let out a ragged breath, asking the questions that had made his gut wrench too many times to count in the past fifteen years: Where was a merciful God in something like that? *Are you even there anymore?*

He shook his head, then stooped to retrieve a magnet that he'd knocked to the floor along with the clinic's monthly volunteer calendar—he'd penciled in dates for the skydiving appointment, mountain biking with Rob, a second rock-climbing lesson in Fort Davis. He had them all logged into his BlackBerry, but he liked having them here too. A concrete list of the few things he looked forward to, that made him feel alive—besides the clinic. And who knew how long that would last after the incidents with Gilbert and the girl? He'd go before the clinic board again, prepare his defense for the city council meeting, and rally the few volunteers he had left.

Volunteers . . .

Jack pulled his phone from his pocket and touched its screen, searched the stored contacts. They'd exchanged cell numbers. He found it and tapped to connect.

"Um . . . hi." Riley's voice sounded wary.

"Hi. I wondered if you had an update on Jane Doe." *Besides the one I got an hour ago.*

Riley sighed. "She survived the craniectomy, barely. The injury is extensive, and they expect a lot of swelling. They're keeping her in a drug-induced coma. The police are still trying to identify her and find family. Baby Girl Doe is doing better than expected—five pounds, three ounces. I saw her." There was a soft groan. "What a horrific . . ." Riley's voice faded off.

He nodded, remembering the shell-shocked look on her face as she stood in the clinic after the ambulance pulled away. "Riley?"

"I'm here. Was there something else?"

"I . . ." His brain fumbled. "I want to pay for your dry cleaning. Make that right." *Let me make something right today.*

"Thank you. But that's really not necessary."

"Look, you only came to the clinic because I badgered you into it. Everything that happened wasn't supposed to. It was a mess. I'm sorry about that. But . . . you did good."

It sounded like her breath caught.

"Let me pay for your dry cleaning, Chaplain." He waited for what seemed like forever.

"I'll keep the scrubs instead."

Huh?

"They fit," she explained. "And I can wear them when I come back to work. Friday afternoon?"

His jaw went slack. "Ah . . . sure. Great."

"See you then."

Jack disconnected, shoved the phone in his pocket, then reached for the refrigerator door. The calendar slid and he secured it with another magnet . . . resisting a sudden, irrational urge to pencil in *Riley at the clinic* somewhere between rock climbing and skydiving.

10

RILEY REACHED FOR VESTA CALDER'S DOOR KNOCKER, a pewter woodpecker, but paused and glanced back toward the yard. The guest cottage sat in a lush and private woodland glen with lantern-lit granite pathways, a modest trickling-water feature, and more bird feeders than she'd ever seen in one place. Built with dark limestone to match the hill country style of the main house, it had a standing-seam metal roof and quaint beveled glass windows trimmed in red—the exact shade of a Texas cardinal. It was a complete contrast to the peeling birthday cake of a building that housed Jack's clinic, only half a block away.

Riley breathed a soft prayer, the same as before all of her chaplain's visits, then set the pewter woodpecker to tapping against the carved door. She wasn't sure what to expect. At their last meeting, Vesta was an escaped ER patient, bleeding, hyper-ventilating, and nearly catatonic with panic.

The impeccably dressed and warmly gracious woman who opened the door in no way resembled that frightened patient.

"I'm so glad you came," she said, ushering Riley toward a pair of pink plaid chairs by the bay window. A large set of binoculars rested on the windowsill next to an open birding guide, one of hundreds of books tucked into ceiling-high shelves covering three walls of the cozy exposed-stone room. A graying cedar cross graced the wall behind Vesta's chair, along with a myriad of framed photos.

"You look well," Riley told her, feeling a rush of relief. She hadn't realized until this moment how much she'd dreaded dis-covering that her initial suspicions were true. She'd feared that Vesta's panic disorder—perhaps a hospital phobia—could put her health, her sanity, and even her life at risk. Seeing her this way soothed Riley's soul, especially in light of Jane Doe's situ-ation. The sad case had deeply affected the hospital staff, and Riley had concerns that a few were showing signs of stress. It had been a painful week all around. Riley needed some good news today.

"You seem well-rested and strong, Vesta," she observed hap-pily. "Have your blood sugar readings been stable?"

"Fairly stable. For me." Vesta's smile displayed almost-girlish dimples. She swept a stray wisp of hair off her forehead. "My diabetes has always tended toward brittle. I was diagnosed at age eleven."

"Wow." Riley winced. "That's a lot of needle sticks."

"Not so bad, except for finding new injection sites. That's

always a challenge. After I was married, my husband gave me my insulin. He was an incurable adventurer and we were always traveling . . . climbing this mountain and hiking into that wild and woolly forest." She chuckled. "But he always kept an eye on my health first. Quite the taskmaster about diet, rest, and fitness. Military man, my colonel." Her wistful smile was replaced with a flicker of sadness. "He's been gone sixteen years now."

"I'm sorry, Vesta."

"I am too. But I don't dwell on it—the colonel would *hate* that. 'Don't wallow in sorrow when you have legs to dance!' he'd say." She sighed and then lifted her brows. "Where are my manners? I made tea." She rose.

"May I help you?"

"No, you stay comfortable," Vesta instructed. "I've got everything ready in the kitchen." She smiled. "My diabetes journal is on the table by the chair if you want something scintillating to read."

Vesta disappeared down the hallway, and in moments Riley heard the soft clatter of dishes blending with the sound of distant music.

She sank back into the overstuffed chair, letting her gaze drift to the colorful array of photos on the wall. It was a collage of a well-lived life and proof indeed that Vesta's colonel had been an adventurer. The romantic travelogue offered photos of the smiling couple in a hot-air balloon, posing atop Yosemite's Half Dome, on the rail of a cruise ship at sunset . . . even one of Vesta wearing a fur-lined parka in the snow, laughing as she waved from a dogsled. All evidence that, despite some episodes of anxiety, Vesta was strong, independent, and she—

A sharp rapping at the door interrupted her thoughts.

"Delivery!" a voice boomed from the porch. "I have your groceries, Mrs. Calder."

Riley stood, glanced toward the kitchen. "Shall I get the—?"

The pewter woodpecker pecked again.

"Mrs. Calder, it's Gordy from Central Market. Everything okeydokey in there, ma'am?"

Riley opened the door to a young man in a tropical-print shirt and backward ball cap, holding a grocery sack. A single gerbera daisy rose cheerily from the top of it.

"Mrs. Calder's in the kitchen," Riley explained. "I'll get her for you."

"No problem," Gordy said, his eyes taking in her hospital name badge. "There's no need to sign anything. Mrs. Calder's a regular." He handed Riley the sack and carefully rearranged the daisy. Then smiled, his dark eyes kind. "I always like to check on our housebound customers—say hi, try to brighten their day a little if I can. You know."

"Yes," Riley said, stomach sinking despite her smile. "I do." *Housebound.*

"Okay, tell Mrs. C. that I'll see her next week, same time, same place." Gordy started to turn away but stopped and tapped his cap. "Oh. Almost forgot. Will you tell her that I saw her hairdresser at my last delivery? Billie said to tell Mrs. Calder that she'll be here for their appointment, but she's runnin' a little late. She'll phone first." He clucked his tongue, then grinned. "Gotta love a small world."

Riley carried the sack inside, glad it was light enough that her weakness wasn't an issue. She closed the door, noticing the locks for the first time. Lots of locks. Dead bolts, chains, peep-hole. Security alarm box . . . and an aluminum baseball bat wedged discreetly between umbrellas in a stand beside the small foyer table. *She's afraid. Of what? And how much is it crippling her life?*

"Here we go," Vesta said, arriving with a laden tray. "The cookies are low carb, so . . ." Her gaze swept the living room before moving to the foyer—and the sack in Riley's arms. A faint flush rose on her cheeks.

"I'll take it to the kitchen," Riley offered, noting the discomfort in Vesta's expression.

"It's fine on that little table there—no perishables."

Riley did as she asked, then settled back in the chair beside Vesta. She took a slow breath, reminding herself that she was here to listen, not to judge or to fix. "Gordy said to tell you that he saw your hairdresser at his last delivery. She'll be here for your appointment, but she's running a little late." Riley waited for a response, felt the silence broken only by the ring of Vesta's spoon against her china cup. "You don't drive?"

"I haven't in years," Vesta said, making eye contact for a split second as she handed Riley a cup. "I sold my last car five years ago. Poor timing, I suppose, since this cottage comes with a very nice two-car garage. It's sitting there empty."

Riley shook her head. "I have the opposite problem. Two cars. And after my roommate moves in, only space for one." She thanked Vesta for the tea, cinnamony Constant Comment. She pressed carefully ahead. "You walk to the store for small things? Bread, coffee, creamer?" *Do you go out of this cozy cottage at all, dear lady?*

Vesta toyed with a cookie on the platter. "My landlady goes to the store almost every day. She always calls to see if I need anything. I wouldn't bother her for a larger order."

"Vesta—" Riley set her cup down, leaned forward, kept her voice as casual as possible—"I'm asking if you *ever* go to the store. Or . . . anywhere else." She managed to connect with the woman's eyes. Smiled gently. "I'm asking because I'm concerned. . . . I care. You were so uncomfortable at the hospital. Was your panic attack because you have trouble leaving this house?"

- + -

Vesta set her tea down before it could slosh over the edge. She pressed her hands together to keep them from shaking. A familiar mix of shame and defensiveness swept over her. "I have a treadmill; if you look at my journal, you'll see that I log the time and the miles. Every day." She flexed her fingers, told herself to breathe slowly. She'd begun to perspire beneath her thin cotton sweater. "When I had a dog, I'd walk him for miles. But Corky died, and . . ."

"When?"

Vesta was touched by the genuine concern in Riley's blue eyes. It compelled her to be truthful, despite the pain. "Two years ago," she whispered, her voice thick. *I haven't left this house in two years. Except for the day I met you—and Dr. Travis.* Vesta made herself smile. "So now I have my birds."

Riley was quiet for a few seconds. "You're quite a bird lover, then."

"Yes." Vesta glanced toward the window, feeling a dizzy rush of relief at the turn in the conversation. Familiar, comfortable ground. "Woodpeckers, cardinals, bluebirds . . . and soon, painted buntings. Beautiful. Do you know of them?" She sought Riley's eyes, confidence building.

"No. I'm afraid the only thing I know about birds is not to park my car under a tree filled with grackles." Riley grimaced. "My mother keeps birds, though. Finches, I think—in an aviary in the sunroom. She prefers them inside."

"I like them . . . free." Unexpected tears stung Vesta's eyes and she hurried on to keep them from giving away more than she was prepared to reveal. "I go out and fill their feeders." She lifted her chin a little. "And lately I've been taking some walks around the yard."

Riley leaned forward. "How does that feel?"

"It . . . feels . . ." There was no way to stop the tears.

Riley dropped to her knees beside Vesta's chair, took hold of her hand.

"I'm so ashamed," Vesta said, dabbing at her eyes with a napkin. "I've climbed to the top of Half Dome, sailed across so many oceans, but now—" a sob escaped her lips—"it takes all my courage to walk in a circle around that yard. As soon as I leave the porch, I can't get enough air. I'm dizzy and so certain it isn't safe. I know that something . . . completely horrible . . ." She gripped Riley's fingers, hard, and stared toward the window. "That fire . . . at the clinic . . . The man who was burned . . ."

"Slow breath," Riley instructed, rising to slip an arm around Vesta's shoulders. "Are you concerned about the parking lot fire?"

"The police said it wasn't arson . . . not related to those fires in New Braunfels." Vesta took a shallower breath, blew it out slowly, trying to keep the panic from rising. "Do you think that's true?"

"Yes, absolutely." Riley gave her shoulder a reassuring pat.

Vesta attempted a smile. "Sometimes my imagination runs away with me. I thought perhaps the police didn't give it their full attention."

"They're convinced that the victim—who is doing much better now—fell asleep with a cigarette burning. It was corroborated by the doctor who initially treated the man and knows his past history." Riley nodded. "You know him, Dr. Travis, from—"

Vesta choked, gulped for air, helpless to stop the trembling.

"Slow breath, Vesta. Take some sips of tea. I think we should check your blood sugar."

- + -

In fifteen minutes, Vesta was calm, talkative, and Riley had obtained a relatively normal blood sugar reading of 115. Vesta shared several photos of the painted buntings that visited her yard and an old snapshot of her much-beloved terrier, Corky. And then received the promised phone call confirming that her hairdresser was on her way. Riley helped put the groceries away, found a bud vase for Gordy's daisy, but asked no more questions. She made the offer of a prayer, as she did on most chaplaincy visits—and because she'd seen the prominent cross on the living room wall. But Vesta deferred, saying, "Another time perhaps." She changed the subject and walked with Riley to the foyer.

"You have the card with my number," Riley reminded her.

"Call me anytime. And with your permission, I'll ask one of our social services staff to come by. Coordinating with your doctor, of course. I can arrange for a home-visit diabetes nurse, too."

"All right. But I'd like to have *you* come back. If you would."

Riley smiled. "I will. Next Thursday?"

"I'll be here." Vesta gave a comic shrug, relief quite visible in her eyes. "And in the meantime, please arrange to get your extra car here."

"My—?"

"I have an empty garage and you need space. No argument— you can compensate me in birdseed."

Riley walked back along the crushed-granite path toward her car, feeling the goose-bumpy rush of gratitude that always came when she was able to connect with someone on a soul-deep level. Really help them. Or in the case of Vesta Calder, begin to help. It was obvious that whatever fears trapped the lovely woman inside that house and threatened panic if she strayed too far away ran very deep. They had some powerful triggers. Like those fires, both at the clinic and in the neighboring city. And . . . *Jack Travis?*

Riley frowned. Had she read that correctly? Vesta's reaction to the doctor's name had been immediate and visceral. It was quite similar to the terror she'd displayed at Alamo Grace. Riley stopped at the curb, pulled the Honda's keys from her purse. Was it possible that Vesta's panic at the hospital was caused more by encountering Jack than it was by leaving her house? Why was that? Was The Bluffs' campaign against him that effective?

Riley slid behind the steering wheel without a clue about how to answer any of those questions. She was only certain of two things: she now had a place to store the TYGRR-mobile Mercedes, and she had fewer locks on her door than Vesta Calder did. There was unexpected comfort in both. Somehow it helped to balance the newest looming unknown: how she'd survive her first day of work at Jack's clinic. Tomorrow.

11

RILEY PARKED AT THE BACK OF THE CLINIC near Bandy's camper truck, in the space next to the one assigned to the physician on duty—Jack today, though his Hummer wasn't there yet. Riley was relieved; she was barely more prepared for that encounter than she had been to find Jane Doe lying unconscious on the porch.

"Bandy?" She tapped the doorframe before poking her head in. "I know I'm early . . ." She smiled at Hobo's welcoming bark.

"C'mon in. We're in the kitchen, tending to a bit of a problem."

Problem? Riley walked in, praying she wouldn't be doing CPR on that speckled linoleum.

Bandy was at the table with a cup of coffee and a pair of needle-nose pliers. Hobo sat, cartless, on the floor at his feet.

The little dog wriggled with excitement when he saw Riley, making futile swimming movements with his back legs in a struggle to clamber forward. She hurried to close the gap and stooped to pet him.

"Cart shaft came loose," Bandy explained. "Amazing what can be done with scraps of copper pipe and electrical conduit. Me 'n' Home Depot are on a first-name basis now." He grinned at her. "Grab yourself a cup of coffee. I'll only be a minute; Hobo still thinks of himself as a watchdog, so bein' mobile is mighty important."

Riley smoothed a tuft of fur. "I understand."

"Figured you might."

Riley glanced toward the exam rooms. "May I poke around a little in the clinic? I know another nurse will be with me to start, but I learn best when I get my hands on things."

"Sure. When I'm done here, I'll show you what needs to be done with the lab and medical equipment before each shift—quality control checks. But right now Hobo needs me to quality check this hitch in his get-along."

Riley smiled. "Is there a clinic policy and procedure manual?"

"Doc's office. Shelf above the desk. Help yourself."

Riley made a tour of the rooms, holding her breath as she peered out toward the waiting room. It was scrubbed clean, homey and welcoming once again. She sipped her coffee, hoping it would quell the butterflies in her stomach. She sighed, then headed into Jack's office to find the manual.

Whoa . . . Riley stopped, staring at the photo wall behind Jack's desk. Her gaze moved slowly across the audacious display, mouth sagging open. *Rambo . . . the pictorial perspective.*

Some of the photos were black-and-white, most in color, a scant few framed, but the majority attached to the wall with simple pushpins. Almost all featured Jack as the lone subject. It was a random and haphazard collection with no connecting thread . . . other than the way each depicted a man embracing breathtaking risks. Jack in desert battle fatigues, standing beside a dusty Humvee, rifle over his shoulder and stethoscope around his neck. Jack holding a paddle, his kayak shooting through white-water rapids. Jack tucking low on skis, racing down a slope with his shoulder nearly touching the snow. Bouncing down a rocky trail on a mountain bike, and . . . Riley's breath sucked inward, her stomach dropping at the next one. Skydiving . . . a shot of Jack giving the cameraman a confident thumbs-up. Parachutes dotted the sky below him.

The photo next to it, faded with curling edges, was of Jack at a much younger age, running with a crowd of people down a dusty, walled street, surrounded by . . . bulls? Was that Pamplona?

"Quite a collection, isn't it?" Bandy asked, arriving beside her. Wheels squeaked across the floor as Hobo joined them.

"I didn't mean to snoop." Riley felt her face flush.

"Hard not to notice something like that. I tease Doc that it's his Buckle Wall." He chuckled at the look on her face. "When I was on the rodeo circuit, I won so many buckles that I nearly wore my truck tires bald cartin' them around. But nobody was gonna stop me from chasing better ones." He clucked his tongue. "A big buckle doesn't make a big man. Took me a long time to learn that."

Riley glanced again at the faded photo of Jack running in the crowd. "Is that . . . ?"

"A young fool teasing an animal that's a whole lot smarter than him?" Bandy shook his head. "Yep. Doc and I have that one in common. Both had our moments running with the bulls—him in Spain, me in every town between here and Reno. And both of us liquored up to the eyeballs doing it." Bandy sighed. "My beer-for-breakfast years. I did my best to test the Lord's patience." His smile crinkled the edges of his eyes. "Pull down that policy manual. You've got time to look it over before the patients start signing in. I already stocked the rooms and did most of the quality checks before you got here. Plus put together at least sixteen PB and J's."

"PB . . . ?"

"Sandwiches. Peanut butter and jelly. Or sometimes tuna, when donations are up—they aren't now. Some of our patients haven't had a meal all day. Harder to heal when you're hungry. So I open jars and cans. I fix the sandwiches and stuff them in ziplock bags. Doesn't take that long to stack 'em up. Doc writes a medication script for our patients; I hand them a sandwich. Teamwork." He shrugged. "And maybe, if this old thumb's green enough, I'll have some vegetables to give out too."

Riley smiled, thinking of the woman who had willed this house to the city. "Loaves and fishes. You're still making that happen. But gardening, sandwiches . . . all of your duties, and you're the reception clerk too? How much extra time do you spend here, Bandy?"

"Not extra." He pointed across the room, where a pair of worn slippers poked out from beneath the sofa. "I live here. Sofa couch, nice sheets. Reading lamp. CD player, kitchen, bathtub . . . and now Hobo has wheels. I don't want for any-thing." Bandy met her gaze. "The truth is, I was living in my truck the first day I climbed these clinic steps. I don't mind telling you that I was a sorry son of a gun all round. If it weren't for Doc Travis and the grace of God . . . let's just say that man who caught fire out in our parking lot could've been *me*." He nodded. "I'm grateful. And helping other folks feels good. Sometimes it's sorta like I'm spreadin' hope, not peanut butter." His graying brows drew together. "Speaking of that, how're that poor young lady and her baby doing?"

- + -

Baby Girl Doe.

Kate peered through the viewing glass of the NICU at the helpless infant lying beneath a network of wires and tubing. Peanut-tiny, with a knit cap and no full-term chubbiness, she looked like a frail old woman. Her wrinkled forehead made her appear painfully worried. As if she knew that she was never going to . . . *know her mother.*

Oh, please . . . it was so long ago. Let me get past it.

Kate hugged her arms against her scrub jacket as the familiar wave of pain and guilt returned. She thought she had finally put it behind her. But she'd been caught off guard by the gut punch of feelings that came when the battered teenager rolled through the doors of the ER. A runaway with a baby.

She touched her fingertips to the window, watching the infant's tiny lips pucker in her sleep. An arrangement had been made with Mothers' Milk Bank in Austin, and tomorrow the nurses would start a first trial feeding. Kate's throat tightened. First milk from a stranger, first home in foster care. Then adoption, unless additional family was located.

Jane Doe's condition hadn't changed—drug-induced coma, full life support, a portion of her skull removed to allow for brain swelling. The sedatives were lightened at regular intervals to test the girl's responsiveness and ability to follow commands; at this point, she had shown none. Several of the neurosurgical ICU staff were having a rough time dealing with it. Apparently a veteran night nurse, the grandmother of a preteen, broke down in tears at the sight of the Tinker Bell tattoo.

Riley had teamed with social services to begin some one-on-one counseling, watching staff carefully for signs of critical stress burnout. She'd visited the OR, NICU, neuro intensive care, and the ER with information designed to bolster coping skills. In addition, she was planning a "staff support and fellowship" gathering in the hospital chapel. Kate smiled grimly. Maybe it was a good thing that she'd procrastinated with her packing—not an optimal time to share living space with a woman who was on a first-name basis with God himself. It wouldn't take Rah-lee long to catch on to the fact that . . . *God's tossed me away. The same way I abandoned my baby.*

Kate pulled her fingers from the window, leaving smudges. She shouldn't come here anymore. What was the point? Even if the media was calling Baby Girl Doe a miracle, Kate knew deep in her heart that the true miracle would come only when they identified Jane Doe and found her family. This tiny girl was innocent; she shouldn't have to begin her life like this.

Any more than my son should have been left on the steps of a fire station, minutes old and wrapped in a ratty sweatshirt.

She squeezed her eyes shut for a moment, then squared her shoulders and headed down the corridors toward the ER. The police had brought in the FBI and the search was continuing nationwide. Kate would hold on to that hope for now.

She shook her head, knowing that The Bluffs' action committee was equally hopeful that this second grisly incident at the free clinic would provide the impetus to shut it down. They'd had plenty to say to reporters. But then so had Jack, when he'd answered questions arising from the police report.

In the newspaper article, he'd confirmed that the persons who'd initially found Jane Doe were clinic building manager Bandy Biggs and registered nurse Riley Hale—further identifying her as "chaplain and safety officer at Alamo Grace Hospital and a valuable new member of our volunteer staff." Kate had read it twice, surprised at his enthusiastic statement. Especially considering how tight-lipped Jack usually was around reporters and since Riley had only recently agreed to volunteer at his clinic. Today was her first day.

Kate punched in the door code for the ER, wondering if her friend had seen the *Express-News* article. Riley was protective of her privacy. And there wasn't much doubt how the Houston Hales would feel about their daughter's recent brush with violence.

- + -

Jack watched from the exam room door as Riley applied the last of the bandage tape, surprised that she'd repeated the final instructions in Spanish.

"Por favor, mantener el vendaje seco. Y volver aquí el lunes . . . para que podamos cambiar."

Keep the bandage dry . . . come back on Monday. At least that's what Jack thought she'd said. Though he continued to try, his Spanish wasn't the best; that's what bilingual aftercare instruction sheets were for. Still, Riley's facility with a second language was a definite plus. As was her easy manner with the patients, even the grouchy woman who poked her finger at Jack, complaining that they didn't provide free X-rays. Riley's nursing skills had proved more than adequate for today's simple cases.

Besides, Bandy liked her. Jack smiled. The old bull rider had already given Jack a few pointed watch-yourself-pardner looks to ensure that Jack behaved himself—didn't stage any confrontations with The Bluffs neighbors. Which pointed to the most important reason to have Riley here: the real possibility that her influence, the Hale family name, might be the only thing left to save his clinic from demolition. He'd begun to imagine her standing beside him at the city council meeting, impressing the pants off everyone in the room. It could happen if Jack could manage not to throw a CPR manikin—literally or figuratively—and alienate this woman during the last half hour of her first shift. He was trying.

"Adiós, señor," Riley said, handing their patient a printed discharge sheet.

Jack stepped aside as the man exited the exam room— a gardener who'd gladly offered the ten-dollar pay-if-you're-able clinic donation. And left a trail of boot-embossed topsoil down the hallway.

Jack smiled as Riley glanced his way. "You speak Spanish."

"My nan—uh, babysitter was from Monterrey," she explained, her silky ponytail sliding across her shoulders as she hurried to replace the exam table paper.

Your nanny. And your gardeners, too, I'll bet.

She looked back up at him, a faint flush on her cheeks. "It was great, actually. I knew *Buenas noches, Luna* by heart." She smiled at his confusion. "*Goodnight Moon*—it's a children's book. And Estrella made these amazing, sugary churros, drizzled with chocolate and so fresh you could burn your tongue. And there was *tres leches* birthday cake, piñatas, and . . ." She stopped, flicked her ponytail back with a sigh. "So I speak Spanish . . . *un poquito.*"

He nodded, sorry to see her girlish delight disappearing. If possible, it had made her even prettier. He cleared his throat. "You must feel right at home with Fiesta going on. Battle of the Flowers, river parade, A Night Out in Old San Antonio. Tamales, shrimp tacos, music . . . you know. All the great excuses for an eleven-day party. And the reason I've had to pick confetti out of someone's eye more than once." Jack tried to read the look on Riley's face. He blinked. "Wait . . . don't tell me—"

"I've never been. To Fiesta, River Walk, the Alamo . . . any of that."

He opened his mouth to ask why, but there was something in her eyes that made him decide against it.

"I'll get your last patient into an exam room," she said abruptly, her fingers rubbing the side of her neck. "Asthma. Coughing, no wheezes—I took a quick listen in the waiting room."

"Good, thanks." He stepped away from the doorway and she passed through, leaving the now-familiar scent of peaches in her wake. And more than a hint of a curious chill. It left Jack wondering if his clumsy attempt at conversation had been worse than hurling Toddler Tim.

- + -

Riley had started down the hallway toward a patient room when Bandy emerged from the reception office in the distance, beckoning urgently. "Um . . . out in the waiting room. It's—"

"Coming!" Riley broke into a trot, battling a memory of Jane Doe lying in a pool of blood. *Oh, please. Not again.* She grabbed for the waiting room doorknob, hustled through, and stopped short.

"Mom? How did you find—is everything okay?"

"Yes, darling. I just . . ."

Vanessa Hale's voice was drowned by a fit of phlegmy coughing from somewhere in the crowded waiting room. A giggling child stumbled by, and his half-melted Fudgsicle tagged her immaculate linen skirt like gang graffiti. She ignored all of it, gracious as always, and smiled warmly at Riley. "I was in the neighborhood."

"Mrs. Hale," Jack boomed, wedging into the doorway behind Riley. "Come in. Please. This way."

After a flurry of introductions in the narrow hallway and a quick hug between Riley and her mother, the three of them made their way toward the kitchen, where scents and gurgling sounds indicated that Bandy had already put on a fresh pot of coffee. There was an awkward moment while Jack tried to find Riley's mother the least battered vinyl chair, but she responded with a polite remark about the vintage decor reminding her of a neighbor's kitchen when she was a child. Followed by a few long moments of nice-to-be-here-and-to-have-you-here sort of chatter.

Riley told Bandy no thank you on the coffee and reluctantly

took a seat at the table, knowing that this unannounced visit was happening as a direct result of the article about Jane Doe in the newspaper. Because Riley's name was mentioned, and . . . *I didn't tell her I was working here.* She watched Jack shift in his chair, noticed that he'd pulled a white lab coat on over his scrubs . . . and combed his hair? Damp marks scoring his hairline said that was true.

"You're volunteering here?" Riley's mother asked after thanking Bandy for the coffee. She glanced at Hobo as he crossed the room, cart wheels squeaking. Then back at her daughter.

"My first day." Riley looked anxiously toward the patient rooms. "And as you saw, we do have patients waiting. I should—"

"It's okay," Jack interrupted. "We're good for a few minutes." He turned to Riley's mother. "I appreciate that your daughter is willing to help here at the clinic, Mrs. Hale. We're staffed entirely by volunteers. Though, as director, I make certain each member of my staff is highly qualified. And that we operate under stringent standards. Would you like a short tour?"

Tour? Riley inspected her watch, thinking of the waiting patients. And trying not to imagine what could happen to her mother's sedan in the parking lot.

"No. Thank you." Riley's mother began to stand. "That's kind. But I can see that you're busy. And I really do have to meet friends over in Alamo Heights. We're driving on to Dallas for an event tomorrow. I never intended to take up your time. I was simply too close not to stop and give my daughter a quick hug." She offered her hand to both Jack and Bandy, told them it had been a pleasure to meet them, then turned to Riley. "Walk me out, darling?"

Riley led her outside, grateful to find that her mother's car still had four wheels and that no one was camped alongside it in a drunken stupor. Amazingly, though Riley suspected her mother had wanted to fingerprint both Bandy and Jack, she offered no criticism of Riley's decision to work at the clinic. Only a sigh, a lingering hug scented by her familiar classic fragrance . . . and a discreet glance at the newly installed parking lot lights.

"Motion sensors," Riley explained before she could ask. "I parked close. I'll have someone walk me out."

It's not going to happen again.

"Yes . . . good."

Riley watched her mother drive away, and then mercifully she was back inside the clinic, finding Jack's white coat draped over the chair, Bandy adding jelly to a sandwich, and Hobo yipping in his sleep on the floor. All normal, as if Vanessa Hale's surprise inspection had never happened at all. For some reason, it felt like a small victory in Riley's polite battle for freedom.

"Brianna?" Riley tapped on the door to the lavender exam room, then stepped inside with a gown. "Here you go. I'm new, so it took me a few minutes to find the extra—" She stopped, staring. The young asthmatic was scratching furiously at her neck. "What's wrong?"

"Can't . . . stop . . . itching." The young woman coughed and rubbed at her eye. "I think it's that medicine. From the dental clinic. Penicillin. I took a pill out in the—" she coughed again—"waiting room, and now it feels like I've been stung all over by fire ants."

Allergic reaction?

"Here," Riley said, feeling her own pulse quicken as she noted some redness and mild swelling around the young woman's eyes. "Pull that shirt off, and let me have a quick listen to your lungs."

Hives, swelling of the face and airway, drop in blood pressure . . . Signs and symptoms of allergic anaphylaxis ticked through Riley's brain. She prayed she wouldn't see them and wished she hadn't told the second clinic nurse that it was okay to leave. Riley was glad that she'd assigned Brianna to the room with the quilt—and the crash cart. "Are you having trouble breathing?"

"A little." Brianna stripped off her T-shirt, eyes widening. "Oh, wow, look at this rash." She inhaled and exhaled, following Riley's instructions. "I'm sort of dizzy, too."

"Lie back, please," Riley said, struggling to elevate the head of the exam table. She hauled at the protective side rails with her right arm to no avail and then switched clumsily to her left. "I'll be right back with the doctor." She offered what she hoped was a calm, reassuring smile. "Hang tight, Brianna. We'll take care of this."

Riley caught Jack at his office door. "Our asthma patient took a dose of penicillin in the waiting room. Looks like she's reacting—itching, hives, a few wheezes, no stridor."

They were back in the exam room in seconds, with Bandy and Hobo standing guard outside the door . . . *"Just in case, Doc."*

"BP is 92 over 48," Riley reported, glad the clinic had sprung for a user-friendly electronic unit. "Pulse 112. Respirations . . . 22. I'm getting the pulse oximeter. And the oxygen." She glanced at the bag of normal saline hanging from the crash cart IV pole, remembering the bruises on Kate's arm. *Please, Lord, don't let her need an IV. And don't let this be a mistake that I'm here.*

Jack finished listening to Brianna's lungs, put his stethoscope back around his neck. Then checked the label on the dental prescription. He glanced at Riley. "What's that pulse ox reading?"

"Ninety-six percent." Riley switched on the oxygen and portable monitor.

"Good." Jack reached for the cannula, slipped the prongs gently into Brianna's nostrils. "Only precautions," he assured her. "You're having a reaction to the penicillin. We'll do a few things to take care of that. The medicines might make you drowsy, though. Do you have someone who can drive you home?"

"My sister's in the waiting room."

"Great." Jack stepped back as Riley placed the monitoring electrodes on Brianna's chest. "Keep the oxygen at two liters," he instructed. "Then let's give Brianna some sub-q epi. Zero point three. And fifty milligrams of diphenhydramine IM." He gave a quick nod. "It should be right there, top drawer of the cart."

"It is. . . . I checked." Riley swallowed, mouth suddenly dry. *Please don't let my hands shake. Please let me be able to draw it up from the vial.*

"Um . . ." Jack's brows drew together. "If you'll hand me the epi preload, I'll give that myself while you go to the medicine room. I changed my mind; we'll give that Benadryl by mouth instead. Same dose. It'll be just as effective as an injection." He smiled down at their patient. "No need to feel like a pincushion, right?"

Or overchallenge the disabled nurse? Riley wished the floor would open up and swallow her whole. He thought she couldn't do it. And didn't trust her to try.

She cleared her throat. "I'll go get the Benadryl. Be right back."

She'd dropped the two pink-and-white capsules into a pill cup when her cell phone rang from where she'd stowed it on the counter. It was the ringtone assigned to her mother. No doubt she'd decided to express an opinion after all, to tell Riley that working at the clinic was a big mistake. Riley grabbed the pill cup and hurried down the hallway toward the exam room, refusing to give in to a sudden threat of tears. Her mother's timing had always been impeccable.

- + -

Jack watched as Riley gathered her personal things in the clinic kitchen. She looked tired. No, more than that—weary. She'd been quiet since they'd discharged Brianna.

"I'll go then," she said, after reaching down to stroke Hobo's head. "Unless . . ." She looked to where Bandy crouched in the hallway with a whisk broom and dustpan in his calloused hands. "Are you sure I can't help sweep up, Bandy? I think that gardener left half of someone's yard on the floor."

"Nothin' compared to what I used to track into a house with my bull-doggin' boots. You don't wanna know." Bandy raised his head and winked. "I've got this. I'll have 'er spick-and-span by the time Doc Travis turns down my bed and puts that chocolate bonbon on my pillow. Thoughtful guy, our boss."

Jack snorted, turned to Riley. "Thank you for staying over

until Brianna was ready to go. I appreciate that. And . . ." He watched, distracted, as she pulled the band from her ponytail, letting her silky hair fall to her shoulders.

"It was no problem," she said, sliding her purse strap over her arm.

Jack blinked, realizing that he'd been staring. "Well, I hope you liked working here . . . that you'll come back. We can sure use your help."

Riley stared at him, something in her expression making him sure that she was going to say she'd changed her mind. He started to imagine bulldozers in the parking lot.

"I . . . did like it," she said, lifting her chin. "And I put my availability on the schedule in your office." She glanced toward the door. "I'd better be going."

Bandy stood, meandered through the kitchen with the little cart rolling along behind. "We'll walk you out. Hobo always insists on seeing the nurses safely to their cars." He waved his hand, eyes teasing. "Doctors and dentists—on their own."

Jack smiled, surprised by a strange twinge of . . . *I'm jealous of a dog? Great.*

He'd made it back to his office and was reaching for a pile of patient charts when he heard footsteps from the direction of the lobby.

"Forgot my phone in the med room," Riley explained, passing the office. Her voice was breathless as if she'd jogged the distance from her car.

The enticing scent of peaches swept down the hallway.

"I'll walk you out," he said when she returned with the phone. He shrugged. "I think Hobo's helping Bandy check the corn."

She hesitated for a moment. "I left my car out front at the curb. Thanks. It's pretty dark."

They made small talk as they walked—Hobo, Bandy's sandwiches, the weather—and Jack thanked her again for volunteering at the clinic, raising his voice over the sounds of traffic on San Antonio Street.

They reached the curb, shadowy despite the streetlamps and blinking construction barricade lights. Jack waited while she pulled the keys from her oversize purse and unlocked the door to her Honda. There was an awkward stretch of silence that he filled hastily with "Drive safe" and "See you later."

He'd turned, walked a few yards up the dark driveway, when he heard footsteps slamming the sidewalk, a hoarse grunt . . . and Riley's terrified scream.

12

ANOTHER VIOLENT JERK on the purse strap pitched Riley forward, threw her off-balance, and sent her careening sideways. Her purse slid from her shoulder a millisecond before her knee buckled and she fell, right hip striking the pavement. Her right cheek hit next, scraping the cement, bringing an instant flash of her assault in the Houston parking garage. Bile rose and she struggled not to retch. A hand grasped at her and she kicked out as hard as she could, covering her head with her arms to protect herself from being choked. *Oh, God, please, not again. . . . Please help me!*

Her assailant cursed. It was followed by a loud, guttural shout from the distance.

"Get *off* of her! Let go, or I'll—"

Riley struggled to sit up, heart thrumming in her ears. "Jack?"

Pounding footfalls, a menacing growl. A loud slam as something—somebody?—hit hard against . . . *my car?* What was happening? *Cell phone . . .*

Riley patted the cement desperately, searching for her purse and trying to make out who was where in the darkness. She squinted, trembling, and then saw Jack pinning a man—a teenage boy—against the Honda. Jack's legs were spread wide, his shoulders hunched, as he curled one big hand into a fist and squeezed the other mercilessly around the boy's throat. His face twisted with rage as the boy made desperate choking sounds.

"Don't—" Riley stumbled forward, skidded on her purse, and fell to her knees. "Jack . . . help me!" *Stop killing that boy.*

He whirled, his hand leaving the boy's throat. The boy slid sideways, gulping for air, eyes terrified.

"Jack, please," Riley begged, holding her breath as he glanced back at the cowering purse snatcher and then in her direction again. "Please."

He stepped away from the car, started toward Riley.

The boy cut loose, running like the devil was after him.

Riley gave in to tears.

- + -

"I'm carrying you," Jack told her. "No arguments." Riley had winced when she tried to stand; he wasn't about to let her walk. "I'll get you into the clinic and we'll check you over more carefully. Put your arm around my neck—hang on; here we go. I've got your purse."

She slid her left arm behind his neck, let the other curl against his chest. He lifted her easily and felt how violently she was trembling. Her teeth chattered, and her hair lay softly against his neck. "Shhh," he murmured, lips brushing her temple as he climbed the sloping driveway. "You're safe now." Her body relaxed only slightly.

"I think I'm . . . okay," Riley whispered, her voice sounding like it was coming from the bottom of a mine shaft.

That punk . . . Jack clenched his jaw, sorry he'd had to let the kid go.

"You probably *are* okay," he agreed, seeing Bandy near the porch. "But let's make sure."

"I was out back," Bandy said, hurrying toward them, his eyes wide with concern. "Hobo started barking—what can I do?"

"Grab the door. I'll take her to the office."

Jack carried Riley inside, set her on the couch, then stepped aside to have a look at her. An abrasion marred Riley's right cheek, and her upper lip on that side had begun to swell. Her lashes were sodden and inky dark against the startling blue of her eyes. She swiped at a fresh tear, took a slow breath.

"Headache?" he asked, kneeling down beside the couch.

She shook her head.

"Okay . . ." Jack reached his hands toward her face but stopped as she flinched. "Sorry. May I check your neck?"

She bit her lower lip, nodded. He slid his palms along the side of her neck, walking his fingers back to her spine, then gently palpated the muscles and bones. "No pain? You didn't lose consciousness?"

"No pain." Riley's chin trembled and she jutted it out

stubbornly. "And I was wide awake for the whole miserable thing." She tried to smile. "I should have tossed him the stupid purse; it's a cheap knockoff and I never carry credit cards. All I have in there is about three dollars in change, a mascara that's been dried up for weeks . . . and my ministry cheat sheet."

Jack raised his brows. "Your what?"

"A list of prayers, I suspect," Bandy answered, bringing her a blanket. "Right?" He smiled when she nodded. "Might have done that man some good."

"Prayers?" Jack narrowed his eyes. "Yeah, he'd have needed some if I'd had another few minutes with—"

"He was a purse snatcher," Riley interrupted, trembling again. "A kid. All he wanted was my purse. I'm okay. I don't think . . . it's necessary to . . ." She stared at Jack, face going pale and pupils dilating.

"Right," Jack said quickly, sensing that talking about the incident was the last thing Riley needed. "We'll leave that to police." He glanced up at Bandy.

"Called them."

"Good." Jack turned back to continue his exam, careful this time not to touch her without warning—she'd nearly jumped off the couch when he'd tried to examine her neck. Obviously still shell-shocked. And protective, likely, since she'd injured her neck before. If he didn't know all that, he'd think Riley was afraid of *him*.

- + -

"Bruise, scrape . . . no biggie," Riley said, walking to the clinic's kitchen from the bathroom after washing her face and changing into fresh scrubs. "My hip's fine. See, in working order." She paused, raised her arms, did a few steps of what might possibly pass for a country line dance . . . and winced.

"Mm-hmm." Jack tipped his chair back on two legs, crossed his arms. "I'm still willing to have a look, if—"

"No," she blurted, hoping her face didn't look as pink as it felt. She joined him at the table.

"Put the green beans back on your cheek." He handed her the bag Bandy had pulled from the freezer.

"It's okra," she said, taking it. She glanced at his phone on the table. "Did the police call back?"

Jack frowned. "No. So I called Rob Melton. He said his officers are tied up with a gang situation. And since you still have your purse and you're not seriously hurt, he couldn't pull a man away." Jack shook his head. "He also implied that maybe it wouldn't be such a good idea to have the neighbors see patrol cars here three times in a week."

Riley nodded, thinking of Vesta's binoculars. And her parents' reaction if the incident was made public. "I agree. Really, Jack, I'm okay."

"I gave a description. And I got a report number. You're supposed to call when you get home. Meanwhile, they'll have officers keep an eye out for that . . . kid."

Jack's fingers clenched on the table, and Riley thought of his hand around the boy's throat. The ugly, angry look on his face . . .

He caught her gaze. "I hope you believe me that none of this is normal around here. A man catching fire in the parking lot, that girl dumped on the porch . . . what happened tonight.

I wouldn't blame you if you didn't want to come back, but . . . I want you to, Riley."

There was a stretch of silence, broken only by the faint sound of gospel music from the direction of Jack's office.

Riley lowered the okra. "To tell you the truth, I wasn't sure you did. Not really. I'm rusty, and . . ." She lifted her right palm, cold from the okra bag. She flexed her fingers and sighed. "This hand, my arm . . . I try, but—" Riley stopped short as Jack took hold of her hand.

"Numb?" he asked, his thumb brushing across her skin. His eyes held hers. He turned her hand over, traced his fingertip across her palm. "Can you feel me touching you?"

"I . . ." Riley's stomach did an elevator drop. She remembered the strength of Jack's arms as he carried her in from the street. His solid warmth—his heart beating beneath his scrub shirt. Suddenly she could feel his lips brushing her temple as he spoke to comfort her, the soft hair at the nape of his neck against her bare arm, and—

"No," she said, sliding her hand from his. "I can't feel that. I mean, barely. Pins and needles, that's all." She lifted the soggy vegetable bag. "This needs to go back into the freezer, and I need to go home." She stood, gathering her things for the second time that night.

Jack followed her down the hallway, shaking his head at the music coming from behind the door to his office. "Bandy's . . . whatever that is."

"Ernie Haase & Signature Sound—my mother's favorite." She smiled. "Bandy and Hobo like Southern gospel."

"Well, trust me, Bandy plays it endlessly—but Hobo's

outside. He likes to sleep under the truck. He was a rodeo mutt, never got used to 'civilized life,' Bandy says." Jack grinned. "Though rumor has it our mascot has a thing for Andrea Nichols's Persian cat."

"Nichols?" Riley stopped at the front door. "The woman who heads The Bluffs' action committee?"

"One and the same. Too bad the cat can't speak at the city council meeting." Jack rubbed his fingers across his jaw. "Hey, did you make that follow-up visit to Vesta Calder?"

"Yes . . ." Riley hesitated; conversations during chaplaincy visits were confidential. "Her blood sugars have been pretty stable. She looks great. There've been some transportation issues, so I'm arranging for a few home health visits." Riley smiled. "And I learned some things about birds."

"I'll bet. Did she happen to say why she took off that day—ran away from the ER?"

Maybe because she's afraid of you? Riley again saw the image of Jack pinning the purse snatcher against her car.

"I mean," Jack continued, "do you think it had anything to do with the clinic? You said that her neighbor was spouting action committee garbage. Does Mrs. Calder feel that way too?"

"I'm not sure," Riley answered. "She only said that she was worried about the fire in the parking lot. She seemed concerned that it was arson like those fires over in New Braunfels."

Jack frowned. "The investigation said otherwise; it was in the newspaper."

"She saw it but wondered if they were wrong. I reassured her. It seemed to help. I'm going back to see her again on Thursday. She's an interesting lady. We sort of hit it off."

"You did?" Jack's brows rose. "Great—that's great."

Riley pulled her keys from her purse and reached for the door. "Bandy parked my car so close it's practically in his window boxes. You don't need to walk with me. Or even come out onto the porch . . ." *Or carry me. Or . . . make me babble like this. Get me out of here, Lord!*

"Got it. I'm watching from the door."

The motion lights came on as she went down the steps. She reached to open the door of the Honda.

"Riley?"

She looked up, certain he was going to remind her to call in the police report.

"I'm glad you're working here. You're doing fine."

- + -

Jack aimed the key toward a dark spot that he hoped was the condo's door lock. It wasn't. He prodded the painted steel with his fingers, searching for the lock—the door swung inward. Great. No light, no lock. Maybe he should post a sign like they had in the window of the place that cut his hair: Walk-ins Welcome. He could make it easy entry for a few burglars, gang-bangers, drug dealers . . . purse snatchers? A growl rose in his throat. Sure. Bring them on.

He pushed through the doorway, wondering if Riley had given her report to the police yet. True, she probably hadn't gotten as good a look at the perp as Jack had. It was dark and it happened so fast; she'd been knocked to the ground . . . *hurt.* His teeth clamped together at the memory of her scream and the way she'd covered her head with her arms, trying desperately to keep the guy off her. A terrified woman trying to save herself from being battered, broken, violated. Like Jane Doe was. And like . . . *Abby.* Jack's stomach lurched.

No. Stop this. He strode into the living room, threw his brief-case onto the couch, refusing to let the horrific images come. All these years, all those nightmares—it did no good. It never had. There was nothing he could do to change what had happened to Abby. The same thing was true with the girl who'd been dumped near death on his clinic's porch. All that mattered was that tonight he'd kept Riley from serious harm.

He smiled, thinking of her doing that little dance to prove she was okay, then sitting at the table with a bag of frozen vege-tables on her face . . . that beautiful face. But it was more than that. She was a decent person with a good heart. He'd seen it in the way she'd offered to help Bandy clean the floor and the way she drove a basic nothing of a Honda coupe. And more than that, in the way Riley seemed determined to give it all she had—despite significant injury—to return to being a full-time nurse. A tough and often thankless career; he'd testify to that. She was trying to do all that when she probably didn't need the income any more than Andrea Nichols or her pampered, trespassing cat. Despite what he'd imagined, Riley wasn't a jet-setting debutante. . . . She hadn't even been to the Alamo. He shook his head, incredulous, as he headed for the kitchen.

Jack grabbed a foil-covered plate of leftover *chilaquiles* and a container of orange juice, glancing at his calendar as he shut the refrigerator door. Tomorrow was Saturday, and he had nothing planned. He smiled, thinking of how he'd been tempted to pen-cil Riley's name between his adventures, honoring her first day at the clinic. Today was that day, and it had been more than memorable.

He stood there for a minute, thinking. Then told himself the sudden idea was stupid. He'd be shot down, fall from the sky like a fool with a bad parachute. And then he thought again, remembered all that had happened today. Suddenly he needed to erase the worst of it, continue the best. He set the *chilaquiles* and juice on the kitchen counter. Pulled his phone from his pocket and hit the contact number. Heard her answer.

He made himself breathe. "Hey, Chaplain. I'm thinking of going to the Alamo tomorrow afternoon. And maybe playing tourist down on the River Walk. Having dinner there." He tried not to think of fatally shredded parachutes. "Want to come along?"

There was a silence . . . but not for as long as he'd expected.

"Sure. I should see that. History and all."

Unexpected warmth spread through his chest. "History. Right. Can't argue with that."

13

"IT SEEMED BIGGER IN THE HISTORY BOOKS." Riley pressed her palm against her white linen shirt and peered up at the famous arched facade of the Alamo—the shrine of Texas liberty.

"That's everyone's first thought."

"Really?" *Not mine.* Riley's first thought had been that Jack looked far more natural standing in front of this stone bastion than on the pink-frosting porch of his clinic. The Alamo's stubborn ruggedness suited him.

She watched as he sidestepped a young mother pushing a stroller. He walked a few steps closer to the limestone building and was silhouetted against its huge carved door. *Rugged—and incredibly good-looking.* Riley's gaze swept over him. Close-cropped hair turned golden under the late-day sun. Strong jaw. Broad shoulders under a khaki-colored polo. Tanned and muscular arms. Faded Levi's and cowboy boots. Riley was glad she'd worn her boots as well; pulling herself up into Jack's massive H1 had been challenging enough with her weak arm, without the handicap of cutesy flip-flops. She'd quickly dismissed his offer of help, remembering far too well that her last close contact with him had tossed her senses like a Gulf Coast hurricane.

So then why am I here? Because of the history. That's what she'd told Jack when she accepted his invitation. Or because of her own history? Maybe coming here was one more act of rebellion against her family's protective huddle. Riley pressed her lips together. Her mother had left a phone message suggesting that if Riley wanted to do volunteer work, there were many opportunities in Houston.

"Coming?" Jack asked, dodging a cluster of shiny Fiesta balloons. "Or . . ." The toffee-brown eyes teased. "Does cannon fire scare you?"

Not cannons . . . and not you, either.

She hurried forward, boots tapping the stone paving.

Despite the crowd—diverse in accents, age, and dress—there was a hushed silence beyond the enormous wooden door. Visitors swept off their hats and lowered their voices as they filed along the thick, darkened limestone walls of the Alamo's largest room. There were rough niches in the stone, a rainbow of flags, a detailed model of the fort preserved under glass, and rows of metal plaques. Riley glanced up toward the ceiling, then at Jack. "This was all part of the mission?"

"Mission San Antonio de Valero—it was never intended as a

fort. The walls were built to withstand attacks by native tribes, not armed artillery."

Like . . . She decided against making an out-loud comparison to his clinic. "And this room was the chapel?"

Jack smiled. "You should feel right at home . . . except for the muskets, bowie knives, and bayonets."

For some reason, Riley thought of Vesta in the Alamo Grace chapel. She doubted that weapons could have made her any more frightened.

They filed on toward the row of plaques listing the heroes of the Alamo, and Riley caught glimpses of the names—most unfamiliar, some known to almost everyone: David Crockett, James Bowie, and . . . *Travis*. She'd never thought about that. She stopped, reading the prominently displayed plaque: William Barret Travis. Commander at the Battle of the Alamo.

"No relation," Jack said, beside her. "Although—" he gave a short laugh—"I may have let a few girls in middle school wonder about that."

Riley struggled to steady herself as a child wedged into the crowd ahead of them. Jack caught her elbow, his fingers strong and warm. She felt herself flush, her pulse quicken . . . *like a silly, gullible middle school student. Just shoot me, please.*

"C'mon," he said, guiding her toward a dimly lit hallway. "Davy Crockett's rifle is over there."

- + -

Thirty minutes later, Jack watched with appreciation as Riley walked around the last of the Spanish cannons. She stooped to read the plaque and her hair swept across her shoulders, streaks of it shiny gold even in the dwindling daylight. She'd opened the buttons of her thin outer shirt against the heat, tying its tails into a knot just above where a tank top disappeared into the waistband of her jeans. Somehow it managed to make her legs look even longer, especially with her pants tucked into the tooled tan-and-blue boots. He smiled. Boots. Jeans. He liked it.

She turned and he dropped his sunglasses back into place, became a tour guide again.

"Not the original battle cannons?" she asked, walking toward the bench where he sat. He moved over to give her room.

"No. And since the Alamo garrison lacked real ammunition, they loaded the cannons they had with any metal available. Like nails, blacksmithing supplies, hinges from the doors . . ." He grimaced. "Not all that different from what you might find in an Afghan IED. Colonel Travis wrote letters asking for supplies and men, but I think he got something like thirty reinforcements. Nothing against fifteen hundred Mexican troops. Still, they held out for thirteen days." He shook his head. "The night before the final battle, they say Travis drew a line in the dirt with his sword . . ."

Riley's eyes met his. "And asked every man who was willing to die with him to cross it."

"You remember that from school."

"And the movies." Her smile faded. "Colonel Travis was one of the first to die."

Jack looked back toward the Long Barrack. "After it was all over, the Mexicans set fire to several buildings. Hard to believe this place was almost torn down and turned into a hotel by a New York syndicate back in the early 1900s. But the Daughters of the Republic fought hard to save it a second time, and . . ."

Jack let the thought go, suddenly tired of fights and skirmishes, of grappling with strategies to maintain ground . . . and stall the dark inevitable. Today he wanted peace, respite, sunshine. And to simply enjoy this rare chance to be in the company of a beautiful woman. He hoped it wasn't too much to ask.

He checked his watch. "I don't know about you, but I'm starving. You still up for Fiesta?"

- + -

Riley stopped halfway down the steps from St. Mary's Street, boggled by her first glimpse of the San Antonio River Walk. It felt like she'd been swept up in a Texas tornado and dropped into a south-of-the-border Oz—below the streets of the seventh-largest city in America. She held her breath, staring at a sultry and beckoning tangle of green: water, jungle-thick foliage, and a canopy of trees strung with colored lights and endless streamers. There were bright umbrellas, riverboats, tables on meandering sidewalks, neon signs, balloons, people everywhere. And a rich thrum of sounds: the *chug-burble-splash* of boat engines, childish squeals, ducks, sudden explosive cheers, the brass and string strains of mariachi music.

"Smell that?" Jack asked, pressing close to allow a family in magenta sombreros to squeeze by. "Every kind of food you can imagine . . . on a stick."

She stared up at him, the fronts of their shirts touching in the crush of the crowd.

"I'm serious," he said, laughing at the look on her face. "From German knockwurst to beer-battered shrimp to . . . chocolate-dipped New York cheesecake. And then there's sit-down food, like the St. Mary's oyster bake, A Taste of New Orleans, and every Tex-Mex dish imaginable." He groaned and took hold of her hand. "What are we waiting for?"

They waded into a color-rich blur of tropical shirts and crazy hats, navigating the winding path that followed the river. Their boots stuck to cobbled pavement littered with confetti, popcorn, and the remains of hopelessly toppled ice cream cones. Riley thought of letting go of his hand but decided against it, knowing she'd be lost in the blink of an eye. Her mother's long-ago dismissal of Fiesta flashed across Riley's memory: *"Too far, too crowded, not safe."* But impossibly, Jack seemed to know where he was going. She followed, feeling strangely as though she were heading into the heart of a South American jungle as the humidity increased, musky air scented by slow-moving water, boat exhaust, and beer. Talk wasn't remotely possible in the din of music and shouts.

Within moments the sunset—starting on a horizon she couldn't begin to see—turned the frenzied merriment rosy pink and let the long strings of tree lights compete proudly with the confetti and streamers. She moved her fingers inside Jack's, his hand as damp as hers. He responded with a squeeze. And a tug forward.

She'd begun to wonder if the reason that Fiesta food came on a stick had to do with the obvious fact that there was nowhere to sit when Jack stopped. Stock-still, in front of a narrow staircase that led upward along a pink stucco wall. There was a chain across it and a sign that read *Prohibida la Entrada*—No Admittance.

He unhooked the chain, waved her confidently through.

Apparently rules were suspended in Oz.

Riley started up the crumbling stairs. With each step—and there were dozens—the air grew less humid, the din more distant, and the red roof tiles and canopy of trees came close enough to touch. Her pulse thudded against her throat and she felt dizzy; she reached for a handrail that wasn't there. Two more steps and a palm frond snagged at her hair. Something screeched from above. Riley hesitated in the deepening dusk, thinking of the ever-staring grackles, and then felt Jack's light touch at the small of her back.

"Almost there," he said, promise in his voice.

She climbed again, wrestling with a sudden, ridiculous thought about abduction and a fleeting memory of Jack in camouflage that first day, when she was sure he was a maniac. And then last night, with his hands around the throat of that boy.

She climbed four more steps, felt a tug on her belt loop.

"There," he said, pointing. "That wooden gate, under the arch of vines."

Riley squinted into the shadows, mouth dry. The dizziness returned, making her queasy. And her mother's voice whispered without mercy. *"Godless, greedy people who would do anything . . ."*

"Here, let me." He reached past her for the gate latch, coming close enough that his beard-roughened jaw brushed her cheek. "You'll be safe. I promise."

The gate swung inward into what looked like a magical tree

house. A canopy of branches strung with tiny white lights and jewel-hued paper lanterns spread out over a red Saltillo porch inlaid with painted ceramic tiles. And a private, festively decorated table for two.

Jack's low laugh tickled her ear. "Did you think I was going to make you gnaw your dinner off a stick?"

14

RILEY STEPPED UNDER THE LEAFY ARCH and through the gate, took a few steps . . . then stood there, stunned. She glanced toward a low stucco wall dotted with flickering luminarias, back at the vine-covered exterior of the aging building. The magical array of lights reflected from the panes of partially opened French doors; flanked by espaliered vines, they led into a long, tiled hallway and toward a soft clatter of dishes.

"Where are we?" She met Jack's gaze, realizing she'd whispered. And that the roller coaster of emotions—from confusion to fear, relief, and now delight—had left her knees weak.

"One of the oldest hotel restaurants on the River Walk." He grinned. "The owner is an impressive rock climber. This is her private table."

Her . . . ? Riley untied the tails of her shirt, brushed her fingers over her bangs.

"And—" Jack walked toward the corner of the balcony behind the table—"it's not half-bad for catching a sunset. If you're into that kind of thing. Come look."

"Yes," she agreed, joining him. "Texas knows how to paint her sunsets. Oh . . . beautiful. Purple, pink, and see that sliver of gold?" She looked up at Jack, noticing that the diffuse pink light had turned his skin an almost-rosy bronze. And that he was staring at her. Her stomach dipped and she glanced back at the view, then down through the tree branches toward the river, a breath-stealing distance below. She leaned over a bit farther, spotting the colored umbrellas—haphazard polka dots along the pavement—and the riverboats, Fisher-Price in dimension. She stepped back, suddenly dizzy.

Jack caught her arm. "Are you okay?"

"Yes . . . fine. Sometimes I'm not good with heights." She smiled weakly. "I'm guessing you don't ever have that problem." She tapped her fingertip against the embroidered logo on his polo. "Eagle Skydiving?"

Jack grinned. "It's great. I'm going again next week—hey, you should try it." His eyes lit. "Come with me."

She grimaced. "No way. Not going to happen. Ever." She took another step back from the balcony, feeling Jack's hand slip from her arm.

"Think of it as a prescription," he urged, excitement still lighting his eyes.

"I'll take Bandy's peanut butter sandwich, thank you."

Jack laughed. "I'm telling you the truth. Once you've done it, spit in the face of fear—"

He turned as a man with a huge tray of dishes—steamy and audibly sizzling—arrived at the French doors.

"*Señor? Con permiso?*"

"Yes, please," Jack replied. He turned back to Riley. "I hope you like fajitas."

"Love them," she said, glad the waiter's timing gave her a reprieve. *Skydiving?*

Jack pulled out her chair, and Riley stole a glance at him. She wondered, once again, why she'd come—how she could even imagine herself in the company of this man. They were so different on every level. "*Spit in the face of fear*"? What would Jack think if he knew she could barely face a simple flight of stairs for the first six months after her accident? That even now she fought nightmares of that terrifying fall?

Riley's stomach tensed. Last night she'd lain awake for hours because the incident at the clinic—that boy snatching at her purse—brought the Houston assault back in wrenching detail. How could someone like Jack Travis understand the way Riley had been raised? Caution was practically the Hale family motto. Spit in the face of fear? Not. Even. Possible.

- + -

Forty minutes later, Jack watched as the waiter cleared away the empty dish that had held his caramel-topped flan. He smiled at Riley across the table. She shook her head, blue eyes nearly as bright as the festive wreath on her hair—a rainbow-colored mass of paper flowers and ribbon streamers. His spontaneous gift. Under the endless strings of firefly lights, it made her look like some sort of girlish gypsy . . . *angel*.

"You're completely sneaky," she said, her voice still husky from laughing. "I can't believe you found this so fast; I was only in the ladies' room for a few minutes." She shook her head again, the ribbons shimmering under the tree lights. "I saw a little girl wearing one once. That day you commandeered the conference room with your suture kit."

"And you accused me of being dangerous."

She leaned close and once again touched a finger to his shirt's skydiving logo. "I rest my case. Anyway, I was sitting in the hospital gazebo, and a little girl wearing a flower wreath exactly like this one came flying by. Squealing with terror."

Jack raised his brows.

"Because . . ." Riley tilted her head. She smiled slowly, one hand picking at the table's centerpiece. "Her brother was chasing her with . . ." Riley snatched up a purple-striped *cascarón*. Aimed.

"No."

"Ohhh yes!" She pitched it, whooping like she'd fired the Alamo cannon.

He inhaled confetti. Scrambled for ammunition. Blasted back.

She squealed as it exploded in a cloud of color, then settled on the remains of her flan.

"War!" she declared, reloading.

Jack ducked.

They grabbed the last two eggs and stood, pelting each other without aim, scattering confetti across the patio—and laughing until they were weak.

"Ah . . ." Jack staggered backward toward the balcony as Riley struggled against another wave of mirth. "Truce. Have mercy."

"You looked . . . so . . ." She moaned, swiped at a tear, the Fiesta wreath tipping low over one brow. "Admit it, Dr. Travis. I took you by surprise."

"Completely," he said. *Completely. You did. You do.*

Jack watched as Riley brushed confetti from her shirt and then inspected her coffee cup. She'd surprised him with far more than the egg toss. From that first day, when she'd defended herself in the conference room, then gone to bat for his frightened patient in the hospital chapel. She'd surprised him by volunteering at his clinic, even after his less-than-sensitive ploy to recruit her. And again today, with those jeans and boots. And the way she'd bowed her head discreetly before eating her dinner. She was gutsy, inspired, special. And far different from him. Too different maybe. He wasn't sure if it was a good thing. Or if the difference between them was even surmountable. But . . .

Jack smiled at Riley. "How's the coffee? Salvageable?"

"If you like it with cream and confetti."

He shrugged. "Ask for it every morning at Starbucks—venti. Bring it over here. You should see these parade barges."

- + -

Riley stayed quiet for a few moments, fussing with the coffee, refolding the napkins, and letting herself move from silly battle mode to . . . *what, exactly?* She had no clue; the only thing she knew for sure was that she wasn't ready for this evening to end. She took a deep breath before carrying the coffee to the balcony.

"I spooned out the most obvious speckles and added fresh coffee from the carafe, but . . ." Riley handed Jack his cup.

"I'll take the risk." His eyes held hers for a long moment.

Riley looked down at the river, reminded herself to breathe.

"The height's not making you dizzy?" Jack asked, stepping closer.

"No." *You are.*

She leaned on the railing to steady herself, listening to the music below. Violins, trumpets, high-pitched strains of guitar, drifting upward from float after float of musicians dressed in black, silver-studded *charro* attire. Their wide-brimmed white hats dipped as they played. Crowds gathered on the banks, cheering, clapping as they passed.

"Middle school and high school mariachi bands," Jack explained. "One of many parades over Fiesta." He chuckled. "There's even a Pooch Parade, sponsored by an animal therapy group. I told Bandy he should enter Hobo, but I think our cowboy's had more than his fill of crowds. And he only walks about a block or two around the clinic, with all that arthritis."

"From bull riding?"

"He was a clown, too." Jack smiled at the surprise on Riley's face. "I'm serious. When he stopped competing, after the injuries took their toll. Not that being a rodeo clown isn't just as dangerous—maybe more; pretty easy to become a human shish kebab when a bull's got you in his sights."

Riley doubted Jack had considered that when he ran those streets in Pamplona—spitting in the furry face of fear? "How long was Bandy a rodeo clown?"

"Until his second MI."

Riley winced. "Two heart attacks?"

"Three. The last time he collapsed with cardiac arrest in a pen full of sheep. Volunteering in the kids' mutton-busting event at the Amarillo rodeo. He and Hobo." Jack shook his head. "He's told me a hundred times that he's living on 'God-given bonus time' and he's not afraid to die. Says he knows where he's going—'and it's a long way from west Texas.'"

Riley smiled. "Bandy told me that he was homeless. And you gave him a place to live."

"Officially—if anyone asks—he still lives in that camper truck. Truthfully . . . I think having Bandy in the clinic does far more for me than for him." Jack glanced down as if he was uncomfortable with what he'd revealed. "He's a good man. Better than me, that's for sure."

A big buckle doesn't make a big man. Bandy's words.

"So anyway—" Jack shrugged—"Bandy works his behind off manning the desk, cleaning up, doling out sandwiches. And probably some Scripture when I'm out of earshot. I buy groceries, make sure he has enough cash for the movies, gasoline, and—" He stopped short, staring at her. "Hey, wait. Hold still."

"What?"

Jack set his cup down, reached toward her. "Confetti. Hanging right . . . there." His fingertip brushed the side of her nose.

Riley pulled back. "I can do that."

Jack stopped her arm. "Sure, if you want me to pick it out from under your eyelid afterward. Hold still. Close your eyes. Doctor's orders."

She held still. His fingertip brushed alongside her nose, over her cheekbone. She felt his breath as he leaned closer. "Done yet?"

"Almost." Jack lifted her bangs.

The scars. Riley opened her eyes, saw the questions in his.

"A halo brace," she said before he could ask. "I was in one for three months. After surgery." She tried to glance away, couldn't. "C2. And facets on 4 and 5, with fragments impinging on my cord." Riley curled her right hand into her left, fought a shudder. *Please, Lord, I don't want to talk about this.*

"From a fall at work? How could that happen?"

Riley swallowed. *Oh, please . . .*

"I don't get it. Wet floor? Stumbled over equipment?" Jack stared at her, waiting.

Riley took a breath. "It happened in the parking garage. On the stairs. It was dark, and—"

"You're shaking. Hey . . ." Jack reached out, lifted her chin, made her look at him. "Riley?"

"I was . . . attacked," she said, her voice cracking. "A random assault. Strangled and shoved down a flight of cement steps. They found me on the floor. With a skull fracture, broken ribs . . . and my neck. They still don't know who it was, or—" A sob wrenched free and the brimming tears spilled over, streaming down her face.

Before she could take another breath, Jack's arms were around her.

15

+

"SHHH . . . SHHH. I've got you." Jack held Riley against his chest, cradling the back of her head in his hand. He whispered, lips against her hair, "It's okay."

Assaulted, strangled. Jack's stomach roiled at the memory of Jane Doe . . . of Abby. His attempt at comfort was a lie. There was no way to make this kind of nightmare okay.

"I'm sorry," Riley whispered, her voice thick with emotion. She pulled back, brushing at her eyes. "I'm . . . fine now."

He released her reluctantly, and she peered up at him, a festive speck of pink still clinging to her left cheek. Her chin trembled. "Th-thank you, Jack."

"No problem." He led Riley back toward the table, saw their waiter discreetly close the French doors and switch off the hallway lights. Jack made a mental note to leave the man a generous tip.

"Here you go." Jack shook confetti from a napkin and handed it to her. She blotted her eyes, and his throat squeezed at how vulnerable she looked. And broken. Despite her injury, he'd never thought of Riley that way. Not for a minute.

"I'm sorry I pressed you," he said, moving his chair close.

"I don't talk about it much." Riley tried to smile. "Not since I walked away from the fleet of therapists my parents were paying to listen. Enough is enough. It's been almost a year."

A year is nothing, Chaplain. Especially if you were . . . Jack opened his mouth to ask the question. Couldn't.

"I wasn't . . . He didn't do anything more," she said, reading his eyes. "There's that to be grateful for." She flexed the fingers on her right hand. "And I have more use of my arm than the surgeons expected. Not as much as I want—but enough to make my parents crazy with worry. They want me to give up my nursing career," she explained. "Come back to Houston. They were opposed to my being a nurse from the beginning, think it's too dangerous for me."

Jack suppressed a groan, seeing Vanessa Hale's visit to the clinic in a new light. And then the attempted purse snatching later the same day . . . no wonder Riley had been so frightened.

She sighed. "It's been that way all my life. I had a sister who was kidnapped. She died."

Jack's stomach lurched. "When?"

"Long before I was born. My parents never expected to have another child. So when I came, they went into protective overdrive. You can imagine. And it didn't help that there was an incident with my cousin a few years back. On a church mission trip across the border—an attempt to kidnap her and another volunteer. It turned out all right. But . . ."

"It made your parents even more determined to keep you safe." *So you wouldn't end up like Abby.* Jack wrestled with the nightmarish memory.

"Exactly. So I took a nursing position just a few miles from home. And still ended up with those hands around my throat. It's ironic, I suppose." Her fingers moved inside his, and Jack realized that at some point he'd taken hold of her hand. She left it there.

Riley was quiet for a moment, the sounds of distant music and laughter filling the vacuum. When she spoke again, it was barely above a whisper. "People say that I'm brave. That my recovery was a miracle. I don't feel that way. I want more, and I know that's wrong. I should be nothing but grateful because I could be like Jane Doe is now. Or I could have died on that garage floor."

Jack stood abruptly and took a few steps away, squeezing his eyes shut against the memory of the police officer's voice.

"She's dead, Mr. Travis. Abby's been murdered."

"Jack?" Riley asked, joining him at the balcony. "Are you all right?"

"Sure. Fine," he said without looking at her, hating his selfishness in that—and in wishing he were anywhere else but here right now. Skydiving, rock climbing, or even . . . He stared down at the crowded tables along the river, imagining he was there, knocking back a few beers, laughing at bad jokes and flirting with some half-pretty but completely willing waitress.

An anonymous, numbing free fall from pain, past and present. They were things he hadn't done in years, had lost the stomach for.

"I should get you home," he said in a monotone, eyes still on the river. "You probably have church or something tomorrow."

Riley touched his arm. "I'm sorry," she said with confusion and hurt in her voice. "I shouldn't have dumped all that on you. It wasn't fair to expect you to understand—"

"I *do*," Jack blurted, wishing his voice hadn't sounded angry—and ignoring every instinct to stop right there. "I do understand what that's like," he continued, softening his voice. "I can relate to what you went through. Because . . ."

He braced his hands on the rail, dipped his head, and took a slow breath. Riley's hand returned to his arm.

She waited, her patient silence encouraging him far more than he could have imagined. He hadn't said what he was about to say in years.

Jack finally turned his head to meet her gaze, feeling the same way he had the first time he'd jumped from a plane. "I had this friend, a long time ago. She was murdered."

- + -

Riley breathed through her nose, willed herself not to flinch, though her knees had begun to tremble. She kept her hand on Jack's arm and held his gaze, sensing he wasn't finished. *Lord, help me to listen.*

"I was twenty," he said. "Reckless, no goals, suspended driver's license. Waiting tables part-time at a brewery grill in Fredericksburg." His lips pressed together. "And using my father's cancer as an excuse to be mad at the world, I guess. Abby had been accepted at TCU—on a full scholarship. She was smart and had such a strong faith. She wanted to work with kids, make the world a better place. Needless to say, her parents weren't exactly thrilled when she dragged me home. She'd have started college in another week, if . . ." His wince was discernible even in lantern light. "It's a cold case, no leads. The detectives assumed that after the carjacking, she was raped. Then shoved into the trunk of her car." Jack's expression showed marrow-deep pain. "They weren't sure if she was still alive when it was set on fire."

Riley gasped. "Jack . . ." She flung her arms around him, tears brimming. He hesitated, then hugged her back. "I'm so sorry," she murmured against his chest.

"No, don't," he said, pushing her away enough that he could look into her face. His gaze was intense. Eyes shiny. "You don't need to try to make it better for me. I'm trying to tell *you* that I understand. It makes me sick that you've gone through all this, Riley. You have every right to want what that lowlife stole from you; it should never have happened. To you or Abby or that poor kid who was dumped on my clinic porch." He frowned. "I'm sparing you my doubts about how God figures into that mess, but I'll tell you that I'm sick to death of people who stand by and do nothing to help. It's the same as condoning it." A muscle bunched along Jack's jaw. "And if I'd had a few more minutes with that punk who tried to steal your purse—"

"It's over," she interrupted. "I'm fine. And you . . ." Riley reached up and rested her fingers against his face, her heart refusing to cater to lifelong caution. "You've been a blessing,

Jack. By taking a chance with me at your clinic, and tonight too. Showing me the Alamo, my first Fiesta—" she smiled, watching his beautiful eyes—"and letting me ambush you so badly with those eggs."

"Hey . . ." The corners of his toffee eyes crinkled with his smile. "Not so badly."

Riley laughed, drew back. His hands slid to rest on her waist, their warmth seeping through the thin fabric of her shirt.

"I'd say we were pretty evenly matched egg-wise," Jack said.

And so different on every other level, but . . . Riley shook the thought aside. "I'll concede to a tie because of the hair wreath."

There was a long silence, filled only by the distant strains of mariachi music. And by the merciless thrumming of Riley's pulse in her ears. "Thank you for today," she whispered against the sudden, undeniable swirling of her senses.

"You're most welcome." He traced a fingertip along her cheek. Then brushed her bangs aside and bent close, touching his lips to her forehead, warmth against a scar that went so much deeper. "You're beautiful," Jack whispered, lips against tender skin, "and brave. Don't doubt that, Riley. For even a second."

Jack drew back, smiled down at her. Then his head dipped slowly lower, his eyes holding hers. He took a soft breath, waited.

Riley wasn't sure if she nodded. Or merely closed her eyes.

Jack's kiss was gentle, initially tentative and completely respectful. Then, when Riley responded, it was far more thorough . . . and breathlessly lingering. Somehow she managed to get an arm around his neck and a hand splayed against his back. One capable, one numb—both hanging on for dear life to keep her knees from buckling. His arms were strong, solid, and being held in them made her feel . . . like she was skydiving.

What am I doing? . . . I don't care. I just want to finally feel alive.

- + -

"Grab her! Don't let her get away!"

Vesta's scream stuck in her throat, confusion and terror making her nearly blind as she raced to escape. Her car was so close. And too far. She stumbled, felt a vicious yank on her hair, vise-tight fingers on her shoulder. She whirled, raised her knee, and kicked, feeling her shoe connect near his groin—near enough. He cursed and hunched over, staggering backward.

"Get her!"

Vesta ran, shoes skidding on loose gravel. Her lungs sucked at thick night air fouled by a suffocating mix of highway asphalt, gasoline, smoke . . . and fear. Her car, lights still on. *Open the door—the keys, the keys . . .* Something exploded in the distance; there was sudden heat on her skin. She scrambled to climb into the driver's seat, pull the door closed, and then find the ignition. *Where is it? There.* The engine leaped to life. She grabbed for the gearshift, and—

A face at the window. Backlit by the flames, young, wild . . . desperate, murderous eyes. His hands on the door handle, and—

Oh, God, please save me!

Vesta jerked awake in the dim light, confused and shivering; her nightgown was soaked with sweat, her heart pounding. She swept a hand through her hair, dizzy for a moment as reality—blessed relief—came at last. The way it always did after the nightmare that had plagued her for fifteen years. Exactly the same. No. Maybe not anymore. After what she'd seen from the window yesterday evening . . . *Was it possible?*

She switched on the bedside lamp, swung her legs to the floor. She glanced at the clock: 3:30. *Sunday.* Her gaze swept over the Bible lying next to the clock. Closed, in need of a dusting . . . in need of reading. Familiar regret, laced with guilt, washed over her. She reached for her glass of water, thinking of Riley Hale. Her kindness, the way she'd listened with such compassion and without judgment. She'd no doubt heard a lot of things—as a nurse and as a chaplain—stories, confidences . . . nightmares? Would she listen?

Vesta took a slow breath, shaking off the idea. Then reached for her robe. Her mouth was dry, despite the water, and the nagging dizziness persisted. She knew the symptoms all too well.

She retrieved the test kit from the bathroom and settled into the wing chair in the living room. She pushed up her sleeve, pricked her skin, and watched the tiny drop of blood well up. After collecting it on the testing strip, she transferred it to the metering device and waited for the blood sugar reading to display.

Vesta wondered idly how long she'd spent waiting like this over the span of her years. Up to sixty seconds, three or more times a day . . . She glanced back at the monitor as the reading displayed 205. Nearly double what it should be after her evening insulin. She'd had no sherry, no extra carbohydrates at dinner, spent thirty minutes on the treadmill, and checked her feet carefully for blisters and redness after her shower. Maybe she was coming down with a cold. *Or maybe it's stress.*

Vesta glanced toward the window, its curtains released from their tiebacks and closed securely. She fought an urge to check all the locks, bring the baseball bat back to her bedroom. What would be the harm in that? She'd let it rest against the colonel's pillow . . .

Oh, dear God. What am I doing?

Vesta groaned, squeezed her eyes shut. She hated—despised to the depths of her soul—what she'd allowed herself to become. A worthless, simpering, useless coward. She wasn't fooling anyone. And she had no doubt that Riley Hale suspected it even before those groceries were delivered to the door. That lovely, sensitive girl . . .

What would Riley say if she knew about the reality of that night? Maybe she'd agree that it had been too long ago to do anything about it; that, given the darkness and the horrifying confusion, Vesta couldn't be expected to remember anything helpful. Riley might understand how it felt to get the late-night phone calls afterward. No more than dead silence, but chilling—intimidating. And then to wonder if her dog Corky's poisoning had been more than a mere sad coincidence.

Vesta glanced up at the wall, past the photos of Alaska and Half Dome, to the gray cedar cross.

Maybe Riley could even understand how hard it had been to pray since that night. To believe that after all that had happened, God was still there for her. And to wonder if he didn't want her exactly where she was: trapped, sick, and alone. A prison she deserved.

There was no point in this.

Vesta glanced down at her arm, pressed a cotton ball against the seeping blood, and told herself it was best to go back to bed. Riley would be here on Monday to bring the car, then again on Thursday for their scheduled chaplain visit. They'd talk, but Vesta wouldn't burden her with any of this. Not the nightmares and not what she knew about Dr. Travis. Or . . . Vesta glanced toward the curtained window, fought a shudder.

It wasn't possible that she'd seen him. That man with the wild hair who stank of fear and fire and still chased her in nightmares after all these years. If Vesta told the Alamo Grace Hospital chaplain that he'd walked down San Antonio Street in the direction of the clinic, she'd simply add *crazy* to her diagnosis of *diabetic recluse*.

It isn't possible.

Vesta put her testing kit away and headed toward the bedroom. Then went back to the foyer to check the locks. And to get the bat.

16

RILEY DROVE THE MERCEDES down the Highway 10 off-ramp, its grassy shoulder a Monet canvas of bluebonnets and fiery Indian paintbrush. She coasted to a stop, the breeze tossing her hair and the morning sun warming her bare shoulders. She sighed, feeling it again: the heart-tugging pleasure that came even the first time she drove through the hill country town of Boerne. Each time she'd been here, she'd felt it more.

Charming, arts- and family-friendly, the historic community was only a few miles northwest of San Antonio. It boasted a German band that spanned four generations, an amazing nature center—hosting the upcoming Brandon's Revue outdoor benefit concert—and, Riley had discovered right away, a quaint bakery called the Bear Moon that had the most delectable frosting-embellished cookies she'd ever tasted in her life. She'd immediately bought one decorated like a daisy. And chased it with a sugary red ladybug.

Riley turned onto Hauptstrasse—Main Street—glancing at shops with colorful canvas awnings and barrels of flowers. She smiled as she passed the charming Read All About It Bookstore—it was on her list of places to explore. But Riley knew, beyond the shops and restaurants and history, it was Boerne's inexplicable sense of home that had surprised her most. Almost as much as Riley had surprised her neighbor, Wilma, this morning by driving out of the garage in the convertible.

"Oh my. That car suits you. No doubt about it."

Riley would argue that point. But why she'd chosen the Mercedes and left the Honda behind today was as inexplicable as small-town Boerne's lure for a big-city Houston girl. Unless it was that she'd wanted to take the TYGRR-mobile for one last spin before leaving it in Vesta Calder's garage. Or because she was going to church, and somehow it made sense to drive a car with a Scripture-framed license plate. Or maybe . . . it was that her grandfather had intended his extravagant gift as a reminder of courage. And last night Jack had called her beautiful and brave.

Jack. Her stomach dipped in a way that had nothing to do with the surface of the road. She wondered what Wilma would have thought if she'd seen the huge, black H1 in the driveway, if Jack had dropped her off at home instead of the place they'd arranged to meet for their date. Would her neighbor have thought that the daunting car—and Jack Travis—suited Riley as well? *Do I?*

Her thoughts had tumbled far into the night in a struggle to sort it out. There was no doubt that the kiss—*kisses*—had happened at a moment of emotional vulnerability. For both of them. Riley winced, remembering the pain in Jack's voice when he'd told her about Abby's death. And his tenderness when she'd revealed the details of her assault after he saw the scars from her halo brace. Her stomach dipped again as she relived the warm brush of Jack's lips against her forehead. *"Beautiful and brave."* And then the feel of his fingers trailing along her jaw . . .

Riley pushed the thought aside as she continued down Main Street. Last night's unexpected emotional connection with Jack sprang from a mutual attempt to comfort. Simple as that. They were two people who, incredibly, had been forced to cope in the aftermath of similar horrific incidents. In very different ways.

Riley chewed her lip, recalling Jack's flash of anger when he talked about the assaults, how he was "sick to death" of people who stood by, did nothing to help. He'd insisted that doing nothing to stop injustice and suffering was the same as condoning it. And had implied that same thing before in reference to the attitudes of The Bluffs neighbors toward his clinic: he was helping people; they were hindering that process.

No, it was more than that. It was as if Jack honestly felt they were as guilty as the pimp who had dumped Jane Doe's battered body outside the clinic.

Riley braked to a stop at one of Boerne's few traffic lights, thinking that her comparison of Jack's defense of the clinic to the Alamo siege hadn't been that far off. Commander Travis had drawn a line in the dirt, asking those who weren't afraid to die to cross it and stand with him. Wasn't Jack doing the same thing?

Using his reputation as a maverick and his aversion to rules and conventions to divide the community—triage his supporters, separate strong from weak?

Then why am I there? I don't "spit in the face of fear."

Riley flexed her numb fingers on the Mercedes's steering wheel, thinking of Vesta cowering on the floor of the chapel that first day. It had taken so long to ease the woman's fear, slow her breathing, yet it had all returned the instant Jack appeared. And then Riley thought of the boy who'd tried to snatch her purse outside the clinic. The ferocity on Jack's face—in his hands— as he dealt with him. He'd mentioned the incident again last night. *"If I'd had a few more minutes with that punk . . ."* A threat she'd interrupted with the prelude to a kiss.

What makes him so angry? And dangerous? Is he really dangerous?

Riley blinked into the sun, caught sight of the church on the corner of Main Street and Johns Road—rugged blocks of Texas limestone, steep metal roof, graceful arches, stained glass, and century-old doors. She'd first found it when she was Christmas shopping and saw a sign on the lawn inviting citizens to "Walk through Bethlehem," a living celebration of the Nativity complete with robed kings, Roman guards, the holy family . . . and live camels. She'd walked Bethlehem, swept in by the charm, but she'd returned because of the warm, welcoming people and—like the town itself—a soul-stirring sense of home.

Riley pulled into the parking lot, thinking of what Jack had said about Abby, that she'd wanted to work with children, make the world a better place. That she had strong faith. And her family hadn't been thrilled when she brought Jack home. He'd mentioned having doubts about God. She shook her head, struck by the irony that Jack's goal was the same as Abby's, to make the world a better place. Except that he seemed determined to do it in battle mode, with anger and retaliation . . . and without faith?

Riley switched off the engine and felt a sudden achy emptiness despite the scent of breakfast wafting from the church courtyard and the giggles of ponytailed and frilly twins skipping past her car. Regardless of last night's unexpected emotional connection, she and Jack Travis were far too different on fundamental levels. She still hoped that volunteering at his clinic would help her chance for returning to the ER. But if Jack was to actually draw that line in the dirt—ask her to cross over to anger, defensiveness, and lonely doubt—she wouldn't do it. *Couldn't.* Even if for a few breathless and wonderful moments she'd been tempted to skydive in his arms.

The truth was that Riley and Jack suited each other about as much as the TYGRR-mobile belonged in her garage. And she was evicting it tomorrow.

- + -

"Oh yeah . . . let's fly!" Jack's tires lost contact with the trail, launching his mountain bike into a gravity-defying moment of flight. Air, floating rush, freedom . . . then smooth impact with earth and dust, tires drifting into the turn. His victorious whoop echoed through the trees.

"Nailed it!" He braked to a stop, unclipped his shoe, and dropped his foot to the rocky trail, then looked back for Rob Melton. Jack grinned, watching as his friend carefully navigated the last steep yards of the cedar-lined slope. "Hey, Sarge. You missed the jump. What's the matter? Can't get in the mood without lights and siren?"

"Right . . ." Rob's round face was flushed, shiny with sweat. "Just plannin' . . . to be alive for Sunday supper." He gulped air, grinned. "Which means if you hit a tree, Travis . . . count on someone else to haul your sorry backside outta here. You've tasted Rosie's chicken. I'm not about to be late."

"The only acceptable excuse." Jack smiled. "Let's take a breather."

"No argument there." Rob eased back on the seat of his bike. "Wish I could say the same about your clinic situation. Wish we could all take a breather from that battle. Nothing but trouble there."

Jack bit back a curse. Then reminded himself that he'd come out here to decompress, sort some things out.

He pedaled toward the edge of the rocky outlook and stopped. Pulling off his helmet, he let his gaze sweep the expansive view. White clouds scudding across blue sky. Rolling hills, anywhere from five hundred to more than twenty-two hundred feet in elevation. Anyone who thought Texas was flat hadn't seen the hill country. Boulders rose from the thin topsoil, small ones like he'd just soared over and far bigger ones, like the huge, pink granite domes of Enchanted Rock near Fredericksburg. Native vegetation: thick stands of cedar, sprawling live oaks interspersed with yucca and prickly pear cactus. And thanks to Lady Bird Johnson's famous efforts, Texas wildflowers stretching as far as the eye could see: yellow, pink, red, and blue. Fiesta colors . . . *like that hair wreath.*

The scenery was replaced by a memory of Riley's face under

the colored lights. The ribbons in her hair, pain in her beautiful blue eyes. Tears. And her warm empathy for him. They'd shared more than he'd expected. Laughter, play, raw emotion . . . kisses. Unexpected things that he'd come here to sort out, but right now . . .

He turned toward Rob. "Was there something new with the action committee? Or just continuing plans to smoke me like a slab of brisket?"

Rob took a long swig from his water bottle and wiped his mouth with the back of his glove. "You're still on the menu. But we've had three complaints of vandalism in The Bluffs this past week: a garage door tagged, a streetlight broken, and beer cans jammed into a huge stone planter shaped like a cocker spaniel."

"Time to get a real watchdog." Jack clucked his tongue. "Like to see someone try that with Hobo. Bite marks and wheel ruts."

"Ha! I'd bet on that." Rob's expression sobered. "There were two burglaries last night. A garage, with tools and a bicycle taken. And a car was broken into in a driveway—expensive set of golf clubs missing. Both of them within a quarter mile of your clinic. One of the neighbors made sure my officers understood that proximity."

"Great." Jack narrowed his eyes. "Let me guess. My patients did it. Maybe that girl with the penicillin reaction. High on Benadryl . . . and itching for a round of golf." His fingers clenched inside his biking gloves. "I don't believe these people, Rob! Did I tell you that Bandy got hold of one of their e-mails? It actually criticized us for trying to resuscitate that pregnant teenager." Jack shook his head. "Apparently we should have had the common decency to drag her bludgeoned body somewhere out of public view—never mind that doing that could have made her a quadriplegic." His gut twisted. "Andrea Nichols was trying to connect the crimes to my clinic?"

"Not Andrea. It was the opinion of the man who lives next door to the Paytons."

"Payton? The developer who's planning the condo project?"

"Yes, it was his clubs that were stolen. You didn't know he lives in The Bluffs?"

"Nope." Jack grimaced. "Small, *suffocating* world."

Rob was quiet for a few moments. "You're still going to be there for the city council meeting?"

"Wearing my combat boots." Jack tried to read the expression on Rob's face. "What's wrong?"

"I've been asked to provide an overview of crime stats. A comparison before and after the clinic began its current operations. And since you took over as director."

"You were asked by . . . ?"

"The council." Rob sighed. "You won't like the graphs in the PowerPoint presentation."

"And do those statistics take into account closures of other clinics? The downturn in the economy, job losses, increasing homelessness, or—" Jack continued despite a twinge of guilt— "cutbacks in your police force?"

"You're right. And I'll address all that." Familiar compassion flooded Rob's eyes. "Look, you know I support what you're doing with that clinic. You're helping people who have nowhere else to turn. And you helped us reunite more than a few runaways with families. Countless hours, money out of your own pocket . . ." Rob smiled. "If I didn't think you'd hurl that water bottle at my head, I'd say that helping those folks is a calling for you. A kind of ministry." He pretended to dodge as Jack aimed the bottle. "Despite that, let me say that Bandy's rat terrier has more tact than you. Those neighbors aren't bad people, Jack. They're scared people. Wary of what they don't understand. Protective of their families and their property. So they install security gates, form committees—"

"And stand there gawking while Gilbert DeSoto burns? Snapping pictures? I'm sorry, Rob, but don't ask me to feel empathy because they're scared. And don't ever expect me to turn the other cheek when my patient's *face* is on fire! As long as I'm in charge of the clinic, I'll be fighting for my patients. Keeping them safe. Nobody's going to stop me. I don't care if they outnumber me a thousand to one."

Rob pressed his lips together. "There's some talk that a private investigator's been asking around about you."

Jack's stomach lurched. *And I know what he'll find.*

"Hired by our good neighbors?" he asked, trying to keep his voice casual, unconcerned.

"I don't know. It could be just talk, people stirring the pot. I'll check into it, let you know." Rob glanced out toward the miniature roofs and ribbon roads of the town in the distance. "We were in Boerne for services this morning. You remember our church. You came at Christmastime."

Jack smiled, remembering. "Couldn't say no to your kids— or live camels. Nice bait and switch to get me there." He hesitated, measuring his words. He liked Rob, admired him. "I'm still not good with all that. Church and . . ."

"No problem." Rob raised his gloved palms. "Not pushing. I was only going to say that we saw your new nurse there this morning."

Jack's stomach dropped like his brakes had failed at the edge of a cliff.

"Riley Hale. You know, the nurse you mentioned in the *Express-News* article," Rob said, watching Jack's face with growing amusement. "Come to think of it, the only volunteer you've ever mentioned. In the extremely limited times you've even agreed to talk with reporters . . ."

"Okay. I get it." Jack told himself not to say anything else. Remembered that he'd climbed onto his bike today to find time to think—or escape, maybe. He'd thought of calling Riley today but wasn't sure what to say.

"So how was she?" Jack asked, instantly regretting it. *How was she?* Stupid question. What did he expect? Changed because of what happened between them last night?

"We only spoke for a minute." Rob shrugged. "I try to make sure I don't make folks uncomfortable. Because of my work. You know, there's always that awkward moment after you've introduced yourself, when they try to place you. They finally do and then wonder if you're going to say something about the circumstances surrounding the last time you saw them. Sometimes it dredges up things they don't want to think about." He shook his head. "I'm sure it's the same for you."

"Right." *The last time I saw Riley, I spilled my guts about Abby. And then she ended up in my arms, and . . . Is she thinking about that today?*

"Anyway—" Rob resettled his helmet—"in spite of your

cynical outlook, there are good people out there. And when you're ready, I'll introduce you. But it looks like you've already met one of them." He grinned. "Even without the old camel bait and switch."

Jack reached for his helmet. "You up for that new stretch of trail?"

"Are you crazy? It's not even fully groomed yet. No biggie for you. But these tire tracks are leading toward Rosie's chicken."

Jack grinned. "*Chicken* being the key word." He glanced at his watch. "Meet you back at the Hummer in fifteen?"

"Deal."

Jack picked his way through the brush, found temporary trail markers, and climbed to the first outcropping of rocks. He peered down as far as he could see. Steep, rough, but not that much of a risk. Probably. He checked the strap on his helmet and began the descent, bargaining with himself that if he made it to the bottom in one piece, he'd call Riley. If he ended up on a gurney at Alamo Grace . . . he'd probably see her anyway. She was going to be there. Arranging for some sort of "fellowship gathering" in support of staff caring for Jane Doe and her baby. A prayer group to help them deal with the stress.

Jack's lips compressed into a grimace that had little to do with the jolting impact of the dirt trail. Even a trainload of camels couldn't snag him into something like that. And it proved that despite what he'd started to feel last night, he and Riley were as different as two people could be. He'd tried to bridge that wide chasm with Abby, and look what had happened there. Rob meant well, but he was wrong. There were some things that Jack would never be ready for.

But this trail . . . Jack clenched his teeth as his wheel twisted in a rut, then corrected. He picked up speed, forging down-ward. This rocky trail was exactly what he needed.

17

"IT'S AN INJECTION FOR YOUR BACK PAIN," Kate explained, uneasy. The thirty-one-year-old man had been polite, charming even, but this sudden intensity—hinting at agitation—was making her nervous. "It's a hip shot, so I'll need you to lie back, please." She reached for the privacy curtain, indicating for him to lie back on the gurney. He didn't.

"What's the name of it?" The man's rugged jaw tensed.

"Ketorolac." Kate met his eyes. They were a remarkable jade green, appearing especially large because his brows and lashes were so fair. Still, he'd managed to tan, a warm bronzy gold. From working outside, probably. As a contractor, he'd said. They'd chatted, joked out in the triage office. She'd brushed aside his innocuous attempts at flirting but thought he was a nice-enough guy and empathized with his stoicism against the spasms of low back pain. He'd sustained fractures while working on an oil-drilling operation several years ago.

But now . . . she wished she'd asked the male nurse to handle this. This gorgeous guy was acting squirrelly.

"It does a good job on musculoskeletal pain," Kate continued, tearing open an alcohol swab. "And the bonus is that it doesn't leave you groggy. Which is good, considering that you work around heavy machinery, and—"

"It's the same as Toradol, right?" he interrupted, slipping down from the gurney to stand. Even a bit skewed to one side with the pain, he towered over her, maybe six-foot-three to her own five-two. He was lean and powerful as a coiled spring even beneath the shapeless exam gown. She hated her intruding thought of the psych patient who'd hurled the oxygen tank. And of Jane Doe's battered face.

"Yes," Kate answered, glad she'd left the door open and that Riley was watching from the nurses' desk. She stepped around the bedside table to create some distance. "It's a non-narcotic pain reliever. We use it a lot because it's so effective. Even with kidney stones. And they say that pain's almost like—"

"Childbirth," he said, the charming smile returning as quickly as it had disappeared. "My dad had a kidney stone once. They told him it was as rough as labor pains. Mom was completely sympathetic—I was a nine-pound baby." He reached up to drag his fingers through his thick mane of wavy hair and Kate noticed the scars again: pearly ropes against his tan. They covered the entire back of his right hand and extended up his forearm. A burn, she'd guess. From some years back. They did nothing to detract from his good looks but, added to his spinal fractures, it was obvious this man was no stranger to pain.

"Look," he said, glancing at the syringe on the bedside table, "I don't think I need a shot." He shrugged his big shoulders, his expression sheepish. "I'm sorry. I probably should have told the doctor that I'm not so good with needles. Big baby." He chuckled. "Still."

"Oh." She suppressed a laugh, relieved. A fear of needles. Why hadn't she thought of that instead of making it something sinister? *I need a day off . . . and less caffeine.* "No problem. No one's going to force you, Griff."

He smiled, obviously pleased that she'd remembered his name. "Thank you for understanding. You've been really nice." The amazing green eyes held hers for a moment. "When I can stand up straight and I'm dressed in something that has more basic dignity, I'd like to buy you a cup of coffee."

"Thanks, but—"

"A steak, then? Build you a house?"

She laughed, shaking her head. "I'll ask the doctor to come back and talk with you about medication." Kate lifted a brow. "What kind of house?"

"Any kind you want . . . California Kate." He smiled warmly. "Thank you."

California Kate. She had no doubt Griff was watching her as she walked away—and wasn't exactly sure that she hated it. There was no way she'd breach administrative policy regarding professional behavior. Still, Kate couldn't remember the last time she'd been tempted by the attentions of a man, even off duty; certainly not since she'd moved to Texas. With her

TRAUMA PLAN

history of bad choices—such regrettable choices—a relationship should be the last thing on her mind. But today she was tired, vulnerable.

Around 1:30 that morning, she'd pulled on her clothes and driven back to the hospital. She sat in her car for forty minutes, trying to convince herself that it wouldn't look strange to take the elevator up to the NICU and volunteer to rock Baby Girl Doe. A few of the medical floor nurses and a hospital operator had already done that; the *Express-News* ran photos. It was natural to want to help. The NICU census was high and the night shift always needed an extra hand.

Kate needed to feel that baby in her arms, and—

She'd driven back home. To an apartment emptying into moving boxes.

She was tired. And just now realized that maybe rocking the baby wouldn't have made much difference. Maybe *she* needed to be held. It could be as simple as that.

"Kate!"

She smiled at Riley, mouthed, "Be right there." Then took a few moments to fill the ER doc in on Griff Payton's situation and dispose of the unused syringe. When she returned to the nurses' desk, Riley had refilled her coffee mug.

"Thanks, Rah-lee, although I'm vowing this will be my last caffeine for the day. Too jumpy."

"Jumpy?" Riley glanced toward the exam rooms. "Something to do with that hulking patient you were talking to? Hard not to notice that mass of red hair—he looks like the Lion King. I almost walked over there when I saw you backing away. Problem?"

Kate smiled over the rim of her cup. "My ever-vigilant pal.

No, it was fine. He's needle-shy, that's all. But appreciative—he offered to build me a house." Kate laughed at the look on Riley's face. "He's a contractor."

"And . . . ?"

And I'm a sleep-deprived idiot. Kate waved her hand. "And nothing else." She tapped Riley's briefcase. "So why are you here on a Sunday afternoon?"

"I wanted to check on the staff, how they're coping with all that's been going on with Jane Doe and her baby." She studied Kate's face for a moment. "You know, see if anyone was feeling 'jumpy' or anything."

"Unh-uh." Kate raised her palms in a flash. "Too much coffee. No counseling required here." She smiled slowly. "But how about you? I saw your name in the paper. Jack making you crazy yet?"

"No, I'm fine." Riley glanced away, but not before Kate caught a glimpse of what she'd swear looked like a blush.

"Kate?" The doctor strode to the nurses' desk, nodding at Riley before turning back to Kate.

"I'm guessing you didn't talk my patient into an injection," Kate said, noticing the usually jovial doctor's slight frown.

"No. I'm giving him a prescription for hydrocodone. Don't really want to, but he seems to be allergic—conveniently, maybe—to everything else."

Oh no. "You think he's abusing pain medication?"

"I'm not sure." The doctor pushed his bifocals up his nose, sighed. "His story sounds legitimate, but I don't have access to any records because his last physician was at a walk-in clinic in Odessa." He shook his head. "And honestly, maybe it just galled me that the guy was so sure he'd be tearing down Jack's clinic for that condo project."

Kate's mouth sagged open.

Riley stiffened beside her. "What?"

The doctor nodded. "Griff Payton's father is Ross Payton—The Bluffs' developer. Good man. I teamed up with him at the hospital's charity golf tournament last fall. I doubt he'd like his son shooting off his mouth about that project before the city council's even started the decision-making process." He sighed. "I'll give him a script for a few pills to hold him over until he finds a local orthopedist. Will you see that he gets a physician list along with his instructions?"

"Sure." Kate watched the doctor leave and then glanced toward the closed door to Griff's exam room. She was surprised by an unexpected wave of disappointment as she tossed Riley a grim smile. "Yeah, well, guess I'll be moving in with you after all. No way I'm telling Rambo that some good-looking contractor's building me a house—on top of the rubble of his clinic."

"Trust me, I can't see that happening. Jack Travis could have been commander at the Alamo. And there's no way he'd—" Riley broke off as her text message tone sounded.

Kate watched her friend's expression move from surprise to concern. "What's going on?"

Riley stood. "Family has arrived for Jane Doe."

- + -

"Are they sure it's Stacy?" Mrs. Collins tore her gaze away from her daughter to look at Riley. "She's so bruised and swollen. It makes it hard to tell. Could they be mistaken?"

"They're sure." Riley's heart ached at the anguish in the woman's gray eyes. She had dark hair like her daughter's and remarkably similar features. She couldn't be more than ten years older than Riley and likely hadn't slept more than a handful of hours in the past few days. She and her husband had flown in from Seattle barely two hours ago and had already talked to the FBI, the police, the doctors . . . *Lord, help me with this.* "As the agents said, the dental records you provided were a match. Then today the DNA was another confirmation. Plus, you said something about the—"

"Tattoo of Tinker Bell." Mrs. Collins's voice broke as she grasped for her husband's hand. She looked at her daughter's chest, draped discreetly to reveal the ink image of the little fairy-tale pixie. "We've had so many horrible false alarms in the past two years. Hopes . . . scares. I didn't want to do this again. But when I heard about the tattoo, I think I knew."

Mrs. Collins closed her eyes, hesitating, and the pause was filled by the soft *click-whoosh* of the ventilator and the metallic ticking of medication pumps. "Stacy loved Tinker Bell," she said finally. "We had the movie, and in that scene where Peter asks the children if they believe . . . tells them to clap their hands?" She smiled despite a fresh welling of tears. "She'd clap and clap and clap. Her little eyes were so full of hope." She took a slow breath. "We argued about tattoos when she was fourteen, five years after her father left us. I said no. . . . I may have said, 'Over my dead body.' I was trying so hard to hold things together; she was rebelling. And it only got worse after her father was killed in a boating accident." She brushed at her cheek. "They think the tattoo is recent?"

"Yes, very. Still healing." Riley glanced toward the bed, wishing she hadn't added the part about healing. There was no healing going on here. Her eyes skimmed the nameplate on the wall, recently changed to *Paulson, Stacy*. She knew she'd always think of this tragic girl as Jane.

"Stacy turned eighteen last fall." Mr. Collins's eyes mirrored his wife's pain. "We'd had a few text messages telling us she was fine and to leave her alone. We didn't believe it. There are such horror stories about young runaways being trapped into—" He stopped, tightened his arm around his wife. "The police said we couldn't be sure about that, without proof."

Like a fractured skull and a baby? There was another long silence and Riley heard the faint strains of Brahms's Lullaby in the distance.

"May we sit with Stacy for a while?" Mr. Collins asked.

Riley released the breath she'd been holding. "Of course. As long as you want. Take your time."

She found chairs and Kleenex and coffee, encouraged them to touch Stacy, talk to her—and assured them that when they were ready, she'd accompany them to the NICU to see their tiny granddaughter.

Oh, Lord, please have mercy on this family . . .

Riley gave them her cell number. And made it to the chapel before her tears spilled over.

- + -

Jack pulled the H1 into the Alamo Grace parking space next to Riley's Honda. She was still here. He could have confirmed that with a phone call or text message, but . . . *But I want to see her.* He amended his thought: he wanted to see how she reacted to seeing him after all that happened yesterday. It was curiosity more than anything else. And a polite hello seemed appropriate. So—

What's that?

Jack squinted toward a trio of vans in the distance. TV vans? He hadn't listened to the news since he'd gotten back from riding; he'd hosed off the bike and his car, showered, shaved, eaten a sandwich while he worked on his presentation for the city council. What was happening here? Gang shooting? Car accident? He'd stop by the ER, see if it was something there, offer to help. But he wasn't going to wade through those reporters.

He'd barely punched in the first two numbers of the security code to the employee side door when the door opened inward.

"Oh . . . Jack." Riley blinked in the sunlight.

He stepped back so she could exit. "I was just . . . coming in to see how Jane—"

"Stacy," Riley interrupted, a pained expression flickering across her face. "Stacy Paulson. Her parents are here." She glanced down, pulled her sunglasses from her purse.

"That explains the news vans."

"Yes." She slid the glasses into place. "Vultures."

At least we agree on that.

Riley shook her head. "Our information officer is doing his best to keep reporters at bay, but the family will have to leave at some point. And apparently their hotel's already received calls."

"How are they handling things with their daughter?"

"Still pretty much in shock, but the doctors made it clear that she hasn't responded to treatment and probably never will.

The neurologist broached the subject of discontinuing life support measures, but—" Riley sighed—"they'll need more time. The stepfather seems more focused on who could have done this and why. He was pressing the agents and detectives with questions. He's angry."

Jack nodded. *I understand that.*

"The mother keeps looking for something to hang on to," Riley continued. "She talked about Stacy being a tomboy when she was little—how she's always bounced back, didn't even let a broken collarbone from soccer slow her down. She showed me some old photos. And . . ." Riley's voice choked. "She's sure that Stacy's new tattoo is a sign that her daughter still had hope. That she was clinging to her innocence, despite . . ." She shivered.

"Riley . . ." Jack took a step, then stopped, helpless to know what he should do. He couldn't imagine how hard it must have been to be there for that family, offering help without convenient props like medicine or bandages or even a stethoscope. To give aid just by being there, listening to the family's pain and fears. Riley had done that for Vesta, too, for the nursing staff . . . *and for me, last night. Even with all she's been through herself.*

"They're Catholic," Riley continued. "I contacted the priest on call. He went with us to see the baby—a grandchild they didn't know they had, by a man they don't know. Who could be . . ."

A pimp, a rapist . . . a murderer. Jack's stomach churned. He took a breath—and a risk. "Here," he said, grasping hold of her hand. "Let's get away from this place. Go for coffee or something."

"I . . ." Riley hesitated and Jack realized that he was holding her injured hand, which meant she couldn't feel him. But worse than that, he had a gut-level sense that she didn't want to.

"C'mon," he insisted, wanting more than anything to pull those sunglasses off and look into her eyes, tell her again that she was beautiful and so, *so* brave. Then take her in his arms and—

"No." She slid her hand away. "I'm going home. I want to work out some things for staff support. This is going to be harder for them now. And . . . I need to be alone."

"Okay, but . . . are we good?"

"We?"

"I . . ." Jack bit back a groan, suddenly grateful he couldn't see her eyes. "I meant good for working the clinic. You're coming in this week?"

"Tuesday."

"Good." *Can't I find another blasted word?* "See you then."

"Okay."

Jack walked through the doors, watched them shut. He'd wait a few minutes until he was certain Riley had driven off, then climb back in his Hummer and get out of here.

"Are we good?" Why had he asked such a stupid thing? Hadn't he already decided that they were far too different from each other to even consider a relationship? Did he think that because last night he'd risked spewing out those painful things about Abby, it would lead to something more? Only a fool would think that. Riley Hale was a trained chaplain. That's why she'd listened to him. And the only reason there had been so much caring in her eyes. It was her job. The kisses happened

because they were both upset, hurting. A mistake she regretted, obviously.

"We?" Jack flinched at Riley's response to his heart-level question. It had pretty much said it all: he was an idiot for coming here.

One more thing they were in agreement about.

18

"**BANDY?**" Riley tapped at the clinic's back door. It was only a little after nine, but she felt certain he'd be up. Making sandwiches, no doubt.

She'd dropped the Mercedes off at Vesta's, leaving the keys and saying only a quick hello because the social worker was there. Then she walked to the clinic, wanting to have a peek at the schedule for tomorrow and see if Jack was working. If he was, Riley was going to ask one of the other nurses to trade shifts with her. Seeing Jack at the hospital yesterday had felt confusing and awkward. It would be best if she simply stayed away from him.

"C'mon in, Riley!"

She headed toward the kitchen, sniffing what smelled more

like cake than sandwiches. Then she stopped in the doorway, staring in amazement. "What . . . ?"

"Howdy!"

Bandy was loading mini cupcakes into a Tupperware carrier while dressed in full clown gear: stars and stripes shirt, rainbow suspenders, and baggy, patched pants. "You're just in time." He grinned, red lips rimmed in white, black freckles dotting his cheeks, and a battered red cowboy hat pulled over a neon-blue wig. "I could use a hand with the sprinkles. I'm down to my last bottle, and it's gonna require a surgeon's touch not to spill most of them on the floor. These old paws are more suited to hoeing a garden than baking. I usually ask Doc Travis to help, but he was anxious to hit the road for—"

Riley raised a palm. "Let me guess. Rappelling from the top of the HemisFair tower? Juggling swords?" She glanced at a jar on the sink. "Uh . . . maybe smearing himself with peanut butter and lying down on an anthill?"

Bandy chuckled. "No ma'am. Much scarier than any of that." He handed her the confetti-colored sprinkles. "He's down at the Sunshine Center. Totin' a guitar. And right about now I'll bet stage fright's rearin' its ugly head as he's trying to remember the words of the 'Good Morning' song. While fourteen little faces watch every move."

"Sunshine Center?" Riley shook the last of the sprinkles onto the cupcakes while Bandy tucked the others into another carrier.

"Down in Midtown. It's a program to help kids who've been victims of crime. Either themselves or a family member." His painted lips pressed together. "Those little souls could use some sunshine. We go down there every other Monday and do what we can." Bandy shook his head. "When Doc first got the idea of helpin' out, he told me he thought maybe he'd volunteer to do something medical. I asked him, 'You think pokin' a stick in a kid's mouth and asking him to say *ah* is going to spread sunshine?' I told him what those kids needed was a serious reminder of how to laugh. Hobo and I did that for years and we still have the gear. It took some convincing, but we finally talked Doc into it."

"So . . ." Riley struggled to get her mind around the impossible image. "Jack plays the guitar?"

"Well, he's no Brad Paisley. Don't tell him I said that. But you'd be surprised." His brows, smeared with greasepaint, lifted. "Come along and see."

"Oh no, I . . ." Riley shook her head, still having a hard time imagining any of this. "I walked here from a friend's house, and my neighbor's planning to pick me up."

"Tell her I'll drive you home. Our gig at the center is only for an hour or so. Started at nine. I'm late. I ran out of cream cheese for the frosting—Doc says it has to have some protein. He took Hobo and went ahead; that mutt loves to ride in the Hummer." Bandy handed Riley the last of the cupcakes to pack. "Anyway, I could use your help to get these there." He tilted his head, the blue wig shifting. "Fourteen little faces . . ."

"No fair. You're pulling the kid card."

"You betcha. Is it working?"

Riley sighed. "Yes." She glanced around the kitchen. "Anything else you need from here?"

"Only my red foam nose. I have extras if you—"

"Don't push your luck."

- + -

"'We're all in our places with sunshiny faces,'" Jack sang as he strummed, glad that at least eight of those preschool-age faces were indeed smiling. And focused on Hobo. The little dog was outfitted in a polka-dot hat, ruffled collar, and glittery toenails—Bandy had painted them. In comparison, Jack's red-painted nose, plastic glasses, and star-sprinkled cowboy vest over a denim shirt were practically Dallas-banker conservative. He was almost as grateful for that shred of dignity as he'd been for body armor in Afghanistan. Now if only Bandy would get here.

He nodded as a staff leader, also dressed for clown day, stepped close and added her voice to his. His chest tightened. If things had worked out the way they should have . . . *Abby would be here.*

She'd volunteered at the Sunshine Center all through high school and was still here on weekends right up to a few days before she died. . . . No. Before she was murdered. The dark and unfair irony hit him again: Abby spent countless hours helping these young victims of crime and then became one herself. Her dreams, her future . . . ended.

"'And this is the way to start a new day,'" he continued.

Jack stretched his fingers for the chords as the teacher walked Hobo slowly around the circle. The dog's tail thumped against his cart, decorated with Fiesta stickers by the children. If Jack believed it was possible, he'd even swear Hobo's mouth had quirked into a smile. The truth was that the little dog—half of his body rolling uselessly behind him—was much better suited for offering up emotional support than Jack was. And Bandy was a star at it. Jack smiled, thinking of him whipping up cream cheese frosting in that ridiculous blue wig. A tough and crusty bull rider who never seemed to feel sidelined by his current humble circumstances. It was unfathomable to Jack.

And though it had been Jack's idea to volunteer here at the Sunshine Center, Bandy and Hobo had the real heart for it. Jack was . . . extraneous. He knew that. Not to say that if some lowlife walked in and dared to touch one of these kids again, he wouldn't slam him up against a wall and make him wish he'd never been born.

"'Our day is beginning—there's so much to do,'" he sang in a rush, realizing he'd almost missed the line. Hobo yipped, let out a warbling howl. The children burst into laughter, completely delighted.

Jack smiled. Once again, Hobo had rescued the moment. Bandy would save the morning. They'd have cupcakes with sprinkles, and Jack would try to convince himself that his being here had in some way helped. Not the way Riley could, but—

"'Good morning, good morning, good morning to you!'" he sang, ending the musical selection that began each day at the Sunshine Center.

Sunshine. Jack thought of Riley's face in the afternoon light at the Alamo. And the rainbow ribbons in her hair as the sun set over River Walk. He remembered the way she listened as he talked, words that tore the scabs from the wounds of Abby's murder. There was empathy in her beautiful blue eyes, selfless compassion from the heart of someone who'd suffered such horrific hurt herself. He thought of the pain in Riley's voice even yesterday, after she'd done her best to support the family of Stacy Paulson. She was an amazing woman. And as impossible as it was—despite differences that couldn't be breached—Riley had offered Jack a glimpse of soul-warming sunshine that he never knew existed.

I want to know you better. Understand your hope. I need that sunshine in my life.

"Do you think we can sing one more round of the 'Good Morning' song?" the staffer asked, arriving at Jack's side.

"Sure."

Some things were possible. Some weren't. His fingers found the chords.

- + -

"Is it true that Hobo sleeps outside?" Riley asked as the old truck bumped over asphalt made uneven by the San Antonio Street construction. A small wooden cross, strung from the rear-view mirror, swayed with the movement. "Jack made it sound like he sleeps under this truck."

"It's true. He was born under a stock trailer; his mama was a rodeo dog too." Bandy smiled. "Hobo didn't take to civilization like I did. He's more comfortable outside, though he doesn't argue with the fleece cushion I put down for him. Eats in the house, works all day, then goes out to his bed when I'm ready to make up the sofa sleeper. He's got himself a routine."

Riley caught Bandy's Bible as it slid across the dash from the momentum of a turn. She tucked several handwritten slips of Scripture back inside and held the well-worn book in her lap. "And he's a watchdog."

"Yep. Don't let that cart fool you. The boy's got plenty of bark—and bite if need be." Bandy's painted lips stretched downward in clownish melancholy. "I wish we'd been there to help when that fellow tried to snatch your purse. I'm real sorry that happened to you, Riley."

She nodded, said nothing for a few moments. "Do you think there's truth in what the action committee is saying? That the way Jack runs the clinic invites problems?"

Bandy gave a wry smile. "If you mean does he invite a variety of folks—poor, addicted, troubled and in trouble, homeless . . . hopeless?" He shrugged. "Then, yes ma'am, he's opening the door to 'problems.' But then, I think you'll agree that the book you're holdin' shows a fine example of service to others. No matter how messy it gets."

Riley thought of Jesus among the lepers and wondered what Jack would think of that comparison.

"But," Bandy continued, "if you mean does our Doc Travis go out of his way to rile up those committee members . . . or could he learn a thing or two about compromise, turning the other cheek, loving his neighbor as himself?" He clucked his tongue. "Then yes again. I think he's inviting 'problems' there too. It's sort of like . . . You remember that wall of photos above his desk?"

Riley nodded. Jack with the bulls, skydiving, in camouflage and holding a weapon . . . "You call it his buckle wall."

"Right. Ever notice that every one of those pictures is just him alone? There's the trouble. Thinking you can do it all alone. That you were blessed with broad shoulders so you could carry the world on 'em. When a man does that, pretty soon it all becomes *about* him. That's a lot more dangerous than running with bulls. It's the way your soul gets gored."

A gored soul. Riley watched the weathered cross sway with the motion of the truck, speechless at the unexpected words of wisdom from a bighearted man in greasepaint. Did Jack have any idea how fortunate he was to have Bandy?

"We're here," Bandy said, pulling into the tree-lined parking lot of a small stone building. "If you'll grab those cupcakes, I'll take a minute to pull on my big ol' purple shoes. And . . ." He switched off the ignition, fished around in his pocket, found what he was looking for. "Ah, here you go. Fourteen little faces, all painted up as clowns . . . lookin' for a splash of sunshine?"

Riley took the red sponge nose.

- + -

"I can't believe you're wearing that nose," Jack teased, leaning his guitar against the wall. *And that you're here.*

"And I can't believe—" Riley raised her voice above childish laughter in the distance—"you're *not* wearing one. Your building manager is a persuasive man."

"We compromised on this nose paint—after I got one of those sponge ones stuck in a cupcake. You'll see."

"Great." She wrinkled her nose and the red sponge dipped like a fishing bobber signaling a bite. "So . . ." Riley turned to look at the circle of children gathered around Bandy. "It looks like the age range is from maybe four to six?"

"Pretty much. The boy with the Spider-Man cap, José, is seven." Jack grimaced. "Spent two days hiding under a bed with his mother's body on the floor beside it. Drug-related murder. He saw it happen." He nodded toward the other end of the circle. "Kara's four; her father's in prison. Mother's in a coma. Eddie had both legs fractured before he was two, and . . ." Jack sighed. "I'm not sure cupcakes are strong enough medicine." He caught Bandy's signal. "It's time for the skit."

"Skit?"

"Part of the play therapy," Jack explained. "A different theme each time. Today we're doing something about being afraid. And heads up: plastic scorpions are involved."

Riley's red nose bobbed again. "I'll try not to panic."

- + -

Riley sat cross-legged on the rug beside Jack—and across from Bandy and Hobo—while the young teacher read from *The Berenstain Bears in the Dark*. A story Riley had almost forgotten: Brother Bear trying to scare his sister with a spooky story. Then teasing her about her childish night-light, when all along he was the one who needed it most.

Bandy rose to his feet—stumbling comically over the flapping purple shoes—and took his place in the center of the circle. Hobo, cart squeaking, joined him. Followed, somewhat reluctantly, by Jack.

"Well, that was a mighty nice story," Bandy boomed, hands on his hips as he surveyed the children's faces. "You think so, Jack?"

"Nah." Jack shook his head and his plastic glasses slid down his nose. "Sissy stuff—I don't need a night-light."

Riley looked around at the children—some nodding in

agreement—and then pushed aside a ridiculous, intruding memory of Wilma's remark about her blinding row of security lights. *"You could land a 747 here."*

"Nope," Jack said, pointing his thumbs at his chest. "Not me." He swaggered around the circle before returning to Bandy's side. "Not afraid of nothin'."

"Oh yeah?" Bandy made a show of reaching into a small sack attached to the waist of his baggy pants. "That right?"

"Right as rain. Nothin' scares this cowboy, except—yipes! Scorpions!"

"Gotcha!" Bandy dangled the huge plastic scorpion in front of Jack's face. Hobo barked, and the children howled with laughter.

"And snakes!" Jack wailed as Bandy mercilessly added a three-foot rubber rattler to his taunt. "Okay, okay. You got me. I'm not always brave. And sometimes I worry about things too."

"Worry?" Bandy lowered the plastic creatures. "You mean like when you're all alone and you start thinking about things? And you're not sure everything will be all right?" He nodded dramatically, then reached up to pat Jack's shoulder. "It's okay, Jack. Me too."

"Really? Thanks. Now I don't feel so alone."

Jack's eyes found Riley's. She swallowed, completely touched that he was doing this. *So much more than cupcakes . . . Can't you see that?*

In moments Bandy and Jack returned to their places in the circle, and the teacher offered up her childhood fear of bees. She asked the others if they would like to share.

"Armadillos," Bandy volunteered. "Lately I worry they're

gonna dig out every last stalk of corn in my garden. Then set their beady eyes on my peanut butter jar."

"Dogs," Eddie admitted, his tentative smile revealing a first lost tooth. "But not so much after knowing Hobo."

"Lightning," Kara offered.

"Nuh-uh, thunder's worser. 'Cuz it sounds like guns," a boy with a solemn face added. "You never know . . . it could be guns. For reals."

Monsters. Shots. Getting lost. . . . The little voices continued around the circle until Riley felt Jack fidget beside her. After the next child, José, it would only be the two of them left. What would Jack say he was afraid of? What would *she* say? Riley was embarrassed by the increase in her pulse rate. She didn't have to tell the truth. *But what is the truth? What scares me most?*

"Sometimes . . . ," José began. His dark eyes widened and Riley remembered what Jack had said about this boy.

Bandy gave a discreet nod, and Hobo creaked forward and stopped in front of José.

"Well . . ." The boy stroked one of Hobo's ears, took a halting breath. "Sometimes I'm afraid that . . . I'll always feel scared." He looked up at the teacher, his little shoulders beginning to shake. "Will I?"

Riley's throat squeezed tight. She needed that answer too.

- + -

"There you go," Jack said, lifting Hobo into the passenger seat of Bandy's truck. He clucked his tongue. "Not that there's any room for your dog in here. You could host a garage sale of Bible bric-a-brac." He smiled at Bandy. "Tupperware is in the back—José finished off that last cupcake. So you're all set."

"Going to Starbucks?"

"Not sure." Jack had been surprised when Riley agreed to ride back with him. "Maybe that little place with Mexican coffee. And pecan pralines."

A grin spread across Bandy's face. "Word of advice?"

Jack groaned inwardly, certain he was about to get dating advice from a rodeo clown—and because he knew how badly he needed it. "And that would be . . . ?"

"Wipe the greasepaint off your nose."

"Oh, man. Forgot."

Bandy's laugh set his blue wig to bobbing. "I made that up about being afraid of armadillos. My biggest fear is that I won't live long enough to see you finally get the important stuff figured out."

19
+

"IT'S A PROTEIN SOURCE. You have my word," Jack promised, thoroughly enjoying Riley's pleasure—and the sprinkling of caramelized sugar on her chin. It was the exact shade of her hair.

She groaned. "You said that about Bandy's cream cheese frosting. Now I've had a cupcake for breakfast and . . . *mmm.*" She squeezed her eyes shut, savoring the last morsel of praline. "You're a horrible influence, Dr. Travis."

Jack's laugh riffled the surface of his coffee. "Trying my best."

He *was* trying. And until this moment would have argued that nothing compared to the taste of Tia Rosa's pecan pralines—the best medicine for what ailed a man, hands down. But watching Riley Hale devour one was like a miracle cure. He'd felt the same way when she showed up at the Sunshine Center that morning.

But Jack had been nervous too, about more than picking children's tunes on his guitar. If he'd been forced to be honest in that sharing circle, he would've had to say, "I'm afraid I'll scare Riley away." It was the truth. And he was trying his very best not to. *Because I need her . . . for the clinic,* he reminded himself hastily. And since Riley needed him—the clinic—for her own career goals, they should be able to work around their differences and accommodate each other. He had a plan in mind, and when the timing was right, he'd move forward with it. In the meantime, he'd avoid subjects like religion, the controversy surrounding the clinic, tragedies in their pasts . . . and what happened between them at Fiesta. He'd keep it light.

They'd already agreed on the pecan pralines. So far so good.

"Great hole-in-the-wall bakery," Riley pronounced, her gaze skimming the tiny *dulcería*. Its very air was buttercream thick with the aromas of coffee, cinnamon, and burnt sugar. Piñatas, lacy paper flags, and string after string of dusty Christmas lights and twisted streamers festooned the too-low ceiling. Jack had to duck to escape a crepe paper cut. Strains of Mexican music from a scratchy old radio floated from the direction of the kitchen.

"And," Riley continued with a smile, "no decor is complete without one of those." She pointed to a stuffed armadillo standing upright on the bakery's glass counter—wearing a cowboy hat and miniature gun belt.

"You bet," Jack said, thinking of what Bandy had said earlier. That it wasn't armadillos he was afraid of; it was that Jack would never figure out the "important stuff." He had an uneasy hunch that the rodeo clown had meant far more than simply a teasing comment about the paint on Jack's nose.

"This morning at the Sunshine Center . . . ," Riley said over the rim of her brightly painted cup. Her gaze met Jack's, all teasing gone from her eyes. "It's good what you're doing there, Jack. Important."

"It's . . ." He started to say something about Abby, stopped himself. "It's all Bandy. He's a natural with kids."

"Does he have family?" Riley asked.

"A married son. Up near Austin. And a granddaughter. He spends Sundays with them. Bandy and his son were estranged until recently, so it's all fairly new."

"And Bandy's wife?"

"Divorced him years ago. She couldn't deal with his lifestyle, and Bandy says he can't blame her."

"The rodeo?"

"And the booze," Jack added, knowing Bandy would freely admit it. And then find some folksy way to segue into an applicable message from Holy Scripture. "It took its toll on his health—and his wallet. That last heart attack essentially put him out on the street."

Riley shook praline crumbs from her napkin into her coffee. "I'm surprised his son doesn't insist he come live with them."

"They're looking at a home foreclosure. Bandy's son lost his job six months ago. There's another baby on the way and they're struggling to get by. Bandy feels bad that he can't help financially and would never add to their burdens."

Riley nodded. "How's his health now?"

"He doesn't complain, except when I make him put on an

exam gown for our internist. Gives me that old 'not afraid to die 'cause I know where I'm going' spiel." He hesitated, wondering if he'd already managed to offend Riley's faith. Navigating the mountain bike trail was easier. "Anyway, I prescribed some pain pills for the arthritis, but he says they make him too sleepy." Jack shook his head. "I doubt Bandy has ten bones that some bull—or lousy street thug—hasn't pulverized. Has to hurt like the devil every day of his life. But he doesn't complain." Jack's throat tightened unexpectedly. "I don't know how I'd do this without him."

Riley was quiet for a moment. "He admires you, Jack. For reaching out to people who might otherwise have no place to turn. And because of how much you obviously care about them. But Bandy's concerned about what's going on with The Bluffs neighbors. And—" she met his gaze—"about how you deal with that. He's concerned you're not leaving room for compromise and that you're trying to shoulder all the responsibility—"

"Compromise?" Jack's coffee sloshed as he set it down. "And what would that be? Turning the clinic back into a thrift shop? So someone could peddle crocheted toaster covers and Andrea Nichols's cast-off handbags?" He grimaced. "Yeah, sure. Maybe Bandy could learn to make those cucumber sandwiches with the crusts trimmed off and pour tea."

"Jack . . ."

"No, wait." He had to make her understand his point—needed her to see the truth. "Those neighbors won't be satisfied until they've torn down my clinic. And don't try to sell me that load of bull Rob Melton is shoveling: that they're good people who are scared. The only people who should have any claim on fear are folks like Gilbert DeSoto and Stacy Paulson. Who's going to 'shoulder the responsibility' for protecting them if I don't? Those neighbors? Or God, maybe?" Jack told himself to stop, not to cross the line, but it was too late. "The same God who left Abby in the trunk of a car? And allowed some maniac to nearly choke you to death in that parking garage?"

Riley flinched, glanced down at her hands. Somewhere in the distance, the Mexican radio station scratched out a rendition of "La Paloma Blanca"—"The White Dove."

"Old melancholies, things of the soul . . ."

"I'm sorry, Riley. I . . ." Nothing he could say would help now. Somehow he'd managed to cross every line he'd promised himself he wouldn't. Except kissing her. And Jack had as much chance of that happening again as that stuffed armadillo had of blending into Andrea Nichols's home decor.

"So . . ." Riley looked up, brows pinching. "When did you stop trusting him?"

"Trusting who?"

"God."

Great. He should have kissed her. Far less risky.

- + -

Vesta slid into the Mercedes's driver's seat, telling herself to concentrate on the softness of the upholstery and its scent: buttery leather mixed with a faint trace of Riley's perfume. Or the cool heft of the chaplain's key chain—a pewter and crystal cross. She reminded herself to appreciate the speckled morning sunlight filtering through the trees to light the garage. Sensory details—as many as Vesta could absorb—might distract her from the beginnings of an anxious hum in her ears, dampening palms, and a wave of nausea.

No . . . I'm okay. I'm fine. All the symptoms could be related to the fact that her blood sugar was still hovering close to 200; she'd left a message at the doctor's office.

Vesta took a slow breath and managed a smile, recalling the license plate on this vehicle: *TYGRR.* There had to be a story in that. And in the verse on the plate's frame: 1 Corinthians 16:13.

She'd opened her Bible, looked it up: *"Be on your guard; stand firm in the faith; be courageous; be strong."* Riley's favorite verse, perhaps.

Vesta had no problem relating to the Scripture's advice regarding caution. The fact that she locked the door to her house every time she ventured into the yard to fill the bird feeders proved that. But *"be courageous . . ."*

The keys rattled in her trembling fingers and Vesta lowered them to her lap. Courage had become a fair-weather friend.

The last time she'd been in a car was when her neighbor drove her home from the hospital, the return trip after she'd traveled lights-and-siren to the ER. But the last time Vesta actually drove a car herself was more than two years ago.

She took a slow breath, rested her hands on the sun-warmed steering wheel. It had been an Audi. Red, with a sheepskin seat cover and a favorite wedding photo tucked into the sun visor. Her little terrier, Corky, rode beside her, hanging his head out the window and loving the wind in his face. They did that often, visiting friends, traveling to the flower-lush grounds of

Wildseed Farms, ordering car-delivery burgers at Sonic. Corky ate her pickles, squinting his eyes like a little comedian. She'd felt almost free then, finally hopeful, even after all that had happened.

And then Corky died. A malicious rash of antifreeze poisonings, the vet had said. Pets lured by the sweet but deadly fluid. She tried to believe that his death was one of several in the county, a cruel act by misguided kids, and that she hadn't been targeted personally. After all, there had been no middle-of-the-night phone calls for years. And even the source of those was uncertain. But the nightmares started up again anyway. Horrible memories of that night fifteen years earlier. She'd been driving a Camry then, and—

Her heart slamming against her ribs, Vesta whipped around to stare at the window, expecting to see the face staring at her through the glass. The angry eyes, wild hair. In moments the terrifying cycle began. The acrid stench of smoke and gasoline. The shouts of *"Grab her! Don't let her get away!"* And the frantic memory of slamming the Camry into gear, flattening its gas pedal to the floor. Roaring away, praying aloud, nearly blinded by fear. Seeing only a narrow tunnel of light in inky darkness, her headlights on the black asphalt.

And then that other man, staggering along the side of the road, face bloody, blinking into her high beams and waving his arms as if to flag her down. She'd sped on, survival the only priority.

She'd told no one. Traded in the Camry. Moved. Changed her phone number. Moved again and again and again. And now . . .

She had no dog. No car and . . . Vesta moaned. And no right to sit in the car of a young chaplain who so beautifully exemplified the Bible verse on its license frame: *". . . stand firm in the faith; be courageous; be strong."*

God knew Vesta's weakness. And she knew there was no magic number on a glucose meter or treadmill, no series of visits from a social worker or even from a dedicated and caring chaplain, that could make her free again. Nothing could erase her fear and guilt. Or forestall the dangerous possibilities if that murderer was really back.

Vesta's landlady had mentioned a visit from an investigator, asking questions about the clinic and about Jack Travis. He'd be digging into the past.

Are you there, God? What am I supposed to do?

- + -

"I'm making you uncomfortable." Riley thought of the photo of Jack and the Pamplona bulls. He'd looked far less anxious then.

He gave a short laugh. "When did I stop trusting God? That's a loaded question. You know, like the old 'When did you stop beating your wife?' routine." He scraped his fingers along the side of his jaw. "A question that assumes I did at some point trust God. Believe in him."

"Yes," Riley admitted, noticing that there was still the smallest bit of red makeup on the side of Jack's nose. She thought of his boast in the skit: *"Not afraid of nothin'."* He didn't look so sure right now. "When we were talking that night at the River Walk, you said something about sparing me your doubts about God. So I thought . . ." She watched his expression, not sure if his faint wince had to do with her mentioning that night or with her questions. Then she reminded herself that it didn't really matter.

Jack's eyes met hers. "My family went to church. I can't remember a leg of chicken that didn't get prayed over. Or a touchdown. I sang in the choir for a couple of years." He scrounged up a smile. "You could probably tell that at the Sunshine Center. But . . ."

Riley realized she was holding her breath. *It does; it matters to me.*

Pain flickered across Jack's face. "It took a year for the cancer to finally take my father. I watched him sort of wither away. A football coach, six-foot-three, two-fifty pounds. Big guy, bigger heart." He swallowed. "I carried him from the couch to the bedroom those last few weeks; he was light enough that I could hold him in my arms. It seemed so impossible. I couldn't understand how it could happen. I started to think God wasn't listening, you know?"

Riley nodded, her throat tight.

"And right about the time he went into hospice—the same month—Abby was murdered," Jack went on. "It wasn't like we were in love, even. I was twenty; *love* wasn't in my vocabulary. But she'd been there for me while Dad was sick. Gone to the hospital—watched me punch walls afterward. She was a really good person. With more faith than anyone I'd met. I couldn't make sense of why she had to die. All I knew was that prayers didn't help—don't help."

Riley cleared her throat. "All that . . . made you give up on God."

Jack frowned. "I think it's more that he gave up on me. I'm the first to admit there are a whole lot of valid reasons for that. But—" he took a slow breath—"I'm out of coffee, and . . ."

"And I've intruded." Riley reached across the table, touched his hand. "I'm sorry, Jack."

"No problem," he said, visibly relaxing. The toffee eyes warmed. "Chaplain thing. You can't help it." A smile tugged at his lips. "But maybe I can help you now."

"What do you mean?" Riley tried to pretend that his thumb brushing the back of her hand wasn't making her foolishly giddy.

"I had a phone call from the nursing supervisor at Alamo Grace. She was returning my call about clinic volunteers. We're pretty short on help."

"Yes." Riley nodded, feeling a quick stab of guilt about going to the clinic this morning to change her work schedule.

"And," Jack continued, "I took the opportunity to tell her that I'm drafting a recommendation for you. For that triage position."

Riley's mouth sagged open. "You did—you are?"

"I haven't sent it yet. I know your assessment skills are sharp and I've already seen you handle at least a couple of challenging cases, but I should observe you at least another shift. We'll be working together tomorrow . . . unless there's been a schedule change?"

"No," Riley said, her heart wedging into her throat. "No change. Written in stone—I'm there."

"Good." He leaned back, let go of her hand. "And I thought I'd check with Kate and see if she can help us out for a few hours next week. You think she might?"

"I'm not sure," Riley said, still breathless about the offer of a recommendation. "Give her a call or stop by the ER. She's working today."

- + -

"No! No way I'm taking the blame," the big woman blustered, her breath pungent with alcohol fumes. She glared down at Kate, swayed, and planted a hand on the nurses' desk to steady herself. "I didn't do nothin' to that child. He's not mine; I explained that already. He's my sister's foster kid. I told her I was having a little Fiesta party last night and wouldn't be in any kind of condition to watch one of her rug rats today. But she dumps him off anyway." The woman glanced toward the three-year-old in the resuscitation room, eyes widening. "Why did they shove that nasty tube down his throat?"

Because you're an irresponsible idiot. "We needed to rinse his stomach. His heart rate is too fast. And that twitching you saw . . ." Kate struggled to keep her tone under control. The morning had been bad enough without getting punched too. "It could mean that in addition to sips of tequila from those paper cups the medics found in your apartment, he may have gotten hold of some—"

"Drugs?" The woman took a step toward Kate, narrowing her eyes. "Are you standing there accusin' me of something like that?"

"I'm explaining that for this boy's safety we have to consider all possibilities. Of course, the blood and urine samples will show—"

"Unh-uh. No way am I goin' down for something like that!" A fine spray of spittle escaped the woman's lips. She jabbed her finger, brushing the snaps on Kate's scrub jacket. "You are *not* blaming this on me, you skinny little—" She caught sight of an officer at the nurses' desk and bit back the obscenity. Only one of a number she'd spat at Kate during the past thirty minutes. "You called the cops?"

"Yes," Kate answered, feeling the officer's presence like Kevlar body armor. "And DFPS—child protective services." *Poke that finger at me again and I'll find Rambo, too.* "It's required by law." Almost on cue, the officer walked toward them, and Kate took the opportunity to go back into the exam room.

"Nearly finished with the charcoal slurry," her staff nurse, Linda, reported. "I saw some white fragments when I washed out his stomach—but mostly what I suspect was Pop-Tarts. So maybe his tummy was full enough not to absorb the entire drug dose. What do you bet someone at the party got sloppy and dropped some meth on the floor?" She depressed the plunger of a big syringe, pushing the charcoal through tubing that led from the boy's mouth to his stomach. An ER tech, wearing a guitar-print surgical cap, steadied the boy's head.

"Could be." Kate glanced at the boy's pale face. The blue of his eyes was only a narrow rim around dark, dilated pupils. Her heart tugged. *Was he taken away from his family . . . abandoned by his mother?* Guilt prodded as effectively as the drunken woman's finger.

"You can see that his oxygen sats are great. And his heart rate's down to 120," Linda continued, glancing through her protective face shield toward the monitor. "Bless his soul, he's still shakin' like a little leaf." She smiled tenderly down at the child wrapped in a Papoose body restraint. "Aren't you, Daniel?"

"The PD is talking with the aunt." Kate frowned. "I mean the foster mother's sister. She made that pretty clear."

The tech sighed. "My cousin and her husband have foster kids; you've never seen finer folks. I know this sort of thing happens, but . . ." His brows puckered. "Speakin' of things going south, did you get your scratches cleaned up?"

"Soap, water, bacitracin—and an incident report." Kate had been clawed on the arm by an agitated dementia patient even before she'd had a chance to pour her first cup of hospital coffee. It had foreshadowed her day. "Between that and our foul-mouthed Fiesta party hostess, I'm a shoo-in for Most Unappreciated Nurse."

The tech smiled. "I appreciate you. Especially if you take over here for a few minutes while I check on that patient in X-ray."

"Sure."

"Okay." Linda pushed the last of the charcoal through the tubing. "I'm about ready to take this out."

Kate gloved and masked, pulled the suction catheter close, then bent down and cradled the boy's head between her hands. His hair was silky soft, cheeks wet with tears. "We're trying to help you, honey." She brushed a thumb across his skin. *Did my son go into foster care? Was he loved, or . . . ?*

"Here we go, little man," Linda cautioned. "Taking the tube away. One, two, three."

She pulled the tubing as the boy gagged and Kate manned the suction. "Great. All done." Linda watched as Kate wiped Daniel's face gently with a damp cloth. "I saw Baby Girl Doe's grandparents down in the NICU this morning. At least there's something hopeful going on around here."

Kate stripped off her gloves, battling a growing ache in her chest. "I'm going to find that cup of coffee I never got."

"Put some of that hot cocoa mix in it. Chocolate endorphins. As far as I'm concerned, that'll fix whatever ails a person."

"Right." Kate summoned a halfhearted smile as she left the room.

Hopeful? A belly full of Pop-Tarts protecting a boy from amphetamine poisoning; a demented, lonely woman terrified enough to scratch her nurse; and a teenager dying in the ICU, leaving her premature infant motherless. Where was the hope in any of that? It was about as hopeful as Kate ever getting her boxes packed . . . or finally getting her life together.

She hugged her arms around herself as she walked past the nurses' desk. Her only real hope was that someone had made fresh coffee. She'd drink it black. And the entire carton of cocoa mix couldn't dredge up enough endorphins to fix—

"Kate, hold up."

She turned.

"Look what came for you." The ward clerk peered from behind the huge vase of flowers in her hands. Roses—at least two dozen blooms—yellow, bubble-gum pink, and orange, in clouds of baby's breath and purple heather. With little decorated eggs on sticks and a giant rainbow-bright bow of shimmering metallic ribbons. "This is what I'd call Fiesta in a vase."

Kate was stunned. "For me?"

"Must be." The ward clerk's cheeks dimpled. "The envelope says 'California Kate.'"

20

THE DOOR TO THE NURSES' LOUNGE had no lock, and Kate was fairly sure barricading it with chairs would violate safety code. Which meant there was no guarantee of privacy while she waited for her face to stop flaming and devised a plan to get the massive vase of flowers out of the ER.

She'd seen less conspicuous displays around the necks of Derby winners. Within scant but mortifying moments, the outrageous bouquet had inspired a feeding frenzy among the staff, rivaled only by the arrival of pharmaceutical reps with boxes of hot pizza. There was a chorus of envious sighs, followed by wild speculation and comments. Even the finger-jabbing woman—moments from criminal arrest—felt obliged to speak up: *"Someone sent her flowers? Now there's a serious lack of taste."*

Kate groaned. Then, holding her breath, she reread the handwritten florist's card.

Meeting you was the best medicine. Please let me
reward your kindness. Griff.

He'd included his phone numbers, cell and home.

Griff Payton. The patient who flirted with Kate in triage yesterday, offered to buy her coffee . . . build her a house. Tall, great-looking, funny. A patient who'd refused an injection of an anti-inflammatory medication for his back pain because he was squeamish about needles. Or because . . . Kate's stomach sank as she recalled the ER physician's concern—nothing he could confirm, but an educated hunch that Griff had refused the shot because he wanted a prescription for narcotics.

Great. Perfect. So true to form. Kate squeezed her eyes shut and leaned against the lounge wall, feeling a bitter laugh rise in her throat. Not once in her life had her instincts about relationships been right. Or even healthy. Why should it be any different now? A change of geography didn't cure flaws like that.

What would Riley say if she saw the flowers? Would she care that Griff had a connection to the proposed condo project? Riley hadn't made any comment one way or the other about the future of Jack's clinic or her feelings about The Bluffs' complaints. She certainly hadn't taken sides; she'd only taken the opportunity to practice her skills by volunteering at the clinic. Completely understandable.

Kate flicked her fingernail against the florist card. Riley would probably have plenty to say about the flowers. In psychobabble chaplainspeak, of course. *"How does that make you feel?"* And if Kate were honest, how would she answer that? Embarrassed? Bothered? Flattered? . . . Intrigued by the risk? Probably.

Which only proved what she knew about herself: bad instincts.

But Kate knew that if asked directly about Griff Payton, Riley would have no problem expressing an opinion. After all, she hadn't had any qualms telling Kate exactly what she thought of Jack Travis. Riley might be using Jack's clinic as a means to an end, but she didn't like him one bit.

- + -

Jack glanced into the hallway that led to the kitchen, where a tinkling of ice confirmed that Riley was fixing the tea. "Your neighbor looked a little concerned," he said, raising his voice so she could hear. "Are you sure there's no problem with parking in your driveway?"

There was a soft laugh. "Wilma is my guardian angel. And your Hummer probably makes the other cars look like Tonka toys, but it's fine there."

And is it fine that I'm here?

Jack was surprised that Riley had invited him in. She'd planned to return to the clinic and call for a ride from there, but he'd insisted on driving her home. She'd been unusually quiet the whole way. Still flustered about his offer to write a recommendation for her, he guessed. *And maybe wondering if I want something in return?* Was Riley thinking that? Jack acknowledged the guilty truth that there was a certain amount of mutual back-scratching in their working relationship.

A second possibility for Riley's reticence stopped Jack cold. Did Riley think he was expecting something more? She was a beautiful and desirable woman. Did she think he'd try to take advantage—?

"Here we go," she said, carrying two ice-filled glasses. "I decided against sweet tea, considering the amount of sugar we've managed to consume this morning. I'm usually careful about that."

And now you're being careful about me.

"Thanks," he said, taking the glass and feeling suddenly awkward. He'd drink the tea and get out of here. There would be another time to approach her about coming to the city council meeting. In no way did he want to make Riley uncomfortable. She'd gone out of her way to help him, empathized to a degree he'd never thought possible. Especially since they obviously had so little in common.

His gaze swept the warm, inviting, and tastefully decorated living room. Then came to rest on a Bible atop a glass coffee table. Proof of their differences.

"You said that you have a town house too?" she asked after sipping her tea.

"Not like this. It's more like a great garage for my Hummer, mountain bike, and skydiving gear—with an attached house where I reheat dubious leftovers and crash on the couch. And drive the cleaning lady crazy by asking her to dust around my piles of medical journals and paperwork." He shook his head. "I've tried to bribe her, but she draws the line at changing the water in the fishbowl."

"Fish?"

"Just one. A Siamese fighting fish—Rocky." He grimaced. "Not my idea. Or my fish. It's a long story." Jack glanced past Riley's cream-colored leather couch toward a small limestone fireplace, its logs replaced by white candles in glass holders. "Those photos on the mantel—is that your family?"

She nodded.

He set his tea down, took a half step. "May I?"

- + -

Riley watched as Jack's gaze moved across the grouping of framed photos. Nothing like the collections at her parents' home in Houston: formal family portraits, a wall in the library papered with three generations of Hales posing with religious leaders, celebrities, presidents, and Texas athletes. And then there was the commissioned oil of Riley at six, sitting ladylike in a designer sundress under her grandparents' pecan tree.

"This is you, as a kid?"

"Eight or nine, maybe," Riley confirmed as Jack lifted the rumpled snapshot she'd framed. It was slightly out of focus, with shadow-dappled lighting and a tear where it had stuck to a plastic drawer of her play kitchen. "I could see past the fences of my grandfather's ranch when I crawled out onto that branch. Miles and miles. Sometimes I'd pretend I was a bird, that I could spread my wings and fly away." She shook her head. "My best friend took the photo; her parents showed it to mine after it was developed. They had a volcanic fit. Always sure I was going to get hurt."

Riley met Jack's gaze, saw the concern in his eyes before he turned back to the photos. She realized that he was the first person who'd looked—really looked—at this little display of photos. Disordered and random slices of her life.

"You look like your mother. I noticed that when she stopped by the clinic. Same smile . . . chin." Jack moved from her parents' portrait to the next frame. "College graduation?"

"Yes," Riley confirmed, assuring herself there was no way Jack would read the vanity license plate on the shiny new convertible in the photo. "That's my grandfather with me."

"And this one's of you at . . ." He held out a photo in a pewter frame. "The Golden Gate Bridge?"

"Yes." Riley took it from him. "With a doctor friend—a coworker—from Golden Gate Mercy Hospital. I . . ." She hesitated, seeing the sling on her arm in the photo. "It was my first position as a chaplain. Several months after I was injured."

Jack stepped closer, his arm brushing hers. "I'd imagine your parents had qualms about you being so far from home."

"It was a toss-up, I think. They didn't want to let me go but wanted me as far away as possible because that man was still on the loose." She felt Jack's body tense. "Ultimately, I forced the issue. I needed to go. I was . . . suffocating.

"My parents were against my going to nursing school. Completely. And when I ended up on that parking garage floor . . ." She set the photo back on the mantel. "I have no doubt they pulled strings to get me that chaplain's position in San Francisco. And that they expected it would be a first step toward getting me out of nursing altogether. When I came back to Texas, I was supposed to go straight to Houston." Riley gave a short laugh. "Sort of the Hale version of a Monopoly play:

'Go directly to Home. Do not pass Go. Do not collect a salary in San Antonio.'"

"But you wanted to climb out on that branch and spread your wings," Jack said softly, his eyes holding hers.

An ache crowded her throat. *You understand.*

"Being a nurse, part of the ER team, was incredibly important to me," Riley explained. "More than I can say. And since the assault, nothing's been the same. Nothing at all. It's like I'm waiting for . . ." Her gaze moved to the mantel, and for the first time she realized that her little photo collection wasn't at all random or disordered. The little girl in the tree, the rebellious graduate, the woman in a sling two thousand miles from home—it was a chronology of her life, of a struggle to claim it as her own.

She turned to him, blinking back tears.

"What?" Jack asked, brows scrunching.

"Thank you," she managed despite the lump in her throat. "When you threw that stupid training manikin at me, I was sure I'd drop it. And I was *so* furious at you. But I needed that nudge, that chance. You were giving me a way back. But I still had all these doubts. And now you're writing a recommendation for me, and—"

"Wait, Riley." Jack grasped her arms. "There's something I need to explain."

- + -

Jack sat down next to Riley, the leather cushion compressing like a toasted marshmallow under his weight. "There's no guarantee that my recommendation will help your chances. In fact—"

he frowned—"considering my reputation, you could end up making peanut butter sandwiches with Bandy full-time." *And I could learn to like that idea.*

Riley took a sip of her tea, nodded.

"You need to know that I'll be completely honest in that letter," Jack continued, picking his way toward what he needed to say. It felt like he was starting down the steep grade of an unfinished bike trail—and not sure of his brakes. But he'd be a fool to risk having his intentions mistaken for harassment. "I can only report competencies in skills that I've actually seen you perform. And I'd have to address any deficits related to your injuries. . . . Here, raise your arms."

"What?"

"Like this." Jack demonstrated, raising both his hands. "Face me full on and raise your hands shoulder high. Now press them against mine. Right—like that." Her palms, warm and soft, met his. "Now hold steady. Hold me back. Don't let me get close."

"Okay." A faint flush rose on her cheeks.

"Hold me back," he repeated, pressing his palms against hers. He pushed harder, felt her resistance—the left hand noticeably stronger than the right. "Keep them up; don't let that arm sag. It's drifting down."

"I'm trying." Riley's right hand trembled. "It's . . . hard."

"Keep it up," he told her, seeing her pupils widen, her determination despite the fact that her entire arm had begun to tremble. *Ah, Riley . . .* His throat tightened as he recalled her expression in the photo with the tree, that innocent bravado as she crawled out onto the high branch. Jack wrestled with a

CANDACE CALVERT

sudden rush of anger at the violent act that had injured Riley's spine. And might close so many doors for her.

"*Aagh,*" she groaned, fighting to raise her weakened arm higher.

"Okay," Jack said, lowering his hands but still clasping hers. "Enough."

"Well . . ." Riley swallowed. "I guess that was more straightforward than a manikin toss. My doctors say I've shown an amazing recovery, but you can see that there are still problems." She leaned a little closer, enough that he could see tiny flecks of gold in the blue of her eyes and the pulse fluttering in the hollow of her neck. "Jack, I don't expect you to be anything but honest in your evaluation. I've known you long enough to understand that it's part of who you are. Honest, fair. And kind. To Bandy, your patients, those kids at the Sunshine Center today. And to me, too. If I have even half a chance at returning to the ER, it's in large part because of your willingness to trust me at the clinic."

"I do . . ." Jack cleared his throat. "I do trust you. And admire your determination." He sighed. "I'll get that recommendation to the nursing supervisor. But—" he told himself he had to say it—"I want to be sure you didn't get the wrong impression about my offer to do that." He let go of her hands. "You know, considering . . ."

She tilted her head, brows drawing together.

Oh, great. How soon could he get to the Hummer? She had no clue what he meant.

"I mean that I wouldn't try to dangle a recommendation,"

Jack explained, "in order to take unfair advantage. As an employer with a female . . ."

"Oh." Riley's eyes widened. "I wasn't thinking—"

"Good!" he blurted, then laughed. "Anyway, you're a volunteer, so I'm not technically an employer. Which means that when we . . ."

"Went out for . . ." She glanced away, the color returning to her cheeks.

"For pralines today," Jack finished, "it was totally on the up-and-up. So any recommendation I write is valid, regardless of how I might feel personally."

"About—" her smile crinkled her eyes and warmed his chest—"Tia Rosa's pecan pralines."

"Exactly." Jack grinned. *And about wanting to kiss you. Right now. Bury my face in that mass of hair that's making me crazy with its scent of peaches . . . then kiss you again, and—*

"I should get going." He stood.

She walked him to the door and thanked him again for the ride home. He said something appreciative about the tea and that her town house was nice. Then they stood there awkwardly for a few seconds.

Riley chuckled. "Really—a Siamese fighting fish named Rocky?"

"Hey—" Jack narrowed his eyes—"I also have a modest share in a fine dog that comes with a cool set of wheels. It's just that my dog prefers to live in another neighborhood." He shook his head. "Where he manages to flirt with a cat that is way out of his league."

Something we apparently have in common, Hobo.

- ✛ -

"May I?" Vesta rested her hand on her pole-mounted mailbox to steady herself, willing the dizziness to pass. She forced herself to meet the man's gaze. *I can do this. . . . I can.* Even if The Bluffs' curb felt like Dallas rush hour and was the farthest point she'd ventured in two years. "Is it all right if I pet him?"

"Right as rain," the man replied, his blue eyes as warm as his smile. "Hobo was hopin' you would ask."

"I've seen you walking with him. From my window," Vesta said, bending low. The little dog whined eagerly, front legs dancing in place. "It must be hard for him to pull that cart with the streets disrupted by the gate construction. Oh . . . he's so soft."

"I think it's harder for Hobo *not* to get out. He'd pull the cart loaded up with rocks if it meant seein' folks. Making them smile." The man clucked his tongue. "It reminds me of a song we heard on the road. Let's see if I remember the words. Something like 'Out in the highways and byways of life . . . Carry the sunshine where darkness is rife . . . Make me a blessing to someone today.'" He shook his head. "Yep, if Hobo could talk, I think that's what he'd say: 'Make me a blessing to someone today—right after breakfast. And hurry that up, wouldya?'"

Vesta's laugh squeezed past the lump in her throat. "Well, he's been a blessing to me." She stroked Hobo's ears, scratched his chin, watching his melted-chocolate eyes blink in pleasure. "He reminds me of my little dog, Corky. I lost him two years ago." Vesta glanced up at the dog's owner, tears pricking her eyes. "I miss him so much."

"Yes, ma'am."

"It's . . . Vesta."

"And I'm Bandy Biggs." He glanced skyward for an instant and then bent down to shake her hand. "You go ahead and pet a patch of fur right off that dog if you need to, Vesta. He's got plenty—and it's our great honor to see you smile."

- + -

Kate poured an icy glass of cucumber water and moved a box out of the way so she could lean against her tiled kitchen counter. Leaving the flowers at the hospital had been the right thing to do; that much had seemed clear to her. And once she'd decided, taking them to the neurosurgical ICU seemed the logical choice. Anonymously. And minus the cutesy Fiesta eggs, of course—there was nothing festive about the Collins family's situation. But somehow Kate imagined that a girl who loved Tinker Bell would be crazy about such a colorful bouquet, and having it there might remind her parents of some half-forgotten joy. She hoped so and that it would bring them comfort.

Would it have comforted my father when I ran away? Would he have wanted to be a grandfather to my baby? The ache, a well-deep hole in her belly, returned without mercy.

Kate took a long swallow of the water, tasting the faint hint of lime and mint. It was refreshing after her workout and an hour of packing boxes, but far from the remedy health spas liked to claim. *About as helpful as leaving flowers for the family of a dying girl.*

She touched her fingertips to the scratches on her forearm. It had been a thoroughly horrible ER shift—from the clawing incident, to the child who'd swallowed party drugs, to screaming threats from both the foster mother and the aunt. Then she'd had to intervene when a sensitive and skilled male nurse—distraught from an impending divorce—showed up for his shift intoxicated. And all the while, Kate had been forced to field wisecracks and curious questions about the vase of roses on the nurses' desk.

By 6 p.m., she'd been tempted to walk out, quit, call Riley and say that she'd be putting her packing boxes onto a U-Haul headed for . . . anywhere else. That she'd had it with humidity and scorpions, couldn't bear to hear another country song on the PA system of one more grocery store. She'd wanted to say that the charm of fireflies and genuinely friendly strangers— even having Riley as a new friend—wasn't enough to make up for the aching hole in her life. A hole she had been trying and failing to fill for as long as she could remember.

The loneliness of it had made Kate stall for a few seconds before entering Stacy Paulson's room. She'd sniffed the roses, tried to forget all the red flags—her bad choices—and started to imagine the comfort of . . .

Kate set down the glass and reached for her cell phone. She searched the contact list for the number she'd entered and started to call at least half a dozen times in the past few hours. She told herself she was being polite. No more than that. Then held her breath, hit the Call button. Recognized his voice.

"Griff, it's Kate Callison." She took a breath, exhaled slowly. "The flowers are beautiful. And exactly what I needed today."

21

"WILL YOU TELL BANDY that the woman in room 3 could use some sandwich therapy?" Riley asked, spotting Jack in the clinic kitchen. "I'm getting her flu vaccine, but we were talking and she let it slip that she spent the last of her grocery money on her mother's prescriptions—Alzheimer's." She sighed, remembering the worry on the woman's face. And the weariness. "Between that and taking care of her teenage children, she's running on fumes. I doubt she had any dinner."

"I'll bet you're right." Jack refilled his coffee cup. "She said she's afraid she'll get the flu, miss work, and lose her job. They're a single-paycheck family; it would be more than difficult to be looking for work at her age." He frowned. "Her situation proves it's not only 'indigents and drug addicts' we're serving here. Not that I can seem to convince that blasted action committee." His eyes met Riley's and his expression softened. "Thanks for taking the extra time with her."

"Sure," Riley said, heading for the medicine room. "I'm glad I could." *And I'll be glad when this shift is over, too.* She'd been praying from the moment she hit the door, reminding God of how important it was to get through the day without any incidents that might change Jack's mind about writing that recommendation. Surely she could manage to look organized and competent for another ninety minutes.

Riley reached for the flu vaccine, shook her head at the sight of the Band-Aid on her thumb. Barely thirty minutes into the shift she'd managed to stick herself with a needle—fortunately unused, sterile. More fortunate that she'd noticed it and didn't go dripping blood around the clinic, since it was a numb finger she'd jabbed. Mostly numb. *Some things I can't help but feel.*

Her stomach dipped as she recalled pressing her palms against Jack's yesterday when he'd tested her injured arm, how close he'd been, that little spot of clown makeup on his face, those incredible eyes, and his strength. His warmth, too. She could feel it even in her injured arm. But mostly Riley kept remembering how Jack instructed her, *"Hold me back. Don't let me get close."* He'd been testing her ability to push, assessing the damage to her brachial plexus from the spinal cord trauma and determining her muscle resistance. *With no clue that he was testing my ability to resist him?*

It was becoming difficult. She'd been so wary about him at first, unnerved by his volatility, at odds with his methods of management, lack of tact, and his dismissive attitude toward faith. But yesterday, seeing Jack with those children—his willingness to put aside all pride and play Patch Adams in order to help them—had amazed her. And when she pressed Jack about God, he responded by sharing his gut-level feelings about his father's cancer and Abby's death. That Jack trusted her enough to be so painfully honest had touched Riley's heart.

"Hold me back. Don't let me get close." She tried to ignore a new, prodding question: what if keeping Jack Travis away wasn't at all what she wanted?

Riley stuffed some alcohol swabs into her pocket and walked out of the medicine room. Then glanced at the clock on the kitchen wall. Six thirty, ticking toward eight. *Please, Lord, no more glitches. Medical or personal.*

- + -

Kate waited at the table while Griff paid for the coffee. He'd chosen the St. Mary's Street bistro because it was a comfortable distance from the Fiesta crowds on River Walk. And because, in addition to coffee, it boasted wine, appetizers, live music, and "sinful" desserts. Kate grimaced; she could have done without that particular adjective. It only underlined her queasy feeling that this was a huge mistake. Still, he'd been polite and charming on the phone last night, with no undercurrent of the volatility she thought she'd glimpsed during their interaction in the ER exam room. Plus, she'd been so curious to discover if . . .

Yes. Kate looked up as deep masculine laughter rumbled in the distance. The flushed and completely delighted expression on the barista's face seconded Kate's answer to the question that prompted her to accept this invitation: was Griff Payton as gorgeous as she'd remembered? Jade-green eyes, memorable mane of hair—stylishly cut despite its thickness and length. Shoulders even broader under a striped Ralph Lauren shirt worn with faded jeans and full-quill ostrich boots. He seemed impossibly taller now that he was standing fully upright. *Because he has no need to fake back pain to secure narcotics?* Suspicion pricked at the giddy balloon that had too often dragged Kate to breakneck heights. Still . . .

She smiled as Griff turned toward her, raising two steaming cups of coffee aloft. He wove his way through an influx of happy hour arrivals, and Kate reminded herself that she had questions to ask before she even considered trusting this man. Then, with a sinking feeling, remembered that her father had asked questions, too. When she'd finally returned home after that ugly, wasted year. *And oh, how I lied.*

"Coffee for California Kate," he said, settling into the chair opposite her. "Though I'd hoped you could stay long enough to eat dinner. They have these incredible salmon quesadillas, with black salsa and this sort of . . . cilantro and sour cream dip." He raised his brows, green eyes fixed on hers. "Can't I tempt you?"

"Not this time," Kate said over the brim of her cup, then realized her answer implied there would be another time. "I promised to stop by a clinic where I volunteer sometimes, to see if I can help them out next week." She reminded herself to keep her tone casual. "That free clinic down the street from The Bluffs development?"

"Ah." Griff was quiet for a moment. He took a sip of his coffee and Kate noticed, once again, the scars on his hand. From the same explosion that injured his back, most likely. Then

Griff spoke, meeting Kate's gaze directly. "You're wondering if you should date a man who's associated with a movement to shut that good and charitable effort down." He tilted his head, his expression hardening just a bit. "And maybe you're extrapolating that thought into . . . if I'm mean-spirited enough to deny poor people health care, then maybe I also park in handicap spaces and pick the wings off butterflies and—"

"Are you?" Kate interrupted.

"An insect abuser?"

"No." Kate couldn't help but smile. Griff Payton, contractor, had hit the nail on the head; he knew she was checking him out. Fine, then she could be direct. "Are you associated with the action committee that's trying to close the clinic?" She raised her voice to be heard over the musicians warming up a few yards away. "Is that what you want?"

"Two separate questions," Griff acknowledged. "And I don't have a problem answering either of them. First of all, no. I'm not associated with The Bluffs' action committee. I have no issues with the work that's done at the clinic. I honestly don't know much about it." His smile came back, charming again. "But if you volunteer there, I have no doubt that it's valuable."

"Your father's company plans to bid on the property."

"Yes. It's adjacent to The Bluffs—his development, my parents' neighborhood—so it makes sense. Convenient and close to his heart. He'd envisioned condos there years ago but the property was never available."

"Still isn't," Kate said, imagining Jack in this conversation. Wearing Army boots.

"That's right. It will be up to the city council to decide what happens with that property. I accept that, absolutely. But you also asked if shutting down the clinic is what I *want*." Griff met her gaze. "I'm going to be honest with you, Kate. I've been waiting for a project like this. Obviously because it would help my career. But also—" he swallowed—"because working along-side my father could go a long way toward fixing some things between us. I don't know if you can understand that. But I've disappointed my father in the past. Now I'm back, and I just want a chance to—"

"Make him proud," Kate murmured. She'd felt the same way when she'd returned home after running away.

"Yes. Exactly." Griff nodded. "I guess that sounds corny."

"It doesn't." Kate released the breath she'd been holding and wondered if she'd jumped to the wrong conclusions about this man. He wanted his father's approval. There was nothing wrong with that. Maybe beneath Griff Payton's handsome exterior and arrogant charm, there was a decent, good-hearted man. *Now that would be a first.* But there was still that other question. The red flag waving furiously since he'd refused the shot in the ER.

"So," Kate began casually after glancing toward the musicians. Several couples had moved to the small dance floor. "How's your back? Pain medication helping?"

Griff laughed, raised a palm. "No disrespect to the hospitals, but I'll take a good chiropractor over a pill pusher any day. Snap, crackle, pop—fixed."

"Fixed?" Kate asked, surprised at how much she wanted to believe him.

"Not enough to heft cement sacks. But . . ." Griff rose from his chair, extending his hand toward her. "I'm definitely healthy enough for a slow dance." He chuckled at the look on her face. "I think we've established that I don't pick the wings off butterflies, and I promise not to step on your toes."

"Okay," she said, her face warming. "One dance."

You've tempted me after all.

- + -

"Se cayó?" Riley asked her patient, pulling the stethoscope from her ears. She turned toward the man's son, trying to understand. "He fell on the stairs?"

"Uh . . . right." The boy, about fifteen and dressed in dusty work clothes, glanced toward his mother before continuing. "At home." His father moaned with pain, and anxiety flooded into the boy's dark eyes. "The doctor's coming?"

"Yes." Riley's gaze moved to the monitoring equipment. Blood pressure 94 over 32. Pulse 102. Oxygen saturation 95. A fit thirty-six-year-old man, somewhat pale despite his olive complexion and guarding his breathing because of pain in his left lower ribs. "Will you please help him get undressed? Everything off but his undershorts. Here's a gown."

Riley patted her patient's arm and noted with concern that he'd begun to perspire. *"Vamos a ayudarle,* Hector." *We're going to help you.* She glanced up at the clock, thinking with a sudden foreboding that the last half hour of her shift was headed in the wrong direction. She hoped she was wrong about that.

In moments Riley returned to the exam room with Jack. She pushed the buttons on the automatic blood pressure cuff as he introduced himself to Hector and his family. Despite her hopes, the man looked even paler stretched out on the exam table; he grunted softly with each breath. The Velcro crackled as the blood pressure cuff inflated, and she watched the digital display as the machine attempted to locate a systolic pressure. It reinflated, tried again. Not a good sign. Riley's pulse kicked up a notch.

"Breathe in . . . *Respire, por favor*," Jack repeated in Spanish, attempting to listen to Hector's lungs.

"Blood pressure is 87 over 46," Riley reported. "Pulse 112."

Jack glanced at the oxygen saturation display, then turned to Hector's son. "Do you know if he lost consciousness, or—?" Hector groaned as Jack palpated his abdomen. "Were you there when he fell?"

Riley saw panicky confusion on the son's face and then fear on his mother's as she gave a terse shake of her head, lips forming the word *no*.

"I didn't see . . . ," the boy said, chewing his lip. His face was nearly as pale as his father's.

Riley set the blood pressure monitor to take readings every five minutes.

"Belly's distended," Jack said, turning to her. "He's guarding in the left upper quadrant. I don't like—" He stopped short as he spotted something on the floor beside the exam table. "What are these? Roofing nails? Did these come from his pocket?" He stared at the son, forehead wrinkling. "Was your father on a roof?"

A fall from a roof? Riley's breath caught, mind racing. Left abdomen . . . spleen? Or even a vascular tear? *Oh, please. Don't let him bleed out in front of our eyes.*

"Yes. *Lo siento, Mamá.* I'm sorry, but . . ." The boy nodded, tears brimming. "We were on the roof together. It's two stories. I saw *Papá* fall."

"I'll get an IV," Riley said, anxiety crowding her throat. "Ringer's?"

"Or normal saline, if we don't have it. Large bore needle. Two lines if we have time. I'll get him on some high-flow oxygen. Tell Bandy to call for a Code 3 transport. Blunt trauma abdomen, status post-fall from roof. Grab me a neck collar too."

"Will do," Riley said, praying she could do any of the things she'd just promised. She yanked open the door, took off in a jog toward the supply room, and caught Bandy in the lab.

"Just tell me what you need," he said, reading her expression.

"Your finger on the phone to 911." Riley grabbed for the IV tray. "Tell them we have a man who fell from a second-story roof. That he has abdominal pain and shocky vital signs. We need a Code 3 transport."

"You got it," Bandy assured her. "Anything else I can do?"

"Tell our other patients there'll be a delay, and . . ." Riley met Bandy's gaze, her numb fingers tightening on the handle of the IV tray. "Pray. Please."

- + -

"What's going on?" Kate asked Bandy, after hearing Jack on the kitchen phone giving a report to Alamo Grace ER.

"Man fell from a roof. Belly pain, shock. The medics are on their way. Riley's—"

"Which room?" Kate interrupted, hating what she was thinking. *She can't handle this.*

"Two."

Kate was through the exam room door in seconds and confirmed that she'd been right; the chaplain was in way over her head. The trauma patient, his moans fogging the rebreather mask, was pale and glistening with sweat. A blood pressure alarm sounded: 76 over 38.

"Riley . . ." Kate snatched a pair of gloves from a box, nodded at the family.

Riley glanced up, her cheeks flushed, neck blotchy, pupils wide—adrenaline rush. And anxiety, Kate would bet. "I had an eighteen-gauge in, but the vein blew . . ." Riley pressed her gloved fingers against a gauze square soggy with blood from the failed stick. "I think there's another good-size vein here."

"Think" isn't good enough. Kate knew Riley wanted a chance to prove herself, but . . . She struggled against the image of the bruises from Riley's practice attempts and the way Riley had demonstrated her clumsy fingers with that cookie. Crumbs everywhere.

"I got it." Kate snatched a tourniquet off the tray. She extended the man's other arm, applied the tourniquet, and tapped her fingers against the space at his elbow. Big vein, but flattening . . . because he was bleeding out. The blood pressure alarm sounded again. The family whispered in Spanish. Some of it sounded like a prayer. Kate pulled the tourniquet tighter, flicked the vein with her gloved finger, and—

"I'm going for this one," Riley said from the other side of the exam table. "A twenty-gauge, but that will still infuse—"

"Hand me the needle," Kate instructed, reaching out her palm.

"I'm already under the skin. And it's looking pretty . . ."

"Stop—save a vein for the lab. Give me a sixteen-gauge instead. I've got this." Kate's eyes met Riley's over the patient's chest, and she wished her voice had sounded less brusque.

Riley passed her the sixteen-gauge needle set. Kate prepped the vein with surgical iodine, then touched a fingertip to it once more. "You'll feel a needle stick, sir." She held her breath, slid the needle through the skin bevel up, felt the pop as she entered the vessel . . . advanced it, and—*yes!*

"I'm in," Kate breathed, watching with relief as the blood flashed back into the needle set. She glanced up to ask for the IV tubing and tape and saw that Riley was already beside her, supplies in hand. "Thanks," she whispered, wrestling with guilt she knew was irrational.

The door opened and Jack stepped in. He glanced from the patient to the monitor to Kate . . . then at Riley. "You got a line in?"

"Yes." Riley glanced down, exhaling softly. "A sixteen-gauge, running wide open. Kate—"

"Team effort," Kate interjected; she wasn't sure anyone heard over the sudden wail of sirens.

- + -

Jack strode past his office, hearing the familiar strains of music through the door. It was barely nine, and Bandy didn't usually start up this early; he was probably hoping some divine message would get through to Jack, derail the anger train. Fat chance of that. *Heartless hypocrites.*

He forced himself to take a slow breath; Riley was in the kitchen. He wasn't going to bring this up with her.

"Well," he said, watching as she tucked her stethoscope into her purse. "The only thing I can offer to compete with that adrenaline rush is skydiving. Thursday at noon. Still time to change your mind." He raised his brows. "This is my second and final offer."

"No thanks." Riley smiled halfheartedly. "After Hector, falling from heights is the last thing I want to think about." She pulled the band off her ponytail, then closed her eyes for a moment as she rubbed the back of her neck. Jack wondered how she'd react if he offered to do that for her. "I called the ER," she continued. "You were right. Ruptured spleen. And maybe a kidney contusion. Hector's in the OR. Apparently he responded well to fluid resuscitation in the ER." Riley's teeth scraped across her lower lip. "Which reminds me that I should probably tell you . . ."

"What?" Jack saw the discomfort in her expression.

Riley sighed. "Kate started that IV. I had an eighteen-gauge in, but the vein blew. I found another one. I think I could have gotten it in, but Kate—"

"Hey." Jack stepped close. "The man's in the OR. We did our part. It's done."

"I know. I guess I just wanted my part to matter more."

"Matter? Oh . . . that." Jack shook his head. He'd almost forgotten. "You mean because I offered to write your letter."

"Yes," Riley said with raw honesty. "And because I needed to know, for myself, that I could do it."

"Look . . ." Jack spread his hands, knowing anything he said was likely futile. Her determination was as clear as Bandy's gospel music floating down the hallway. "The ER is a team situation too. Veins blow. Some days a buddy has your back; then it's your turn to help him. The important thing is that we're in there, doing something, trying. And as for here in the clinic . . . It's not every day we have a guy fall twenty feet from a roof, to—" He stopped, barely biting back the curse he'd been wanting to shout for the past half hour. A low growl escaped his lips instead.

"What's wrong?"

"I got more information from the son while they were loading Hector into the ambulance. The roof he fell from was a block away—in The Bluffs. Apparently it was suggested that they bring him here because hospitals are expensive. And because the free clinic doesn't ask so many questions."

Riley's mouth sagged open. "Suggested by whom?"

"That's the million-dollar question. Want to take bets on the chances of anyone owning up to it?"

Riley grimaced. "That's why Hector's son said it happened at home. They didn't want to take the chance of anyone prying into their work situation. Or maybe even citizenship status."

Jack nodded. "And our neighbors sure weren't going to take responsibility for someone injured on their property. If Hector's family had taken him home instead, he'd be dead right now." Jack paused as the ugly irony hit him in the gut. "They're itching to haul me before the city council and call *me* reckless and irresponsible, claim there's no good reason to have my clinic here. But when it's convenient for them . . ."

"What are you going to do?" she asked. The wariness in her eyes reminded Jack of why he'd decided against telling her any of this.

"Don't know." He glanced toward the hallway as the music seemed to swell. "Bandy's telling me to let the police handle things and stay out of it."

"That sounds like good advice."

Jack shrugged. "Maybe. But it's not going to stop me from taking a little detour on my way home. To see who's got a brand-new roof. And no heart."

- + -

He can't see me. . . . It's not him.

In the darkness, Vesta squinted through her binoculars toward San Antonio Street, and her breath caught. The enormous Hummer slowed to a crawl at the curb, then rolled slowly on—the second time in the last fifteen minutes. It was impossible to see the driver in the hopscotch pools of light from The Bluffs' elegant streetlamps. Or even identify the color of the vehicle, though Vesta thought it was black. If she could make out the license plate, she'd report it to the neighborhood watch. And if she got a real glimpse of the driver, recognized him, she'd report it to the police.

Or would I? She shivered, remembering the face that haunted her nightmares. Startling eyes, fair lashes, angular face, and that tangled mass of Medusa hair. Fear on his young face, panicky desperation validating unimaginable violence. *It's not him. . . .*

The Hummer moved on, and Vesta's shoulders fell as she exhaled. The neighbors were keeping watch and there was talk of hiring private officers until the security gate installation was complete. The action committee had called a special meeting at the clubhouse on Saturday, with a police officer in attendance.

They would be discussing the recent incidents of neighborhood crime. And ranting about the clinic, no doubt.

Vesta set the binoculars down, reached for her water, and took a long swallow. She hated all the strife concerning the clinic. She hadn't told Bandy Biggs that she knew he worked there—her landlady was a tight link in the local gossip chain. But meeting him, little Hobo, and Riley had finally put a face on the clinic. A warm, friendly face. It made Vesta feel more secure than she'd felt in a long time, even with her own conflict surrounding Dr. Travis. And how that continued to affect her.

If I didn't go to the police then, what makes me think I could now? Even if . . . it's that man out there.

A shaking chill, one of several she'd had today, caused water to dribble down the glass. Her teeth chattered and she hugged her robe close. Fever. She wouldn't worry unless it stayed above 101 despite the Tylenol. Vesta was no stranger to bladder infections; she'd recognized the symptoms this morning and had started taking the antibiotics she kept "just in case." It explained the dull backache she'd had for several days, the headache, and her stubbornly high blood sugar readings. She'd take the medicine, drink extra fluids, rest, watch her diet—be careful. The last thing she wanted was to end up in the ER again.

No . . . Vesta glanced toward the window, shivering again. The last thing she wanted was to find out that a murderer was really out there.

22

+

RILEY PEERED through the NICU window at Baby Girl Paulson—
the Doe nameplate had been ceremoniously dumped. The
Express-News was calling her "a healthy dose of hope in a tiny
pink cap." Riley hoped this baby could provide that for the
Alamo Grace staff as well, relief in the midst of too much tragedy.
But the infant had developed a low-grade fever and episodes
of vomiting, requiring her to be poked, prodded, and x-rayed
in order to determine the cause. It called a temporary halt to
the mother's milk shipped from Austin and to the long line of
volunteers eager to rock the babe. Last evening, one of those
volunteers had been the baby's shell-shocked grandmother.

Riley's heart cramped, remembering. The Collinses had
decided to discontinue life support measures for their Tinker

Bell last night; without the ventilator and resuscitation drugs, it would only be a matter of time before she was gone. Riley had barely arrived home from the clinic when she got the call. She hurried in, sat with them at Stacy's bedside for another heartbreaking hour. Offered prayers and much-needed hugs. A sad ending to Riley's long, stressful, and disappointing day.

"Rah-lee," Kate said, her voice husky-soft as she joined Riley at the window. She glanced away before Riley could read anything in her eyes. "I heard the grandmother held her last night."

"Yes." Riley's stomach sank. Seeing Kate was usually a bright spot in her day, but after last night's drama in the clinic, it felt awkward. She hated that.

"I was here." Riley saw Kate's confusion. "After the clinic. I got a call because they'd decided to sign the DNR papers. I came in to be with them."

Kate winced, pressed a hand to her chest. "I don't know how you do that."

"Sometimes," Riley admitted, meeting Kate's gaze fully, "I don't either. But it's my job." *Until I can get back to the ER. You do remember how much I want that, right?*

Kate cleared her throat. "I called the SICU about your patient, Hector. Two units of blood in the OR. Kidney looks fine. He's stable and awake, doing well."

Riley nodded, deciding not to reveal that she knew all that because she'd dropped by his room after leaving the Collins family last night. She sensed Kate had more to say.

Kate tugged at a lock of her hair. "You did good at the clinic. You handled it well."

"I . . . appreciate your giving me a hand," Riley said despite her bruised pride. Their friendship was far too important. *Even if I needed that chance.* She summoned a smile. "In the drama of the moment, I didn't get a chance to say that you looked great—clothes, hair. Date?"

"Uh . . . sort of." Kate shrugged, the flush on her cheeks far less noncommittal. "But nothing newsworthy." She glanced at her watch. "Gotta go. I lost the coin toss on washing wax out of a trucker's ears." Her nose wrinkled. "You should rethink coming back to—" Kate stopped, the look in her eyes saying she wanted to swallow those last few words. *Coming back to the ER.*

"I'll stop by later," Riley offered in the awkward silence, "and bring you a mocha."

"Great. I'd love that."

Riley watched as Kate hustled down the hallway toward the ER, regretting this new mix of feelings. She wasn't proud of the fact that a huge part of it had to do with ego—she'd so wanted to prove herself with the IV. If she'd threaded that needle into the vein on a second try, it would have meant everything to her confidence. And it would have shown Jack that he wasn't simply doing her a favor by writing a recommendation. But in the end, it had been about saving Hector's life. As it should be. She knew that.

Still, Riley wished Kate had been less abrupt. Her mistrust less obvious. *"Save a vein for the lab."* Translation: *You're going to blow another one.* What real hope was there if her best friend didn't think she was competent?

Riley's phone made a plinking noise in the pocket of her blazer—a text message. She slid the phone out, dreading bad

news about Stacy Paulson. Then pressed the View button. It
was from Jack.

    I sent that recommendation.

                      - + -

Jack glanced into the wheelbarrow and then headed toward
the back steps of the clinic just as their nurse practitioner,
Gretchen, stepped out the door. A smile lit her round, freckled
face. "Hey, Jack."

"Morning." He grinned back, squinting against the sun.
"Bandy con you into gardening?"

"He hinted," she said, clumping down the steps. She wore
cutoff jeans with tall, stitched Justin boots. The stacked heels
added little to her half-pint height. "But I've got patients to see
at the office. I came in to add a few more shifts to my availability.
I'll be taking some vacation from the other job in May, so I could
be here." Her brows scrunched. "If the clinic's still here, that is."

Jack frowned. "Count on it."

"Heard something yesterday . . ." Gretchen pulled her sunglasses out of her purse. "My aunt does catering out of her
house and told me she got a call about providing appetizers on
short notice for an 'emergency' meeting of The Bluffs' action
committee. They copied her on the Evite. You can probably
guess what's on the agenda."

A report from a private investigator? "No clue."

Gretchen rolled her eyes. "I think the wording went something like 'Free clinic: We pay with our safety. Make your voice
heard.'"

"Around a mouthful of appetizers in The Bluffs' fancy club-house—I'm shaking in my boots."

"In the library, actually. Scheduling conflict with an oil exec's business party. Now *that's* the gig my aunt really wanted to cater. I thought I'd never hear the end of it." Gretchen tossed him a wry smile as she slid her glasses on. "Well, I'm off to rid the world of pinkeye, croup, and—oh yeah. Talk Bandy into taking those pain pills you prescribed, would you? I threatened to put a cast on his green thumb; he's torturing his back, dig-gin' out there. Never met anyone more stubborn. Except maybe you, Travis."

"Guilty as charged." Jack smiled. "But thanks. I'll talk to him."

Jack said good-bye, climbed the steps, and found Bandy in the kitchen making sandwiches.

"Loaves and fishes," Bandy said, tossing a crust to Hobo. "Tuna fish today. Found an anonymous cash donation poked under the door this morning, with a nice note saying that not all of our neighbors hold the same low opinion of our work here."

"Guilty conscience," Jack grumbled, deciding not to say anything about the action committee's emergency meeting. "Any roof tar smudges on that note?"

"'If you have faith as small as a mustard seed' . . . you wouldn't doubt our good neighbor's motive."

Jack rolled his eyes, smiling regardless. "You can save the mustard for your tuna. And you'll probably be relieved to know my covert drive around the neighborhood revealed *three* houses with roofing construction going on. No single person I can point my finger at." He raised his palms at the look on Bandy's face. "Not that I was going to. Rob told me the police are look-ing into it, and I'm sure the hospital billing office will be, too, so—" He stopped, seeing Bandy grimace. "Your back?"

Bandy took a slow breath. "Back, shoulder . . . hair." He managed a smile. "Getting old isn't for sissies." He pointed his mayonnaise-smeared knife at Jack. "And don't you start with the pill pushing. If I wanted to stumble around half-doped, I'd go back to having beer for breakfast—I'm done with those days. I'm fine, Doc. Just don't like when it gets bad enough that I can't sleep."

"Take a pain pill at night," Jack suggested. "Who cares if you're groggy then?" He tossed Bandy a teasing smile. "And it could only improve things when you croon along with that CD player."

Bandy chuckled. "You're talkin' me into it."

"Good. And my shift in Kerrville doesn't start until three, so if you need something done in that garden, I'm your man."

"Thanks, but I'm taking off in a few minutes." His eyes lit, all outward traces of pain gone. "Meeting the family at SeaWorld. My son's taking a day off from his job hunting. I can't wait to watch that grandbaby's face when she sees Shamu, tastes some cotton candy . . ." He clucked his tongue. "Just a sticky pinch. I promise." Bandy's eyes shone with sudden tears. "Yessir, bonus day in a bonus year. I never would have expected these blessings. I . . ." He reached for a paper towel, swiped at his eyes.

"Here." Jack reached for his wallet. "Let me contribute a little—"

"No thanks, Doc," Bandy said, clearing his throat. "Appreciate the thought, but got it covered. And I'll be back in plenty of time to open the clinic. The kids have a long drive home, so they can't stay late." He was quiet for a moment, then grabbed two coffee cups and filled them. "Biggest mistake I ever made was making no time for family. Making everything else more important. Daredevil ambition, personal glory, booze . . . all that worthless stuff that a man thinks it takes to prove himself. I lived my life like it was all about *me*." Bandy shook his head. "Best thing I ever did was find out it isn't—not even close. And it took God pointing me to the porch of this clinic to make that happen. That's the truth."

Jack had no clue what to say. He'd never seen Bandy cry.

"So . . ." Bandy took a sip of his coffee, peered at Jack over the brim. "Riley Hale. Now there's a fine young woman."

"And that's . . . right out of left field."

"Just thinkin' out loud." Bandy raised his brows. "It makes sense . . ."

Jack crossed his arms and had no problem imagining this man in the blue wig, teasing a bull.

Bandy glanced up at the ceiling. "Yessir. Could be the good Lord had a plan pointing her to the porch of this clinic too."

And could be the devil chucked a CPR manikin at her because he had a plan to use her.

Bandy waited. Hobo squeaked his cart in a circle, then trod in place, staring up at Jack.

Jack threw his hands up. "Okay, I give in. What are you saying?"

"That maybe you could make time in your life for someone like her."

Jack shook his head, trying to dispel the memory of Riley

in his arms, the sweet scent of peaches. "What is this? A super-size deal? Get the girl who comes with a generous side order of redemption?"

"Works for me."

Jack scraped his fingers across his jaw. "Well, not for her, apparently. I invited Riley to come along to a sports thing I'm doing. She turned me down. Twice."

"What kind of 'thing'?"

"Skydiving."

Bandy snorted. "Fine young lady—and smart, too."

- + -

Kate slipped into the Alamo Grace chapel but stayed discreetly toward the back, telling herself it was because she didn't have time to stay, didn't want to disturb what had already started. She was curious more than anything else. As she'd said earlier at the NICU, Kate found it hard to understand how Riley could do all these things, open herself to such painful turmoil. Like right now, offering support for staff affected by what had turned out to be a miserable—and high-profile—week.

A surprising number of people had taken her up on the idea, gathering in a small circle of chairs near the altar: nurses Kate recognized from SICU and NICU, an ER ward clerk, the caseworker assisting with the toddler who'd ingested amphet-amines, a teenager in a striped volunteer's smock, and two stu-dent nurses.

"I want to thank you all for being here to support one another," Riley said, her profile backlit by sunshine spilling through the stained-glass window. "It's been a tough few weeks.

Many of you have put in long hours and worked extra shifts to make certain very sick patients get the best of care. Doing that day in and day out can take a toll." She smiled gently at the student nurses. "Some of you may just be learning that." Riley glanced around the circle. "Unfortunately, we caregivers often hold ourselves to impossibly high standards."

Kate nodded, remembering the frustration on Riley's face the day she'd tried so hard with the CPR manikin. And the look in her eyes last night when Kate told her not to try that IV.

"We tell ourselves to buck up, be strong, because we're afraid that feeling overwhelmed, sad, or angry as a response to emotional stress is a sign of weakness." Riley shook her head. "Nothing could be further from the truth. Which is that sometimes we need to give ourselves permission to feel rotten."

Kate thought of Stacy Paulson's arrival in the ER and the painful memories it stirred. *Rotten* didn't begin to describe it.

"Those are the times that we have to be especially kind to ourselves," Riley continued. "Do things that make you feel good. Take that run, listen to favorite music, rent a funny movie . . ."

Accept a date and not tell you about it, Rah-lee.

Kate drew a deep breath, hoping to settle the confusing mix of feelings. Then listened as a SICU nurse spoke up.

"I was doing fine," she said, hugging her arms around her purple scrubs, "until this morning, when Stacy's mother brought out this old hairbrush. A kid's brush." The nurse lifted her chin. "She was nervous because of the bandage. But I helped her with the hair we could reach below it. We got the tangles out and she braided it. All the while she kept telling me things about Stacy—that she loved to draw and her bedroom wall had been covered with crayon pictures, finger paintings, and glitter art. She wondered if the baby would have that gift too. Then . . ." The nurse's voice broke, and the ward clerk slipped an arm around her shoulders. "She said she had to believe that, somehow, even this tragedy was part of God's plan for their lives."

Kate moved toward the door. She'd heard way more than enough. The only plan she knew of required her to spend the next four hours in the ER. Whether it made her feel rotten or not.

Her cell phone buzzed with a text message an hour later—the ER director asking Kate to come to her office. Scheduling issues, she assumed. One of the nurses had unexpected problems with her pregnancy that required her to go out on disability, and vacations for other staff might need to be adjusted. And there was still that issue of the male nurse on leave for counseling. She checked in with the triage nurse and the doctor—who'd plugged his ears with his stethoscope while suturing the chin of a shrieking toddler—and told them where she'd be.

Kate started off toward the director's office but ran into Riley as she rounded a corner.

"Your mocha," Riley said, holding out the green-logo paper cup. "A promise is a promise. I meant to bring it earlier, but I needed to talk with one of the nurses after the gathering in the chapel."

"Thanks." Kate took the cup, telling herself that Riley probably hadn't seen her there. And if she had, what did it matter? That Riley was chaplain and Kate had issues with God had nothing to do with their friendship.

"How's the packing going?"

"Good—slow, but . . ." *Am I stalling?* "I've been busy with some other things."

"Well—" Riley smiled—"remember, if you need help, I'm there for you."

"I know," Kate managed. All at once she wanted more than anything to tell Riley she was sorry about the IV, admit she'd had coffee with Griff Payton. *And finally let you know how "rotten" I feel most of the time.* She had no doubt that Riley would listen, be there for her. But . . . "Thanks again." Kate lifted the coffee. "Gotta run. Meeting."

Twenty minutes later, Kate was certain she was about to hit a new low in feeling rotten.

"I hate putting you in this position, Kate." ER director Joanna Berry bridged her hands together, snowy French-tip nails touching. "But this is an unusual situation and you're my best hospital resource."

"There are three other charge nurses. And relief staff."

"I've talked with them. And I received a letter from Dr. Travis today. All somewhat helpful, but the fact remains that you've had the most contact with Riley in the emergency department setting because you work day shift. Granted, that was in her capacity as chaplain. But I understand that you've been helping her with some manikin practice. Perhaps worked with her at the clinic?"

Oh, please, no . . .

"Riley's proposing that she be considered as a full-time triage nurse," Kate explained.

"Exactly the dilemma, I'm afraid." Joanna sighed. "That position—a dedicated triage position, exclusive of acute care nursing tasks—has never existed in this hospital system."

"And neither did the position of trauma chaplain." Kate met her gaze, knowing full well she was pointing to the Hale-size elephant in the room. Kate gritted her teeth. Why should she have to weigh in on a problem the hospital created?

Joanna's pretty fingers interlaced, thumbs wrestling each other. "That's true. And while I'm not at liberty to discuss that decision, my personal opinion is that it was one of the best moves this hospital has made. Riley's doing a remarkable job as chaplain. That she's a nurse and a trauma survivor herself only adds to her abilities. I can't tell you how many letters I receive from patients, their family members, and staff. My own mother calls her the Alamo Grace angel." She shook her head. "If only I could clone her for every team in every department."

"As a chaplain."

"Yes." Joanna frowned. "We come full circle again. So . . ."

"What are you asking me?"

"I want to know this: if the triage position were taken off the table and Riley was being considered as an ER staff nurse, could you recommend her?"

Kate glanced at the sheaf of papers in front of the director, stomach plunging. "Officially—on the record?"

"Only as a guideline to help me. I'm meeting with the nursing supervisor and the head of human resources in an hour. We'll be looking over résumés from some very qualified trauma nurses and considering the department's immediate needs, now that two of your staff are out." Joanna exhaled, met Kate's gaze.

"The ultimate decision regarding Riley's employment will be based on several factors, of course. Not only the nurses' input."

Kate took a sip of mocha that suddenly tasted like sawdust. She thought of Riley's words only minutes ago: *"I'm there for you."*

She cleared her throat. "I . . ."

23

"I'M SORRY TO HEAR THAT, VESTA." Riley held her cell phone with one hand while opening the clinic's medicine cupboard. "Are you keeping up with your fluids? You don't want to risk getting dehydrated." *And ending up in the ER again, sweet lady. Neither of us wants that.*

"I'm being careful. And I'm sorry about your visit tomorrow. I was looking forward to it."

"Me too," Riley said sincerely. "I'll call you on Saturday to check in. We'll reschedule for next week, when you're feeling better."

"I'll be better. I'm not going to miss another chance to visit with you . . . or pet that little dog from the clinic."

"Yes, Hobo's quite the charmer. I'm glad that you got to meet him."

Riley said good-bye and disconnected, thinking that maybe she'd just found more evidence of the hope she'd been looking for this morning. Vesta had met Bandy and Hobo, which required her to walk to the San Antonio Street curb. Maybe some first steps in broadening her world. She smiled to herself. Not that Vesta would be taking the TYGRR-mobile for a spin anytime soon, but—

"Last patient, last sandwich," Bandy reported from the doorway. His smile crinkled the corners of his eyes. "I like it when it works out like that." He watched as Riley tapped a couple Tylenol into a paper medicine cup. "Doc Estes and I appreciate your coming in to help at the last minute."

"I was glad to. And to hear that he asked for me specifically. It gives me hope." *Especially after Jack's text about the letter. And soon, my medical clearance, then . . .* She replaced the lid on the medicine bottle and turned to Bandy with a sigh. "I'll be honest with you. I may have been working as chaplain this past year, but that doesn't mean I haven't had doubts. Even after I got past peppering God with the 'why me' questions about my injury." She wrinkled her nose. "At least I think I'm past that. But what I'm saying is that I've worked so hard to get back to where I was. And most of the time it feels like I'm slogging through waist-high mud in some east Texas bayou. When just over there—" she extended her numb arm—"is the river I'm supposed to be floating down. Does that make sense?"

Bandy nodded. "I've done some time in hip waders."

Riley stared down at her right palm. "I can't understand why

God would only take me so far. Why he'd tease me with what I want most, then hold it back, and . . . It's so hard, Bandy."

"I hear you. It is tough. And that's exactly when we have to believe that God is still faithful, worthy of trust. That's the time to close our eyes, stop keepin' tally of this and that, and just feel his hands holding us. Feel his hold . . . and trust it." Bandy winked at her. "There's no eight-second buzzer on that grip."

Riley watched as he walked back through the kitchen, noticing how stiffly he was moving today, and remembered what he'd said about pulling some muscles in the garden. He'd finally agreed to take the pills Jack prescribed, even if they'd knock him out "deep enough so I wouldn't hear a train roarin' past that sofa bed." She smiled to herself—like The Bluffs would tolerate a train. She hoped Bandy got some much-needed rest.

Despite the doubts she'd just admitted, Riley was starting to feel more optimistic about things like Vesta's situation and the fact that Jack had sent that recommendation to the ER director today. She'd felt good about the chapel gathering at the hospital and elated when Dr. Estes had requested to work with her. And she even felt better about Kate. *You did good at the clinic. You handled it well.* She'd said that to Riley and—even if she'd been hesitant about Riley starting that IV—it meant something. It meant hope.

- + -

Kate sat cross-legged on an old beach towel in the deepening dusk, wondering which would chase her out faster—the infamous Texas chiggers or The Bluffs' neighborhood watch. She didn't really care; all she needed was time enough to see if . . .

She hunched forward, peering down the knoll toward the creek that threaded through the exclusive golf course, searching the dense cedar and dark stands of old oaks. She'd been told that April was early to spot them, but the evening was warm and humid . . . *Ah, there—fireflies!*

Her breath caught at the magical blink-blink of beautifully eerie light. Green, glowing—there and gone. Then she smiled at the impetuous answer: a zigzagging glimmer stumbling down the creek like a smitten lover holding a minuscule flashlight, asking, "Are you there? I'm here. Are you there?"

Incredible. Kate sighed. Fireflies were Disneyland made real. She'd needed that today. Something that simply . . . felt good. Riley had said much the same thing to the stressed staff she'd gathered in the chapel.

Riley . . . Kate pulled her phone from the pocket of her hoodie and once again scanned her missed messages. A call from Riley, followed by a text:

> My senior house call canceled 4 tomorrow. Have extra time and bubble wrap. Packing party?

Kate winced; she should call Riley back. But . . .

A blinking trio of fireflies flickered close enough to touch and Kate watched, spellbound, until they disappeared. She stared at the dark vacuum left in their wake. Had Stacy Paulson lived in Texas long enough to see fireflies? Kate hoped so. She needed to think that their elusive magic had helped that runaway forget about being pregnant, alone . . . and scared to death.

Kate sighed, recalling what she'd heard in the chapel this morning—that Stacy's mother had brushed her daughter's hair, braided it, and talked about the good times they'd had. Kate swept her hand over her bangs, and her throat tightened the way it always did when the ifs tumbled forward. If Kate's ugly mistakes had left her in Stacy's situation and her mom were still alive, would she have done that for Kate? *Brush my hair, sit beside me all night, talk about* . . . Kate chewed her lip. Were there enough good times to outweigh all the bad?

"Do things that make you feel good."

What if there wasn't anything?

Kate frowned in the darkness. What was she doing here? Fireflies weren't magic—they were bugs, same as chiggers. And she was too old for Disneyland. She was an adult who'd put her mistakes behind her, moved nearly two thousand miles to start a new life and take on a demanding leadership position that sometimes required tough decisions. Feeling good wasn't always in the equation.

She stood and shook her beach towel, stopped as her cell phone rang. Riley? Kate reached into her pocket, thoughts staggering toward what she'd say.

"Griff?" she asked with surprise.

"The one and only. What's up?"

"Uh . . ." Kate glanced toward the creek, feeling foolish— and for some reason remembering his quip about picking the wings off butterflies. She wondered if his no-harm agreement extended to fireflies.

"Kate? Did I catch you at a bad time?"

"No," she said quickly, "not at all. I'm just winding down after work. It was a miserable day."

"I can only imagine—and don't want to." His breath sounded close enough to warm her ear, like it had when they'd danced. "I have this idea. I know I said I wouldn't push, but I've got tickets to the Majestic Theatre on Saturday night. It's an incredible historic building; you'd love it. I'm in Dallas till Saturday, but I'll be back in plenty of time to make the performance. And these are great seats."

Kate glanced down at her old beach towel. "What's the production?"

"*Wicked.*"

She made no attempt to hide her laugh.

"Well then . . . Saturday night . . . ," Griff persisted, the faint Southern gentleman accent as tempting as firefly magic. "Does that sound good?"

Do things that feel good . . .

"Yes." Kate smiled in the darkness. "*Wicked* sounds good."

- + -

"Good," Jack said, continuing his cell phone conversation with Bandy. He glanced at the Kerrville ER's status board: belly pain awaiting labs, fractured hip, motorcycle road rash . . . "I'm glad Riley came in. And it sounds like there won't be any problem with staffing tomorrow. I've got that appointment—"

Bandy snorted. "You versus gravity."

Jack smiled. "Yes. But I'll check in to see if you need anything. How's your back?"

"Still holdin' me up. Even after walking a bunch of miles at

SeaWorld—worth every step." Music swelled in the background. "After I get Hobo settled outside and do my rounds in the parking lot, I'm going to try one of those pills you gave me. Break it in half and see how that goes."

Jack shook his head, agreeing with Gretchen: stubborn.

"And hopefully there won't be any more shenanigans in the neighborhood," Bandy continued, referencing the reason for his call. A Dumpster fire at the dress shop down the block from the clinic. No serious damage, but plenty of commotion. "You'd think folks could find better things to do than play with matches."

"Rob thought it was kids?"

"He suspects so. Though . . ."

Though we'll get blamed. Again, Jack finished Bandy's unspoken suspicion.

"I'd better get back to work." Jack nodded as a ward clerk caught his attention, indicating that another call was waiting. "Sleep well, pal."

"Jump safe, Doc."

Jack reached for the desk phone, frowning at the thought of the action committee using tonight's Dumpster fire as more fodder against the clinic. No doubt it would be mentioned at their "emergency" meeting on Saturday at the library.

Then a tempting thought struck him: unlike The Bluffs' clubhouse, the library was a public place. Anyone could show up.

- + -

Riley nearly dropped her phone. "I don't understand. What are you trying to tell me?"

Kate sighed. "That Joanna pointed out what we both knew all along: you applied for a job that doesn't exist."

"Proposed," Riley said, sensing that she was spitting into the wind. "It's different. I *proposed* that I be considered for a position as full-time triage nurse. I asked them to consider it."

"I know." Kate's voice had diminished to a near whisper. Not good.

"So . . ." Riley paced across her living room, mind whirling. "What do you think she meant by leaving me that phone message? I wish I'd gotten it before it was too late to call."

"I think she meant just what she said, Riley. That she'd met with the hiring committee. And your proposal, along with Jack's letter, was presented with the applications from other qualified RNs currently employed in emergency departments."

Qualified. Riley squeezed her eyes shut. *Oh, please, God . . .*

"And," Kate continued as gently as if she were explaining a painful procedure to a frightened child, "she wants to discuss their concerns."

"Which might be . . . ?"

"Riley, please. You don't want me to second-guess this."

"I do." Riley clenched her numb fingers, fighting a rush of feelings. "I wouldn't have called you if I didn't. Though I would have thought you'd call me after your meeting with Joanna."

"I thought about it. I did. But she said input from the charge nurses was only one factor in their consideration. They'll need that medical clearance from your doctors."

"I'm expecting it this week."

Kate sighed. "I didn't think Joanna would contact you until tomorrow, and I didn't want you to be worrying all night."

Riley groaned. "So much for that." She sat on the couch, got back up, paced toward the fireplace. She winced at the photo with the TYGRR-mobile, then told herself to stop stalling and ask. "What did you say to her?"

The silence was long enough that Riley thought she'd lost the cell connection. "Kate?"

"What do you mean?"

Riley swallowed. "I mean, when you talked to the director about my return to the ER as a staff nurse."

"Riley . . ."

"What did you say?" Riley held her breath and imagined Kate's direct gaze, knowing that she was honest. Loving her for that, but dreading . . .

"I said I wouldn't be comfortable with you in a staff nurse position. I'm sorry—*so* sorry—but I don't think you're ready, Riley."

- + -

Jack had almost dozed off in front of the TV when he realized he'd left his BlackBerry in the Hummer. He headed for the door, backtracked to the kitchen to get a flashlight—he still hadn't replaced the porch light—and went to the garage. The phone was right where he'd left it on the console. It showed a missed call . . . from Riley? He climbed into the driver's seat and retrieved the message. His brows pinched together at the sound of her voice: thick, ragged, like she'd been crying.

"It's Riley . . . and, um . . . about eleven, I guess. Don't call me back tonight; I'm going to try to get some sleep. But—" she cleared her throat—"if that invitation is still open . . . you know, for jumping from that plane, I might be interested. I don't know. Maybe. I'll call you in the morning."

Jack played the message again, checked the current time on his watch. One thirty. Too late, but she'd sounded so . . . He hit the Call button. Heard it ring a half-dozen times.

"Jack?" She sounded groggy, half-asleep.

"I got your message. Are you okay?"

"Um . . . sure. I'm sorry I called so late. I just . . . I don't know—I wanted to talk. And thought of you."

Of me. "We can talk now. Or I could come over there, or . . ." She'd given him the security gate code. He'd take off right now. Be there in—

"No." She sighed. "Thanks, but no. I'll call you in the morning."

"Skydiving? Did you mean that?"

Riley gave a half laugh. "Yes. Your 'spit in the face of fear' thing. Something about it suddenly sounded . . . good. Scary but good. Can I let you know tomorrow?"

"Absolutely. I don't jump until noon."

Jack said good night and sat there for a while, wondering if he'd imagined that Riley had been crying. Wondering what could have changed her mind about skydiving. Even the balcony at the River Walk restaurant had made her nervous.

He shook his head at what Bandy had said about Riley turning down his jump invitation before. *"Fine young lady— and smart, too."* What would Bandy say if he knew they had a mutual date with gravity? That Riley wasn't as smart as she looked? Or would he simply gloat about his suggestion that Jack find time for someone like her in his life? Not that he was doing that, of course. But . . .

He pushed the phone into his pocket and slid out of the Hummer, smiling. He wasn't taking it for more than face value, but he really liked what Riley had said. That when she'd wanted to talk . . . *"I thought of you."* That felt good.

Now if he could just stop imagining her in a skydiving jumpsuit and get a few hours of sleep.

24

+

"BLUE SKIES, TRAVIS!"

"Blue skies!" Jack gave a thumbs-up to the man waving in the distance—a bearded sixty-year-old veterinarian from Bandera outfitted in a vintage leather aviator's helmet and an orange jumpsuit that made him look like an escaped prisoner. Jack squinted against the sun, scanning the San Marcos drop zone: three planes at the ready, skydivers heading out at their twenty-minute call. There was a familiar rainbow of jumpsuits and faces this morning: Parachute Club members, the husband and wife videographer team, a recently retired pharmacist, and that female K9 officer from Hondo who was well into her accelerated free-fall program. Standing near the wind sock, holding cameras and binoculars, was the usual clutch of curious onlookers and skydive groupies. The sky, under perfect conditions, was dotted with a dozen rectangular ram-air parachutes in fuchsia, purple, electric green, chili-pepper red . . . drifting, gliding, maneuvering like the wings of huge Pixar movie creatures. Five thousand feet above the ground. Jack's pulse kicked up a notch, eager to join them. *And because . . . Riley's here.*

He stepped into the converted metal hangar, blinking as his eyes adjusted, and heard the buzz of excited voices accompanied by seemingly endless strains of Tom Petty's "Free Fallin'." Then spotted the small group of first timers, wide-eyed with excitement and nerves after their preflight training. One of them was Riley. He still couldn't believe it. And from the look on her face, neither could she. *Why did she change her mind?*

"All signed up?" he asked, noticing that she'd changed into the navy-blue jumpsuit and swept her long hair into a loose knot at the back of her head. She looked even more beautiful than he'd imagined, making him regret not having an instructor's certificate. Being hooked together for a tandem jump would be . . .

"Liability waivers, medical waivers . . ." She took a breath. "Signed my life away. If I so much as slip on a banana peel on the tarmac outside the plane and break my neck . . ." She grimaced. "Poor choice of words."

The Petty song began yet again.

"She's a good girl, loves her mama.
Loves Jesus and America too . . ."

"Hey." Jack reached for Riley's hand—and found it damp. Despite last night's phone call saying she needed to talk, she had said little this morning. She'd simply called him at nine and said, *"Let's do it."* On the drive to San Marcos she gave no indication of why she'd changed her mind. He suspected something had happened but didn't press her. "Are you sure you're ready for this?" he asked now.

"And I'm free, free fallin' . . ."

"Ready. I've got it all down." Riley took a halting breath and licked her lips. "The plane is a Super Otter. We climb to 13,500 feet. I'm snapped to Margo, my back to her chest and stomach. I sit between her legs, wait for my turn." She glanced upward like a nervous student reciting in front of the class. "At the door of the plane, I cross my arms across my chest, holding my harness. The plane's speed is around 90 miles per hour, and the terminal velocity of the human body falling is 120 miles per—"

"I meant—" Jack stepped closer—"are you sure you really want to do this?" He drew her hand against the chest of his jumpsuit as he studied her face. "You don't have to."

"I know that." Riley lifted her chin. "I'm doing it because I want to." She slid her hand away, narrowed her eyes. "You're not trying to talk me out of it, are you?"

"Not me." Jack laughed. "I saw that photo of you in the pecan tree, rebel girl."

"Keep that in mind."

"Oh, I will," he said, missing the feel of her hand. He glanced up at the PA system. "We should get our twenty-minute call soon." He pretended not to notice the anxiety that flickered across her face. "Got your goggles, Chaplain?"

She nodded, swallowing. "I think I'll run to the ladies' room for a minute."

"Sure." She'd done that right before her training, too. Fortunately, Jack had reminded her to eat a light breakfast. "I'll be right here."

He watched her hurry away, trim flight suit *swish-swish*ing as she moved, and was glad—whatever her reason for coming—that Riley was with him today. He'd always thought of skydiving as a solitary pleasure. In fact, he'd guarded that aspect of it. But last night, after they'd talked and while he was trying to get to sleep, he'd had this completely corny thought. A memory of that old Christopher Reeve movie. The scene where Superman takes Lois Lane flying for the first time.

"*I wanna write her name in the sky,*" the Petty song continued without mercy.

Jack shook his head, then heard the twenty-minute page just as Riley headed back toward him. She was smiling, despite a hint of pallor.

"That's us?" she asked.

"You and me," he said, reaching for her hand. "Let's go fly." *Blue skies, Blue Eyes.*

- + -

What on earth was she doing? No. Not *on* earth . . . thirteen thousand feet *above* the earth.

Riley had a sudden, horrible realization that this was exactly what all those vile grackle birds were staring at: fools jumping from planes. And now she was one of them.

The laughter and conversation of the other skydivers blended with the roar of the plane engines as Riley clutched the seat in front of her, not sure if the trembling in her legs was from the motion or pure fear. She stared through her goggles at the flimsy Plexiglas covering the open door of the twin-engine plane, watching as a skydiver squatted close by, awaiting her turn. The woman looked confident, excited. A police officer from Hondo, she'd engaged Jack in lively jargon-smattered conversation as the plane climbed to altitude. Easy for her, since she likely still had saliva.

Whoa. The plane tipped for a turn, giving Riley a dizzying view from the windows and making the butterflies in her stomach threaten escape through her lips. She perched forward on the seat that she was sharing awkwardly with her instructor— sitting between the woman's legs—trying not to squash her. Riley concentrated on the view. Blue sky, miles of brown dotted with miniature trees and Lego-size buildings.

"Welcome to my office," Margo said from behind Riley's left ear. "How are you doing?"

"Great," Riley fibbed, resisting the urge to ask if they should retest the snaps holding their bodies together. They'd done it, Riley literally hanging from Margo's chest, before they'd boarded the plane. "You'll tell me when?"

"Yes," Margo assured her, "and we'll sort of wobble toward the door like we're crabs glued together." Her face moved from Riley's shoulder. "Ah, Jack. Have some words for our girl?"

Margo shifted to make room for him to move up beside them. Riley did her best to smile. And Jack . . . looked like he belonged up here. Goggles resting casually atop his leather helmet, zippered gray jumpsuit with the Eagle Skydiving patch, parachute harness . . . those amazing toffee-colored eyes. He smiled back at her and the butterflies in her stomach shifted to accommodate several more.

"Ready to spit in the face of fear?" he asked, raising his voice above the drone of the engine.

"You bet—stay upwind, Doctor."

"Good girl."

The pilot called the altitude, and the Plexiglas door was opened for the policewoman.

"I'll jump immediately after you," Jack said, managing to move closer despite the jostle of the plane. "If you think of it, look for me."

"Okay," she managed, the butterflies merciless. "I'll . . . try."

"You'll do great." Jack held her gaze for a long moment. "I don't have any doubts."

Doubts. Tears stung her eyes without warning. "Thanks."

Somehow—in spite of the cramped situation it afforded poor Margo—Jack managed to lean forward and brush his lips against Riley's forehead. "Blue skies," he whispered before lumbering backward into his seat.

There was a loud whoop and Riley stared, eyes wide, as the policewoman disappeared through the doorway of the plane.

"Now," Margo told her, "hunker down and make your way toward the door."

Oh, please, God . . . Riley's heart wedged into her throat. She started to move, remembering what Bandy had said about God's hands. That they held you, even at times when you doubted they could, and you had to trust—

"Closer to the door, Riley. Right to the edge—right up there."

The wind snatched at her hair. The ground blurred below.

Why am I doing this? Riley's heart pounded in her ears. She thought of the pecan branch . . . her parents . . . the staircase in the hospital garage. A fall of less than fifty feet had broken her neck.

"Cross your arms and grab your harness." Margo placed a palm on Riley's forehead, pulled her head backward to cradle it against her shoulder. Margo leaned forward, and Riley's backside lost contact with the doorway. "Here we go!"

Oh, God, help . . . Riley braced herself for a fall . . . that didn't happen.

Instead there was an incredible sense of simply merging with the air. An outward, lifting stretch and forward momentum, as if riding a wave. Like a feather in an updraft—or those childish dreams of flying. But with ear-buffeting noise: rushing air and crisp flapping of jumpsuit fabric. Riley responded to Margo's prompt to spread her arms wide. And at once her palms crested the air currents like a kid's from the window of a car on the interstate. Cold wind whipped her hair, jiggled her cheeks, puffed her nostrils . . . chilled her teeth. She giggled and shouted against the wind, teeth going numb. "I'm . . . doing this! I'm—" She turned her head, looking as Margo tapped her shoulder again and pointed.

A flash of gray, big and spread out like an eagle riding a thermal. A hand, a thumbs-up—the windswept but familiar grin. *Jack!*

Riley grinned back, felt air floss her teeth. "Look, I'm—"

Margo tapped again, grabbed Riley's forehead, and deployed the parachute.

Oh! There was an abrupt upward yank, the harness grabbing

at Riley's hips and shoulders, legs dancing like a marionette's . . . and then complete, pristine silence. She glanced down at an impossible view: her shoes dangling free, silhouetted against a patchwork panorama of Texas countryside. Ribbons of highway, minuscule buildings and vehicles . . . *God's view.*

Margo loosened the harness for comfort—causing Riley a split second of panic—then pulled expertly on the strings, making the canopy swirl as they changed direction. Riley relaxed, awed by the graceful silence and an unparalleled sense of peace. She floated downward like dandelion fluff set free by a child's wish.

If only my life could compare . . .

- + -

Jack gathered up the last billowing yards of his black parachute while keeping one eye on the sky. He'd maneuvered his canopy to land before Riley. And . . . *She's there. She's fine.*

He shook his head, still confused by the unexpected rush of feelings that had started while he was in the plane. He'd started out as stoked as ever, joking with the other divers, eager to free-fall and excited to be sharing the experience with Riley. It was the ultimate high: thin, fuel-scented air, the roar of engines, the secure bulk of his parachute, a chilling rush of air through the exit door—and a beautiful woman to share it with. *Incredibly beautiful.* If possible, Riley was even more attractive at thirteen thousand feet—in that jumpsuit, with her breathing quickened, cheeks flushed, and long strands of hair coming loose. Truthfully, if she hadn't been harnessed to Margo, Jack would have had a tough time keeping his hands off her.

It had been his Superman fantasy made real—until the fear

in Riley's eyes hit him like a bucket of cold water. Then suddenly Jack was remembering that she'd spent a full year recovering from bone-shattering trauma and was still struggling to reclaim her life. He started to worry. What if she had a bad landing, reinjured her neck . . . or worse? Her parents had already lost a child. With a wave of guilt, he'd reminded himself that Riley wouldn't be in the plane if it weren't for him.

He'd found himself questioning Margo's expertise, the integrity of the equipment, the sobriety of the pilot, the accuracy of the blasted wind sock. And in a stomach-churning instant, he remembered Abby's funeral. If he hadn't known that Riley was probably praying, he'd have been tempted to try it himself.

But instead, Jack had kissed her, whispered, "Blue skies" instead of "Don't do it." And he still had no clue why he'd felt all of that.

Jack turned his head, spotted them on final approach, and exhaled in an audible rush. Margo's feet touched ground, then Riley's. They were down, safe and sound.

In mere minutes he was beside her, watching as she chattered to Margo in the breathless superlatives typical of first timers. She pulled off her goggles, fussed to control her wind-scrambled hair.

"Jack!" she said, noticing him finally. "I—oh, I'm dizzy." She took a step and staggered sideways. "But I did it. You saw. I did it and I'm still alive, and . . ." She smiled, tears welling in her eyes. And then began to tremble—chin, shoulders . . . all of her. "I d-don't know why I'm crying. This is . . . so crazy."

"Here." Jack slipped an arm around her, "Let's get away from the landing area. Over there." He guided her toward the shady side of the hangar, the swishing of their flight suits filling the void in conversation. They stopped, and before he knew it, he was holding her. Tightly. *Safe, where you're supposed to be.*

It finally struck him—the reason for his jumble of feelings on the plane. It was that he couldn't risk losing her. Talk about free-falling . . . *What am I doing?*

25
+

"I'M SORRY." Riley pulled back to look up at Jack. Traces of goggle lines etched her forehead. *Skydiving marks and surgical scars.*

She struggled against another wave of trembling, managed a short laugh instead. "I'm an idiot for crying. And so embarrassed—I don't know what got into me."

"Altitude. Thin air," Jack said, trying to ease her discomfort. He brushed wind-wild hair away from her face. "And First-Timer Syndrome," he added with feigned seriousness. "Giggling, shaking, dizziness. Miserable hives . . . and relentless retching."

"Hives? Retching?" Riley eyed him warily.

"And a sudden infatuation with your tandem instructor." Jack smiled, enjoying her expression. "Which is why I suggested Margo. Even with her really bad safety record, and—"

Riley punched at him.

He captured her hand, laughing. "C'mon," he said, leading her toward a picnic table a short distance away. "Let's sit down a minute."

They sat side by side on the bench, quiet for a stretch of time. The endless loop of "Free Fallin'" in the distance blended with excited chatter of passersby, several of them with arms full of parachute. Riley's gaze swept skyward, and Jack saw the almost-imperceptible shake of her head. As if she still couldn't believe what had happened. He knew the feeling. Even after more than thirty jumps, today was different. And whether he liked it or not—even if it felt riskier than a failed chute—Jack had to talk with Riley about it. Had to know . . .

He cleared his throat. "When I took my first jump in New Mexico, it required an hour or so of ground school. A video, the waivers. All that. They asked the first timers, 'Why do you want to skydive?'" He frowned. "At the time, I thought it was a stupid question. A no-brainer. I was doing it because I wanted to. Period. That's who I am. But other people started giving reasons. A woman who'd been divorced wanted to prove she could make it on her own; a guy said he was going to start chemotherapy the next week; two people insisted it was on their 'bucket list.' And this elderly woman who'd been a card-carrying Audubon member for fifty years explained that she needed to know what it felt like to be a bird."

Jack met Riley's gaze. "When you left that message last night, you sounded upset, like you were crying."

"I . . ." Discomfort flickered across her face. "Tough day."

When she didn't say more, Jack made himself go on. "Like

I said, for me it's always a matter of taking the risk, thinking about it later—maybe. But you don't operate that way, Riley." He smiled. "You're like the safety officer of life, and—" He stopped, not expecting her frown.

"Is that how you see me?" Her chin lifted in that way he knew too well. "Like an overprotected hothouse flower? Or some gutless—?"

"Whoa, whoa—hey." Jack groaned, remembering what Rob had said about his lack of tact. "Wait. I guess what I'm asking is, did I coerce you into doing something you didn't want to do?" He hurried on, insisting she hear him. "I wouldn't want to do that. That's all I'm saying. In my inept way." *Because I care. More than I want to.*

"No. It wasn't anything you did." Riley took a deep breath, exhaled. "Yesterday I heard that I'm not going to be considered for a triage position at Alamo Grace. After all my planning and all that focus, it's not going to happen. Joanna confirmed it this morning."

"She got my letter?"

"Yes. And in the end, it doesn't help. Because I was proposing a position that doesn't exist. There is no full-time triage nurse. Only staff nurses who triage." Riley shook her head. "I knew that."

Jack knew where this was going. Maybe he'd always known.

"They can only hire for an ER staff nurse position. I'll have to make a formal application. And show competency in all areas: be precepted in manikin practice, IV therapy . . ." Riley glanced down at her hands. "And first, they want medical documentation from my neurosurgeons that I'm physically capable of all that it entails. I'm expecting it any day now . . ." She looked back up at him, tears gathering again. "They asked . . . Kate's opinion."

Oh no . . .

"She told Joanna she wasn't comfortable with the idea of me on her team."

"Ah, Riley . . ." Jack reached for her hand.

"No," she said, sliding it away. Riley blinked stubbornly against the tears. "I don't want you to feel sorry for me, Jack. I'm not really surprised by what's happened. And I am going to keep at it. I'm not giving up. Mostly, I'm just plain mad. Not at Kate, even though that hurt. I'm more ticked off that after an entire year, I haven't made the progress I expected. I've been fighting and trying—using everything I have—to prove I'm not overprotected and gutless. And incompetent and broken." Her voice cracked.

"And that's why you jumped," Jack whispered, understanding that kind of anger better than anyone.

"Yes. Not because I wanted to feel like a bird; I don't like them that much." Her half smile was comically sad.

"Hey . . ." He reached for her hand again and this time she didn't object. "There's something I didn't tell you about skydiving."

"Besides the rash, gagging, and the way I'm going to feel about Margo?"

Jack laughed. "Besides that. You have to celebrate your first time. Beyond the certificate and that little pin they'll give you." He brushed his thumb across the back of her hand. "Whatever the reason you jumped, you have to go out and celebrate. With me."

Her fingers curled inside his. "What do you have in mind?"

"Dinner. Then somewhere for live music." He wondered if she could feel how much he wanted this. "And after that, to this great place I know for watching the sun go down."

"'Blue skies' . . . then a sunset?"

"Required—it was in the fine print."

- + -

It was no use. Vesta set the binoculars down. A painted bunting would look the same as a house sparrow with her vision so blurry. And it wouldn't clear up until her blood sugar stayed under 300. It had done that only once in the past twenty-four hours. She glanced up at the photo of her colonel, knowing that if he were alive, she'd have been marched to the doctor at the first inkling of illness. No excuses. He'd remind her that health was a gift and that they had to be good stewards, even if it meant sugar tests three times a day, insulin injections, and homely but foot-friendly shoes. He'd promise there were mountains yet to climb, rivers to raft, foreign starlight to dance by.

And now the mailbox seems as far as Africa. Vesta glanced away in shame and reached for her reading glasses. She'd give the antibiotics another forty-eight hours, and if things didn't improve . . . what? Her landlady was in Colorado for a week. If Vesta even managed to work up the courage—or desperation—to venture out for help, she'd have to call a cab. Or . . . walk down to the clinic?

She glanced toward the open laptop beside her and reread the e-mail reminder from the action committee about Saturday's emergency meeting at the library. And a reference to yesterday's

Dumpster fire at the dress shop. She'd heard the sirens. The *Express-News* printed a short article, saying that the police attributed the fire to a stunt by local juveniles and doubted it could be linked to the far more damaging fires in New Braunfels. But that all the fires were still under investigation.

Vesta shivered, not sure if it was caused by the continuing fever or because there had been another arson. One block away. She shed her glasses and reached for the binoculars again, struck by the irony that she was beginning to feel suffocated by the safe confines of her home. She'd come to depend on that stingy glimpse of the outside world more than she'd realized. And now it was disappearing. If she couldn't see the street, there would be no hope of spotting Bandy Biggs and the sweet little dog that so reminded her of Corky. No way to see fire trucks. *No warning if that man is out there.*

Vesta's hands trembled with another chill, making the rubber eyepiece bump against her cheekbone. She wished she hadn't canceled Riley's visit. There was something about the young chaplain that made her feel connected and . . . hopeful. Not much else did these days.

- + -

"I can't . . . believe . . . I'm in Luckenbach!" Riley shouted over the sharp twang of steel guitar and a cattle drive of boots against the historic dance floor. "Doing the electric slide and— oh, brother, wrong way. Again. Sorry. I'm so rusty." She whirled back around, faked the grapevine step to catch up, and saw Jack grinning beside her as the classic Brooks and Dunn tune swelled.

"Oh, get down, turn around, go to town. Boot scootin' boogie . . ."

"Good thing there was only one way out of that plane!" he shouted back, the light from drooping swags of bulbs bouncing off his hair and the shoulders of his worn-soft black henley. He grinned, rocking forward along with the whooping crowd. Then pointed in the direction of the next turn, nodding as she hitched the step and followed the line of the dance. "You nailed it that time." Jack's gaze swept discreetly over her. "But in those boots . . . with that skirt . . . I'd probably follow you into oncoming traffic."

"Yeah, heel, toe, do-si-do. C'mon, baby, let's go . . ."

Riley was glad she could blame her blush on the overly warm dance floor. And that she'd decided against the German knockwurst at the Fredericksburg restaurant. The butterflies she thought she'd left at the drop zone were threatening to polka in her stomach. She'd had no idea that Jack was taking her to his hometown or even that he'd grown up in the beautiful Texas hill country. They'd walked the quaint streets of Fredericksburg, Jack ruggedly handsome in faded Levi's and boots, pointing out the Pacific War museum and the *biergarten* where he'd waited tables, talking about Wildseed Farms and Enchanted Rock. Seeing him like that, learning where he'd come from, had felt so—

"C'mon." Jack slid an arm around her waist. "Let's get out of here."

He guided her through the dancers, out of the huge open-air dance hall and back toward the outdoor theater, a ramshackle stage embellished with hundreds of license plates under gigantic spreading oaks that gave roost to chickens. There was another boisterous crowd out there, every age and all attire, from biker leather and bandannas to designer linen. Hands hoisted old-fashioned sarsaparilla bottles and longneck beers, and laughter was the common language—along with music. This time it was an aging, bearded guitar picker wearing an "Everybody's Somebody in Luckenbach" T-shirt and Willie Nelson braids.

Riley shook her head. "I think we'll have to stand," she said, her voice already hoarse. "There's no room."

"Not staying." Jack tugged her hand and pointed toward the famous wooden post office and a chrome and leather sea of Harleys. "Back to the car. Sunset time."

Blue skies and a sunset . . . Riley climbed into the Hummer.

In twenty minutes they'd navigated miles of hilly roads past huge private ranches with lush native grasses, herds of spotted axis deer, and the occasional exotic, twisted-horn blackbuck antelope. Then they turned onto a dirt road, climbing steeper still, through pink granite boulders, stands of cedar and live oaks. Tires crunching, the Hummer finally came to a stop at a huge gate. Locked with a chain.

Riley glanced sideways as Jack cut the engine. "I'm adding trespassing to my adventure day?"

He smiled. "My uncle's property. Grab that ring of keys in the glove compartment."

Jack opened the gate, snagged a camping blanket, and they left the car behind and walked. Up a deer-narrow trail that climbed toward the crest of the hill—crushed pink granite, clumps of wildflowers and prickly pear cactus, hemmed by wispy knee-high prairie grass. Not so steep that Riley couldn't manage it in boots and a skirt, but enough of a hike that her heart quickened. Until they reached the top, and then the view took her breath away.

26

+

"IT'S . . . INCREDIBLE," Riley murmured, senses swirling. "Those hilltops and the bluebonnets down below—they're like a lake of flowers. And all those fruit trees. Acres and acres. What are they?"

"Peaches." Jack stepped closer, pointing to the tidy rows. "Red Globe, Regal, Bounty."

"They're my favorite fruit." Riley slid her fingers down a tendril of her hair. "Even my shampoo is peach."

"No kidding?" Jack looked like he was trying not to laugh. He pointed along the horizon. "There was this annual event called Easter Fires, where people started fires in barrels and set them up on the hills. It started from an old German tradition that got tangled up in local history involving a treaty with the Comanche Indians. Apparently some Indian signal fires scared the kids. So the Fredericksburg settlers explained that the Easter Bunny used the fires to boil water for coloring eggs." He chuckled at the look on her face. "Trust me. Until a few years back there was a pageant. People dressed up in bunny suits. Whole families for generations."

"Did you . . . ?"

"I plead the Fifth."

Riley laughed, glanced back down. "I don't see a house. Your uncle doesn't live here?"

"No. He's in New Mexico. Leases the orchards out, comes back to hunt."

"And your mother?"

"Moved to Santa Fe two years ago to help my sister with her kids. She sold the house after my father died." Sadness flickered across his face. "I'd come and gone for years—backpacking across Europe, in the Army, school—so there wasn't much sense in Mom staying. At that point, it was only a matter of ending her condo lease." He shook his head. "And conning me into taking the Siamese fighting fish."

Riley smiled. "Rocky."

"Yes."

"Do you miss having your family close?"

"I . . ." Jack hesitated, his brows pinching together. "I go there a couple of times a year. To ski and for a conference. I call; we text. You know."

Riley didn't know. Couldn't fathom it at all. It had only been two weeks since her last visit to Houston, and despite her mother's drop-in visit, her folks were well past pout stage about "never seeing her." She'd call them tonight. With no mention of the failed job proposal, skydiving . . . or that she'd been seeing Jack outside of work.

"Well . . ." He slid the blanket from under his arm. "Sun's sinking fast now. Let's find a spot without cactus and fire ants and get set for the show."

Riley helped to spread the blanket and sat, not surprised that Jack settled close beside her. After the plane, the dancing, and sharing so much over the past couple of weeks, it felt natural. Visiting his hometown and this beautiful place made her want to know even more about him. Despite Jack's reckless reputation—which he managed to bolster at every opportunity—Riley sensed some vulnerability when it came to his family. *We have that much in common.*

"There," he said, pointing toward the west. "First streaks of pink. The peach blossoms are that same color. In March, sunsets are pink from sky to tree . . . to the shower of petals on the ground below. My aunt called it Ballerina Valley—not the best tactic to recruit a boy for orchard labor."

"You worked here?" she asked, easily imagining him as a boy, sun-browned, scurrying up a ladder. "Picking peaches?"

"Picked them, ate them, pitched them. And squashed the mushy ones on my sister's head." Jack touched a fingertip to Riley's hair, a smile teasing his lips. "I invented peach shampoo."

She smiled, watching the pink horizon changing moment to moment, its wispy purple clouds now burnished with orange and gold. Travis property, pieces of Jack's past.

"Why New Mexico?" she asked, turning to look at him. "Why did your family go there? Work?"

"Partly." Jack pulled up his knees, leaned forward. "Roots,

too. My great-grandmother is from there. Via Mexico. Maria Alma Flores . . . Travis."

"Ah." *You have her eyes.* She took a slow breath, noticing how the color of the sky highlighted the gold in his hair. Blond hair, dark eyes.

"Plenty of stories regarding that page of family history, trust me." Jack shook his head. "It wasn't easy for her. Foreign country. Prejudice." A muscle bunched along his jaw. "People can be so cruel."

"Yes." It made sense—Jack's generosity toward Bandy and his passionate defense of Gilbert DeSoto, Jane Doe, Hector; the whole idea of the free clinic . . . *Your grandmother's eyes and her cause, too. It's personal for you.*

"I was thinking," Jack said, shifting beside her, "about those competencies you need for that staff nurse application. What if you give me a list and we work on them at the clinic? One by one, in a targeted strategy. Gretchen could help, and—" He stopped, brows furrowing. "What's wrong?"

"Nothing," Riley said, her heart cramping at his generosity. *And now you're fighting for me.* "It's just that . . . Thank you, Jack." She touched his arm. "For wanting to help and for wishing me blue skies in that plane. For dinner and Luckenbach . . ." Riley took a slow breath, watching the ember-orange horizon. "And for my first hill country sunset. I don't know how you do it, but somehow you seem to understand exactly what I need, and—"

"Wait." Jack leaned forward, sought her gaze. "Don't give me so much credit. The truth is, you can add *selfish* to everyone's long list of complaints about me." His eyes held hers for a long moment. "Today wasn't just about helping you. It has a lot more to do with what *I* need. Which, I've recently figured out, is . . . to be with you."

"Oh." Riley's breath caught as Jack brushed the back of his hand gently across her cheek. Her heart stalled. "I . . ." *Can't think. Or breathe or . . .*

There was a stretch of silence made deafening by the drumming of her heart.

"Mmm . . ." Doubt flooded into Jack's eyes. "I'm scaring you." He drew his fingers away. "I'm sorry. I shouldn't—"

"No," she said in a rush. "I'm not scared." Slow breath. *Talking skills—I'm supposed to have them.*

"Are you sure? For a second there, you looked like I was pushing you out the door of a plane."

She smiled, foolishly dizzy. *He needs me?* "You surprised me, that's all."

Jack looked wary. "Surprised like a scorpion in your shoe?"

"No." She took hold of his hand, warmth spreading.

His head tilted. "Nervous because I was raised by wolves?"

Riley laughed. "I'm taking that back. Now that I've seen your hometown. And your sunset." She leaned a little closer, watching Jack's eyes in the deepening dusk. "You did surprise me with what you said . . . about needing to be with me. Only because I'd been thinking the same thing about you." His immediate smile made her pulse quicken. "And I don't think you're selfish, Jack. Far from it." She reached up, rested her palm along his jaw. "You're generous and caring. You have this incredible courage of conviction. And honesty . . ."

Jack grimaced slightly, and Riley suspected she was making

him uncomfortable. It was the last thing she wanted. She brushed her thumb along the stubble of his jaw and chuckled. "For a reckless maverick, that is."

- + -

The rosy light had turned Riley's eyes from blue to smoky lavender, and Jack was feeling more and more like a nervous adolescent. But something about this—about her—seemed more important than anything had in a long time. He had to handle it right.

"No," she said, shaking her head, "you're not a maverick. And I'm not a hothouse flower. Today it's far less complicated, simple. I'm a first-time skydiver, and you are . . ." She smiled. "The inventor of my shampoo. Thank you, by the way." She leaned forward, brushed her lips against his cheek.

He slipped his arms around her before she could move away and then hugged her close, burying his face against the soft, fragrant tumble of her hair. Her arms twined around his back. It felt so different from that time at the River Walk, when their embrace sprang from pain and comfort. And much better now . . . *because I care for you more than I ever thought was possible.*

"Riley . . ." Jack nuzzled her neck, felt her pulse against his lips. He breathed in the dizzying scent of her, reluctant to let go, then leaned away far enough to search her eyes in the shadowy light. The sweet vulnerability in her expression made his heart ache. *Sweet, beautiful, brave.* Jack cradled her face in his hands, then dipped his head to lightly kiss her brow, cheek, the soft corner of her lips . . . before covering her mouth with his own.

27
+

RILEY PADDED BAREFOOT from her bathroom to the kitchen, shower-damp hair brushing across the shoulders of the hooded terry tunic she'd pulled on over leggings. A quick breakfast—coffee, bagel; did she have any cream cheese?—then she'd change into a skirt and blouse, pick up her linen blazer at the cleaners, and head to the hospital.

She glanced at the clock—7 a.m. Way too early. So . . . she'd slow down, dawdle over the coffee and poach some eggs, then return her mother's call. Maybe do that on the cell phone . . . while she walked the bike trail? Good idea. Or see if Wilma wanted to walk along with her, then . . .

Oh, brother! Riley leaned back against the granite counter, laughing out loud. Where was her brain? She'd been far less indecisive perched in the doorway of that skydiving plane. *With Jack.*

Aaah . . . Her stomach did another in a series of dips—the most ridiculous having occurred when she took the cap off her bottle of peach shampoo. Now that was certifiably crazy. And dangerous. She laughed again, imagining how she'd explain her swoon and subsequent near drowning to the paramedics. She needed to get a grip. Coffee would help.

She poured herself a steaming cup, took it back into the living room, and sank onto the leather couch. It was cool—too much so—from the overnight air-conditioning. She set the coffee down while she spread out a knit throw . . . which made her remember the blanket on the hill overlooking the peach orchard. And the sunset. *With Jack.*

She grabbed her coffee and took a gulp, hoping the milk-laced brew would calm the new giddiness. Returning doubts did a better job. *Can I trust this?*

The same whispering doubts had kept her awake long after Jack walked her to the door and gathered her close for one last, lingering kiss. Riley held the cup to her cheek, adding even more warmth to the memory. She'd hoped that sleep would smooth out the confusing tumble of emotions—giddiness, uncertainty . . . fear? But she suspected that her feelings came from more than yesterday's heart-skipping moments. The past two weeks had been a roller coaster of hope and despair for herself and for so many around her. Stacy, her family, the baby, the staff at Alamo Grace . . . her attack outside the clinic, the bad news about the job proposal. How much of that colored what she was feeling for Jack? It was more than a possibility.

If Riley were counseling traumatic stress victims, she'd dispense the experts' advice: delay any serious decisions until your life becomes more normal. Don't change jobs, move, enter into contracts, make decisions about key relationships . . . or fall in love?

Riley clutched her coffee cup as her stomach swan dived again. Was Jack someone she could love? And could she even recognize love when her life was still so far from normal?

She lifted her right palm away from the cup and flexed her fingers, testing the faint tingle that had been a source of hope. For her career. And maybe even her faith. *If* God healed her, *if* she could get back to the ER, *if* the nightmares ended, then she'd feel like herself again and all doubts would go away. Everything hinged on that fragile hope.

She flexed her fingers again and glanced toward her Bible on the coffee table. *You know how much I need this. Please . . .*

Her cell phone buzzed, trembled on the surface of the table—a text message. Riley reached for it, thoughts leaping to scenarios at Alamo Grace: Stacy Paulson, the baby . . .

Her pulse quickened, oblivious of her heart's doubt—it was from Jack.

Check your porch.

Her porch?

Riley stood, battling suspense, and padded to the door—wishing, for the first time ever, that she didn't have so many stupid locks. Slider, chain, dead bolt . . . she forced her numb fingers to deal with them while her pulse did a two-step worthy of the Luckenbach dance floor. She reached for the knob at last, took a breath, opened the door . . . and jumped, covering her ears as the security alarm began wailing without mercy.

Eeep, eeep, eeeeeeep. Brinnnnnng. Whoop! Screee . . .

"Aagh!" Riley slammed the door and whirled to the keypad, punching the code as quickly as her fingers would comply. *Unbelievable.* She leaned back against the wall, hands over her mouth, torn between a laugh and a groan. Heat flooded her face. Never once in the year since her attack had she forgotten to arm—or disarm—the security system. It had seemed a veritable lifeline. And now one little text had changed things. . . .

She double-checked the alarm status. *Green light: go.* She opened the door and saw the bakery box on the mat. Tied with string, pink as a hill country sunset. It was topped with a fistful of just-picked Texas bluebonnets. Her breath caught.

"Everything okay, Riley?" Wilma asked, holding a newspaper against her robe. The neighbor's kind concern floated over the silvery sage bushes dividing their driveways.

"Yes—I'm so sorry about that." Riley picked up the box and glanced quickly toward the street, half-expecting to see . . . "I was hurrying to get this bakery . . . delivery."

"Ah." Wilma nodded graciously, respecting Riley's privacy as always. Her lips tugged toward a smile that hinted she understood a bit more. "Good, then."

Riley waved and carried the box inside, the scent of just-baked pastry stirring her senses. She set the bluebonnets on the coffee table, slid the strings aside, lifted the lid . . . and warmth flooded through her. Peach cobbler. *How on earth did he . . . ?*

Riley's phone danced on the table again.

You forgot something on the porch.

She didn't know how she got back to the door, walking or floating. Only that when she opened it, Jack was there.

- + -

"So all things considered," Jack teased, standing in the foyer with Riley in his arms, "it's a good thing I decided against wearing the Easter Fire bunny suit." He chuckled against her damp hair. "Your alarm would have blown my ears off."

Riley's shoulders trembled with laughter, and Jack tightened his arms, enjoying her blushing mirth. He glanced discreetly at her collection of locks. *You're safe with me. I promise you that.*

"C'mon," she said finally, leading him toward the living room. "After that embarrassing welcome, the least I can do is offer you coffee."

Riley insisted she didn't need help, so Jack waited on the couch while she poured the coffee and gathered plates for the cobbler. It was comfortable here. The couch, the colors Riley chose, and the way the morning light filtered through those honeycomb window shades. Upbeat music—contemporary Christian, Jack guessed—spilled softly from speakers near the mantel. He noticed, once again, the Hale family photos displayed there. Today felt very different from the last time he'd been here . . . except that he was thinking about kissing her then too. At least this time his odds for success had improved considerably.

Jack relaxed, reassuring himself that despite her exasperation with the alarm, Riley seemed glad to see him. He was relieved that his instincts had been correct, because for the first time ever, he was hesitant to trust them. As he'd explained to Riley about skydiving—all his sports, all his endeavors, really—Jack's tendency was to leap in, ask questions later. But now, with her, Jack sensed he should proceed with caution. Be careful. Take it slow. But what did that look like in practice? He shook his head. The Army trusted Jack to carry out a trauma plan in the chaos of combat, yet he was having trouble formulating a plan to handle a new relationship. Why was that? His gaze moved to the Bible sitting next to the bakery box. Maybe because he wasn't sure if he was prepared for—

"Here we are," Riley said, arriving with a tray. "All set. I'm sorry it took so long. I had a message from the chaplain's office." Sadness flickered across her face. "The Collins family requested last rites for Stacy."

Jack winced, remembering the girl on his clinic porch. "Do you need to leave?"

"No." Riley sat down beside him. "The priest was already there. And our social worker is standing by. They were reminding me that I'm on call for the weekend. In case . . ."

He nodded. In case the brutalized girl died . . . *like Abby.*

"And if that happens, I'll go in. Be there for them." Riley exhaled softly and then reached for the serving spoon.

Jack raised his plate, watching as the morning sunlight slanted through the windows and played over her freshly washed hair. *Beautiful woman with an amazing heart.* Riley would be there for the Collins family; Jack had no doubt of that. He admired her more than he could say. But right now he was selfishly grateful that she was here with him. They'd be working opposite shifts today, which meant he probably wouldn't see Riley until tomorrow, Saturday. Jack wasn't going to waste a moment of the time they had right now. Or do anything to spoil it.

- + -

Collins . . . Stacy Paulson's mother? Kate winced, wishing she'd checked the name of the patient sooner. She would have traded places with the staff nurse stanching that stubborn nosebleed. This was too painful.

She took a breath and walked in.

"Mrs. Collins, I'm Kate," she said, glad to see the woman already had a box of tissues. And her husband.

"I'm . . . sorry," Lorna Collins's voice choked. Her gray eyes, red-rimmed and smudged with mascara, met Kate's. "I'm usually so much stronger than this."

"Our daughter's a patient here," her husband explained, his expression no less shell-shocked and grim. "We had the priest give her last rites . . ." He paused and his wife clasped his hand.

"The doctors say that Stacy probably won't live through the weekend," Lorna continued. Her fingers moved to a small gold cross lying against her blouse. "She was beaten so badly. Brain damage. We've been searching for her for two years. Ever since she . . ."

Ran away. Like I did.

"I'm so sorry." Kate glanced up at the woman's husband, trying not to think of her own father. "I was here when Stacy was brought in."

"Then you know that there's a baby," Mr. Collins said.

Kate's knees went weak. "Yes."

"She's having problems too. We've been running back and forth between intensive care and newborn intensive care. The doctors thought that if Lorna could get a sedative to help her sleep tonight . . . There will be decisions to make and arrangements. You can't imagine how hard this has been."

I don't want to . . . but I can.

"I'll . . ." Kate cleared her throat. "I'll let our doctor know."

"Thank you so much, Nurse."

Kate stepped out into the corridor, willing herself to stop trembling. To push aside the sick, sad feeling. She took a deep breath, squeezed her eyes shut for a moment. She was leaving early today because one of the other charge nurses wanted some extra hours. And tomorrow started Kate's weekend off. She very likely wouldn't be here when the Collinses' runaway daughter died and they were forced to choose a future for the baby they never knew she was carrying.

Kate sighed. The last couple of weeks had been filled with misery, not the least of which was the painful new conflict with Riley, the first real friend she'd made here. Kate had no idea how that would resolve. An ache rose in her throat. She was no stranger to loneliness—she'd handle it, either way. But tomorrow night she had a date with Griff Payton. Dinner and then the Majestic Theatre to see *Wicked*.

Right now there was no better prescription for what ailed her. A handsome and charming man, the opportunity to break out the little black dress and the eBay designer pumps she hadn't worn since leaving California. Maybe she'd end up in Griff's arms by the end of the evening. Kate's face warmed at the thought.

She needed that connection. And its validation that—despite her obvious flaws—she was still someone special. Even if it was only a warm good-night hug. Everyone deserved at least that much.

- + -

If Riley could stop time, she'd do it in a heartbeat. Nothing had ever felt so safe, so wonderful, as being cradled in Jack's arms. Except maybe . . . She smiled as his lips brushed her temple.

"I don't want to let you go," he whispered, shifting his position on the couch. He laughed, his breath puffing against her hair. "But my arm's falling asleep. No, wait. Don't," he groaned as she moved away, his handsome features morphing toward a boyish pout. "Unfair."

She waggled her fingers. "One numb arm's more than enough." Riley's heart tugged as Jack grasped her hand and then gently folded her fingers back to press a kiss against her palm.

"You're working in Kerrville today?" she asked.

"Yes." After kissing her fingertips, he sighed and reached for his coffee. "Not till three, but I need to go over some things for the next board meeting." He caught the confusion on her face. "The clinic's monthly board meeting—lately I'm more of a firefighter than a director. Putting out the hostile bombs the action committee keeps hurling at me." A muscle twitched along his jaw. "They're holding an emergency meeting at the library tomorrow."

"And the council meets next week. To hear the neighbors' . . . concerns."

"Complaints. About me. Never mind that they trusted me to patch up Hector Silva when he fell twenty feet from one of those hallowed roofs." Jack's expression darkened ominously.

"When they couldn't be bothered to call for an ambulance despite the fact that he could've died before their eyes. I wonder how that gritty revelation would taste with the fancy finger food they'll be serving in the library."

"You're not . . ." Riley's breath stuck in her throat. "You're not planning to confront them?" Her stomach tensed at the look on his face. Anger, aggression . . . *worse.* "That would just fuel them more. Wouldn't it be better to wait until the council meeting and—?"

"What? Ask Bandy to pass peanut butter sandwiches around? Or bring those clown noses and do a happy little skit about saving lives?" His mouth twisted into a bitter smile. "Yeah, maybe I'll let them shoot Nerf balls at me, get it out of their systems. Then we'll all hold hands and sing 'Kumbaya'—you can loan Andrea Nichols your Fiesta wreath."

"Jack . . ." Riley set her cup down before he could notice that her hands were beginning to tremble. "Please."

"What?" he asked, his hand clenching atop his thigh. "Accept it? Let them put a stop to everything I've been doing to help people who have nowhere else to turn?" His voice lowered to a near growl. "I can't, Riley. I won't let them do this to me."

"Please . . ." *Oh, God, please . . .* Riley squeezed her eyes shut against the image of Jack's hands around the throat of the boy who snatched her purse. "Don't."

- + -

What had he done? She was shaking. "Riley?"

"I'm sorry," she said, finally meeting his gaze. "When you get angry like that, it . . . worries me."

Scares you. Her beautiful eyes were dilated with fear. Jack's chest constricted—he'd sworn to himself that he'd be careful.

"Here," he said gently, taking hold of her hand. "I'm the one who's sorry. I shouldn't dump this on you." *Please don't look at me like that.*

Riley exhaled. "It's just that I know that isn't who you are. This hostility and bitterness—it's not *you*, Jack."

What if it is? What if that's all I am?

She managed a smile. "I know you now. You're kind and caring and so generous. Every good thing you do comes straight from your heart."

Riley . . . Jack tried to swallow past the sudden ache in his throat. He wanted what she was saying to be true—he'd never wanted anything more.

Riley rested her hand along his jaw. "I'm going to come to the city council meeting. Tell them all the good things that you're doing at the clinic—and how much I believe in you." Her thumb brushed his skin. "I do, Jack. I believe in you."

"I . . ." He swallowed, not trusting himself to speak. Breathing was hard enough. After all his plans to persuade Riley to help him, she was freely offering this?

"So," she continued, tipping forward to plant a kiss against his cheek, "it's settled. Bandy, Hobo, and I will be Alamo heroes to your Commander Travis." Riley smiled at him.

"Okay." Jack brushed his thumb across her lips. "Except the Alamo didn't finish so well, if you recall."

"We'll rewrite history—think you can handle that?"

"Yes." Warmth flooded through him. *With you . . .*

He cradled her face in his hands and kissed her lightly, then chuckled.

"What's so funny?"

"First your shampoo and now . . . you taste like peaches too."

"Oh, please. You are *not* going to say—"

"Yes, ma'am." He drew Riley close again. "Peach lipstick. My finest work by far."

She tried to laugh, but Jack barely gave her time to breathe before his lips found hers again.

28

WAS IT SATURDAY? Vesta stopped in the hallway and tried to think. Her brain was becoming as blurry as her eyes. Yes, Saturday. Friday she'd found the business card wedged under her door: *Eric Erikson, Private Investigator.* There was a penciled scrawl on the back of the card, almost illegible even with her reading glasses: *Would like to speak with you at your convenience.*

It wasn't convenient. And it wouldn't happen—Vesta couldn't talk about Jack Travis. To anyone but God. And she was fairly certain he didn't want to hear her cowardly excuses anymore. Guilt swirled, compounding her dizziness. She put her palm against the wall to steady herself, then moved on toward the living room.

Saturday. The action committee would hold that meeting

in the library in a few hours. She'd been surprised—awakened, truthfully—by a reminder phone call this morning. A woman too new to the neighborhood to know that Vesta never went out. She'd told Vesta that the committee was hosting a police sergeant, that there would be catered food, and that the topics of discussion were "vital matters of personal safety and well-being." Vesta smiled grimly. The caller had no idea that Vesta had long ago taken those matters into her own hands. With a securely locked door and an aluminum baseball bat. But it was hard to find that comforting when she could no longer see much beyond the closest bird feeder in the yard. *Can't see if he's out there . . .*

Riley Hale would be calling today to check on her. The chaplain cared; it was obvious in everything she did. That fact had become more comforting to Vesta than the locks on her door. Riley would ask how Vesta was feeling and she'd get the truth: no more chills, no more backache, less of a headache . . . just so very weak. She'd slept most of the day away already. And even now felt too tired to eat or measure her sugar. When had she done that last? Vesta wasn't sure. But she'd taken her insulin . . . she thought. She'd check her log. After she slept a little more.

Vesta turned and headed to the bedroom. She'd refill the water pitcher in the bathroom—*so thirsty*—and crawl back into bed. Just for a little while. Until Riley called. She'd watch TV while she waited. It was close enough to the bed that she could see it fairly well. The woman from the committee said they'd hoped to get some news coverage of the meeting.

What they were trying to do to Dr. Travis wasn't right, but there was nothing Vesta could do about it now.

- + -

"Fever?" Bandy asked, leaning against the doorway to Jack's office. He adjusted the brim of his SeaWorld ball cap. "From the way you've been acting today, I figure you're runnin' a mighty high one. Or—" he smiled, the edges of his eyes crinkling— "it might have something to do with an especially enjoyable day off." His gaze did a quick dart toward the ceiling as if he'd made some divine arrangement for that.

"Nope. No fever," Jack pronounced, feigning cluelessness— and trying to decide just how long to torture his friend. He'd already dodged Bandy's hinting questions when he called yesterday to check on the clinic. He leaned back in his chair. "Went skydiving . . ." Jack dragged it out, toying with the man's infinite patience. Hobo barked. Jack shrugged and then slowly smiled. "With Riley."

"No." Bandy's mouth fell open; the space was immediately filled by an immense, toothy grin. "Well, I'll be . . . You don't say!"

"I do say. And then we went to dinner and dancing in Luckenbach, and . . ." Jack inhaled, warmth spreading enough to give support to Bandy's fever diagnosis.

"That's okay. I won't pry." Bandy's eyes twinkled. "Even a gentleman who runs with bulls shouldn't kiss and tell."

"No one mentioned kissing."

Bandy snorted. "No one had to, Doc."

Jack shook his head, still amazed. "Riley wants to come to the city council meeting. She said she plans to tell them that she believes in me. Not just in the clinic and what we're doing here, Bandy. She said she believes in *me*." He met Bandy's gaze. "I can't quite get my head around that."

"Well, I'd say that's something a man can get his whole heart around." He was quiet for a moment, then winked. "Grab you some fresh coffee?"

"Sure. Thanks."

Bandy went to brew the coffee and start the patients' sandwiches. Jack glanced at the clock. The clinic would open in less than an hour. But he'd arranged for Gretchen to cover him for a while. So that he could—

Jack was hit with a memory of the look on Riley's face when he'd talked about the action committee's emergency meeting at the library. She'd been frightened by his anger. *"You're not planning to confront them?"*

He hadn't answered her directly. And it wasn't as if he had a solid plan. But he had to be there. He couldn't simply stand by and do nothing. Riley didn't understand. And it made Jack sick to think that something he did could frighten her. But he had to show up at the library today. Being there, doing whatever it took to make things right . . . *is who I am.*

- + -

Kate skimmed her bare foot over the bath bubbles and caught a faucet drip with her big toe. It was painted a shade called "Do You Think I'm Tex-y?"—an impulsive clearance-bin purchase more for the crazy name than the berry-pink color. It was apparently from a past season's Texas collection, popular enough that there were few remaining choices. But hoot-worthy, all: "Houston, We Have a Purple," "Suzi Loves Cowboys," and "Big

Hair . . . Big Nails." She'd laughed out loud in the Walgreens cosmetics aisle, looked around for someone to share it with, and wished so much that Riley were there.

Rah-lee . . . Kate sank lower in the tub, knowing she had some repair work to do in her relationship with the chaplain. At this point she wasn't even sure Riley still wanted her as a roommate. They'd missed each other at the hospital yesterday because Kate left early. But they had spoken briefly by phone later; Riley cut it short to answer a page. Kate didn't think it was because Riley wanted to avoid talking to her. And she did promise to call Kate back. That was hopeful. Meanwhile, maybe the neurosurgeon's report would come through and prove that Riley could be cleared for employment as an ER staff nurse. Riley seemed convinced it would happen. Kate wasn't so sure. As difficult as it had been to admit—to the ER director and to Riley—she honestly believed Riley wasn't ready yet. Kate hoped she was wrong. It wasn't as if she'd never been wrong before.

Kate glanced toward her little black dress hanging on the closet door. And the Italian heels waiting for freshly painted toes. Griff had called to say he was back from Dallas but was going to be unexpectedly detained at a meeting he hadn't planned for. He had concerns regarding their dinner reservations, so Kate insisted on meeting him at the restaurant—Bohanan's near the Majestic Theatre. Griff protested in that deep Rhett Butler voice and then finally agreed—*"Promise I'll make it up to you, darlin'."* And in a blink it was there again, that confusing mix she'd felt from the first moment she'd met him at Alamo Grace: undeniable attraction, curiosity, and temptation. Along with a breath-catching frisson of risk—which, she reminded herself, she'd already safely dismissed. The simple fact was that Kate *needed* tonight.

She smiled, wiggling her feet in the bubbles. California Kate with Tex-y toes. Something about that felt like firefly magic.

- + -

The air was thick, cloying, and the darkening sky rumbled with thunder. The grackles had their eyes on it.

Ugh. Riley plowed through a stubborn flock of the birds gathered at the side door of the hospital, shuddering as a feather brushed her ankle.

Stacy Paulson's condition had deteriorated overnight. And despite a prescription for sedatives, Lorna Collins slept poorly and was having a rough time. Riley promised the nurses that she'd offer whatever she could. She pressed her numb fingers against the door's security pad and headed for the elevators.

The ICU charge nurse greeted Riley like she was there to heave a life preserver to drowning victims—always a bad sign. And the sad scene at Stacy's bedside confirmed it.

Lord, help this family . . .

"Stacy's having a hard time breathing," Mr. Collins said, watching his wife sponge their daughter's face. "Lorna thought that if she kept her lips moist, it might help." He flinched as a monitor alarm began a muffled but insistent dinging.

Heart rate . . . 39.

"Yes." Riley stepped closer. "That will be a comfort." She glanced toward the IV equipment, glad to see the morphine pump in place. Chemical comfort, too. Thank heaven.

"Father Ned was here," Lorna said, barely above a whisper.

Her eyes met Riley's. "Everyone's been so kind." She winced, face paling as her daughter drew in a deep, snoring breath. "She was croupy as a baby. I think we wore out half a dozen humidifiers. But Stacy never wanted a night-light—such a brave girl."

Brave. Riley thought of her grandfather. He'd said that about her.

Lorna reached for Stacy's hand as the hungry breath was followed by a second and third. And then by shallower ones until there was an agonizing moment of apnea. Broken by another deep breath as the painful cycle began again.

Cheyne-Stokes breathing from the head injury . . . and impending death.

Riley ached for them all. She stepped up beside Lorna, touched her arm. The woman turned to her, eyes shimmering with tears.

"I tried . . ." Lorna's voice dropped to a whisper. "To keep her safe. Protect her. All of her life—even before she was born. I was so careful." Her eyes seemed to plead for Riley to understand. "Maybe I tried too hard . . . should have given her more freedom. Maybe then she wouldn't have run away. But I was afraid. I worried . . . loved Stacy so much. I couldn't bear the thought of something bad happening to her. A mother is supposed to protect her child."

Riley struggled against a rush of emotion. And a truth that she'd never seen before. Lorna Collins was watching her daughter die and giving voice to the same soul-rending pain that Riley's parents had lived with since the death of her older sister. And then lived through again when Riley was attacked.

"She . . . knows," Riley said, voice choking. "I don't have

any doubt that your daughter knows you were trying to protect her. Just as I believe—" she swallowed—"Stacy knows you're here now."

Lorna held Riley's gaze, her chin trembling. "You do?"

"I believe that with all my heart," Riley whispered. "As a nurse and a chaplain . . . and a daughter." She glanced at Mr. Collins, nodded. "Your being here is a huge comfort for Stacy. A blessing."

"I . . . oh, thank you . . . thank you." Lorna grasped Riley's hand, tears spilling down her cheeks. She let Riley lead her to a chair, sighed as Riley settled a blanket around her shoulders. Mr. Collins pulled a second chair close and sat, his big shoulders stooped.

Stacy began another series of deep, irregular respirations, eclipsing the mechanical bleeps of the monitoring equipment.

"Now," Riley told them, "I'm going to the cafeteria to get some soup and whatever else looks good down there. I'll set it up in the lounge—" she pointed through the doorway—"right over there, not far. Then I'll sit here with Stacy while you two take a break. I insist." Her heart ached at the weariness and loving loyalty on their faces. "And after that, I'll be here for you. For as long as you need me."

- + -

Jack slipped into the back of the library conference room twenty minutes after the start time, surprised at the number of people who'd shown up. He hoped it was because Gretchen's aunt was a talented caterer, but . . .

Jack hunkered down in his chair as Rob Melton entered from

a door nearer the front of the room. The sergeant took a seat in the first row of chairs next to a man who looked suspiciously like the reporter who'd asked for Jack's statement regarding Stacy Paulson. And there were several other people Jack recognized: the owner of the dress store with the recent Dumpster fire; the president of homeowners' association; Ross Payton, the developer with the plan for a condo project; and . . . Jack squinted, trying to place the man sitting next to him. Younger, tall, and powerfully built . . . reddish hair. Bandy had pointed him out. *Payton's son, a contractor.*

There was no mistaking Andrea Nichols, either. Or her obvious pleasure at the size of the turnout. She preened from behind the podium.

"Well, then . . ." Her chuckle puffed against the microphone. "I'm glad I doubled that order for the garlic shrimp skewers. What I'm seeing from here is proof positive that this community is ready to take action!" Andrea raised her arms, beckoning for a response. "Am I right, Bluffs citizens? Am I right?"

There was a smattering of applause and then enthusiastic hoots from two teenage boys, one of whom brandished the wooden skewer from his appetizer. Jack frowned, easily imagining the two of them stuffing beer cans into a cocker spaniel planter. Or . . . snatching a purse?

He clenched his hands, turned his attention back to Andrea Nichols.

"And here are just a few of our concerns." She dangled a poster-board collage of newspaper clippings over the podium. "A fire started by a homeless person, a pregnant teenager beaten nearly to death, theft, and several counts of malicious vandalism all within two weeks' time. Each vile act—" her finger poked the air—"can be directly linked to one single element. An atrocious blot on our beautiful community."

"That clinic!" the teenager with the skewer shouted. The room rumbled with sudden conversation. Andrea crossed her arms, smiling.

Rob Melton stood. "Please, folks—listen," the sergeant insisted, replacing Andrea at the microphone.

Jack's teeth ground together. He told himself to hang back and let Rob handle it, forced himself to remember that look on Riley's face. *"When you get angry like that, it . . . worries me."* He'd felt awful about that. But . . . he thought of the boy filming Gilbert DeSoto as he burned, of Hector falling from that roof with no offer of help . . . and of the private detective they'd hired to dig into his past. Jack's stomach churned; he wasn't sure hanging back was an option.

- + -

Riley gathered her papers from the chapel table and slid them into her briefcase. She was going home at last. She felt drained but was glad that she'd stayed until Lorna Collins's sister arrived. The two women seemed close, and though seeing Stacy had brought on another wrenching deluge of tears, the sisters would be a comfort for each other during the remaining vigil. *Family.*

Riley sighed as she remembered how deeply Lorna's words affected her. They'd made sense of the struggles she'd had with her own family—those smothering efforts to protect her. Riley understood it better now. She hadn't changed her mind about wanting her independence, but . . .

She smiled, thinking of how she'd do it. Tell her parents about . . . *Jack.* Her stomach did the dip she'd come to expect, and she glanced at her watch. He was at the clinic until eight. She could bring dinner, and . . . The dip did an encore as Riley imagined them sneaking a quick kiss when no one was looking. And then later she'd tell him she was finally going to be honest with her parents, explain to them that once she got the medical clearance, she was going to apply for a full-time position at the Alamo Grace ER. Riley would take Jack up on his offer to help her with her skills. She would make it clear to her parents that while she loved them dearly—and respected all they'd done to help her— she wasn't moving back to Houston. She'd visit and they'd come here. Her breath snagged as she imagined them at the church in Boerne—with Jack there, too. That was still a hurdle. But it could happen. All of it. She was certain, no doubts. After such a miserable year, everything was finally feeling good.

She glanced toward the stained-glass window with the white dove and then at the cross on the chapel wall. *Thank you, Father. Thank you for this beautiful blessing of hope.*

Riley grabbed her briefcase and headed out the door, mentally ticking off a list of to-dos: call Kate, check with Vesta Calder, and stop by Central Market for some takeout. That rosemary grilled chicken and crusty French bread, a house salad with their incredible lemon dressing. Jack would love that.

She waved at an ER tech pushing an EKG machine and then slipped out through the exit door, mind still a whirl of plans.

The outside air was humid but no longer threatened rain. The grackles were still there, but who cared? Even those miserable doomsday birds weren't going to spoil—

Riley's phone buzzed in her pocket and she slid it out. Her mother. She glanced heavenward, smiling. *Okay, Lord, I understand. No time like the present to make good on my promises.*

"Mom," she said, stopping outside the door. "I was going to call you. How are—?"

"Oh, thank heaven I caught you, Riley," her mother said in a rush, the anxiety in her voice unmistakable. "I need to tell you something."

Riley's heart stood still. "Is it Poppy? Dad?"

"No, darling."

"Then . . . what?"

"It has to do with that free clinic where you volunteer."

"Mom . . ." Riley groaned, dread replaced by irritation. She turned away for privacy as a coworker passed by. "The newspapers have it all wrong about the clinic. Anything you heard—"

"He's a murder suspect."

What? Riley blinked. "Who?"

"That doctor. Jackson Travis."

Riley gasped. "That's . . . not possible."

"I have the information right here. 'Fredericksburg resident Jackson Travis . . . held for questioning in a grisly murder-arson claiming the life of TCU freshman—'"

Oh . . . please . . . no.

"'Abby Parrish.'"

29

RILEY HAD NO IDEA HOW SHE GOT HOME. Only that she was tripping the motion sensor lights, opening door locks, disarming her security system—actions that had become routine this past year, each designed to protect her. Except now nothing felt routine . . . *or safe?* Her hand trembled as she locked the door behind her, thoughts staggering. Logic and reason told her to stay calm, but her mother's words ran in an endless loop through her mind. *"We felt we had to warn you . . ."* Riley had trusted Jack, and he hadn't been truthful. About Abby's death. Or about . . . Was her mother right about that too? *Please, God. Don't let this be true.*

Riley reset the security alarm and fixed a glass of iced tea. In minutes she'd settled onto the couch where only yesterday she'd been wrapped in Jack's arms. She brought up her cell phone's search engine, tapped in *murder arson Fredericksburg Texas.* And held her breath.

Instantly, Abby's name cascaded down the small screen—paired with Jack's.

- + -

"All I'm asking," Jack insisted, standing beside the podium and struggling to keep anger at bay, "is to be heard." He shot a look at Andrea Nichols, who was clutching the microphone to her jacket as if keeping an assault rifle from the hands of a terrorist.

"This is a private meeting, Dr. Travis."

"In a public place." Jack saw Rob Melton move a few discreet steps closer, the look on his face saying he wouldn't intervene. Yet.

The reporter stood. "I'd like to hear what the doctor has to say."

"Shut up—you don't live here, buddy." The angry shout from the back of the room set off a chain reaction of comments and hurled insults. Several people rose to their feet.

"He's right. You don't have low-life bums trying to torch your neighborhood!"

"Or exposing your children to prostitutes."

"What's the matter, Doc—respectable folks won't let you touch 'em?"

Respectable? Jack's teeth clenched, blood rising to his face. "If you'll give me the courtesy of listening, I'll explain . . ."

There was a bellowed curse, and a man in the second row

stood so quickly that his chair tipped over. People gasped; the teens eagerly raised their cell phone cameras.

"Courtesy?" the man shouted, lumbering forward. "That's rich. You endanger our good people and ask that we respond with courtesy?" He glanced around the room. "Ask Herb about his house being vandalized. Ask Jody Bader how he feels about someone ripping off his son's bike." His face reddening, the man ignored Rob's signal to sit. "Ross Payton had his *golf clubs* stolen—"

"Golf clubs?" Jack glared as the reporter pressed close and ignored the fact that Rob was now giving him the cool-it look. "You're going to stand there and moan about property— *things*—when half a block away people are struggling to get through the day . . . to even live?" He trembled with anger, realizing he'd somehow closed the short space between himself and the man. Close enough to smell the garlic shrimp on his breath.

"Jack." Rob's voice was calm behind him despite the buzzing crowd. "Hold it."

Jack narrowed his eyes. "What kind of 'good people' stand around doing nothing when an old man's burning alive?"

"Doctor, please," Ross Payton said, stepping close behind. "Let's not do this."

Jack whirled, shot him a look. "Why? Afraid I might mention something about a roofer who nearly bled to death while your 'good' neighbors looked the other way? In fact, aren't *you* having some roofing work done, Payton?" Blood pounded in his temples as the words hissed through his teeth. "I have never seen so many pathetic hypocrites. And I will not stand by while—"

Rob grabbed his arm. Jack pulled it away.

Then someone shoved Jack. Hard.

Any thought of restraint was gone.

- + -

Riley exited the Internet browser. How long had she been sitting here? Long enough that sunlight was waning. And way past the time it took to feel completely sick. She shivered, squeezed her eyes shut against the images prompted by the horrific details surrounding Abby's death. And Jack's undeniable connection to it.

Her mother had been right. He had been a "person of interest" in this girl's murder, enough so that he'd been initially detained and then called in over and over for questioning.

Jackson Travis, son of popular high school football coach Hadley Travis, admits to having been under the influence of alcohol . . . was a passenger in the murder victim's car . . . The vehicle was found torched with the young woman's body in the trunk.

Riley hugged her arms around herself. Jack had said that Abby was a kidnapping victim. Not that he'd been with her when it happened.

Travis continues to insist that he was knocked unconscious by carjackers. Three young men wearing ski masks kidnapped the girl . . . claims he tried to flag down a car on the rural highway . . . Police are trying to locate the owner of a Toyota sedan . . .

There had been guarded statements from the Parrish family, from Jack's mother, and from a neighbor who'd said, "He's a good boy. But he's having a rough time with his daddy's illness and all . . ." Plus a quote from a Fredericksburg biergarten coworker who threw in, "Dude had a serious anger problem."

There had been countless photos of Abby. And Jack. And one of Abby and Jack attending a picnic at the Sunshine Center, where Abby had apparently volunteered on a regular basis. Riley's throat constricted at the memory of her morning there.

There were reports of Jack's futile attempt to describe the alleged carjackers. A medical description of Jack's head contusion, his mental state at the ER, and confirmation of a .07 blood alcohol result. There was conjecture that the head injury could have been self-inflicted to cover a murder committed in a drunken rage—with a sidebar containing statistics on underage drinking and violent crime and a statement from MADD Texas. And some speculation that perhaps the victim had rebuffed unwanted physical advances, that Jack had wanted more than she did from the relationship. Motive for his murderous rage. It was followed by a statement from Jack that Abby was a friend, not a girlfriend. They hadn't fought; he'd been drinking that night because he was upset about his father. And Abby was trying to help him.

But the hardest thing to read was the report from the medical examiner. The beautiful young woman's body had been burned beyond recognition. Her godfather, a San Antonio dentist, provided the records that confirmed her identity. Mercifully, all that happened to Abby prior to being placed in the trunk of her car would remain a mystery. It was assumed, however—because articles of clothing had been found in nearby shrubbery—that she'd been sexually assaulted. And . . . Riley struggled against a wave of nausea. A bone in Abby's neck was fractured. An indication that she was . . . *strangled.*

Riley closed her eyes against the memory of her Houston assailant's hands around her throat, then shivered at an overriding image of Jack confronting the purse snatcher—

She jumped, heart pounding, as her TV came on and the news blared. Her automatic security measure at dusk. She reached for the remote to shut it off, then stopped, recognizing the voice. *Jack.* At the library? She held her breath, watching.

"I won't let you do this to me!" Jack grabbed the collar of a man, shouting at him nose to nose. "I swear, I'll—" A police officer pulled him back. The camera bobbed and there was a disjointed pan over faces in the crowd: Andrea Nichols, that developer Mr. Payton. Then a shot from the exit, a reporter trying to get statements from folks leaving the library.

The camera closed in on the face of a young man trying to squeeze by. Handsome, big jaw, striking green eyes . . . mass of red hair.

That patient from the ER? The contractor?

"No comment." The young man frowned at the camera. "I said no. Get out of my face!" The shot went fuzzy black as his hand covered the lens. Then the camera focused again on someone else.

"Well, I sure have a comment," an older man growled into the lens. "You can quote me: that doctor, Jack Travis, is a dangerous menace!"

- + -

Gretchen stayed for the whole shift; the clinic had been busy. Jack was grateful for her help. After that circus at the library and his conversation with Rob once the meeting broke up, he wasn't sure he had anything left for anyone. Except Riley. And after what Rob had revealed, there might be some damage control to do there as well. *How do I handle that?*

But Riley hadn't returned his calls. He hoped it was because she'd been busy at the hospital and had her cell phone turned off.

"You made the evening news." Bandy glanced up from where he stood at the sink washing the coffeepot. "I suppose that's why Gretchen covered for that first hour? So you could return a library book?"

Jack grimaced. "I had to do it."

"And how did that work for you?"

"Who are you—Dr. Phil?"

Bandy rubbed a dish towel over the glass pot, stayed quiet. Too quiet.

"I'm sorry." Jack groaned. "You're right. It didn't work. It made things worse. But I don't have any respect for people who—"

"And there's the problem," Bandy said, cutting him off. "That's it. On the nose." He shook his head, sighed. "I've never seen anybody try as hard as you do to show respect—and generosity—to folks who are down on their luck, hurting . . . hungry. You did that for me, too, Doc; as long as I live, I'll be grateful. But the plain truth is that we can't pick and choose who deserves good treatment. Those neighbors need it too."

"Mmm." Jack squirmed, feeling a do-unto-others moment coming. He was too tired for this. And sick to death of feeling like he was walking into battle alone. Why couldn't anyone understand—?

Jack's phone rang. He waved a hang-on-a-minute signal to Bandy and pulled it from the pocket of his scrub jacket. Riley.

"Hey, stranger," he said, feeling the full impact of how much he'd missed her today.

There was a prolonged silence.

"Riley?"

"Is everyone gone from the clinic?" she asked, her voice sounding strange.

"Bandy's here." He had a bad feeling. "Where are you?"

"In the parking lot."

Jack's brows scrunched. "At Alamo Grace?"

"No. Here. Right outside. I need to talk with you. Privately."

"Sure . . . uh, I'll ask Bandy to give us some privacy. Come to my office in a couple of minutes." He thought of his conversation with Rob, felt his throat tighten. "Is something wrong?"

"We need to talk."

Riley disconnected without saying anything more, and Jack slowly lowered his phone, his dread becoming visceral. "Bandy . . ."

"I'm going to take Hobo out to get settled for the night," Bandy offered before Jack could finish. "Then do some tidying up in the truck—clown noses everywhere. I should be ashamed." He nodded, gentle concern in his eyes.

"Thanks."

Jack thought of meeting Riley at the door but changed his

mind and walked to his office instead. As if being there would give him more control over what was about to happen. But in his gut, he doubted it. Something was seriously wrong.

30

+

"NO, DON'T." Riley flinched and backed away a step as Jack reached out to her. "Why didn't you tell me the truth?"

"Truth about . . . ?"

Riley's heart stalled. *How many lies are there?*

"Abby's death. That you were there when she was kidnapped." She fought a wave of nausea. "And that you were a . . ."

"Suspect?" Jack met her gaze, his expression somewhere between pain and defensiveness. "Is that the word you're looking for?" His voice lowered. "Is that what this is about, Riley?"

"You could have told me." She hugged her elbows, beginning to tremble. "That first night at the River Walk and even after that. I told you . . . everything. You should have—"

"Told you all the ugly details?" His tone was growing bitter. "Just what every woman wants to hear over dinner."

"Better than hearing it from my mother."

Oddly, something in Jack's expression said that he wasn't surprised.

- + -

Jack stayed quiet for a moment, telling himself not to get angry. And that any blunder on his part could . . .

"Okay," he said finally. "If that's what you want, I'll tell you everything. Right now. Right here." He glanced around the room at his cluttered desk, a stack of newspapers on the extra chair. "Or we could go someplace more comfortable, and—"

"No," Riley said quickly. "I don't want to go anywhere."

You don't want to go anywhere . . . with me.

"Wait," Jack said, beginning to feel sick. "You can't think that I'm actually capable of something like that?" He reached for her hand, desperate to change what was happening. She took another step back. "C'mon, Riley. You know me."

"Do I?" Sudden tears shimmered her eyes. "I thought I did. I'd started to think so many good things, but now . . ." She took a breath, met his gaze directly. "It's not that I believe you were involved in Abby's death—I don't. I'll admit that it scared me. I read those accounts from the newspapers, Jack. All those horrible things. And I've seen you get angry." She swiped at a tear. "Still, I don't think you could do something like that. Not murder. But . . ."

"But what?" Jack watched the expressions flickering across her face. Hurt, doubt . . . anger? "Tell me what's going on."

"You applied for a grant from the Hale Foundation?"

It's about that?

Riley watched his eyes. "She said you did."

Jack told himself to chill, be careful. "I probably did. Okay. Sure. I did." He shook his head. "I've gone everywhere for funding. I'd go to the man in the moon if that's what it took to keep the clinic going. You know how important that is to me."

"Yes. I do." She narrowed her eyes. "Important enough to recruit a crippled volunteer who just happens to have connections to a medical foundation."

"I . . ." Guilt snagged his words. "Riley, wait . . ."

"Why? So you can deny it?" Her lips twisted. "And tell me that you would have wanted me here, offered to help me, if my name were something other than Hale? What if I were . . . Jane Doe?"

"No, Riley—"

"I didn't want to believe my mother," she continued. "But it all makes sense now. You waved my name like a flag. Even before my first shift here. And then you practically rolled out the red carpet when my mother stopped by that day. You *used* me, Jack. Now I can't be sure anything between us was real." Her tears returned, but she pushed on. "But that's not even the worst of it. The saddest part is that you've made this clinic all about you. Not about the patients—about *you*. And your insatiable need to be—" her gaze drifted to Jack's photo wall— "some sort of invincible warrior. That ugly, angry need makes things chaotic and unstable . . . and unsafe." A tear slid down her cheek. "It proves over and over that the action committee is right—they're *right* about you! And I can't—" Her phone's text tone sounded in her pocket. She swiped at her eyes and then reached for it.

Jack struggled for words. There had to be some way to—

"Stacy Paulson died," she announced in a monotone. "I'm going."

"Riley . . ."

She walked out without looking back.

It wasn't until several minutes after she left that Jack realized he'd never told Riley what he learned from Rob Melton. That it was the Hales who'd hired the private investigator to snoop around in his past. Jack had been furious. And he fully expected them to tell Riley what they'd learned. Maybe they'd even whisper it to the newspapers, get the whole ugly mess stirred up again. The timing couldn't be worse; the city council meeting was next week.

Jack sank into his office chair. It wasn't likely that Riley would be standing beside him at that meeting. Blast it; she was wrong about him. And was being completely unfair. He'd applied for the Hale Foundation grant long before they had met. Not that Riley let him defend himself on that point. And even if Jack had considered what her name could lend to the clinic, it had nothing at all to do with how he'd begun to feel about—

There was a sudden frenzy of barking, then a horn blast and a shout.

Jack jogged to the rear parking lot, squinted as the security lights snapped on. Then saw Bandy. Wielding a hose nozzle like a weapon.

"Fool . . . kids," he gasped, soaking wet and struggling to shut off the water. He stopped the flow, then shushed Hobo. "Chased 'em down." He drew a ragged breath. "Scared 'em off."

"What happened?"

Bandy pointed. "Sorry, Doc."

The Hummer. Spray-painted with *GET OUT QUAC—Quack.*

Bandy handed Jack a soggy stack of papers. "They dropped these."

Action committee flyers announcing the city council meeting.

- + -

Kate crossed her legs, uncrossed them, then glanced anxiously at her cell phone lying on the crisp linen tablecloth. Time: 7:47. No messages. She poked her straw at the lime wedge in her third glass of ice water.

"Still waiting?" the silver-haired waiter asked, doing his best to be discreet despite the fact that she'd taken up an undoubtedly valuable Bohanan's table for nearly an hour.

"Unfortunately, yes." Kate pretended she couldn't feel patrons' eyes sneaking curious glances at her. "And now I'm wondering if I misunderstood." Heat crept up her neck. She took a slow breath of air scented with ninety-dollar steaks. "Perhaps I was supposed to meet him at the theater. We have tickets for *Wicked.*"

"Ah." The man's eyes darted to her cell phone.

"He's a doctor," Kate said a little too loudly. Perspiration trickled beneath the bodice of her dress. "My . . . husband is a heart surgeon. He can't always get to a phone."

"Of course."

And I'm an idiot who never seems to learn.

"I think I'll go over to the theater, then. Thank you," Kate said, folding her napkin and standing. "You've been very kind."

She squared her shoulders and walked away from the table, vowing that she would not make another call to Griff—or cut him any more slack. She'd left half a dozen messages in the last hour and invented twice as many excuses for him: the unexpected business meeting had run long; he'd taken a nap after the drive from Dallas and accidentally overslept; his phone battery died; he was stuck in the I-10 traffic. But after an embarrassing hour without a word, Kate could only forgive Griff Payton if he were lying under a bulldozer on some remote building site. She winced and reassured herself it wasn't likely. It was far more plausible that after a successful meeting he'd celebrated with drinks or . . . something else? She recalled the ER doctor's suspicion that Griff was a drug seeker. And then told herself even that thought amounted to giving the man an excuse—too stoned to call.

No. The truth was that the handsome and very charming Griff Payton had simply stood her up. Well, fine. Another lesson learned. Kate refused to be bummed by it. In fact . . .

She smiled, reaching for a mint at the table near the exit. Kate had half a mind to take her little black dress, Italian heels, and Tex-y toes to that Tex-Mex place in Alamo Heights. The one that used to be an auto service business. Taco Garage. Yes. She'd go there, order the Cadillac carnitas, and forget—*forget completely*—that she'd ever believed in firefly magic.

Kate grimaced. First she'd take a side trip to the Bohanan's ladies' room. Three glasses of ice water were more than enough to add injury to insult.

Adiós, Griff.

- + -

"It's been over two hours. They won't be back." Bandy reached down to tuck the flowered dish towel around Hobo where he'd fallen asleep beside the kitchen chair. "Scared silly of my watchdog."

Jack glanced toward the window. "I'll give them something to be scared of. I should have heard them out there."

"What you *should* do is get out of here. It's nearly ten, and—" Bandy shot Jack a knowing look—"it doesn't look good for a man to be knockin' on a young lady's door late at night."

"Who said anything about knocking on doors?"

"The look on your face did, Doc." Bandy sighed. "I'm not asking what all that was about earlier, but you need to go see Riley. Get it straightened out. Even if swallowing some pride is on the menu."

"Doesn't anything get by you?"

"Armadillos sometimes, but . . ." Bandy waited, ever patient.

"Riley has some things all wrong about me. She's upset. I don't know if I can do anything about that."

"She's the woman who believes in you—remember telling me that?"

Jack's throat squeezed. "I'm not so sure that's true anymore. There are things in my past . . . things I did that I didn't get right. And now I don't know."

"We all make mistakes, Doc. We're human." Bandy's eyes did that familiar ceiling inspection. "That's where grace comes in. But even in the beautiful light of that, we can still do a little somethin' to get things squared up."

"What are you saying?"

"Go talk to her."

Jack looked out the window again, uncertain.

"I'll be fine here." Bandy shook his head. "And the truth is, I'm plain tuckered out—too old to be hauling a hose around like a fireman. As soon as I get Hobo settled outside, I'm going to take two of those pain pills and hit the sack. I don't care if it knocks me for a loop. And you . . . you're going to go knock on that young lady's door."

Jack opened his mouth to protest, but Bandy raised his hand and cut him off.

"Maybe you don't know it yet, but you *need* her. Take it from a man who knows. You don't want to fool around and take a chance of losing someone like her."

You need her . . . "Okay . . . I'll think about it."

"Past time for thinking." Bandy rolled his eyes. "I can't believe I'm about to say this, considering our particular history, but it's time to take the bull by the horns, Doc."

31

+

RILEY SAT ON HER COUCH IN THE DARK. She was bone-weary, wrung out. Numb. Empty. Even tears weren't an option. She'd used them all up holding Lorna Collins in her arms. Hearing her heart-wrenching sobs, feeling her tremble . . . helping a loving mother let go. The little girl who'd clapped and clapped to save Tinker Bell, eyes bright with hope, had taken her last breath at 7:39. When Riley was at Jack's office, letting go of him. And now . . . Riley drew her knees up and sank back against the pale, cool leather of the couch. Now there was nothing left. Because just when she thought things couldn't get any worse . . .

Her gaze moved to the stapled trio of papers lying on the table beside her Bible. The long-awaited medical report. A thorough assessment, complete with measurements and comparisons of push-pull strength, grading of paresthesia, muscle tone, and reflexes. And a cover letter signed by her Houston neurosurgeon that, though eminently gracious, did nothing to soften the impact of the bottom line.

> Unfortunately, the patient's dominant arm still exhibits significant weakness and sensory deficit. In my opinion, it would be both unwise and unsafe for her to perform the physical tasks presented in the job description provided . . .

It had gone on to say that while the highest percentage of nerve recovery occurs during the first year, there was perhaps hope for some small measure of improvement. The letter concluded with personal remarks about Riley's "valuable and inspired" work as a trauma chaplain.

She'd screamed out loud, grabbed the papers, hurled them as hard as she could. And watched them flutter pathetically onto her foot because she'd used her unsafe, "significantly weakened" arm. Then Riley screamed at God. But she doubted he heard her.

"You aren't there," Riley whispered to the darkness. "You've given up on me too. You knew the one thing I needed and you took it away." *"Valuable and inspired"?* She groaned. "Because you know that my faith isn't strong enough. That I'm a fraud. And I don't deserve—"

Riley's cell phone jumped on the table with an incoming call. *Jack.* She waited a few more rings before picking it up.

"Your gate code isn't working." His voice was low, hesitant.

"I changed it."

There was a short silence. "Why?"

Because I can't see you anymore. "What do you want?"

"I want to talk with you. I need . . . to see you, Riley."

"We talked. There's no need—"

"There is. Please let me in."

The emptiness began to ache.

"Riley?"

"It's . . . late." The ache choked her like a merciless assailant. "And I can't do this anymore." *The clinic, the hospital . . .* She glanced at her Bible. *I can't even hope.*

"Please . . ."

"Good-bye, Jack." She disconnected, then touched her fingers to her cheek, surprised to find it wet. Apparently she'd had a few tears left.

Before Riley could set it down, the phone rang again. She'd let it go to voice mail, erase Jack's message without listening, and . . . Riley squinted at the display. Vesta?

I was supposed to call.

"I'm so sorry," Riley said quickly. "I promised I'd call, and—"

"Thank . . . God . . . you're there. I've been so frightened, and I couldn't . . ."

"Vesta?" Riley stood. "Are you sicker? Should I call an ambulance?"

"No—oh no. I can't go out . . ." She gulped air. "But I have to. I have to do something. I saw him. That man. Oh, dear God—*he's here!*"

Man? "Someone's broken in?"

"No, no . . . But I saw him . . . on the TV."

TV? Vesta wasn't making any sense; it had to be a panic attack. Or her diabetes.

"And now," Vesta wailed, "I need to do something. But my eyes . . . I'm so dizzy. And I can't find my shoes."

"Wait. Don't move." Riley reached for her purse. "Stay right there. I'm coming."

- + -

The Mercedes's engine roared to life—it had taken Vesta two tries because her hands were shaking so badly. Only minutes before, she'd vomited in the Mexican sage bushes near the oriole feeder. She wasn't sure if it happened because her sugar was too high or because she was scared out of her wits. But it didn't matter now. She was here in the car; she'd made it. In her bedroom slippers, carrying the baseball bat—and the scrapbook. It had taken Vesta some time to find the collection of yellowed newspaper clippings and her handwritten notes; she wasn't sure it would be of help to anyone, but it had seemed important to have it with her. *When I finally do the right thing.*

Strangely, that thought made her feel better than anything had in a long time. She glanced at the passenger seat, where Corky would ride if he were still alive. The colonel's small Bible lay on the leather seat. Vesta wanted that with her too. Maybe because she needed to feel the presence of both—her wonderful husband and God.

"Are you there, God? Even if you aren't, I'm doing this. I have to. I can't die . . . being afraid to live." She shivered, searched for the headlights but turned on the windshield wipers. Then got it right. She squinted as the beams lit the wall of the garage; then she took hold of the gearshift and found reverse. She smiled despite another wave of dizziness. "If you're there, God, fasten your seat belt; I haven't done this in a long time."

- + -

Riley realized two blocks from home that she was low on gas. She pulled the Honda into the nearest station. She could have made the short distance to The Bluffs, but she was still on chaplaincy call at Alamo Grace. And with the way things had been going . . .

As if to prove her point, a fire truck and ambulance sped by with lights flashing, sirens squealing. Heading the same direction she was. Riley dreaded the thought of the traffic delay. And the thought of Vesta becoming even more anxious.

She pulled out her phone, tapped the redial for Vesta's number. Let it ring . . . and ring . . . and ring—and go to voice mail. *"We're not able to take your call right now . . ."* Riley's concern increased. Vesta hadn't made it farther than the mailbox in two long years; surely she wouldn't . . .

"I can't find my shoes."

Riley stopped the pump, replaced her gas cap, impatient to leave. She debated calling the paramedics or the police or . . . who? And why? Because a panic-prone diabetic bird-watcher had been frightened by something she saw on TV? It would take Riley less than ten minutes to get to Vesta's house. And if necessary she'd call 911 from there.

Please, God, I'm asking this for her . . .

Even though it was well after 10 p.m., the San Antonio Street traffic was painfully slow. And it looked as if that ambulance had been dispatched to a location just ahead. The looky-loos brought the line of cars to a near standstill. Riley strained to see as the cars began to crawl again. Then saw the flashing lights, first responders in firefighter gear . . . medics. And—the Honda inched closer—the wreck. A car in one of the shallow trenches excavated for construction of the security gate. Fortunately, it looked more precariously tipped than damaged. Light blue, a Mercedes convertible, and—*Oh, dear Lord!* Riley hit the brake, heard the car behind her blast its horn. She stared, heart wedged into her throat, at the TYGRR-mobile.

In minutes that seemed like hours, she found a place to pull the Honda off the road and jogged back to the accident scene. She brushed past a firefighter trying to stop her, explaining breathlessly, "I'm a nurse. Please let me by." She struggled to see, and it occurred to her that perhaps it wasn't Vesta, that maybe someone had stolen the Mercedes. Maybe a car thief was "that man" Vesta had been so frightened about.

"Vesta!" Riley called out, catching sight of her on the ambulance stretcher. "I'm here. I'm coming." She squeezed past another firefighter, hurriedly identified herself to a medic, and made it to Vesta at last.

"Riley . . ."

Riley reached for Vesta's hand, throat constricting at the sight of her: chin secure in a cervical collar, small laceration on her nose, bloodied lip, a swollen bump above one eye. And a flood of tears. "It's okay, Vesta. I'll stay with you."

A paramedic caught Riley's eye. "You're a family member?"

"A nurse at Alamo Grace. And a friend. I know her medical history, and I'd like to ride along."

Riley left instructions regarding the Mercedes, and in a few minutes they were loaded and on their way. Vesta dozed off en route to the hospital, awakened at intervals by the paramedic so that he could check her neurological status. Riley watched, still amazed at the situation—at this whole regrettable day—as the man checked Vesta's vital signs and performed his assessments.

"Blood sugar's 280," he reported, "so it's not easy to determine how much of her responses are related to that or to the head injury." He pointed to the front of Vesta's shirt. "Looks like she may have vomited. The source of that could go either way too."

Riley nodded, wondering if she'd missed a clue when Vesta called to cancel Thursday's chaplain visit. Then she thought about all the things that had changed since that first day she'd met Vesta in the ER. Riley's job at the clinic and all that had happened with Jack, the rift with Kate. But one thing hadn't changed: Vesta was still afraid. That first day and tonight too. She'd been frantic on the phone. What could have frightened an agoraphobic enough to get in a car?

"Did . . . you . . . see him?" Vesta asked. Her tongue, visibly dry, explored her swollen lip.

Riley leaned close. "Who?"

"The man. That awful man."

- + -

11:15. Jack glanced away from the Hummer's clock and back at the road, sure he was being a fool. But after what had happened earlier at the clinic, he wanted to have a look around before he drove home. He'd cruise through the parking lot, make sure the security lights came on, and check things out. Bandy had taken the pain pills, so he wouldn't even notice that Jack was there. And Jack would sleep better if he knew everything was all right.

Maybe sleep. He thought of his phone conversation with Riley. How could everything have gotten this fouled up? Things had been going so well between them. Better than he'd ever imagined. And now . . .

He shook his head, thinking of what Bandy had said about Riley. *"She's the woman who believes in you."* And that Jack needed her. So off target. *The truth is, Riley's a woman who believes . . . she needs to change the gate code to keep me out.* Maybe Bandy was wise about a lot of things, but he had a blind spot when it came to the chaplain. She didn't want anything to do with Jack anymore. And the only need Jack had was to check on his clinic. He was almost there now . . .

Jack braked, slowing the Hummer so that he could peer at the scene ahead. Aftermath of an accident, it looked like. Flares, tow truck, and a Mercedes in the ditch alongside The Bluffs' security gate construction. There wasn't much damage. Except to the driver's pride, probably. And there was undoubtedly some significant pride—he clucked his tongue as he read the car's vanity plate: *TYGRR.*

Mercedes versus security gate. In no way would he wish any real harm to anyone. But if Jack really was the insensitive jerk those people claimed he was, he'd have to say there was a certain poetic justice in that little fender bender.

He drove the remaining short distance to the clinic and pulled into the driveway, wondering how close he could get before the motion sensor lights came on. He inched forward, watching—then stopped suddenly, staring at the windows in the distance. *What . . . ?* Jack squinted, trying to imagine what could cause so much light. Flickering like a big-screen TV, but there wasn't one, and—

Fire!

He slammed the Hummer's pedal down, roared up the driveway, screeched to a stop, and hit the ground at a sprint. *Bandy . . . no, don't be . . .*

"Bandy!" He pounded his fists on the front door, yelled again—raced along the side of the building, saw that the fire was in the kitchen. Fully involved. Too hot. Bandy was in the office, so . . . He raced back to the front porch, heart slamming against his ribs and breath heaving. He heard the smoke detector shrieking as he dug into his pocket for the key.

"Bandy!" Jack shouted, shoving through the door and seeing the thick cloud of smoke clinging to the ceiling. He coughed, felt the heat even from the distance, and charged across the waiting room toward the inner hallway. "Bandy, where are you?"

"Here . . . I'm . . ." Bandy staggered from the office doorway, coughing. "What's happ—?" A deafening explosion shook the building and scorched the air.

Jack lunged forward, heaved Bandy onto his shoulder, and ran like he was escaping hell.

32

+

VESTA OPENED HER EYES. Even in the dim light of the Alamo Grace hospital room, she could tell her vision had dramatically improved. She could make out the IV pump with the bag of antibiotics, the tray table, and . . . *She's still here. Thank you, God.*

"Hi." Riley moved to her bedside, smiling. "Your blood sugar's coming down." She lifted the melting ice pack from Vesta's forehead. "And so is that goose egg on your head. You dozed awhile. How are you feeling?"

"I'm . . ." Vesta licked her lips, winced as her tongue touched the lower one. "Mostly embarrassed. And so sorry about your car."

"Unh-uh." Riley shook her head. "We've been over this. It's

not a problem. I'm just grateful that you're okay." She patted Vesta's hand. "And I'm the one who should apologize. I promised to check on you. If I had, maybe I could have helped you with whatever it was that had you so upset."

Vesta saw the question in Riley's eyes and wondered if the scrapbook had been left in the car. She still had to take care of—

"Vesta?"

"I'm glad you're here," Vesta said softly, thinking that there was something full circle about being back at Alamo Grace. Looking up and seeing the chaplain. Only this time—even after a car accident and everything that had led up to it—she didn't feel the fear she had before. It was strange, considering. But then, maybe not so strange. She thought of those frenzied moments in the garage as she struggled to start the car. How she told God to buckle his seat belt.

"I'm glad I'm here too," Riley said. "And I'll stay as long as you need me." The question gathered in her eyes again. "I'll listen if you want to talk."

"I think . . ." Vesta felt tears well. "I'd like you to pray with me now. Can we do that?"

Riley nodded. "We sure can."

- + -

"How're you feeling?" Jack pulled up a chair beside Bandy's hospital bed.

"You mean after you lugged me around like a sack of spuds?" Bandy smiled, eyes teasing as if the oxygen cannula were just another clown prop, this whole scene no more than a skit for the kids at the Sunshine Center.

Jack's throat tightened. If he'd lost Bandy . . .

"I'm good, Doc," Bandy continued after glancing at the bed-side monitor. "And ready to go home, if they'd only let me."

Home. How badly was the clinic burned? The fire department had arrived moments after Jack got Bandy out. But . . .

"I'm taking you back to my condo," Jack told him, "as soon as you're released. Probably in the morning. They want to observe you overnight. Considering how long you abused your body by eating rodeo food." He smiled. "As soon as I leave here, I'll go back and look for Hobo. Don't worry."

"I'm not worried. He'll be fine," Bandy said with certainty. "The boy survived being stomped by a bull; a little fire's not going to shake him up. Probably took cover in the bushes for a while. You'll find him." He reached up to touch the oxygen tub-ing, grimaced. "I checked the stove before I turned in. I always do. Can't imagine what happened." He shot Jack an I-told-you-so look. "Our good neighbors called the fire department."

Or started the fire.

"Guess so," Jack said, recognizing the difference between them. Bandy saw hope, and Jack . . . *will wait for the investi-gator's report.* All he knew right now was that he was grateful— beyond grateful—that Bandy was alive.

Bandy's smile was stretched by a yawn. "Pain pills. Still get-tin' to me."

"I'll go. Let you sleep."

"Not before you tell me what happened when you talked to Riley."

"I didn't. She wouldn't even let me through the gate. So . . ."

"So you go back." Bandy rolled his eyes. "The man thinks

nothing of jumpin' out of a perfectly good plane . . ." He pointed his finger. "Promise me you'll go back."

"Sure." *If a promise lets you sleep.*

"And one more thing," Bandy said as Jack started to go.

"What?"

"Thank you. For what you did tonight. I appreciate it. Though . . ." He inspected the hospital ceiling, that knowing look on his face. "You know I'm not afraid to die."

"Because I know where I'm going." How many times had Jack heard that? He shook his head. "You're not dying."

"So they tell me." Bandy shrugged. "But if I'm not afraid to die, then don't you be afraid to *live*, Doc." He smiled the same smile that he offered to the kids at the Sunshine Center—life lessons with a red sponge nose. "Now come here and give me a proper *hasta la vista*."

Jack grinned, stretched out his hand. Bandy grasped it firmly, then hauled him into a bear hug, IV tubing dangling. "*Hasta mañana*, Bandy."

Bandy let go, and despite his smile, his eyes shone with tears. "You're a good man, son. Don't you ever forget that."

Jack's heart cramped. "You need anything?"

"The CD player. But I guess it's gone now." He tapped his fingers over his heart. "Good thing I have the songs right in here."

- + -

Riley leaned forward in the chapel chair, thankful for the quiet. She glanced through the dimly lit room to the cross on the wall. *Thank you, Father. Thank you for being patient with me. For understanding that it would take me time . . .*

She shook her head, still rocked by the rush of feelings. And the truth. In a year fraught with struggles and filled with pleading prayers, she'd completely missed it. Riley's short laugh echoed in the room. She raised her hand and stared at it, flexed her numb fingers. What had Bandy said that day at the clinic about God's hands? *"Feel his hold and trust it."* It was about *his* hands. And she'd stubbornly made it all about hers. Her arm, her hand—her unspoken pact with God. If she got her strength back, if she could get back to the ER, *then* she'd trust him again. The truth was she'd taken the chaplain position as a bargaining tool. In that respect she was a fraud. And then—Riley squeezed her eyes shut at her stupidity—when she got angry at God for denying her all she wanted . . . *I jumped out of a plane and dared him to catch me!* She'd never seen any of it before. Not until tonight.

Riley's heart tugged, remembering Vesta's request for prayer. And the gratitude she'd expressed for the times that Riley had been there for her—the day she'd had a panic attack here in the chapel; at her home when she'd finally admitted to being housebound; and then tonight, when they prayed together. She remembered Vesta's expression afterward. It was the first time she hadn't seen fear in the woman's eyes. It was as if Vesta had opened a far bigger door than the one in The Bluffs, walked through—kept going. And suddenly it felt that way for Riley too. Clear, for the first time in so very long. She had no doubt that God had wanted her there for all of that with Vesta. And for so many other patients and staff, too . . . *as a chaplain.*

Tears welled in her eyes. Riley had been so afraid of being broken . . . that she hadn't seen God's plan to make her whole.

There was another truth she needed to face. And she wasn't sure yet how to do that.

Jack. Riley grimaced at the things she'd said to him a few hours ago. She'd been completely unfair. In the same spoiled, foot-stomping manner that she'd made demands of God, she'd arrogantly accused Jack of using her. When the truth was she'd been using him, too—from that first moment she'd decided to volunteer at the clinic. She wanted the experience and a recommendation. And then so much more. More than he wanted to give? She had no idea if that part was true. But still . . .

Riley pulled out her cell phone and brought up the text screen. She typed in the new gate code and pushed the Send button. She was trusting God on this too. Putting it all in his hands.

- + -

Jack retraced his steps and took the elevator up to the third floor, still confused. He'd stopped by the ER to thank the staff who'd cared for Bandy, and the charge nurse told him that a patient upstairs had called to see if he was on duty. Vesta Calder. Apparently she'd been in a car accident and was hospitalized. She'd insisted it was urgent that she speak with him as soon as possible. It was nearly midnight and none of this made sense, but . . .

Vesta was awake.

33

✝

"YOU CAME." Vesta swiped a hand over her hair, grimacing slightly as she touched a darkening bruise on her forehead. "I'm so . . . relieved."

Why? Why had she called him here? Jack stepped close to the bed rail. "You had an accident, I heard."

"I was trying to get to the police." Vesta nodded. "But now I think it's better that I talk to you first."

The police? Jack glanced at the IV pump. No meds that would affect her thinking. Maybe a concussion was causing her confusion.

"I was there," she continued, her eyes suddenly riveted to his. "I saw those men that night."

His brows bunched. "I don't know what you mean."

Vesta took a breath, her hand moving to her throat. "I saw the car on fire. I saw the men. I didn't know the girl was inside until the next day."

"Wha . . ." Jack struggled to breathe, gut-punched by her words. It couldn't be. Could it? *Abby?* He gripped the bed rail, his legs weakening.

"And I saw you," Vesta whispered. "Staggering down the highway. You tried to wave me down."

"The . . . Toyota," he choked out, mind cartwheeling. "It was you?"

"My Camry," she said, tears beginning to stream down her face. "I'm sorry. . . . I'm so sorry. I should have called the police. But I was scared—they saw me. And then I got phone calls. Hang ups, at night. And—" a sob broke loose—"someone . . . poisoned my dog."

"I'm trying to understand." Jack dragged a chair close, sank into it. He was shaking. *An eyewitness. Someone knows I'm innocent.* The relief felt almost like pain. "If you didn't come forward all these years because you believe you're in danger, why are you telling me this now?"

"Because being afraid was stealing my life . . . and my faith . . . everything good. Then I met you at the hospital and I started to think about how I'd hurt you by not coming forward. And tonight . . ." Vesta took a shuddering breath. "I was trying to go to the police because one of those men I saw that night . . . is *here.* I saw him."

Jack's stomach lurched. "Where—when?"

"I saw him walking down San Antonio Street once. And

then tonight I saw him again. On that TV broadcast, that meeting in the library. You know—you were there too."

Jack's senses were still reeling when he got back to the clinic around 1 a.m. Even in the darkness, he could see the charring. The stench of smoke and sodden wood made his stomach shudder. He'd wanted to be there when Rob talked with Vesta, to find out if she'd been mistaken about the man's identity. But he'd promised Bandy he'd check on Hobo. He stayed clear of the fire inspector's barricade, shone his flashlight toward Bandy's truck, and—Jack grinned at the sight of the terrier's little eyes blinking in the beam of the flashlight. "Hobo!"

He hurried forward and knelt down, laughing as the dog whined and licked at his hands. "Good boy, good boy." Hobo was trembling but seemed okay except for . . . one lost wheel. Jack shone the light, saw the cart tilted sideways and the dog's tail thumping like crazy. "Scary night, buddy, but everything's going to be all right. Everything will be just—"

Jack's phone buzzed in his pocket and he pulled it out. Noted that there was a text message he hadn't checked. And that the incoming call was from Alamo Grace.

"Jack Travis," he said, keeping one hand on Hobo.

"Jack, Adam Bonner here." Bandy's doctor.

"Adam, hey. What's my pal doing, trying to sign himself out?"

"No." There was a pause. "I'm afraid I have bad news."

Jack froze. "What's wrong?"

"Bandy went into cardiac arrest. No warning. His admitting cardiogram looked okay, considering his past disease, but—"

No. No. No . . . Jack sat down in the gravel, barely able to hear.

"Asystole. Refractory after all the drugs . . . I even tried a pacemaker. We did CPR for an hour. But we couldn't get him back. I'm sorry. I know you were close."

You can't . . . begin . . . to know.

Adam cleared his throat. "We have some phone numbers for a . . . son, I think."

"Uh . . . right," Jack confirmed, barely above a whisper. *And a grandbaby. A second on the way. . . . They all went to SeaWorld a few days ago. . . . How can this be happening?*

"I'm so sorry, Jack."

34

RILEY JERKED AWAKE. Her neck hurt, she was all scrunched up, and . . . *Where am I?* The couch. And her cell phone was ringing. She glanced at the clock: 1:30 a.m. She grabbed for the phone, pulse quickening. She'd left that text message for Jack. But it was . . .

"Kate?"

"Yes. I'm sorry. I know it's late, but . . ." Kate's voice cracked.

Riley sat up. "Are you crying? What's wrong?"

She heard a low groan. "Everything. I don't know where to start."

"The beginning?"

"No." A pained laugh. "Trust me, you don't want that."

"What I want is to help you."

There was a prolonged silence. Tears, no question about it. "Kate?"

"You're offering me help after what I did to you? I know how much you want to be back in the ER. I'm really sorry."

"It's okay," Riley assured her. "Some things have happened . . . I'm good with it. But right now I need to know what's going on with you. Please tell me."

"The police just left my place."

Riley gasped. "Why?"

"A man I've been seeing . . . he's being questioned in connection with an old, unsolved crime. Then he tried to use me as an alibi for something that happened last night. And—" Kate moaned—"that's not even the worst part."

"Who is this man?"

"I never told you I was seeing him; I should have. . . . Griff Payton. That ER patient."

"And he needed an alibi because . . . ?"

"They say he set a fire. And—" A sob swallowed Kate's voice.

"It's okay. You can tell me." Riley held her breath.

"It was Jack's clinic that burned. Bandy's dead."

- + -

Jack shifted his cramped leg on the truck seat, careful not to disturb Hobo, who was sleeping on a tattered songbook. Gospel music. He thought of Bandy tapping his fingers over his heart. Saying the last words Jack would ever hear from him. *"Good thing I have the songs right in here."* The ache in Jack's throat threatened suffocation.

He glanced at his watch. He'd been sitting here for nearly

four hours; dawn wasn't far away. It would bring an onslaught of people—insurance and fire investigators, police, reporters looking for a story, and other people simply . . . looking. Curious. Eager to offer an opinion. Pass judgment. Much the same as when homeless Gilbert DeSoto caught himself on fire in the parking lot and a pregnant teenage runaway fought for her life on the porch. But this time it was different because . . . *it's you, my friend.* Jack peered through the windshield at the darkened rubble of the clinic's kitchen. And this time . . . there wouldn't be another time. *The clinic is gone.*

Jack should go. Get out of here, clean up, grab some sleep before he had to be back to answer questions. They would be endless and intrusive. About the fire and about Jack's past, too, if Vesta's story panned out. A cold case solved? Jack shook his head, still not quite believing it. There could even be a sort of final vindication. He had wanted that for fifteen years.

But right now all Jack wanted was to sit in Bandy's truck. He liked knowing that its camper bed was filled with boxes of clothes, sleeping bags, an old saddle . . . and the circus-striped sack that held his blue wig and clown noses, puppets, and a rubber scorpion. Enough junk to start an avalanche. Jack glanced around the cab, remembering how he'd teased Bandy that he could host a garage sale of Bible bric-a-brac. It was true: gospel songbooks, Sunday school workbooks, and a tin of Fish Mints, peppermints shaped like those little Christian fish symbols you saw on car bumpers. There was a wooden cross hanging from the rearview mirror and, on the front seat, beside Hobo's one-wheeled cart . . . *his Bible?*

Jack reached over the sleeping dog, lifted the well-worn

leather volume, and set it in his lap. It really was Bandy's Bible. He was surprised to see it out here. Bandy always read it at night, kept it by his bedside, and then returned it to the truck in the morning. He'd take the Bible out and bring Hobo in—sort of a trade. But last night Bandy had done his reading out here in the truck because . . . *I was talking to Riley in the office.* Jack's fingers brushed the cover. It would have burned except that Bandy had wanted to give them privacy. Because he thought it was important that Jack talk with Riley. Bandy had been insistent about that from the beginning.

Jack smiled in the darkness, remembering the day he'd asked Bandy to show Riley around the clinic. Even from that first day Bandy had been sure that Riley's being there fit some kind of heavenly plan. He felt that way about everything—good and bad. Always glancing up at the ceiling with that knowing look like God had everything covered. Even last night, at the hospital.

"If I'm not afraid to die, then don't you be afraid to live, *Doc."*

Afraid. Me? For some reason, Jack remembered what Riley said last night in the office when she'd been so angry. And hurt. She said that he'd made the clinic about him, not the patients. That he had some "insatiable need to be an invincible warrior." And that because of it, things were chaotic and unstable and she couldn't be part of that. *So she locked me out.*

He waited for the familiar anger to come—about Riley's accusation and rejection and the very real possibility that someone had torched his clinic. An unspeakable day that had ended in ashes. It killed Bandy and robbed Jack of everything he'd wanted. Blistering anger was never more justified—and it was his usual MO. Ask anyone. But right now Jack only wanted peace. He wanted what Bandy had. He needed to feel that the responsibility to make things right wasn't all on his shoulders. He wanted that relief.

But more than anything, Jack needed to believe that even after everything he'd done and hadn't done—all his mistakes— that . . . *"You're a good man, son."* He tried to swallow past the ache, felt tears slide down his face. He glanced at the cross hanging from the mirror and felt the solid weight of the book in his hands. Then, through the blur of his tears, Jack looked up at the ceiling of Bandy's truck and took a halting breath. "Are you there, Lord? I need you."

35

+

"I DIDN'T SLEEP MUCH EITHER." Riley switched the phone to her other hand and opened the shade on the front window. Dawn was painting the sky an amazing rosy gold, almost the color of . . . *peaches.*

Riley took a slow breath and let the memory go. She had to. Today was about moving forward, not looking back. Last night she'd prayed that morning would bring peace and hope. From the sound of Kate's voice, she could use a merciful dose of both.

"You're at the hospital, then?" Riley asked, padding barefoot to the couch.

"Yeah. Pathetic, right? When the world spins off course, the ER is the place that feels most normal to me. Hospital coffee. Sirens. Cold pizza. Even that confetti-sprinkled drunk singing

Fiesta songs." Kate sighed. "You know, the usual aftermath of a Saturday night."

If only that were true.

"And because I was here," Kate continued, her voice softening, "I wandered down to the NICU. The Paulson baby's fever is gone. The nurses said she's chowing down on the donated mother's milk. And . . ." Kate's voice cracked. "Her grandparents gave her a name."

Riley waited, throat tightening.

"Nadia," Kate whispered. "It was her great-grandmother's name . . . and it means 'hope.' I think I like it."

"Me too."

There was a pause and a distant garbled sound of singing before Kate said, "I tried to call Jack. He didn't answer."

Riley nodded mutely. She'd left three messages.

"He was scheduled to work in the ER today," Kate continued, "but he got one of the docs to cover his shift. Someone said he probably went to Santa Fe; Jack has family there. I can only imagine how hard he's taking this."

Santa Fe. Riley hugged her arms around herself. *He's gone.*

Kate's voice was achy soft. "I feel like I keep making all the wrong choices, Riley. I can't get it right. I didn't trust you for the ER position—you, the best person I know. But without so much as a blink, I was willing to trust a man who could be an arsonist, a murderer even! How can I be such a complete—"

"Don't do that to yourself, Kate. Come here. I'll fix breakfast. I'm pretty sure I have some eggs, maybe bagels. If not, we'll go out. Come, please."

"I . . . Okay. I might go home first and take a shower." She gave a short laugh. "I'll bring you a bottle of nail polish I just bought. It's a great color, but it's not me."

"Good. I'll see you when you get here—oh, wait. I almost forgot. I changed the gate code. Let me give that to you."

Riley disconnected, glad Kate had agreed to come. It felt like months, not weeks, since they'd spent any real time together. So much had happened in those few weeks . . . for so many people. Her heart ached for the grieving Collins family, yet Riley was thankful for the sweet blessing of their newborn . . . *Hope.* And though she was unclear about Vesta Calder's reason for leaving her house last night, it was obvious that something pivotal had happened in the woman's life. Something that challenged the fear that had held her painfully captive for years. Vesta's request for prayer had seemed an important part of that. Riley was relieved that she had survived the accident without serious injury, but the fact that Vesta chose the Mercedes as her means of escape seemed somehow fitting. *"Be on your guard; stand firm in the faith; be courageous; be strong."* Whatever the motivation, Vesta Calder had been courageous, indeed.

Kate thought the world had spun off course, but Riley saw it differently; despite all the turmoil and tragedy, she'd finally found a measure of peace. She was certain now that God's hand was in all of these things. And that he'd wanted Riley there, that she was part of the plan. She wasn't broken and useless. The long and painful struggle had helped to make her exactly who God needed her to be, a trauma chaplain. Whether she'd continue to do that here at Alamo Grace or in Houston, Riley wasn't sure. But right now the only decision she needed to make was about breakfast.

Riley started a fresh pot of coffee, then opened the refrigerator, hoping she'd been right about the eggs and bagels. But there on the shelf was the peach cobbler. Sitting next to a jar of peanut butter. *Bandy* . . . Tears stung her eyes. She thought she'd cried them all.

The doorbell rang, and Riley swiped at her eyes. God's perfect timing—Kate must have decided against the shower. And the nail polish. Riley couldn't wait to hug her.

She opened the door . . . and her legs nearly gave way.

"You sent me the gate code," Jack said, more tentative than she'd ever heard him. His clothes were rumpled, face rough with beard growth; his eyes looked bruised by pain. He smelled of smoke. "I know it's early, but . . ."

"Jack . . ." She wasn't sure who reached out first, but suddenly they were hugging each other, and her heart was breaking for him.

36

"I THINK I'M IN SHOCK," Riley said, trying to take in all Jack was saying. About the fire, Bandy's heart attack—and that Vesta had been a witness to Abby's murder? He sat next to her on the couch, smelling more of soap than soot after using the guest bath to wash up. One side of his forehead was mildly blistered from the heat of the explosion. Her throat tightened. *Jack risked his life for Bandy.* "It's all so incredible."

"You can say that again." Jack blew on his coffee. "Even Rob was amazed at how it came together—questioning Griff Payton about the cold case, then discovering a new crime. Apparently our contractor was too stoned to get rid of his smoky clothes." He shook his head. "Or clean up the dog bite on his ankle."

"Hobo the watchdog." Riley nodded. "Griff set fire to the clinic so his father's company could get the land for that condo project?"

"And because he's always been a firebug. Arson, drugs, petty crimes as a juvenile—all reasons his father sent him away fifteen years ago." Jack frowned. "Of course, Ross Payton had no idea how bad it really was—that his son was connected to a murder. The recent rash of arsons gave Griff an opportunity to hurry his plans along; he thought the clinic fire would be passed off as more vandalism. I'm sure it didn't help his state of mind when I mouthed off at the library." Jack's expression left no doubt he regretted his actions. "Rob's inclined to believe Griff didn't know Bandy was sleeping inside the clinic. And maybe even about his part in Abby's death. He claims he only agreed to steal a car, not . . ." Familiar sadness flickered in Jack's eyes.

"And Vesta held the key to it all."

"Yes."

Jack was quiet for a moment and Riley noticed how different he seemed. Apart from the grief he was obviously feeling, there was something more. His anger seemed to be missing. Last night's tragedy should have had him pacing, agitated and even vengeful. But now . . . She cleared her throat. "Abby's murder will finally be solved."

"Looks like it. Griff offered up names. The FBI took charge since it was a kidnapping. It's all coming together." He shook his head. "Because a frightened woman had the courage to climb into her car and—"

"My car, actually. She let me store it at her house."

"I should be surprised, but . . . it makes sense somehow."

Jack set his coffee down. "I've been thinking about some things, Riley. That's why I came here. I need you to listen."

Riley nodded. She saw it again. That change in him. *Father, please. You've made me a listener. Help me to do that now . . . for Jack.*

- + -

"I heard the news about Bandy when I was at the clinic last night. I'd promised to check on Hobo," Jack explained, needing to share everything. "He was scared, shivering. So we climbed into Bandy's truck. After a while, Hobo fell asleep. And . . . I started thinking about things Bandy had said over the time I knew him. He was always doing that. Peanut-butter-and-wisdom sandwiches. You know?"

Riley nodded, her expression solemn. "I do."

"At the hospital he'd told me he wasn't afraid to die. I blew it off; Bandy was always saying that. But while I was sitting in the truck, I got to thinking about how easygoing he was. He always tried to see the best in everyone—*everyone*. Even me, at my worst. . . . And then I remembered what happened when you came to the clinic last night. Those things you said to me."

Riley winced. "I shouldn't have—"

"No," he said, stopping her. "The point I need to make is that you were right, Riley. I did make that clinic about me. I was angry and defensive and willing to go to battle—I wanted to fight. Anybody, everybody. I told myself I was doing it for people who couldn't defend themselves. Because it was the right thing to do. But . . ." Jack took a slow breath. "The truth is that I was angry with myself. Abby saw it when my dad was dying.

That's why she picked me up that night. I was circling the drain and she wanted to help me. Then Abby had a flat tire and we got carjacked. And I was too drunk to stop them from . . ."

"Jack." Riley reached for his hand. "Don't."

"It's all right," he said, holding her hand between his—her warmth like balm for his soul. "It's a relief to finally see this. I couldn't save Abby—maybe I even felt guilty that I lived. I don't know. But I understand now that everything I've done since that night was a lame attempt to prove I was better than that loser kid who got left on the roadside. I took every kind of risk I could because . . . I was afraid I was a coward." He shook his head. "And then, last night . . ." *Help me, Lord. Give me the words to explain this.*

"I'm listening," Riley said, barely above a whisper.

"I found Bandy's Bible in the truck. And it got me thinking. It wouldn't have been there if Bandy hadn't gone out to the truck to give us privacy. You and me, Riley. If he hadn't taken it there, that Bible would have burned—along with all those idiot photos above my desk. Do you understand what I'm saying? It was there for me to find because you had the courage to tell me the truth about myself. And then because you encouraged Vesta, she had the guts to climb into your car and come forward about the murder. Abby's parents will finally have some peace. And maybe—" Jack's throat constricted—"I can look in the mirror and not be ashamed of the man I see. Stop taking it out on everyone else. I'm so tired of feeling that way."

Riley's eyes filled with tears.

Jack went on. "So I sat there holding Bandy's Bible and I

knew none of this was coincidence. It can't be. Bandy, Vesta . . .
you. Everything that's happened and how it's all connected. I
have to believe that God planned this. That . . . maybe he hasn't
given up on me." He shook his head. "Does this make sense?"

A tear slid down Riley's cheek. "Perfect sense."

"Good. And to tell you the truth, I'm not sure where I'm
going from here." His heart thudded in his chest. "But right
now I need to clear up a couple of things. Okay?"

- + -

Riley nodded, suddenly as dizzy as she'd felt in the skydiving
plane. Hope was heady stuff. But no matter what happened
next, this was already enough. *Thank you, Father.*

"It's true that I applied for the Hale Foundation grant," Jack
told her. "But that was weeks before I met you. And it's true that
I asked you to volunteer because I was hoping you'd give credi-
bility to the clinic. In that sense, I did use you. I'm sorry. I think
we've already established that I've been a selfish fool. But . . ." He
reached out, brushed a tear from her face.

Her skin warmed at his touch. "But what?"

"Everything that happened afterward was real. I knew you
were special from that first day, when we found Stacy on the
porch. I care for you, Riley. More than I've ever cared for any
woman before. And . . ." Jack paused, a question forming in
his eyes.

"Don't stop," Riley whispered.

"I'm trying to say that I need to know there's a chance for us.
I need that chance as much as I need . . . to breathe."

Breathing. Yes, she should do that.

"Riley?" Jack's brows pinched. "Will you give me another chance?"

"Yes," she managed finally. Not easy, considering the fact that her heart was skydiving. "More than a chance."

"Good—great." Jack's eyes lit. "One more thing."

"Wha—?" She stopped as he drew her close. *Oh.*

"This," he whispered, kissing her temple. "And this . . ." He touched his lips to a corner of her mouth.

"That's two things," she teased, wrapping her arms around his neck.

"Stop counting."

His kiss was warm, tender, then eager . . . and nearly endless. She wasn't sure she'd ever breathe again. Or if that was even a problem. Riley's senses swirled as she returned Jack's kisses, measure for measure.

When at last they broke away, she didn't trust herself to speak. She snuggled close, her head against Jack's chest as he stroked her hair.

She heard his heart beating, smelled the remaining traces of smoke on his shirt—evidence of courage. He'd carried a man from a burning building. But in the end, it was much more. She thought of something Bandy said the day she'd first seen Jack's "Buckle Wall." He'd said, *"A big buckle doesn't make a big man."* And that it had taken him a long time to learn that.

Then Riley thought of Jack sitting in that truck until dawn with a crippled dog and an old Bible, of the lessons he'd learned there. She had no doubt that Bandy Biggs was smiling in heaven. The same way she knew that her heart was safe with this hero.

Epilogue

Jack glanced down from the porch, doing one last check: traffic barricades in place, circular driveway and wheelchair ramp swept and hosed, reflecting tape on the steps. Safety first. There was a designated parking area for the catering truck, press, and—

He smiled, his heart doing what it still did every time he saw Riley Hale. Even after almost six months. Especially today.

"I think we're all set, Dr. Travis," she said, stepping out the front door wearing an apron and an oven mitt. She smiled. "I do love the fragrance of new lumber and fresh paint . . . mixed with the scent of six dozen peanut butter cookies hot from the oven." Her blue eyes glittered. "I think you should invent a shampoo." Her expression grew wistful. "I'd send a bottle to Kate so she'd know what she's missing."

Riley had been disappointed when Kate accepted a position as emergency department manager at Austin Grace Hospital. But it was easy to see that the incident with Griff Payton had affected her more than she admitted. Jack sensed that Kate Callison was searching for something but wasn't quite sure what it was. He'd felt that way himself. Until Riley.

Jack was grateful beyond reason. For that and for so many things, including the phone call he'd had from Bandy's son this morning. They'd received the fire insurance check in time to stop the foreclosure on their home. He'd started his job, and their new baby boy was doing fine.

Jack's pulse quickened. He hoped that today would mark two more new beginnings, starting with . . .

"C'mon," he said, making his way down the steps. "They got the sign up. Have a look."

"Great." She glanced back toward the doorway. "But I still have a batch of cookies in the oven."

"Wilma's in there. She'll take care of it," Jack insisted, realizing that he was nervous. Excited too, but nervous. Today had been a long time coming. "And people will start arriving in another twenty minutes. I want you to see this—with me."

She came down the steps . . . wearing that oven mitt. He smiled at the unexpected complication. Fitting—they'd had more than a few complications in their history. Then the sun caught Riley's hair and his breath staggered. The world had never felt so right.

She joined him on the circular driveway, and they turned to look back at the newly constructed stone building that smelled of milled lumber, fresh paint, and peanut butter.

Riley shielded her eyes from the sun and glanced up. "Oh, Jack," she breathed, pressing the oven mitt to her chest.

"It's good, isn't it?" He read the sign again, his throat constricting.

Bandy Biggs Community Clinic

"It's perfect." Riley's gaze moved from the sign to the window boxes on the porch, freshly planted with the beginnings of a winter garden. "Everything."

He smiled, loving her even more. "Good enough for the city council members?"

"Absolutely." She grinned at him. "Especially since two of their wives have signed up as volunteers." She shook her head. "The new volunteer coordinator is a miracle worker."

"She assured me there would be photographers here for the ribbon cutting."

"*Aagh.*" Riley's brows shot up. "Ribbon. We need to do that. And I should make a quick call to Alamo Grace, to see if everything's okay there. My assistant's taking calls, but—"

"Hold it, Chaplain." Jack caught her arm. "Not so fast. You forgot something."

He reached into his pocket, handed her the engraved name tag:

Chaplain Riley Hale, Clinic Director

"Oh." Her eyes lit. "It came. I'll pin it on as soon as I get this apron off."

"Good." Jack took a slow breath, feeling his heart climb toward his throat. "One more thing and you're official."

"Official?" She peered at him warily. "Tell me you are *not* going to toss a CPR manikin."

"Hardly." He laughed as he reached into his other pocket . . . and found the small velvet box. "You think I was raised by wolves?"

"Then what—?" The oven mitt rose to Riley's lips; her eyes went wide. "Oh, Jack! Is it . . . ?"

"It is," he said, opening the lid to let the Texas sun hit the facets of a princess-cut diamond solitaire. "I love you, Riley. Please say you'll marry me."

She caught her breath, fresh tears shimmering. "I will. Of course I will."

"Good." He started to laugh. "Now if you'll take that pot holder off your hand . . ."

"Oh, right."

He slipped the ring on her finger, and she flung her arms around him. He hugged her close, squeezing his eyes shut—and feeling everything fall into place at last.

"I love you so much," Riley whispered, her lips warm against his neck.

He released her just enough to cradle her face in his hands and kiss her. Once, twice, and—

They both looked up at the sound of barking.

"Hey, you two!" Vesta Calder walked briskly up the driveway, an eager Hobo and his cart leading the way. She waved a sheet of paper, her cheeks a healthy pink and her smile completely contagious. "I have two more volunteers. And some neighborhood news."

"We have news too." Jack smiled at Riley, slid his arm around her waist. "But you first."

"Nothing earth-shattering," Vesta said, arriving beside them. She squinted up at the clinic's new sign and released a deep sigh. "Only that Andrea Nichols's house has a For Sale sign on the lawn. Thought you might be interested in that. Though it might take some time at the price she's asking. I suppose that's because she spent all that money a while back on the new roof."

Riley nudged him and Jack knew she was thinking the same thing he was. Hector's fall all those many months ago. It made sense, Jack supposed. But so many other things made far more beautiful sense. Like the fact that Riley was going to be his wife, and—

"I'll have to figure out a way to break the news to Hobo about Andrea's cat, of course," Vesta continued. "But right now we'd better stop this dillydallying and snap to it. We have a clinic to dedicate!"

Riley laughed, offered a hearty thumbs-up.

Jack glanced heavenward. A habit he'd recently adopted.

Sounds like a plan. Yessir.

About the Author

CANDACE CALVERT is a former ER nurse and author of the Mercy Hospital series—*Critical Care, Disaster Status,* and *Code Triage.* Her medical dramas offer readers a chance to "scrub in" on the exciting world of emergency medicine. Wife, mother, and very proud grandmother, Candace makes her home in northern California. Visit her website at www.candacecalvert.com.

An Interview with Candace Calvert

Where did you get the idea for this story?

The character of Riley Hale sprang from my own experience of being a nurse sidelined by serious injury. In Riley's case, it was an assault that left her with debilitating fear. It reminds me of a profound question I once heard in a Beth Moore Bible study: "Down deep, what are you most afraid of?" Fear (at odds with faith) is such a universal human experience. I wanted to explore it with this story and show the triumph of hope.

Are any of the scenes pulled from your personal experiences as a nurse?

As with most authors, my stories have a base in personal experience. In the ER there was heartbreaking tragedy but also stress-relieving humor and the warm camaraderie that came from being part of the medical team. I strive to offer all of that to my readers. I also draw from many "out of scrubs" life adventures. Yes, this author did indeed skydive! For the sake of romance, I spared Riley the indignity of having air rush up her nostrils. Not pretty.

As a former nurse, how do you write realistic medical scenes while avoiding the use of too much technical jargon?

When possible, I try to show medical scenes through the eyes of a layperson. That helps. My readers tell me they are more interested in the relationships between characters—the hearts and souls behind the stethoscopes—than they are in medical jargon and technical detail. So my goal is to use the "sirens and adrenaline" imagery to add tension and enhance setting without making folks feel they need to stop reading and consult a medical dictionary.

In the story, Riley is coming back to work after a traumatic injury. How is that similar to your own personal story?

It's quite similar, though my injuries came from an equestrian accident that landed me in my own trauma room—with back and rib fractures, a bleeding lung, a broken neck, and spinal cord damage. Like Riley, I had weakness and numbness in my dominant arm and serious doubts I'd be able to continue my career as an ER nurse. I could easily understand Riley's frustrations and fears. When I begged to return to duties too early, my department manager asked me much the same question posed to Riley in *Trauma Plan*: "What if a panicked mother rushed in, shoved a critically ill child into your arms—could you carry him to the treatment room?" It shook me to the core. The inspirational essay that chronicles my experience as a trauma victim, "By Accident," appears in *Chicken Soup for the Nurse's Soul* and started my writing career.

Was there a specific inspiration for Jack? How did his character come about? Do you usually know your characters fully before you start writing, or do you discover new things about them as the story takes shape?

I wouldn't say there was a specific inspiration for the character of Jack Travis. But as an easygoing, nonconfrontational, go-by-the-rules person, it was fun to create the opposite: a volatile maverick willing to take a stand like Commander Travis at the Alamo. Though I make notes about my characters before I begin, I don't really know them until they start telling me their secrets. They whisper; I type. For instance, I had no clue that Jack played the guitar, had a Hispanic great-grandmother, picked peaches as a boy, or would soon learn valuable life lessons from a rodeo clown. These discoveries are blessings that enrich a story beyond any author's plan.

San Antonio comes to life in this story. Why did you decide to set this series in Texas? And how did you research the setting for this book?

Though I'm a native Californian, my husband is a fifth-generation Texan and wanted to return there after retirement. We spent six years in the beautiful hill country northwest of San Antonio. Texas is beyond colorful, so different from what I'd known, and such fun to "research"! From gorgeous sunsets, the confetti whirl of Fiesta at River Walk, and the dance floor at Luckenbach to cannons at the Alamo, Tex-Mex food, and the surreal magic of fireflies, it was an experience I'll never forget. And I'm eager to share it with readers!

Readers fall in love with the animals in your stories— and Hobo is sure to become one of their favorites. Do you have pets of your own? Do any of them have physical disabilities similar to Hobo's?

Right now, we have no pets. Sadly, we lost our elderly mini schnauzer while we lived in Texas. I once had a Manx cat named Franklin, who lost the use of his back legs, and a beloved horse who suffered from seizures. Pets bless our lives and teach us valuable lessons about courage and unconditional love. Somehow animals always seem to wag, meow, swim, squawk, or gallop their way into my stories!

I think we learn a lot about people—and fictional characters—
when we see them interact with animals.

**The people of The Bluffs are against having the clinic in their
community because they are afraid it will bring crime into
the neighborhood. Did you feel there was any validity to their
fears? Have you experienced this kind of resistance during
your nursing career?**

I think Rob Melton nailed it when he told Jack, "Those neighbors aren't
bad people, Jack. They're scared people. Wary of what they don't
understand. Protective of their families and their property. So they
install security gates, form committees—" It's human to fear what we
don't understand. And it's wise to be cautious sometimes. But I think
people are far more alike than different. Trauma and tragedy spare no
one. I once worked at a hospital that served people from very poor
neighborhoods as well as a new, affluent community. The ER waiting
room was a melting pot. Was there ever intolerance, friction? Sure.
But not as much as you'd think. Everyone can understand a mother's
worry over a sick baby, the wrenching pain of losing a loved one. You'd
be surprised at the number of times I heard suffering people say,
"Take that person ahead of me. He needs help more than I do." I try
to convey that grace via my stories.

Discussion Guide

Note: Book clubs that choose to read *Trauma Plan* and would like me to "attend" your gathering, please e-mail me at Candace@candacecalvert.com. I'll try to arrange a speaker-phone conversation to join your discussion.

1. In the opening scene of *Trauma Plan*, Dr. Jack Travis rushes to help a man set afire in the clinic parking lot. He's furious that the gathered crowd has done nothing to help the victim. How do his attitude and actions here set the stage for his behavior as the story continues? What was your initial reaction to Jack? If you were in that crowd, what would you have done? Have you ever felt compelled to provide aid in a similar situation?

2. Former nurse Riley Hale struggles to accept her physical limitations after a vicious assault. It's a miracle she survived, yet she can't help wanting more—to be "whole

again." Have you ever been grateful for blessings while sensing a nagging need for more? How did that make you feel? How did you handle it?

3. Fear plays a prominent part in the theme of *Trauma Plan*: Jack attempts to "spit in the face of fear"; Riley fears she'll never be whole; Vesta's panic attacks leave her housebound. When Jack, Bandy, and Riley entertain children at the Sunshine Center, the teacher asks each child to name a fear. If you had to do that, what would your answer be? What helps you most when you're afraid?

4. Birds are a recurring symbol in *Trauma Plan*: the grackles that Riley so despises, the birds Vesta loves to watch from her window, the Eagle Skydiving logo on Jack's shirt, the caged finches Riley's mother keeps, and the white dove in the stained-glass window of the hospital chapel. What do you think each represents?

5. Bandy Biggs tells Riley, "Sometimes it's sorta like I'm spreadin' hope, not peanut butter." Do you think that is true? How does Bandy touch (and change) the lives of the people around him? How important is his character to the story? Discuss.

6. After Jack's explosive confrontation with clinic neighbors at the library, Bandy tells him, "We can't pick and choose who deserves good treatment. Those neighbors need it too." He is, in effect, reminding us of God's commandment to "love your neighbor" (see Matthew 22:34-40). Have you ever been involved

in community conflict? How difficult is it to "love your neighbor as yourself"?

7. When chaplain Riley Hale comforts the parents of a dying girl, nurse Kate Callison tells her, "I don't know how you do that." Have you ever had a nurse, physician, chaplain, or other hospital staff member offer support or prayer for you or a loved one? If so, did it help? How?

8. Riley must accept the fact that she will never return to full nursing duties, that God has another plan for her. Have you ever struggled to accept an unexpected plan that God had for your life? Did you find it to be a blessing after all? Share.

9. How important was setting to your enjoyment of this story? Did you feel that you were in San Antonio and the Texas hill country? What was your favorite "taste of Texas" scene?

10. Was there a moment in *Trauma Plan* that caught you by surprise? One that made you laugh? Cry? Share your favorite story moments.

Please visit my website at www.candacecalvert.com for more information on upcoming books in this series.

Thank you for reading *Trauma Plan*.

Warmly,
Candace Calvert